His Rejected

Game Of Wolves: Book 3

Lindsey Devin & Skye Wilson

© 2024
Disclaimer

This is a work of fiction. Names, places, characters, and events are all fictitious for the reader's pleasure. Any similarities to real people, places, events, living, or dead are all coincidental.

Contents

Chapter 1 - Kira

The all-consuming darkness slowly faded, leaving me confused and disoriented. What was this place, and how did I get here? What had happened? I couldn't remember anything after seeing Leif break off from the pack of feral wolves. Everything else lay behind a gauzy barrier in my mind.

Not knowing who might be around, I pretended to be asleep. Keeping my eyes closed, I focused on the sounds around me and did my best to figure out where I was. I heard bubbling, faint beeps, the scratch of a pen furiously scribbling on paper, and most disconcerting, the soft and disturbed chuckle of a man laughing to himself.

In an instant, it all came back. The jungle, Leif, Simon. I'd been taken. A dart or spell or some sort of gas had knocked me out—I couldn't remember exactly what. The last thing I remembered was Leif dragging me toward the volcano.

I was a prisoner. The thought set my heart hammering. It took all my training to keep the placid, slack look of sleep on my face.

Speaking of training, I *had* to get my bearings. One of the first things I'd been taught as a Tranquility operative was to gauge and memorize your surroundings, especially if you were taken as a hostage or prisoner. The only way I could truly do that was to open my eyes and look around, but a strange, pervading dread swelled within me at the thought. I did *not* want to see Simon again. Something about the look he'd had in his eyes made my blood run cold.

I wanted Wyatt. I'd never been the type to want or need a man to save me, but lying there, helpless... I wished he was there. If nothing else, he'd have given me strength, and knowing we were going through this together would have given me comfort. Had he gotten back to Haven? Was he still searching the jungle for me? If nothing else, I had to get out of this alive to make sure Wyatt was okay.

Steeling myself for what was to come, I inched my eyelids open. Bright spears of light sent pain spiking into the backs of my eyes, and for a moment, the harsh glare blinded me. Blinking, I managed to look around the room. No windows—only bare, solid concrete walls. The entire room had the sterile look of a lab, with stainless steel shelves and tables, autoclaves and incubators, Bunsen burners, racks of glass beakers and cylinders. There were also strange magical implements on several tables: stone runes, flasks of brightly colored potions, dried herbs, and ancient-looking texts that lay scattered across benches and shelves.

A faint but unyielding ache and burning sensation tickling at my wrists and ankles pulled my attention away from the room. Glancing down, I found the cause. The acrid stench of wolfsbane finally registered in my mind. Strong leather cuffs buckled around my wrists and ankles held my arms and legs in place. Another larger band crossed my midsection an inch below my ribs. The leather was saturated with wolfsbane oil. The stink of it burned my nostrils. I should have been able to snap the cuffs easily, but with that shit soaked into them, it was impossible.

My senses continued to return and strengthen as the effects of the drug they'd given me wore off. The disturbing laughter had given way to a haunting humming. The tune came from above me, relative to the table I lay on. Craning my neck did no good, and there was no way to see what awaited me in that direction.

A familiar scent caught my attention. Leif. He had to be in the room, too—the scent was too strong for him not to be. Closing my eyes again, I tried to send all my power to my sense of smell. That was my best bet to garner as much information from my surroundings in my current state.

My nostrils filled with the smells of Leif, dozens of chemical and plant residues, and a very slight whiff of coppery, metallic smell that told me vampires were nearby. Strange. Stranger still was the scent of another alpha wolf in the vicinity. Most of the smells were too feeble and too far away for them to be in the room with me. How big was this place?

The humming grew louder, the voice more distinct. My skin pricked with fear. Up and down, the song became a leech, latching onto my brain, filling me with a bit of Simon's madness. He had to be the one humming, but it still made no sense. How was he alive?

For over a decade, I'd told myself that I'd torn him apart in the madness of my first shift. Hell, I'd been covered in blood when I woke up sprinting through the forest. Now here he was, alive and well.

On second thought, he definitely wasn't *well*, not mentally. That had been obvious even as the drug had begun shutting my mind down. Even there, strapped to a table with wolfsbane, a small sliver of my mind leapt with joy and relief. I *hadn't* killed an innocent person all those years ago. The weight of that sin had warped and shaped me into the person I was, but now I could finally peel off that shame.

The humming stopped, and my thoughts froze. The *clap-clap* of hard-soled shoes on a stone floor drew near. Simon. Every part of me screamed to run, to get away even though that wasn't possible.

Cool, latex-encased fingers slipped across my forehead, making me flinch despite my wishes to stay motionless. A moment later, the finger lifted my eyelids.

"Ah, yes," Simon said. "She is awake. Did you have a good nap, my dear? I do hope it was refreshing." He gave a mad little chuckle. Leaning over me, his face upside down, he appeared even crazier than he had in the jungle.

"Why am I here?" I asked, my voice a rasp.

Simon walked around the table until he could look me in the eye straight on. "Oh, that is a *very* exciting question indeed." His eyes glittered with menacing excitement. "Now that I have my first success back, we have a lot we need to do together. I'm sure you're as thrilled as I am."

Now that my mind had broken free of the drug he'd injected me with, I could see something was deeply wrong with this fae man. Corruption was my first thought, but he didn't have the telltale look of pale skin and blackened eyes. Nor did he have the spoiled-milk scent I'd always noticed from corrupted fae. No, something else was going on here. Simple madness, perhaps? Whatever it was, his very aura and presence near my body made me mentally recoil from him.

"What's that?" I asked as I spotted the strange device in his hand.

Simon's eyes widened, as did the freakish smile on his lips. "This?" He raised the device. "A little toy of my own design."

He held it closer for me to see. A leather cuff of some sort, with buckles to strap it to something. On the outside, a few small devices and magic stones were attached to a small mechanism. A long, thin, and flexible hypodermic needle protruded from the inside of the cuff. It looked like a torture device, and cold sweat sprang out all over my skin.

"See?" Simon asked, pushing the device closer to my face. "Maybe you need a better look?"

He lowered it inch by inch, until the needle filled my vision. The hair-thin metal drew nearer my right eyeball. Cold panic burst through my heart as I tried to pull my face away. Was he going to stab my eye with the fucking thing? The thought nauseated me. I imagined it piercing my eyeball, the quiet *pop* as it burst through and slipped all the way down to the optic nerve, then toward my brain. Breath hitched in and out of my lungs in panicked bursts.

Simon pulled the device back and let out a manic titter. "Oh, that was good. You looked truly scared." He shook his head and wagged a finger at me. "Silly. This must be placed in the bloodstream to be effective. A direct injection to the brain would have, um, *very* bad results." Again, that awful laugh echoed throughout the room.

Simon bent low and attached the cuff to my bicep, buckling the strap tightly to my arm. I winced and hissed as the needle threaded itself into the muscle.

"What the fuck is it?" I gasped, unable to hold my tongue.

Without looking up, Simon answered, "This is a simple tracking device that will keep me up to date on your location. The needle itself is designed to pull small samples of blood and analyze them at random intervals. All to see how your body is reacting to the next experiment I have planned for you." He finished attaching the device and patted my arm. "There we are. All done."

Simon grabbed a stainless steel rolling stool, moved it to the side of my table, then sat. Resting an elbow on the table, he gazed at me lovingly. It wasn't a lustful look; it reminded me of how a child would look at an ant farm they dearly cherished. Like I was nothing more than a beautiful specimen in a jar of formaldehyde.

"I can't tell you how ecstatic I am to see you again, Kira. You've grown into a strong young woman. So similar, yet so different from that awkward girl I pulled aside at that party all those years ago."

Gritting my teeth, I glared at him. "I'm glad I could make your day."

Simon gave me a faux-shocked, open-mouthed smile and pointed at me. "Testy, aren't we? Perhaps that's why you proved such a good guinea pig all those years ago." He burst into a laugh. "Maybe I should have said guinea *wolf*, huh?"

"Very clever," I mumbled.

Ignoring me, Simon went on. "You know, I didn't even *want* to go to that party for my niece." He clicked his tongue in disgust. "She was always quite boring. A simple child with simple desires. Truly, the only reason I accepted my sister's invitation is because my theories and experimentations had grown beyond what could be done in a lab or computer. I *had* to have a live subject, and there would be children at the party. Any live subject would have worked, of course." He waved a hand as if shooing a fly away. "But children are, shall we say, easier to convince."

My skin crawled. He'd come to the party for no other reason than to conduct an experiment on a child? He really was a monster. Part of me wished that I had actually ripped his guts out all those years ago.

"And I fit your parameters?" I asked.

Simon's eyes locked on mine, and I inwardly flinched away at the look of hunger in them. He nodded and patted my shoulder. "Indeed you did, my lovely. You can't begin to appreciate my shock at seeing another latent shifter like me there. You were *perfect.*"

"What?" I asked, brow furrowing in confusion. "I wasn't a latent shifter. How could you know that, even if I was?"

Simon's smile grew wider, revealing too many teeth. "Ah, I see. You were unaware of your true nature."

My fear of the man and the situation faded as my anger and curiosity grew.

"What do you mean? What was my true nature?" I asked, blinking rapidly. Remembering what else he'd said, another question popped out before I could stop myself. "How can you be a latent shifter? You're fae."

Simon crossed his arms and sat back on the stool, still looking at me with those mad, beady eyes. A look of contemplation crossed his face, and he ran his tongue over his lower lip.

"Kira," he finally said, "you were a latent shifter. I had developed some detection spells. When I strolled by you while you and my niece were dancing that evening, those spells locked onto you and showed me what I'd been waiting for. Not only had a shifter been invited to the party—a child shifter, no less—but a *latent* shifter like me.

"You see, I am a bit of an anomaly. A half-breed: part shifter, part fae. My mother had a tryst with a wolf from a random unofficial pack. That was a year or two before she met the man who would be my younger sister's blood father. The pairing between fae and alpha created offspring." Simon touched his own chest. "Myself. Quite rare indeed. A one in a million chance, as you well know."

I stared at him, horror-struck. I'd never met someone with that type of lineage. They were whispered about, but rare enough that they were thought impossible. It all began to make sense.

I glanced around the lab again, Simon's purpose becoming clear. "You wanted to access your inner wolf?"

Simon snapped his fingers and leaned forward hungrily. "Exactly. And you were the *first* step in my process. My dear girl, you have no idea how important you were to my research. I'd spent years developing a concoction that would unleash a suppressed latent wolf. A potion that would be strong enough to bend the will of nature herself.

"I believed the special tincture to be ready, but I needed to test it first—"

"So you forced it on a child?" I snarled, cutting him off.

Simon waved my outburst away and frowned in annoyance. "Not important. What matters is that I was *right* to test it first. When I lured you deep into the forest with a bit of fae glamor and gave you the potion, there were immediate and violent side effects."

"And those were?" I asked. As angry as I was, I wanted—*needed*—to hear everything that had happened that night.

"The induction of ferality," Simon whispered. "Almost instantly, I knew I'd been successful." He bobbed his head back and forth. "There was a bit of... screaming and shouting. Pain, yes, but you shifted. The problem was that the wolf that appeared did not come into this world peacefully. The thing erupted, fully formed and mature, yet completely out of its mind. Feral beyond belief. I, being a scientist by nature and not a warrior, was not well-equipped to fight for my life in such tight confines as the cave to which I'd lured you. Had I not been anticipating *some* side effects, you very nearly would have done me in. As it was, I received numerous and rather severe injuries. As a last-ditch effort, I cast a somnambulism spell on you. You sleep-walked out of the cave and ran into the forest while I writhed in pain and neared death."

Rather than looking sad, he had the look of someone giddy with happiness. "With nothing else to risk, I took the potion myself. It forced my own long-repressed latent wolf to step forward and show itself to me. You see, being a half-breed, I never had the gifts of most shifters. No enhanced senses, no inner wolf to bond with—the enhanced speed and strength were all nowhere to be seen. Also missing? That wonderful rapid shifter healing. Once my wolf revealed itself, all of that came to the fore. Isn't that exciting, Kira?"

Swallowing hard, I nodded hesitantly. "Yeah. Amazing," I said dryly.

"Still, it was a slow process to heal. Even for a shifter, my wounds were grievous. In my agonized stupor, only one thought kept me going: I had been successful. I'd brought about a shift in a latent shifter." Simon clenched his fist in front of his face, staring down at his knuckles. "I had harnessed the power I'd sought for all those years. I would survive. Which was good, because I had too much work to do."

Simon was lost in thought for several long seconds, almost like he'd put himself into a trance. Every second I spent with the man showed me more and more how crazy he was. Not only crazy, but possibly fully psychotic.

A giggle from his mouth broke the silence, and he looked at me again. "You were a fiery little thing. Yes, you were. Robust and powerful. Not only had I managed to pull your wolf free from you, but some part of my magical potion had also converted you into an alpha. A female alpha. Rare beyond words. By my own hands, I'd pulled a wolf from its prison. Not any wolf, either, but the most powerful and rare of its kind." Simon held his hands out, palms up for me to inspect. "You see? I have the power of a god in these hands."

The way he described that night, it was as though he were talking about some happily nostalgic evening we'd shared as friends—the polar opposite of how I'd always viewed that day. My stomach churned as I remembered how terrified I'd been, how I'd hated myself for years. All that time I'd wallowed in self-loathing, this psycho had been thinking fondly about the day. When I'd run, I'd been drenched in blood, enough that when Wyatt found me in that smaller cave, it had looked like I'd butchered someone.

Simon had to be telling the truth. He'd lost too much blood for even fae healing spells to have saved him. Nothing made sense, other than the fact that he'd become a shifter that night. Had he become an alpha, too?

I thought so. I could catch the whiff of his scent in the air.

"Anyway," Simon said, grabbing a clipboard and scanning it. "After recovering, I used the little incident to fake my own death. It worked perfectly. I'd been trying to figure out a way of slipping away for some time. I needed time and freedom to continue with my experiments." He chuckled and glanced up from the clipboard to pin me with his eyes again. "Things truly worked out for the best. Honestly, I should thank you for almost ripping me to shreds. You should thank me, too."

"I'm not thanking you for anything," I said, momentarily unafraid.

"Kira, don't you see? You *should* thank me, because without me, you still wouldn't have your wolf. I granted you the greatest gift anyone could give a shifter. My experiment that night unleashed your true self—a self that never would have been there without me. Right?"

Pressing my lips into a thin line, I gave him a belligerent look. I hoped he could feel the hate radiating off me. He hadn't given me a gift; he'd made me think of myself as a monster for years.

Instead of taking my silence as an affront, Simon just giggled in that mad way. "I like you! Most of my experiments are overly dramatic." He rolled his eyes. "All the screaming, the pleading, the begging. Ugh." He shook his head sadly as if remembering all the terrible moments from his past. "It's exhausting, listening to it all. I like silence for a change."

The next words slipped from my mouth against my better judgment. "You're crazy."

Simon's eyes grew steely and deep, like pools of inky black madness. "Only those who don't understand true genius call the gifted crazy. We aren't crazy. It's only that everyone else is too dense and can't see our vision."

With that, he stood, his lab coat swishing behind him, and began to hum that awful song again. Near where I lay strapped down, a strange contraption was bolted on a rolling upright rod that looked almost like an IV stand. Simon tinkered with it, using a combination of magic as well as a few small, delicate tools he extracted from his pocket.

The scent of an alpha tickled my nose again, and I sat up as far as the leather strap on my chest would allow. To my amazement, Abel lay on a table across the room, strapped down exactly like I was. We'd all thought him dead, yet here he was, alive. The same strange needle device was attached to his bicep.

A wave of relief and happiness washed over me. I'd been so sure that Abel had been killed that I'd already begun mourning him in my mind. Seeing him alive, his chest rising and falling in sleep, was the best thing I could have seen—other than Wyatt and Zoe crashing through the doors to save me, of course.

My solace faded quickly. If Abel was locked up here in Simon's lab, it meant the mad fae scientist had plans for him, too. Did he want to make him feral like he had with Leif? Or did he have some other atrocity planned? For a moment, I recalled those hodgepodge creatures we'd fought, those random combinations of other beings put together with some awful form of magic. The thought of that happening to Abel made me sick to my stomach.

What did Simon have planned for me? He'd strapped that weird machine to me, too. Thundering terror echoed through my chest at the idea of being turned feral. I'd spent so many years thinking that was what I'd done the night Simon kidnapped me, I'd basically developed a phobia of becoming that type of monster again. Even knowing it had all been a lie didn't wash away my horror at the idea.

Neck protesting, I lay back against the hard metal table. The burning itch of the wolfsbane on my skin was a distant but irritating sensation. I still couldn't believe that I *hadn't* killed someone that night. As awful as my current situation was, I could take heart in that one truth: I hadn't been a killer. I had never been a monster. Reaching deep within myself, I sent apologetic sympathy toward my inner wolf. She hadn't forced me to murder anyone, and I'd shoved her away because of that. I didn't know if she would ever forgive me, but I had to start somewhere.

A whimpering acceptance came back, echoing from the deepest recesses of my mind.

"Let's see how this works," Simon said, pulling my attention back.

He'd rolled the strange IV stand to the very side of my bed. With a few quick movements, he had it attached to the device already on my arm. A hose of some sort ran into it. He muttered to himself and cast a few waves of magic across both devices.

Before I had time to really see what he did, I felt the magic thrumming through my body, coursing in as something moved from the device on the pole into the device on my arm, then finally into my body. Dizziness and vertigo slammed into me. Blinking did nothing to abate it. If anything, opening and closing my eyes made things worse.

"What... what are you doing to me?" I muttered. It took all I could do to stay conscious as sleep threatened to drag me under.

Simon leaned across my body, checking me over. "Prepping you for a new experiment I want to try next." I could smell peppermint on his breath as he lifted my eyelids high and flashed a penlight on my irises. "A little something I've been working on to instill *utmost obedience* in my more volatile subjects. As you are the strongest specimen I have, I thought it would be smart to test it on you."

"I feel... weird," I mumbled.

"Yes, yes, a bit of lethargy is to be expected, but other than that, you should notice nothing else. As long as you don't pass out like that one"—he nodded toward Abel—"I'll reward you by giving you a thorough tour of my laboratories. It's the least I can do for your help that night many moons ago."

The dizziness faded, leaving me with a strange exhaustion. He'd said I wouldn't notice any other side effects, but the weird hum of magic still vibrated in my veins.

Simon turned, looking at a doorway, and snapped his fingers. "Come."

Two vampires scurried into the room, obeying Simon's summons. Each wore a lab coat similar to Simon's. These vampires weren't mad like the ones in the jungle I'd fought over the last few weeks. A sane clarity shimmered in their eyes. When they looked at Simon, they did so in a subdued, even cowed manner—they both respected and feared him. Odd to see.

"Do not frighten—or *feed*—on my first success," Simon instructed them as he pointed at me. "I have a deep and particular liking for her. Without this specimen, none of this would be possible. I'll be back shortly. Monitor her and the other wolf." He gestured toward Abel.

Without another word, he strode from the room. As soon as he left, it was like a heavy blanket had been lifted. The man had such a powerful, oppressive aura about him.

After Simon's departure, the vampires set about inspecting the devices attached to Abel and myself, noting random things on clipboards. Even with whatever magic-and-scientific hybrid formula Simon had pumped into me, I was more aware of my surroundings than just a few seconds before. My TO training compelled me to study the environment even more thoroughly. Maybe something would give me some clue or hope for escape.

Leif's scent still lingered, but there was no sign of him in the lab. He must have been in one of the rooms off the one they held me in. There were a few doors that led out, and several were open, which meant he could still be nearby.

The vampires hovered around the room like spectral shadows, writing notes, adjusting dials, examining readouts on displays, and creeping me the fuck out. I'd never been a bigot toward other species, but Von Thornton had turned me off vampires. For the time being, at least.

Even as I tried to catch the vampires' eye, they actively ignored me. Probably for the best. I didn't have the strength to try and talk to them, either, and I could see it would be pointless. Simon had them right under his thumb in a way no simple conversation could sway.

The room didn't give up many secrets. It was as generic as anyone could imagine, exactly what a secret lab on an uninhabited dangerous island would look like. I'd have to wait and see what my friends could do to save me or jump on any chance Simon might give me in the near future. Maybe I'd get lucky and could somehow get Abel and Leif out as well. Those were my only hopes.

Thinking about my friends brought images of Wyatt to my mind, sending a pang of longing through me that was physically painful. I begged whatever fates or gods might be listening to keep him safe. Stuck here, I had no way of being there if he needed me. If he had made it out of the jungle and back to Haven alive, I had no doubt he'd come for me.

He'd have to find me first, though. That would not be easy. It also looked like Simon really was as well-funded and organized as Crew had suspected.

My entire world had been flipped upside down in the last hour. Everything I thought I knew had been shown to be false. Now I was lying here, helpless, and it pissed me off. Terrified me, too.

Please be safe, Wyatt. Be safe and find me. Please find me before it's too late.

Chapter 2 - Wyatt

The rotting flesh stink of the wendigo still burned in my nostrils, mixing with the green scent of the jungle. As badly as my lungs burned from running, and as much as I didn't want that thing to catch me, my mind still screamed at me to go back.

Kira. We'd been separated, the whole group rushing off in different directions. I had to get back to her. Gods only knew what else she might run into out here.

After another hundred yards, I stopped and crouched, listening hard. Silence. Lifting my nose to the air, I sniffed. The wendigo's scent still lingered, though it was fading.

Fuck it. Kira needed me. Doing my best to remain quiet, I began retracing my steps to where we'd originally been when the creature had come upon us. The going went slower than I wanted, but that thing would still be looking for us. I would be no help to Kira if it caught me and decorated the forest with my guts.

Looping around to give a wide berth to the area where the wendigo's scent was strongest, I continued on until a faint whiff of Kira touched my nostrils. Hope and excitement flooded through me, and despite the danger, I rose from my crouch and jogged forward.

Beneath a large palm tree, I found the area where we'd scattered. The ground was torn and disturbed from when Kira, Crew, Eli, and I had bolted. From that location, I managed to find Kira's trail, her scent growing stronger the farther I moved down the path.

"Where are you?" I muttered, worry building with each step.

Several hundred feet on, I froze, sniffing harder, and my worry morphed into panic. Leif. His scent was faint, but easily recognizable. He'd been in this same location. Hands trembling, I knelt and checked the path, pushing aside moss and twigs, looking for tracks. Sure enough, paw prints intermingled with human footprints. Footprints that matched Kira's size.

"Son of a bitch," I hissed.

With a huge effort, I tore my eyes from the tracks and saw what lay ahead. Rising above the tree line, black and monolithic—the volcano. Dread and oily fear dripped down my spine, and a flash of memory broke through. Only a few days before, Leif had tried to drag me up the slope toward that place where the whirring mechanical sounds emanated from the cave entrance.

No. Kira couldn't be there. She would have fought Leif off. She must have.

Bending like someone looking for a lost contact lens, I followed Kira's path. Rather than finding something to allay my fears, they only got worse. After another twenty yards, I found something that made my blood run cold. With numb fingers, I picked up what lay discarded on the path: a metallic hypodermic dart. For a moment, I thought another storm was rolling in. It took a few seconds for me to realize it wasn't thunder, but my own heart slamming against my ribs and booming in my ears.

The tip of the dart only confirmed my fears—it was rusty red and smelling strongly of Kira's blood. Only one person on the island could have done this. *Simon.*

Tossing the dart aside, I moved along, keeping my eyes glued to the ground. Soon, the picture of what happened formed. I came across another set of tracks—adult male. Leif's paw prints. Kira's prints stopped, but a dragging track formed, interspersed with the paw marks. Simon's dart must have held some kind of sedative. Afterward, Leif had dragged Kira's body to Simon's lab. The same way he'd tried to drag me.

Too preoccupied with figuring out what had happened to Kira, I'd allowed myself to forget that I stood in the most dangerous place on the planet. From my right, a dark figure erupted from the jungle, slamming into me. The thing hit me hard enough for every ounce of breath to burst from my lungs as we tumbled over.

Spitting, hissing, and growling, the feral vampire had me at an immediate disadvantage. Unable to draw a breath, I struggled with the creature laying on my chest. It wasn't as emaciated as others I'd seen on the island, which meant it was stronger and more powerful. Fresh blood that smelled of bear shifter wafted from its mouth as its teeth clacked together at my throat.

"Fuck... you," I grunted, finally managing a thin stream of air.

The vampire's wiry strength made it impossible to push him away. With every passing second, its teeth drew closer to my neck. Then, in a spastic surge of twitching energy, the vampire slammed its knee into my crotch. Any strength that *had* returned suddenly flooded out of my body, along with what little breath I'd managed to pull in. An explosive, pain-laden groan burst from my lips, and my limbs went slack. That was all the vampire needed.

The wickedly sharp canines sank into the soft flesh on my neck, a few inches below my right ear. My vision went fuzzy as the vampire's saliva sedated me, allowing the creature to feed unhindered.

For several moments, I lay beneath it in a strangely blissful state, allowing it to suck my life's blood from my neck. The snuffling, gulping, and hungry growling noises didn't seem that bad. It was good to help a fellow creature, to give him what he needed. What was a little blood between friends?

My mind swam as my heartbeat grew ever more rapid. Everything faded in a peaceful haze. There was an almost sexual pleasure to what was happening.

Something massive slammed into the vampire, sending it crashing into the ground beside me. As soon as my flesh was free of its teeth, my own mind fully returned. Shivering with disgust, I scrambled to my feet, ready to rip its damn arms off.

Unfortunately, I was too late for revenge. A dark one-eyed wolf, Crew, already had the thing pinned down, his sharp white teeth puncturing the beast's skin below the jaw. With a quick, vicious jerk of his head, Crew tore the vampire's head free of its body, ending the thing in a second. The body began to shrivel almost immediately.

Standing on shaky legs, I leaned over and spat on the darkening corpse. "Prick."

Crew shifted to his human form and adjusted his eyepatch before gesturing to my neck. "Are you good?"

I touched the spot below my ear. The bite wound had already closed, my healing erasing the punctures. "I'm fine, yeah. I don't think he had me for long."

Crew nodded and glanced around, surveying the area before addressing me again. "Okay. This is what we do: you and I head back to Haven. Eli and Kira will know to find us there."

My brow furrowed in irritation. "Are you trying to order me around? I'm not going anywhere other than after Kira."

"Listen, I'm not having this fight right now. We need to—"

"No!" I snarled, pointing at the ground and the tracks. "Simon has Kira. I'm sure of it. There's a fucking spent tranquilizer dart with her blood on it. We're going after her."

Crew shook his head before I'd even finished. "That's not how things work here. We've all survived this long on this stupid island because everyone listens to what I say. I know this place better than anyone. There are lives at stake, people who rely on me. I say we head back to Haven and regroup."

A growl vibrated in my throat as I took an aggressive step toward the man. "Are you trying to tell me you'll stop me if I try? Because I'd *love* to see you try."

Crew's one good eye went steely cold, and he pressed his chest against mine. "Maybe I will stop you. You may be a Tranquility operative, but I've lived in this fucking place for two years, day and night. I've seen shit—dealt with shit—you can't even comprehend." He grinned savagely. "Even more than TOs have seen."

It took all my willpower not to shove him back. "I've seen what this island has. I've survived just fine. And I'm going to survive while I look for Kira."

Crew gave me a sarcastic smile. "Yeah, really tough life you had on the show. Go out into the woods for an hour or two, then head back into the mansion. Nice hot food, massage therapists, healers, showers, a warm bed. Such a *struggle* you had."

"Fuck you—"

"Can you two boys put your dicks back in your pants? I'm not in the mood to watch that kind of sword fight."

Crew and I spun to find Eli trudging out of the jungle toward us. Seeing her and not another monster, we both relaxed, but I was still spoiling for a fight. The seconds ticked away like a banging drum in my head. Every moment I didn't go after Kira was another moment that Simon could do something awful to her.

Eli placed a calming hand on our chests, gently pushing us away from each other. "We will help you get Kira back," she said to me. "But rushing into Simon's lair with no plan and no backup is suicide. We have to think rationally, or it will go bad for everyone. Worst-case scenario? Simon kills her and cuts his losses. Best case? We underestimate him and we all get captured, too."

An irritated wince creased my face. She was right, of course. I knew better than to go off half-cocked. It was the kind of thing that would get you killed on the job. Hell, it was the same thing I'd always chastised Kira for at work.

Still, it made me crazy to not search for her. Everything in me—my mind, my inner wolf, my instincts—told me to rush after her.

Crew, visibly calmer, nodded in agreement. "I promise we'll help Kira. The last thing I want is Simon messing around with anyone else. I'm not going to cut her loose to fend for herself, but we have to make a plan before attacking Simon. We've tried to find intel, but even after all this time, we know too little. We don't know if he has staff or security in his bunker, what kinds of weapons or magic he has, nothing.

"For all we know, Simon has access to the show broadcast. He may very well know that you and Kira are an item," Crew added to me. "He could try and use you to hurt each other. Unlikely, but possible. A good, strong plan is the only way."

What they said made sense. I knew it, understood it, and on a deep level, agreed with it, but my wolf wasn't having it. When I glanced over my shoulder toward the volcano, he snarled and growled in my mind, demanding I run after her. The urge and desire was so strong that I was ready to argue with Crew and Eli again, but a cacophony of howls from deep in the forest stopped me.

"Shit," Crew said, looking in the direction of the noise. "The ferals."

Eli stepped forward, gazing into the jungle. "I think there's lots of them, too. We have to run. They're headed this way." She turned and looked at me, giving me an assuring nod. "We *have* to. The three of us can't take on a dozen feral shifters alone. You know that, Wyatt."

My fists clenched at my sides, shaking with impotent rage. "Fuck," I hissed. "Fine. Let's go, but," I leveled a finger at Crew, "we come back for her as *soon* as possible. Got it?"

Another set of howls ripped through the trees, closer than before. Crew and Eli both nodded, Crew putting his hand out for me to shake. "I swear. You have my word."

Gritting my teeth, I clutched his hand and shook once. "Fine. Let's go."

Eli and Crew took the lead, as they knew the island better, but all three of us moved with haste as the sounds of the feral pack grew closer. Soon, I could even hear the faint sounds of breaking twigs and tearing leaves as the group headed our way.

The danger behind us should have taken all my attention, but I couldn't stop thinking about Kira. For all I knew, Simon could have already turned her feral, or worse, killed her. The thought alone made bile rise at the back of my throat, and an icy ache pierced my heart.

Eventually, the wind shifted. Crew and I glanced at each other as the mangy stench of the feral shifters reached our noses.

"Change course," Crew said, pointing in a different direction. "Use the wind while we can."

If we could smell them, then we'd finally gotten upwind of the beasts. They would have an almost impossible time catching our scent while we were in that position. Crew was smart and quick on his feet—I had to give him that. He'd come to the same realization as I had, though even quicker.

The three of us hurried, taking a forty-five degree angle from the path we'd been on. Eli explained that this route would add three or four hundred yards to our journey, but not having the ferals on our tail would be well worth the extra time.

Easy for her to say. The woman she loved wasn't locked away with a psychopath. Every second mattered.

The plan worked, though. We'd gone about a quarter mile before the scent of the ferals became so faint as to be almost nonexistent. We'd put enough distance between us and them that we were comfortable talking as we continued our light jog back to Haven.

"I'm positive this Simon guy has his lab *inside* the volcano," I said. "The side closest to the mansion, from what I remember."

"That's one of the main areas we've suspected," Crew said. "That, and a fairly well-hidden underground cave near the swamps, and some caverns in the face of the ocean-facing cliffs to the north. Honestly, the volcano was our best bet. Easier access for air-dropped supplies, more access to all the different parts of the island, plus it's fairly centrally located."

"It's part of why we've always tried to give it a wide berth," Eli added. "A lot of weird things happen near it. Simon has seen Crew before. Has his eyes on him."

"Really?" I asked in surprise.

Crew nodded. "He's tried to capture me at least four different times. I don't think he likes failure. Now, it's more of a matter of pride, I think. It's one of the main reasons I don't like anyone other than Eli leaving Haven. There's no reason for others to get hurt or captured just because Simon has a hard-on for me."

Within ten minutes, we were back at Haven's hidden entrance. We'd barely gotten through all the traps and tunnels that led to Haven proper before J.D. came rushing up the tunnel toward us, a hopeful gleam in his eyes.

"Did you find Leif? Is he okay?"

Knowing Kira was lost somewhere had put my temper on a short leash. "Yes, dammit," I hissed at him, unable to stop myself. "We fucking found him and then lost him. We lost Kira, too."

J.D. shrank back a bit as I glared at him. From farther down the hall, more footsteps hurried toward us.

"What do you mean you lost Kira?" Zoe asked. Mika, Chelsey, and Gavin trailed behind her.

A deep, weary sigh shuddered out of me. I couldn't talk, terrified I might actually burst into tears of fear and frustration.

Zoe, obviously far less afraid of me than J.D., stomped over and shook me. "I said, what do you mean? Where is Kira, Wyatt?"

"Gone. Gods almighty, she's gone, okay?" My voice was strained, on the verge of breaking. My hands shook.

"Motherfucker," Gavin growled, rounding on me. "I knew she wouldn't be safe with you!" He pointed an accusing finger at me. "This is your fault. If I'd been out there, you could fucking guarantee I wouldn't have let Kira out of my sight."

"You piece of shit," I snarled as I leapt toward him, ready to paint the walls with his blood, and damn the consequences.

The only thing that stopped Gavin and me from mauling each other were the others. Crew and Eli wrapped their arms around me, while Mika and J.D. did the same to Gavin. All Gavin and I could do was stare daggers at each other.

It would so fucking good to slam my fist in that Fell fucker's face, I thought.

"Enough!" Crew bellowed, silencing all of us. "We have bigger things to worry about."

His words were like ice water splashed on my rage, and I shrugged out of Crew and Eli's grip. "Everyone calm down," I said, holding my hands up to show I wasn't going to fight anymore.

Crew eyed me warily, but he and Eli stepped back.

"Bickering like kids won't stop anything," Crew said. "It's a waste of time. Simon has taken Kira— we're at least we're ninety-nine percent sure of that. We have to figure out a plan to storm his lab and get her back. We need a few days to organize, then we can head there to rain hell down on Simon."

I nodded along with his words. "Yeah. The only issue is, I'm not waiting a *few days*. We need to head back out ASAP. I plan on heading to the volcano by nightfall. If the whole plan is ready by then? Great. If not? I'll go by myself."

Eli sighed. "I thought we talked about this, Wyatt."

"We did," I said. "I promised I'd come back here and let Crew formulate a plan before heading back for Kira. I never said when *I'd* go back for her. If you all are ready, that's fine, but regardless, I'm leaving tonight."

Gavin's lip curled in disgust. "Kira wouldn't need to be rescued if she'd stayed in Haven in the first place. Who thought this was a good idea, anyway?"

"Please," Zoe hissed, pressing her fingers to her temples, "shut up. Stop talking. All this macho bullshit is making my head hurt. There's too much angry dick in here and not enough level-headed vagina. Am I right?" She glanced at Chelsey, who shrugged, obviously confused by her statement. Zoe rolled her eyes. "*Anyway,* can those of us who are capable of discussion without fighting move this to the meeting room? Then can we get this plan together?"

Before anyone could respond, Zoe turned and headed down the corridor. Gavin sneered and shook his head at me as he followed her. All the while, my wolf raged inside my mind. Part of him was ready to tear off back into the jungle to find Kira, the other part ready to rip Gavin apart for daring to accuse me of endangering her.

Off to the side, J.D. stood still as the others filed past to follow Zoe. He looked more distraught than I'd ever seen him.

I swallowed my pride and anger. "Are you good?"

J.D. shook his head helplessly, mouth agape. "This is my fault. All of it. I asked Kira to do everything she could to get Leif back. I thought about going, but she's better trained. I mean... I'm a fucking alpha. I should have gone with you all. Maybe it would have been different if I'd been there."

I put an arm around his shoulders and led him down the hall toward the meeting room. "You can't blame yourself. Knowing Kira, she would have gone after Leif whether you'd put the idea in her head or not."

But my reassurances didn't seem to penetrate J.D.'s head, and bone-deep guilt still marred his face as we walked into the meeting room. Chelsey entered ahead of us, and even in my misery, it was easy to see how she avoided Crew as she moved to the opposite side of the room. Instead of speaking to Crew, she made a show of probing Eli for information.

"I want to help get Kira back," she said. "She's my friend, and I know she'd do the same for me."

Eli patted her on the arm. "We'll figure all that out. For now, we need to get the basics."

"Absolutely not," Crew barked. He was resting his weight on his fists against the large meeting table, glaring across the room at Eli and Chelsey.

"You aren't going anywhere," he added, this time directly addressing Chelsey.

"Excuse me?" Chelsey looked at Crew like he'd slapped her. "Are you talking to me? Because I don't remember giving you jurisdiction over my decisions."

Ignoring the jibe, Crew waved a hand in frustration. "It's bad enough you're on this gods-forsaken island to begin with. I'm not letting you anywhere near Simon. That's final."

Chelsey, her face blazing scarlet, took a few steps toward Crew. I'd almost never seen her look that way. The woman was usually calm and easygoing, but now she looked ready to kill. The last time I'd seen her with a similar expression was when the show had thrust her little brother into danger. Even then, it had been more of a terrified anger.

This? This was unmitigated rage.

"I'm sorry, *Ben*," she spat. "But of everyone in this room, of everyone on this entire *fucking* island, you are the last person allowed to tell me what I can and can't do. You gave up any say in my life when you turned your back on me on your parents' porch a few years ago." She suddenly frowned as though pretending to remember something. "Or wait... was it someone else who rejected me?" Sarcasm coated every word.

The entire room had gone quiet as we all watched the argument play out, none of us daring to interrupt.

Crew looked like he'd been kicked in the gut. "This... Chelsey, it's not about—"

"Not about what?" she snapped. "Not about ripping my heart out and leaving me to suffer alone?"

Crew slammed a fist onto the table. "I have to keep my mate safe. Don't you understand that?"

My jaw dropped. I didn't know the whole story, but from what Chelsey had explained, this guy had *zero* right to call her his mate.

Chelsey took another step closer, kicking aside a chair with a clatter. "Ben, I don't know if being on this island has given you brain damage, but do I need to remind you how things went down? *You* rejected *me*, not the other way around. I am *not* your mate... you made absolutely sure of that. Not only that, but you did it in the most embarrassing and cowardly way possible. So, how about you shut your mouth?"

The two stared each other down, anger fading into mutual hurt. If one good thing came of this weird fight, it had taken my mind off Kira for a few moments. Now that it seemed to have fizzled, her plight returned in full force. A lance of worry speared into my heart.

Chelsey crossed her arms and stomped out of the room, her sobs echoing back to us. Crew's shoulders slumped and he made to go after her, but Eli grabbed him before he made it to the door.

"Maybe give her some time to cool down," the fallen angel said.

Crew stared after Chelsey, but nodded absently. "Okay. Yeah."

"You guys can talk it out *after* we get Kira back," Eli added, nudging Crew back to the table.

The alpha nodded and wiped at his face. Even though he now had himself under control, Crew waved at Eli to start the meeting.

She addressed us all, giving her leader more time to recover. "Well, back to the problem at hand: Simon. We've had heavy suspicions that his lab was located in the volcano somewhere. With Wyatt's firsthand knowledge, we're pretty positive that we were right. Over the last several months, we'd made preliminary plans to infiltrate with a small but elite team of our best here at Haven. Obviously, that wasn't going to be possible until we knew the location."

"So you guys have never gone on the offensive?" Gavin asked.

"Not as of yet," Eli replied. "Simon is slippery, and not only that, but the show and its security teams make life difficult on the island. It's been all we can do to survive, honestly."

"Well, you guys have lots of supplies," Mika said. "It looks like you're doing all right."

Eli pointed down the hall. "The supplies are from sporadic shipments sent to the show—and I do mean *sporadic*. Their magic staff is too preoccupied with their duties for the show. That means that instead of teleporting the items to the island, they have them air-dropped in. *Maybe* once every eight or nine months, one of them will get blown off course and end up somewhere where I or Crew can raid the supplies before the show staff gets there. Everything else we have are things manifested by our fae or witch citizens. Even then, there's only so much they can do.

"If we can take Simon down, and possibly use his equipment and supplies, we may be able to use what he has to finally get off this island. If we don't deal with him soon, Crew and I are afraid he'll find our location and destroy what little safety we have on this island." She cut her eyes toward me. "Wyatt, are you sure you can find the area where you saw the entrance?"

"I can," I said. "I remember what it looked like and the basic direction of the entrance. I'm trained for stuff like this. I've got you."

She nodded and gave a slight victorious smile. "Good. Crew?"

She glanced back at the alpha, who seemed to have fully shaken off the argument with Chelsey. Stepping forward again, he scanned all of us. "We need to figure out a team who are the most capable and able to handle themselves. We know for sure Simon has magic on his side, but there could be anything from standard weaponry to some of his more unsavory experiments to deal with. I'm not forcing anyone. This will be volunteer only."

"Well, I'm going," Zoe said. "When I get pissed, I can do a fair bit of damage with my magic. And I can tell you now, I'm freaking *pissed*."

Crew and Eli shared a worried look.

"What's wrong?" I asked.

Addressing Zoe, Crew said, "I don't know if it will be a good idea for you to go."

"Why the hell not?" Zoe demanded.

"Simon tends to be more aggressive when it comes to fae," Crew answered. "He seems to target them more than shifters, so it may be best if you sit this out. I don't want you in even more danger than we're in."

"Bullshit," Zoe said, flipping her hair. "You can try to keep me here, but I'm *not* leaving my bestie hanging. I'm going, no matter what."

He held up a placating hand. "Okay, okay, fine. But keep close to me or Wyatt so one of us can keep an eye on you."

Zoe looked happy at the compromise and settled back down.

"I'll go," Mika said quickly.

Maybe I was imagining it, but I thought he gave Zoe a sidelong glance as he said it. It made me think that her volunteering had encouraged him. Strange.

"Count me in," Gavin said, leaning against the far wall.

Crew cut his gaze back and forth between me and Gavin. "Are we going to have a problem here? I'm don't want to have to break up some schoolyard scuffle in the middle of a battle."

Gavin locked eyes with me. After a few seconds, we both nodded. Neither of us wanted to be the cause of Kira getting hurt or put in more danger.

"We're good," I muttered.

"All right, then," Crew said. "I think that's enough. Eli and I will go with three other Haven citizens who already volunteered weeks ago when we started putting this plan together. Any more of us, and the team will be too big to move swiftly and quietly. I think if we can get our supplies and final kinks worked out, Wyatt's plan to go tonight may work."

A shuddering sigh escaped me, and I pressed a hand to my mouth to hide the sound. My wolf was struggling for control of my mind. He wanted to run *now*. It was all I could do to hold him in check. Knowing that we'd go soon did little to alleviate the need.

When J.D. put a hand on my shoulder, I flinched.

"Easy man," J.D. whispered. "How you doing?"

Gazing around, I saw the others were in deep conversation about the mission. I should have been participating, but my head wasn't in the game. All I could do was worry about Kira.

Shrugging helplessly, I said, "Not great. I can't stop thinking about Kira with that lunatic. Every second away from her feels like an eternity."

"We'll get her back. Don't worry. Crew and Eli are pretty damn competent. They know what they're doing."

"I hope so," I muttered, biting at my thumbnail.

J.D. gave me a quizzical look. "You know, if I didn't know better, you're already acting like you're Kira's mate."

"I love her, okay? Labels don't matter. Love is what matters, and I will do anything it takes to get her back safe."

Chapter 3 - Kira

Whatever the machine pumped into my arm had made me lightheaded. There were no clocks or windows in the room, which gave me no clue to how long Simon had been gone. Regardless of how much time had passed, it felt like an eternity. The only thing I had for comfort was the whirring of machinery, the beeps of medical devices, and the low hum of the air conditioner. Even the vampire assistants had left after a while, leaving me alone with Abel's unconscious form.

Whatever was being fed into my body wasn't putting me under. A small blessing. It gave me time to inspect the room, though that proved to be useless. I'd gone over every square inch with my eyes. It was impossible to get out, not only because of my wolfsbane binding, but the doors had locks that required a code—a code I didn't have. The few open doors I *could* see must have been storage or mechanical rooms, or possibly other exam rooms like the one Abel and I were in. No amount of training would get me out of this room by my wits alone.

If escape with my current information wasn't possible, then I needed more details. Simon had told me earlier that he would give me a *tour*. When he returned, I vowed to turn on the charm. I'd make that psycho fucker believe I was the best patient or experiment he'd ever had.

One thing I could count on, above all else, was that Wyatt would come for me. Once that happened, I needed to have some idea of how to get out of the facility. Being able to navigate the deeper recesses of the lab would help keep me from running in circles.

The door of the lab opened, but it wasn't Simon. The vampire assistant bypassed me and went straight to Abel. After checking the machines hooked up to him, she made a few notes on a tablet and strode out again, heels clicking on the stone.

Waiting until the door closed, I lifted my head to get a better look at him. "Abel?" I hissed. "Abel? Can you hear me?"

The other alpha didn't so much as twitch to indicate he'd heard me. Whatever they'd done to him must have been stronger than what they'd done to me. That, or I wasn't easily susceptible to the drugs and potions. Still, it worried me that Abel had been out for so long.

Before my worries could increase, the lab door opened again. Both vampires returned. The one who'd checked on Abel carried a flask of bright yellow liquid and headed back to his bedside. The other pulled up a stool and sat beside me, checking my own instruments.

"What are you doing to him?" I asked, hating how groggy my voice sounded, almost like I was drunk.

Ignoring me, the vampire at my bedside glanced at his colleague. "You know, I've never seen a female alpha shifter in person before," he said.

"They are rare," the female vampire responded.

The male lifted a tool that looked like a gun and inserted a small metal pellet into a gas injection chamber.

"What the hell is that?" I asked, eyeing the implement.

"A little something to keep track of you," he muttered without looking at me. "In case you somehow find your way out of here. Not likely, though. Probably overkill, but... orders are orders."

Without pause, he latched the tiny pellet in place, pressed the gun muzzle against my shoulder, and pulled the trigger. A quiet *psst* burst from the tool, and a sharp, white hot pain crashed through my shoulder. It was like I'd been stabbed with a dull needle.

"Fuck," I hissed, grimacing in pain.

Setting the injection gun aside, the technician leaned closer, hungry eyes taking me in as he gazed up and down my body. "Fascinating," he murmured. "Supple, strong, and that smell?" He leaned over my body and breathed in deep, like a hungry man taking a whiff of Thanksgiving dinner. He sighed in pleasure. "So good."

The attention he was giving me wasn't quite what one would expect from a scientist or doctor. There was a hunger in his eyes that made me nervous.

"Don't get too close," the female warned. "You know how Dr. Shingleman feels about that one. It'll be your ass."

He waved her off. "I know, but... I can't help it. If you could smell the blood in her, you'd understand."

The female tech shrugged and turned away, checking over Abel again. The male vampire leaned close again. "Such a wondrous anomaly."

His gloved hand slipped across my stomach, up to my sternum, then across the mounds of my breasts. My skin crawled at his touch.

"What would that blood taste like?" he whispered as if murmuring to a lover.

Before I could spit in his face or cuss him out, he jerked his hand back, slapping a palm to his temple. A wretched look of agony folded over his face as he clawed at his head, a gurgled gasp of pain escaping his lips.

Behind him, Simon strode into the room with his hand up, looking down his nose in distaste. He must have cast some sort of spell on the vampire.

"Very unfortunate, Trevor," Simon muttered. "I thought you knew how to follow orders. Perhaps when you wake up, you'll have better manners."

The vampire let out a bloodcurdling scream. His left eyeball burst, sending a spray of blood across the room. It spattered my stomach before he went slack and tumbled off the stool onto the floor.

"Holy shit!" I shouted, staring at the lifeless form on the ground.

Simon lowered his hand, ending the fucked-up spell. "No worries. He'll reawaken in five to ten minutes good as new. And, hopefully, with a new respect for his superiors."

The scientist stepped over the body of the dead vampire. Across the room, the female hurried to the door, sending terrified glances at Simon over her clipboard as she left.

Simon hovered over me with that mad gleam in his eye. He clapped his hands once like a giddy child. "I am excited you're still awake. I knew you were strong, but this is beyond my best expectations. I truly have created something formidable in you. How are we doing here?" The question seemed to be addressed to himself rather than me as he leaned down to inspect the device on my arm. Within a few seconds, he grinned. "Good. All the preparatory serum has been infused."

Simon unhooked the IV from the device and then began working on undoing the straps on my wrists. "I have so many fun things to show you. The serum will need time to begin working, but while that happens,

I'd love to show you what has come of our meeting all those years ago."

He slid the wolfsbane-saturated leather strap off my arm. A red welt had formed across my wrist. Once the strap was off, I raised my arm experimentally, and all thought of attack vanished. My muscles were sluggish and slow. The wolfsbane and whatever the hell he'd pumped into me had weakened me to the point that my training would do me no good. Plus, after seeing what he'd done to the vampire, it was pointless to try and overpower him in my current state. I'd have to stick to the plan and do my best to be obedient.

Simon undid the other straps, finishing with the one across my chest. When I sat up, the room spun for a moment, the back of my head throbbing from suddenly being upright.

Though mad, Simon wasn't dumb. Before I'd even managed to get my bearings, he helped me off the table, put my hands behind my back, and tied them with more leather straps, also soaked in wolfsbane.

"Come, let me show you the facility." He winked at me. "I'm sure you'll be very impressed."

I shuffled after him. The lethargy wasn't as bad as before, but the weakness was still enough to make walking exhausting. That didn't stop me from analyzing everything, logging it away for later. Any ounce of information would come in handy when I finally managed to escape. I also wanted to see if I could lay eyes on Leif.

Simon led me down a long corridor lined with LED lights embedded in the stone. At the end, a large and brutally thick steel door stood sentinel. It almost looked like a bank vault. Placing his hand on a glass panel, Simon waited until a thick band of laser light scanned his palm print. A heavy *chunk* sounded from the entryway as it unlocked and swung outward.

My jaw dropped in horror at what lay beyond. A hallway lined with glass walls looked in on holding cells. Each cell held one of the monstrous creations we'd encountered on the island. Combinations of various species melded together in a disgusting tableau, each one as awful—or worse—than the things I'd already fought.

"Come, come. See the wonders I've created," Simon said, ushering me into the hall of horrors.

There was nothing for me to do but gape in terror at the things Simon had brought into the world. Some looked like they shouldn't have been able to survive. One creature swung its head around to glare at me, and a shiver thundered up my spine. It had a human head and face but the teeth of a gator shifter and the slit-pupiled eyes of a lion. Its body was a crisscross of lion fur, plate-like scales, and small patches of pink human flesh.

"Ah, yes," Simon murmured with a smile. "This was one of the first. I think the human face gives it a, uh, I don't know how to say it... a poetry? An immediacy, perhaps. It speaks to the soul. I truly view them as individual works of art. This is my newest." He gestured to the next holding cell.

This one had been totally sealed and filled with water. Inside, a being swam and thrashed in the water. It had the body and tail of a merperson, but from the chest up, it had the bulbous head of a great white shark. Serpentine legs moved in time with the tail, propelling it around the small enclosure. As we neared, the thing pressed itself against the glass, pushing its webbed merperson hands on the wall, and gazed out at us with lifeless black shark eyes.

"Mother of gods," I whispered.

"I know," Simon whispered enthusiastically. "Very exciting, isn't it? It took a long time to get the spell right, but this one can survive in water *and* on land. Very difficult."

"Why?" I asked, the word leaving my lips before I could stop them.

Simon turned and stared at me, a quizzical look on his face. "What do you mean *why*, my lovely?"

Huffing out a breath of exasperation, I pulled my eyes from the horror in the tank. "Why would you create these things?"

Simon let out a slight chuckle. "Money, of course. Money, and to find out if I *could* do it. It's like they say, when you see a mountain, why not challenge yourself to climb it?"

What? I couldn't understand what he was saying. Money? How?

"You... sell these?" I asked, incredulous. "To whom?"

"Whoever pays the most. *Lots* of people interested in killing machines these days, what with the war raging on the mainland. It's still in the early days, with small skirmishes here and there, but soon? It will take off like a wildfire. When it does, the sides that have my beauties will have a marked advantage, and the money these bring in will help fund more of my experiments. Preorders have been rolling in. Many of these have already been sold. Once they are ready, they'll be shipped to the mainland. That's when the real fun will begin."

Before I could ask more questions, a roar erupted behind us. I spun around to face another cell. Inside were three beasts of varying combinations. The thick glass muffled the noises, but the sounds of battle still came through. Snarling mouths, snapping teeth, ripping claws. A spray of blood spattered the glass as the three beings waged their own war.

"Oh," Simon said, a disappointed look on his face. "This is not what I'd planned. They're supposed to try to mate with each other, not kill each other. Hold on a moment."

He raised a hand, passing it over the glass in an arc. The air shimmered faintly with magic. Immediately, the creatures stopped fighting and slowly sagged to the ground, unconscious.

"Still a bit hard to control," Simon said when he was done. "All of them are. As I said, it's why I haven't shipped any of these creations out yet. But that's where you come in, Kira."

The look Simon gave me sent spiders crawling all over my skin. "What do you mean by that?" I asked.

Was he going to turn me into one of these things? The thought sickened me. I'd die first. I'd rip out my own throat with my bare hands if I had to choose between that and being turned into one of these... these *things*.

"A new experiment that I think your particular genetics will help with," Simon said. "I feel that with the strength you showed in the first experiment, you will be the key to creating a new substance that can help to control these dear creatures. You see, my first shipments *will* be leaving the island soon, and they need to be ready for battlefield control.

"Of course, it's not only these hulking beautiful weapons of war. Other, more... let's say, *subtle* tools have already been sent out over the last several months. I have devices that can nullify fae and wiccan magic. A new concoction that can send even sane vampires into a feeding frenzy like sharks in bloodied waters. Along with those are other items as well, like a potion that can force shifters into heat. Very powerful.

It's hard to fight when all you can think about is humping the person standing beside you." Simon dissolved into a fit of laughter.

He'd created the heat potion? The thing that had helped ruin my career and ultimately sent me to this island? Somehow, this man had had a hand in two of the most defining moments of my entire life. Both had sent me down a dark and depressing path. Now, it appeared he'd be on hand for *another* equally awful moment.

Recovering, Simon wiped a tear from his cheek. "The forced ferality serum is still in the development stage, though. That is my only development that is yet to sell."

"Why are you showing me this?"

"Why?" Simon looked at me like I was crazy. "Well, for one thing, all my assistants are quite boring. When I found you in the jungle, I was ecstatic. To have someone who would truly appreciate my genius? I cannot tell you how marvelous it feels. You, more than anyone, must realize how amazing all this is. My experiment unearthed your inner wolf, made you whole. The same can be said of me. For many years, as a half-breed, I had access to my fae magic, but not my shifter side. After testing the concoction on you, then using it myself and releasing the power of my inner wolf? It was like nothing I'd ever experienced. The wolf not only gave me my shifter powers, but also enhanced my magical abilities."

"So, you're saying this is all my fault?" I gazed around at the horrors in the cells, feeling the crushing weight of guilt.

Either Simon didn't hear the shame in my voice or chose to ignore it. He nodded eagerly. "Indeed. With my increased magical powers, my experiments grew in complexity at an exponential rate. My inventions and developments progressed at leaps and bounds. Soon, I'll be able to show the world what true power is." Simon pulled his eyes away from me and stared into space, voice dropping to a whisper. "Perhaps one day, my father and his pack will look upon me with pride."

That last bit was barely audible, and it confused the hell out of me. Maybe there was even more going on in Simon's head than he let on. Desperate to learn more, I kept my mouth shut, hoping he'd give more glimpses into his mind. Instead, he ushered me into another corridor, leading me away from his abominations.

"Here is where I keep much of the *fuel* for my most intense magical work," Simon said.

He punched a code into a panel. A section of that wall slid aside, revealing floor-to-ceiling racks filled with angel wings. Despite myself, I gasped. There were feathers of over half a dozen different colors and sizes. Some were single wings, while others sat beside their matching partner. Several racks were empty, either waiting on new additions or disposed of the wings that *had* been there.

"Where did you get all of these?" I asked. Wings from fallen angels weren't technically rare, but they were hard to find and almost prohibitively expensive. I'd been shocked when the show had us look for them in the forest during one of the last challenges, but *The Reject Project* basically had a blank check to work with.

Simon shrugged and punched the code back in to hide the wings. "Here and there. Angels fall, wings are lost. You have to know the right people to get these, of course. There's no substitute for the magical power they contain." He smiled. "This next area should be of utmost interest to you, though. Follow me."

Simon's excitement bordered on fanaticism. He couldn't even see the cruelty and pain he was inflicting on other beings. Everything was about his brilliance, his experiments, his goals—everything else was beneath him. The guy was a fucking sociopath.

The *next area* Simon was so excited about was even more disgusting. He led me to a huge, glass-walled corral filled with feral shifters in their animal forms. Bears, tigers, lions, panthers, wolves, and a half-dozen others all snarled and snapped at each other, fighting over scraps of bone and meat scattered on the ground. In the upper portion, feral bird shifters sat on beams, nervously plucking out their own feathers and twitching their heads back and forth madly.

"Good gods," I muttered, gazing through the glass at the awful living conditions.

"I know." Simon beamed. "These are my absolute favorites. The others are left to roam the island at will. Though, your little friend Leif is an exception. He is exceptional at finding other specimens for me."

At Leif's name, I scanned the group of animals, but caught no sight of him. Instead, through the glass walls of the opposite end of the corral, three more assistants walked by, rolling a massive plastic bin filled with hunks of meat. The team inserted them into a feeding trough in the wall, and the creatures inside immediately ran over and snatched the food, only to begin fighting once more.

Between these assistants and the techs I'd seen in my room, Simon had a total of five staff members. How many more could there be? Everything here was well-run and professional. When discussing this man with Crew and Eli, I'd imagined some dirty, mad-scientist lab with limited resources carved into a muddy cave. This was... beyond anything I could have guessed. I realized I'd need to double the number of staff in my mind from whatever I counted during this tour. Safer to be too careful than not careful enough. The last thing I wanted was to expect nine or ten people when there were actually twenty.

Simon took my bound arm and led me down the hall. "Speaking of Leif, I thought you might like to see him. Here we are."

I caught a whiff of Leif's scent and found him alone in a cell. Unlike the other ferals, he was in his human form, sitting on the ground. His back rested against the wall, but he rocked back and forth, tearing at his hair. Whatever Simon had done to him, he was mentally and physically struggling with it. My heart hurt to see him fighting the madness that threatened to drag him under. If I hadn't been bound and weakened, I thought I might have butchered Simon right there in that hallway.

A doorway beside Leif's room opened, and yet another assistant came out. This one was a human.

"Dr. Shingleman? The subject still hasn't become fully feral yet. I think the newest version of the potion isn't as strong as we'd hoped."

Simon sighed and gazed at Leif. "True, but it does keep him more pliable. Let's continue tweaking the formula, see if we can find a happy medium. Thank you for the update. We'll continue assessing each time he returns from his excursions."

Simon and the assistant led me back down the hallways to the vault door. Passing the ferals and abominations, I kept my eyes down, not wanting to see them again. On the walk, I grew lightheaded and dizzy again, probably from whatever they'd pumped into my body. It also could have been from fear. What *did* Simon have planned for me? The unknown was almost too much to contemplate. Would I end up like Leif, half-mad and suffering? It was too terrifying a thought. Getting torn apart to be melded with other creatures would be even worse. A fate worse than death.

Hurry, Wyatt, I thought as we stepped through the vault door.

As badly as I wanted Wyatt to come swooping in like a white knight to save me, I also feared it. Gods only knew what kind of security measures Simon had built into this place. The creatures he had contained here alone would be more than Wyatt could handle on his own. Still, he *would* come for me. I *knew* it. He would fight tooth and nail to save me. It was a quality I'd spent years hating, but now? When I needed it most? I realized it was one of his greatest qualities. He'd never leave someone he loved to fend for themselves.

We reached the exam room, and I spotted the vampire Simon had tortured on the floor. His burst eye had regenerated, but he still gazed out with dead eyes. Whatever Simon had done must have been severe for him to still be healing.

The other tech sat beside Abel's unconscious form, scribbling notes on a tablet.

Before Simon could return me to the table, a Klaxon alarm ripped through the dull silence of the lab. Everyone, excluding Simon, flinched in surprise. The scientist merely stared up at the warning lights that flashed in time to the *whoop–whoop–whoop* sound of the alarm.

"Son of a bitch," Simon growled, looking angrier than I'd seen him thus far. "That's the proximity alarm." He spun to glare at the assistant who'd walked back with us. "Someone has broken through the perimeter. Unleash the gods-damned ferals. *Now.*"

The assistant sprinted from the room. A surge of hope flushed away the worry that had been gnawing at me. Was this Wyatt coming to save me? I didn't want to feel the crushing disappointment if it wasn't him, but I couldn't help myself. A faint smile played at my lips as I imagined Wyatt storming the lab in search of me.

"You," Simon snapped at the vampire tech. "Secure this one, and hurry."

Before she could even stand to obey his order, Simon vanished, stalking down the corridor away from the room. This was my chance. No other time would be as perfect as now.

The tech laid her tablet down and hurried over to me, unbuckling the leather straps keeping my arms bound behind my back.

Digging deep into my mind, I summoned my wolf. I apologized for having suppressed her and hating her all those years, for thinking she'd gone mad and killed an innocent person. I asked her for all the strength she could give me, enough to do what needed to be done, even with my body sedated and weakened.

She responded with a happy, hungry growl.

As soon as my hands were free, I pulled every ounce of strength and power I could summon, pushing away the effects of the drug and wolfsbane. Spinning and lashing out with the back of my fist, I hit the vampire in the chin.

Even with my wolf giving me all she had, it wasn't enough. The hit was feeble and close to ineffective. It startled more than hurt the vampire, sending her stumbling backward. Surprise was replaced with fear.

If I let her recover, it would be over. My *only* chance was surprise.

Leaping forward, I kicked out with both my feet, using mass instead of strength. My heels smacked into her chest. She was flung backward as I crashed to the floor. The assistant careened into the wall, fell forward, and slammed her temple against the edge of the metal table I'd been strapped to earlier. The solid steel corner burst through her skull and into her brain. She fell to the floor, likely dead, even if just temporarily.

The other vampire would be awake any second. I had to move quickly. Rushing to Abel's side, I ripped the tube from the device on his arm, then began to unstrap the binds that held him. My hands stung as I tugged at the leather straps, and the wolfsbane leached out onto my fingertips. As I struggled, the best sound I'd ever heard in my life echoed from deep within the mountain laboratory: the howl of a familiar wolf. Chills ran down my spine and a grin spread across my face. Wyatt.

Farther away, gunfire erupted. *Pop-pop-pop.* Trying to ignore it, I finished unbuckling Abel's arms and went to work on his ankles. After a few moments,

I'd freed him. Without the IV pumping shit into him, his eyes fluttered open, but he was in no shape to walk on his own.

I'd managed to get his legs off the table before a hulking shape slammed into me from behind. Crashing to the floor, I found the male vampire, now healed and awake, atop me.

"I see you've been busy while I was asleep," he hissed into my face. "Maybe I will get a taste of that blood after all." He grabbed my hands and pinned them at my sides, easily overwhelming my weakened strength. His face leered mere inches from my own, and a nasty smile crossed his vampiric face. "Maybe..." He nudged his knee between my legs. "I'll taste more than your blood."

"Fuck you!" I used every bit of strength I had left to pull my knees up between us and kick out.

He didn't go flying like I'd hoped, but he released my hands and tumbled back a foot or two. In a blink, he was back on his knees and coming at me again, an even angrier look on his face. That look of rage and hunger vanished when a furious snarl erupted from behind him. The vampire's face collapsed into terror before he spun to find Wyatt's dark wolf stalking toward him, his torn ear twitching, teeth bared.

"No," the vampire moaned. "No, no, no n—"

Wyatt lunged forward, slamming his jaws against the man's skull. Wyatt thrashed his head back and forth, sending the vampire's body flopping side to side like a rag doll. Eventually, the vampire's head parted from its body, and the bastard was dead for good. The decapitated body tumbled into a corner, where it immediately began to decompose.

Wyatt tossed the head aside and shifted to his human form, rushing toward me. Unable to help myself, tears of relief flooded my eyes. "Wyatt."

He had me in his arms before I could blink. Collapsing into him, I allowed myself one sob before I forced myself to regain control. We had to be ready to fight our way out. His scent intoxicated me, sending shivers of pleasure through my body. Clutching at him, I basked in his strength. He was alive. He'd come to rescue me. I was a strong woman, but sometimes it was nice to be saved.

Especially if it was by the man you loved.

Chapter 4 - Wyatt

Feeling Kira's body pressed against mine sent a shiver of relief through me that surged all the way to my bones. My inner wolf howled deep, letting out all the stress that had been building within him since Kira went missing.

"Are you okay?" I asked.

She pulled away from our embrace to look into my eyes. "I've never been so relieved to see you in my life. That's saying a lot."

She hadn't answered my question. "Kira, I need to know that you're okay."

"I'll be fine, but we've got to hurry. There's no time to talk."

The sounds of howling and snarling shifters, gunfire, pulses of magic, and screams of confusion echoed from deeper in the compound. The cacophony made me feel like we were in the middle of a war zone. Which, on second thought, was exactly where we were.

"Let's go," I urged, tugging on Kira's hand. "We underestimated Simon's defenses. This rescue mission is going to fall apart if we don't hurry."

Kira yanked her fingers from my grip. "Help me with Abel. We can't leave him."

I froze and looked toward the other exam table, where an unconscious man lay. It really *was* Abel. I'd been so focused on finding Kira and killing the vampire attacking her, nothing else about the situation had sunk in. The tunnel vision of battle had kept me from getting the whole picture.

I gaped down at him. "He's alive?"

"Yeah. Help me."

Together, we got him off the table. Abel was unconscious, and Kira weak and drained from whatever Simon had done to her. Rather than weigh her down with Abel, I lugged him over my shoulder like a sack of concrete.

With my free hand, I gestured at the door I'd come through. "Down this hall, first corridor on the right. That's where I left Eli and Zoe. They were going to destroy as much of Simon's equipment as they could."

"Zoe?" Kira's head whipped toward me, and I wasn't sure if it was terror or relief that flashed through her eyes.

"She wouldn't take no for an answer. Come on."

Taking the lead, I hurried down the hall, Kira close behind me. The battle sounds grew as we rounded the corner and walked right into a full fight.

"Stay down," I hissed at Kira, pushing her against the wall as we entered.

Zoe and Eli were using their abilities to fry equipment, computers, and everything in between. On the far side of the room, Crew, Mika, and Gavin fought a group of vampires and demons. Three of the Haveners fought Simon himself and a couple of feral shifters.

Simon looked irate as the battle played out. Irate, but not scared or nervous. More like he was pissed his day had been disturbed.

"Filthy idiots!" Simon screamed over the roar of battle. "Don't you realize what you're doing? How much work you're destroying?"

Even from my distant vantage, I could make out the look of utter disdain and disgust he directed at Zoe. She had her back turned to him, and he raised his hand and sent a blast of magic her way. Eli jumped in front of the ripple of magic and blocked it, sending the spell careening into the wall. It slammed into the concrete, tearing a four-foot-wide hole in the wall. Had that power struck Zoe, she never would have survived.

Kira couldn't stay here—things were too dangerous.

"Crew!" I called out over the cacophony.

He turned his wolf head toward me after dispatching a vampire.

"Fall back," I said. "I've got Kira. Let's get the fuck out of here."

Crew nodded and shifted back to his human form. "Fall back! To the entrance. We have the target in hand. Fall back!"

The others immediately fell back toward us even as Simon and his team continued their assault. A stray spell slapped into the doorjamb beside me, bare inches from my face. A lick of purple fire washed across the wall, sending wicked, blistering heat toward me. Flinching away, I shouldered Abel more firmly and grabbed Kira's hand to get her to the exit.

"Shit!" Kira shouted, pressing a hand to her forehead. "Leif. We have to save Leif."

"What?" I barked at her, confusion and incredulity in my voice.

"They have Leif here. They had him in a cell. We can't leave without him."

A deep, angry growl rippled from my throat. The look in her eyes told me all I needed to know. Kira Durst had made a decision, and that was final. Either I helped her, or I knocked her out and dragged her out of here... and if I tried the latter, she'd never forgive me. Arguing would only ensure we were stuck in this damned place even longer.

One of Crew's Haven guys, a burly bear shifter, rushed through the door.

"Hey!" I yelled at him. "Take this guy. We've got to save someone else." I handed Abel's limp body to him.

"What the fuck?" he asked, surprised. "I thought we were coming for her."

"Change of plan. Tell Crew we're going after Leif. He'll know what that means." I gripped Kira's hand tighter. "We have to hurry."

Before the bear shifter could argue, Kira and I sprinted down the hall, Kira taking the lead. As we ran, it became evident that she'd had some time to explore the compound, as she rounded corners and rushed through doors like she'd memorized the place. Knowing her, she very well may have.

Eli had managed to shut down the lockdown security mechanism in Simon's facility, which was how we'd breached the compound. Every door that had been locked now stood wide open, which looked to be a good thing. Kira led me through what looked like the biggest, heaviest door I'd ever seen in my life, where a horror show of unspeakable monsters awaited beyond it. We were going too fast for me to get a good look, but those I did see made my stomach flip wildly, and I had to swallow down the vomit that threatened to spew from me.

The sounds of fighting had faded to almost nothing by the time we reached Leif's holding chamber. Sitting with his back against the wall, Leif looked much like he had the last time I'd seen him—rocking monotonously back and forth, holding his head. His hair lay in greasy lumps between his fingers, and he was covered in a thick layer of mud and muck.

"Are you sure he's okay?" I asked.

"No idea, but we have to try," Kira said. "He's obviously fighting whatever Simon did to him. Be ready, though." She stepped forward to unlatch his cell.

Rather than electric locks, Leif's cell was secured by three massive sliding metal bars. Kira pulled each aside with a loud *clunk* before pulling the door open.

Leif froze mid-rock and stared at us. "Kira? Wyatt?"

"Thank the gods," I said with a sigh of relief. Maybe he was okay.

"Come on, Leif," Kira said, extending a hand toward him. "We're gonna get you out of here."

A smile played at his lips, and he reached out as well. Then, like a switch had been flipped, the smile vanished. His lips peeled back, turning the grin into a vicious grimace. Growling a warning to Kira, Leif snatched his hand away and shifted.

"Kira, get back." I grabbed the back of her shirt and yanked her into the hall.

I'd planned to slam the door shut and lock him back in, but Leif was too fast. He leaped forward, banging the door back open with his shoulder, and crashed straight into Kira, the two of them tumbling to the floor. I grabbed Leif's tail and wrenched him away from Kira before he could sink his teeth into her. Now fully feral again, he spun, snapping his maw at me. Ivory white teeth clapped together an inch from my hand.

Startled, I lost my balance and fell backward. It was all he needed. In a second, he was on top of me.

Before he could tear my throat out, I shoved my forearm under Leif's jaw and pushed him away. Saliva dripped onto my cheeks as he growled and snapped. With my free hand, I held a fist full of his fur, keeping him from twisting to get a better angle at my neck.

"Kira," I grunted. "Help. He's fucking strong."

Before Kira could get to me, the sound of boots running towards us filled my ear. Great. If Leif didn't rip my head off, some of Simon's guys would blow my brains out. Those thoughts were bouncing through my mind when Eli rounded the corner. Not Simon's men, but a friend.

"Little help!" I called out, still struggling to keep Leif at bay.

Eli rushed forward and placed a hand on Leif's head. "Peace, brother."

With those words, Leif's eyes rolled to the back of his head, and he slumped sideways onto the floor before unconsciously shifting back to human.

Kira, still slowed by what Simon had done to her, smiled up at Eli. "Good timing."

Eli shook her head disapprovingly. "When Crew heard what you two were doing, he sent me to find you." She nodded to Leif's sleeping form. "I guess he's coming with us?"

"He is," Kira said, wincing as she got to her feet. "We'd never leave him here."

"We have to run," Eli said. "Who's carrying him?"

"You guys are slow as hell, aren't you?" another voice called.

Kira and I whirled to see Mika jogging up. He shrugged. "I figured Eli might need some help."

The fallen angel looked affronted by the suggestion, but said nothing. Mika stepped forward, and with my help, heaved Leif up onto his shoulder. He gave the three of us a meaningful look. "There are ferals running through the halls. I think Simon let them all loose. So far, he hasn't let those damn monsters out yet, but that's probably coming if we don't get the fuck out of here."

"Then I suggest," Eli said, "we get moving."

Eli and I took the lead, with Kira behind us and Mika carrying Leif at the back. The compound had gone strangely silent, now that the main battle had followed Crew and the others toward the entrance we'd breached. Our first roadblock came about a hundred feet past the lab where I'd last seen Crew and the others. Two tiger shifters fought and snarled at each other over the lifeless body of one of Crew's men.

Eli tore past me in a rage, leaping on and attacking one of the tigers. I shifted and went to work on the second. It slashed out with a paw, claws slicing the air in front of my face. In a lucky turn of fate, the tiger slipped on the blood coating the floor and crashed to its side. Before it had time to right itself, I lunged forward and clamped my jaws on the thing's throat as hard as I could, shaking my head for good measure. It managed to swing a paw toward me, raking its claws painfully down my side before the cartilage of its throat snapped and crumbled between my teeth.

On the opposite side of the hall, Eli had dispatched the other feral. She knelt next to the dead Havener, a devastated look on her face as she ran a thumb along his jawline.

"Jackson? Dammit," she muttered. "We aren't leaving him. Gods only know what that sick fuck will do to his body."

"Are we gonna carry him?" I asked, glancing back at Mika, who was still carrying Leif. I didn't see how we'd make it out with two bodies.

Eli gave me a pained look and shook her head. "No, but I'm not letting Simon experiment on him. Jackson was a friend. He deserves better. Hang on."

She put her hands on the man's body. While she closed her eyes to concentrate, I glanced around nervously. Time had gone strange. It somehow felt as though it was going really slow and really fast at the same time. We had to get out of here, but I didn't want to rush Eli. Kira stayed silent as well, though she looked as concerned about the time we were losing as I was.

A moment later, a strange blue flame engulfed the body, and Eli stood, backing away. In seconds, the Havener had turned into nothing but a faint cloud of ash.

"Sleep well, my friend," Eli murmured. She turned to us and nodded. "It's time. We need to hurry."

"Fine by me," I agreed. "Let's go. At this point, we'll be lucky to get out of here alive ourselves."

The rest of the compound remained deserted as we drew near the entrance. Gunfire erupted again, along with the howls and roars of battle.

"Damn," Eli grunted. "We can't go that way. Simon's men will be blocking the tunnel."

I nodded and pointed down a side corridor. "From what I saw when we came in, if we go this way, there should be another corridor that connects to the one we came in. It'll spit us out right by the door, hopefully ahead of Simon's men. We have to hope that Crew and the others can hold them off long enough for us to get out."

Eli didn't look happy about the plan. To be fair, it was a shit plan. Too much unknown, too little recon, too many things that could go wrong. But our only other options were going into the fray or staying here and becoming another of Simon's sick experiments.

"Fine," Eli said.

"Kira, are you good?" I asked. She didn't look good.

She waved me away. "I'll be fine. Let's keep moving."

Her words didn't have the intended effect on me. If anything, she looked even worse than when I'd found her in the midst of that vampire attacking her. Her complexion was pale, and she was sweating more than I thought was necessary, even with all our running.

Whatever Simon had done to her had taken a toll. Her wrists and ankles had telltale wolfsbane burns. She'd been drugged *and* poisoned. Even with her shifter healing, it was a testament to her strength and training that she was even walking, much less running through this place.

The secondary hallway led in the direction I thought, but we'd only managed to get twenty feet down it when Simon lunged from a doorway, blocking our path. Kira and I, in the lead, skidded to a stop, the others almost running over us.

Simon didn't bother speaking. No quick jokes, no monologue about how we'd ruined his plans. Instead, he swept a hand through the air. Magic pulsed out of him, cascading toward our entire group, except he wasn't aiming at all of us. Only Kira.

She screamed, not in pain but surprise as she shifted into her wolf form. It didn't take long for me to realize she hadn't done it on purpose—Simon had somehow forced the shift. Kira thrashed her head around, eyes wide and panicked, hackles raised in terror along her back.

"Now we see her true nature," Simon said with a twisted grin.

I shifted and moved between Kira and Simon, growling at him, daring him to try to touch her.

He smiled even wider, no fear in his eyes. "Ah, yes. You could be a nice addition to my prized collection, Mr. Rivers."

Down the hall behind Simon, Crew and Gavin appeared, both covered in blood. Crew saw us and waved a hand. "Move! Come on."

Knowing we didn't have more than a few seconds, I lunged at Simon, slamming my paws into his chest and pressing him to the wall. The others, even Kira in her distraught state, took the opening I'd made and rushed past us.

Simon hadn't even flinched as I attacked. He reached down, took hold of my front paws, and leaned in close. "Pathetic."

Fast as lighting, he shoved a foot into my stomach and pushed me away. His strength shocked the hell out of me. A fae *couldn't* be that strong. No way. As I tumbled to a heap, the thundering sound of boots running from the opposite end of the hall echoed forth. Reinforcements for Simon.

Flipping over and regaining my stance, I bared my teeth at Simon. If I wasn't going to make it out of here, I'd take this asshole with me.

When Simon shifted into a wolf, I could do nothing but gape at him. My canine jaw hung open in horror. I'd scented a shifter, but had assumed it was from all the others. Simon was a shifter? But he was a fae. What the hell was going on?

Though thickly muscled and sleek, Simon's wolf had a twisted look to it, as though it was slightly deformed. Snarling, he took an aggressive step toward me. As strong as he'd been in his human form, I did not want to start a fight with him now, especially with how strange he looked. I couldn't figure it out, but something about his wolf looked bizarre, like it shouldn't have been possible.

"Wyatt!" a scream sounded from down the hall.

I glanced toward it. Kira. She'd managed to shift back and was trying to come for me, but Crew and Gavin had her by the arms, trying to drag her away. The bootsteps drew ever closer, and now I could make out voices. Simon inched closer, saliva hanging from his maw.

We weren't going to make it.

Zoe, her face covered in blood but showing no injuries, rounded the corner like the answer to our prayers. "There you are, you assholes! I thought you'd left me."

Simon swiveled his head around and growled at Zoe, who sent a massive cloud of pitch black smoke toward him. The tendrils of the ink-black mist enveloped him, and barking wolf coughs erupted from the fae/shifter's mouth as he tried to breathe.

Zoe turned and sent an additional cloud down the hall behind her. It swarmed the corridor. The sounds of screams and coughing echoed down the hallway, Simon's reinforcements overcome by the magic.

Zoe rushed toward me. "Move it or lose it, fuzzy boy."

Shifting back, I ran after Zoe, and we joined Crew and the others. Kira collapsed into my arms and ran with me. The gunfire and spell-casting had stopped. All we could hear were confused shouts as the entire compound staff dealt with the cloud Zoe had manifested.

Exiting the final hallway, we rushed out the door that hung from destroyed hinges from our earlier breaching. That had only been ten or fifteen minutes ago. How was that possible? In my mind, we'd been in there for hours, fighting, searching, and battling our way out.

The darkness of the night embraced us as we ran.

"We need to hurry," Zoe said. "That smoke spell only lasts two or three minutes."

Her insistence that we hurry was unnecessary—we were all moving as fast as we could with our injuries and hindrances. After the sterility and man-made nature of the compound, being in the green and brown of the jungle made my head spin, like we'd stepped out into a different reality.

"Has anyone seen Jackson?" Crew asked as we ran.

"He didn't make it," Eli said sadly. "I took care of it. Simon won't get his hands on him."

"Son of a bitch," Crew hissed.

We went on in silence for a few minutes. Crew seemed to be going through a gamut of emotions. Losing one of his people was hitting him hard. The man had a deep sense of responsibility for those in his care—that was easy to see. But he also understood the peril we were in and pushed his mourning aside.

"We can't go straight back to Haven," Crew said. "Simon might try to track us. There's a river ahead. Some of us need to go upstream, the rest downstream. Find someplace to hide, then we'll make our way back to Haven when we're sure he's not following."

"Got it," I said. "I want you to take Leif. Eli can keep him asleep. I'll take Mika, Zoe, and Kira with me. The rest of you, branch off."

Gavin glared at me as we ran, obviously wanting to argue. At least he was smart enough not to start with his shit in a middle of a crisis.

Crew gestured to his other team member, who took Leif's limp body from Mika. Crew's team was heavily laden, with Leif and Abel both unconscious. It'd be slow-going for them.

"We'll hang back after you guys run," I said. "Try and make sure our scents are the heaviest when they eventually get to the river. That should give you a head start."

"The river is only a couple of feet deep," Eli pointed out. "Too shallow for any nasty beasts. We'll cross to mask more of the scent. Make it as difficult as possible for them to follow."

"Good call," Crew said. "There it is." He pointed at the river through the trees.

We all crossed, and Crew called us over, pointing first in one direction, then another. "I'll take my team this way," he said. "You guys head that way. Once we're sure we aren't being followed, we can all loop around and head to Haven. You guys already know how dangerous this place is, but watch your backs." He tapped his eyepatch. "Lots of nasty things out there. I don't wear this as a fashion statement."

We were running for our lives, but curiosity got the best of me. "How did you lose that eye, anyway?" Shifters healed from almost any wound unless it was truly terrible.

"Nasty thing got a hold of me about a year ago," Crew said. "Looked like the grim reaper. Swiped at my face with this big scythe. I dodged, but the silver blade took my eye. Even the fae and wiccans in Haven couldn't fix it."

I shuddered, remembering my own run-in with the revenant. "Understood. We'll see you soon."

Crew gave me a meaningful look as he departed. "Be careful. We'll see you soon."

I nodded and led my team away from the river. Knowing that Simon's people might be right on our tails pushed most thoughts from my mind, but we were still on Bloodstone Island. Any of a hundred different dangers might be lurking around each tree and shrub. Worry ran through me like a high-voltage wire.

"Wyatt?" Kira said, putting a hand on my arm. "We need to talk."

"Is now the best time for a heart to heart?" Mika asked, raising an eyebrow.

Kira shook her head. "It's not like that. Simon put a tracker in me."

We all froze, and my eyes widened. "Inside you?" I asked.

Kira nodded, yanking her sleeve up. "Here, in my shoulder. We've got to get it out. Otherwise, they'll follow us. We'll never get away from them or be able to hide."

"Damn," I hissed. "We've got to get somewhere safe. Then we can work on that." I glanced up an incline and saw an overhanging rock, high on a ridge.

"Up there." I pointed. "We can hide in the shadows under that rock. It gives us a view of the surrounding area, and we'll see them coming if they do end up following us. Let's move."

The hike up the hill to the rock outcropping was silent. Even Zoe was too exhausted to do more than gasp for breath as we trudged to our hiding spot. With the overhang hiding us from the moonlight, I was able to sit with Kira.

"What did that asshat put inside you?" Zoe asked her. "Was it a magic gemstone? Metal? Glass? What?"

Kira, still looking drained and tired, lifted her sleeve again. "A pellet sort of thing. Probably metal, but I'm not sure. I didn't get a good look at it. I don't think it was magical, though. A vampire inserted it with some sort of injector gun."

I looked at Zoe. "Can you get it out?"

She cocked an eyebrow at me. Her face still had a smear of blood across it, making her look like some kind of warmongering fae goblin. "Do you doubt my skills?"

"Just want to make sure Kira is safe."

"You and me both, buddy," Zoe said with a humorless chuckle. "If there are no counter spells and it's a simple mechanical device, it should be easy. But medical magic isn't my forte."

Zoe placed a hand on the spot Kira had indicated and closed her eyes. A few moments later, Kira winced in pain.

"Shit," she cursed, jerking her shoulder away from Zoe's hand.

A small bead of blood trickled from her shoulder, but when she moved away, a tiny metal pill hit the stone at our feet, bouncing once, then coming to rest. Mika lifted a foot, ready to slam his heel down to destroy it. I put a hand on him to stop.

"Hang on," I said. "If this is what they're tracking, then we can use it to keep them off our asses and get back to Haven faster."

Zoe's eyes widened in understanding. "Oh, nice. A diversion?"

"Exactly," I said. "Can you enchant this thing to move on its own or something?"

"A locomotion spell?" She shrugged. "Yeah, probably. It won't last long, though. Maybe only fifteen or twenty minutes."

"That's perfect," I said. "Send it in the opposite direction of Haven. Someplace really dangerous."

"Send it to the swamps," Kira suggested, tugging her sleeve back down. "Make those fuckers work for it."

"Say no more," Zoe said, picking up the pellet.

The tiny metal object hovered along the ground, moving in a relative pace toward the swamps. With our pursuers most likely headed in the wrong direction, we left the safety of the outcropping and took a circuitous route behind the volcano to head back toward Haven.

Kira still looked a bit shell-shocked, and I walked beside her. "Are you sure you're okay? Anything else hurt or injured?"

"Wyatt, I'm okay," she said. "I promise." She slipped her hand into mine.

The touch of her skin calmed my worries. I couldn't see any outward signs of injury other than the few bumps and scrapes she'd gotten in the escape. Even the wolfsbane burns had faded as her healing kicked in. But she wasn't acting like herself. Something had been done to her in that godsforsaken place, and I dreaded hearing about what Simon had been planning, what Kira had gone through. There would be time to talk when we were back to safety. For now, I wouldn't push.

Nearly an hour later, we caught sight of the entrance to Haven. We'd been lucky not to run into any creatures on our trip back. A few aggressive harpies had swooped near us, but Zoe's magic had made sure they headed off for an easier meal.

Crew stood at the hidden doorway, waiting for us. Even in the darkness, the relief on his face was clear, though he tried his best to hide it.

"Thank the gods. I was starting to get worried," he said.

Eli gave him the quick and dirty explanation about Kira's tracking device. Crew looked at her, then to Zoe, his face clouding with worry. "We need to check Leif and Abel. Simon might have put trackers in them as well."

Hearing that was like getting ice-cold water poured on my head. I hadn't even thought of that. If Crew was right, then Simon could be on his way to Haven right now.

"Zoe, come with me," Crew said. "I'll take you straight to the others." Turning to us, he said, "Get in here. I had some folks cook up a meal for you all. I'm sure you're starving."

Kira put a hand to her stomach. "You could say that." She sounded happy, but it didn't disguise the worry in her eyes. She was just as worried about the possible tracking devices as I was.

Crew led us through the hidden entrance and down the hallway of traps and magical spells. Once we were back inside the safety of Haven, Kira and I broke off, heading toward our assigned room. Crew and Zoe sprinted down the corridors to wherever they were keeping Leif and Abel.

Kira and I stopped at the kitchens and grabbed some food, but the stress and worry had diminished our appetites. After nibbling a bit, we headed on to our room. Haven was buzzing with activity, and I couldn't help wondering how much more chaos would erupt if they all found out Simon was on his way, following the tracking devices that might or might not be lurking inside our friends.

I gave Kira time to process as we walked. It wasn't until we were back in the room that I realized she was crying. Kira never cried... well, almost never. Knowing her, she probably viewed it as a sign of weakness.

I took her face in my hands, gently cupping her cheeks, terrified that she had some injury I hadn't seen. "What's wrong? Are you okay?"

"I didn't do it," she sobbed. "I never did."

"Huh?" I frowned. "I don't understand. What didn't you do?"

She cried even harder and wrapped me in a hug. Putting my arms around her, I rested my cheek on her head, letting her get it out. These weren't sobs of sadness, pain, or misery, but relief. Maybe even happiness.

After a few moments, I probed again. "Kira, what's going on? Are you sure you're okay?"

She nodded and pulled her head back, looking up at me with bloodshot eyes. "I'm innocent. I *didn't* kill that man when I was a kid. I was never a murderer, or a monster, or any of those things."

All I could do was stare at her. How had she discovered that? "Did Simon tell you that?"

Kira laughed and wiped an arm across her face to dry the tears. "*He* was the guy, Wyatt. Simon. He was my friend's uncle. He gave me something that forced me to shift, and I almost killed him, but he managed to get away. He faked his death. That means none of it was my fault. I spent years thinking I was a monster, but that wasn't true."

"You were never a monster," I said firmly. "I always knew that."

She chuckled and shook her head, fresh tears spilling down her cheeks. "That's great, but your faith couldn't wipe away the guilt I'd locked up inside me all those years."

I put my thumb under her chin and tilted her head up so she'd meet my eyes again. I smiled at her. "Even if you had made some awful mistake during your first shift and accidentally killed someone, no one would have thought you were a monster. You've been nothing but selfless and empathetic your whole life. All you do is try to protect people who can't protect themselves. It's what led you to become a Tranquility operative, and it's why I love you. That's the only truth you need to know."

Before we could say more, a frantic knock sounded on our door, making both of us flinch. I opened it to find Zoe, breathing heavily as though she'd just sprinted here.

"What's wrong?" I asked. "Is it bad?"

Zoe waved a hand, then spoke between gasps as she tried to catch her breath. "All good...no trackers on them...wanted to...tell you...before you...started banging each other or something." She eyed our fully clothed bodies. "I guess I made it in time."

My relief was like a stream of cool water on a burn. I let out a shaky sigh.

"Why did he only put one in me?" Kira asked.

"He probably had different plans for you," I said. "If I had to guess, he was going to do some kind of experiment, then set you loose to lead him back here. He didn't put trackers in the others because he had Leif fully under his control, and he was going to do the same to Abel."

"I have no clue, Kira," Zoe said. "I'm going to leave now." She wagged her eyebrows up and down. "Let you guys get back to whatever it was you were getting to."

Zoe left, and I closed the door. Kira pulled me to her and kissed me long and hard. When we were both slightly out of breath, she said. "I love you, too."

"All I want to do is take care of you," I said. "Speaking of, do you want me to get some more food? Are you still hungry? We didn't eat much."

Kira grinned, her eyes still red, but the guilt that had always swirled in her eyes was now replaced with desire. Heat flooded through me.

"I'm hungry," she murmured. "Not for food, though."

I grinned as my cock hardened. "Is that so?"

"Uh-huh. I feel better than I have in a long time. I've got some energy to burn." She slipped her hand down between my legs, squeezing my dick through my pants. "Do you think you can help me with that?"

As she ran her fingers along my crotch, I groaned. "I think I can."

Kira gasped as I picked her up and carried her to the bed, laying her down quickly but gently. I gazed down at her as I stripped my clothes off. She kept eye contact while doing the same. Every inch of flesh she revealed sent me into more of a frenzy. I'd never wanted her more. Knowing she was in danger, being unable to help her, had driven me nearly mad. Now that she was here, safe and sound, within these walls with me? I couldn't help myself.

My pants were still around my ankles when I dropped to my knees, spread her knees apart, and buried my face in her pussy.

"Oh, fuck," Kira moaned as I flicked my tongue over her.

Sliding my tongue as deep into her as I could, I reached up and took hold of her breasts, caressing the skin and pinching her nipples. My lips glided over her pussy and her clit. Kira tasted like heaven, and I wanted more. Wanted to feel her come on my tongue.

Lowering my hands to grip her thighs, I held her open for me and wrapped my lips around her clit, alternating between sucking and flicking my tongue over the engorged nub of flesh. She quivered beneath my hands, shivering in pleasure.

Glancing up, I found her staring down at me, watching me ravish her, her mouth hung open in ecstasy. My cock throbbed as our eyes met. I ached to be inside her, but I had to do this first, had to give her all I could. This day had shown me that nothing was promised, and every moment mattered.

Without taking my eyes off her, I raised my mouth an inch. "Come for me, Kira."

As I resumed devouring her, I slid a finger into her, then another, thrusting lazily in and out. Kira pushed her hips into my face in demand, and I moved my fingers faster in time with her pelvis. At last, she shuddered beneath my mouth and hands.

"Fuck, Wyatt, I'm coming," Kira hissed through clenched teeth.

I grinned against her as her orgasm crashed over her, her hips bucking harder and faster with each wave. Before she'd finished climaxing, I rose, keeping her legs apart with my hands, and slid balls-deep into her soaked pussy. Resting my weight on my forearms, I caught her left nipple in my mouth and sucked on it as I crashed my hips into her.

Kira ran her fingers through my hair and wrapped her legs around my waist, locking her ankles to hold me inside, urging me to go faster. Sweat already glistened on our bodies, and our labored breaths mingled.

Each time I slammed into her, the wet, velvety softness of her pussy elicited a grunt of happiness from me. Gods, being inside her was so good. More than good. It was fucking fantastic. Nothing had ever, or would ever, feel as amazing as her body. I raised my face to hers, finding her lips, and kissed her deeply as we fucked with ever-increasing abandon. The first ripples of pleasure grew deep in my balls and pelvis, the massive and explosive climax building, ready to burst.

Kira threw her head back, stuffing her fist in her mouth to stifle the scream that erupted from her throat as she came a second time. Seeing her face twisted in the throes of pleasure sent me over the edge. A deep growl of satisfaction rumbled in my throat as my own orgasm erupted from me. Each thrust sent another wave of ecstasy through me. Tingling electric tendrils ran up and down my back, my arms, legs—every fiber of my being. Happiness and contentment flooded through me as I collapsed onto her chest, panting to catch my breath.

After holding each other like that for several silent minutes, I finally managed to get my pants fully off and slid down to lie next to Kira. She settled herself in the crook of my arm, resting her head on my chest.

"Is everyone all right?" Kira asked after a few minutes of silence.

"What do you mean?"

"The others. Leif, Abel, the rest of Crew's people. I was too out of it to ask earlier."

"Oh," I said. "Not sure. I think the plan was to take Leif to some kind of holding pen or something if we found him and got him back. I'd assume Abel was taken to the healers. As far as I know, other than that one guy who got killed, everyone else just has some scratches and bruises. Nothing too serious. Don't worry about all that now, though. You were the reason we went in."

"I know." She gave a sad shake of her head. "I feel guilty about it, anyway."

"You shouldn't. Hell, if you hadn't been taken, we'd have never gotten Abel or Leif back. Yes, we lost one, but we recovered three. It's a shit trade, but at least it wasn't for nothing. That guy did a brave fucking thing going in there with us. You can feel bad, that's allowed, but remember that two other innocent people were saved along with you."

Kira relaxed against me. "Okay."

Squeezing her shoulder, I turned my head to look at her. "Crew can handle things without us for a while. You've been through a lot. I almost lost my mind not knowing if you were okay. I just want you to myself for a little while. We can check on Leif and Abel tomorrow."

She nodded, but I could already tell she was slipping away. Her eyelids drooped shut as sleep took her under.

With a smile, I closed my own eyes, happy to be holding her in my arms, to know she was safe. After all she'd been through, she was obviously shaken up and needed the rest. As I slipped off to join her in sleep, I wondered how many more close calls we'd have before this was all over.

Chapter 5 - Kira

When I awoke later on, I was shocked by how rested and relaxed my body felt. It hadn't been until I was somewhere safe and calm, with someone I loved, that I realized how stressed I'd been in Simon's compound. Tension and worry had pulled me so taut, I'd been on the verge of ripping in half. The metal table I'd been strapped to and the sterile environment hadn't helped, either. Haven's dirt and stone tunnels weren't as luxurious as the Reject Mansion's, but they were a thousand times better than being locked up as some science experiment.

Rolling over, I reached out for Wyatt, but the bed was empty. The room was dark and quiet. He must have gotten up earlier. Gods only knew how long I'd slept. It could have been midday, for all I knew. My stomach growled. I had barely touched the food we'd been given when we returned last night, and I hadn't had anything to drink. A half-empty, lukewarm water bottle sat on a block of wood that served as a makeshift nightstand. I twisted the cap off and sucked down the entire thing in three fast gulps.

"Man, that's good," I moaned to myself as I put the cap back on.

Throwing off the covers, I stood and gathered my clothes from around the room. I'd tossed them away with abandon the night before with Wyatt. A ball of heat formed in my stomach at the memory. It was a lovely celebration of being safe.

Once I was dressed, I sat back on the bed and took stock of myself. My lethargy was gone. The wolfsbane burns on my body had faded to almost nothing. As far as I could tell, I wasn't suffering from any lingering effects of the shit Simon had pumped into me. My shifter biology must have cleared it from my system. I didn't want to think about what might have happened to me if Wyatt had been even an hour later in rescuing me. An involuntary shiver ran up my back, sending gooseflesh rising along my arms.

I had to get out and about, see some people, get my mind off what I'd been through. I tugged my shoes back on and headed out into the tunnels of Haven.

I wasn't out of my room for more than thirty seconds when Zoe crashed into me, hugging me so tight, I was afraid my ribs would crack.

"Oh my gosh. I'm so glad you're back," Zoe gushed.

Hugging her back, I smiled. "Glad to *be* back."

Zoe held me at arm's length and looked me over. "Are you all right? I was *literally* coming to check on you. I was worried. You've been asleep for, like, forever."

"I'm good. I came out to get something for breakfast... or lunch?"

Zoe smirked. "You mean dinner? You slept the entire day. We don't have a huge selection here. Limited supplies, you know? How about some oatmeal?"

The whole day? Good gods. My stomach gave another warning rumble at the mention of food. "That sounds fucking fantastic," I said. "Plain food would be fine at this point."

"We do have some dried fruit and stuff. It won't be like prison food. Come on." Zoe pulled me along toward the dining area.

In the little carved-out commissary area, Zoe spoke to a younger witch and asked for a serving of food. It seemed that everyone in Haven pitched in and helped where and when they could. Again, I was impressed with the society Crew had managed to build in such an inhospitable place as Bloodstone Island.

Zoe joined me at a small table with a bowl of oatmeal filled with raisins, chunks of coconut, and a drizzle of honey. It was incredibly basic, but by the gods, nothing had ever looked that good. I ate the whole bowl in about a minute. After finishing, I was still hungry, but it would keep me going for a while.

"How is everyone else?" I asked, tossing my spoon into the empty bowl.

Zoe's face fell a bit. "Okay, I guess. We lost another guy on the way back to Haven last night."

"What?" I sat forward. "Besides the guy we lost in the lab?"

She nodded, picking at a spot on the table. "Yeah. Jackson was the guy who got killed there. On the way back, we ran into a few ferals. They weren't Simon's, they came out of nowhere. This panther shifter, Terrance, saved Crew in the fight but...well, he didn't make it."

"Dammit," I hissed, that all-too familiar guilt leaching out again. "I'm sorry, Zoe."

There were only a few dozen people in all of Haven, which meant they were probably a really close-knit group. Any loss would be like a kick to the stomach. Losing two citizens in one night had to cut deep.

Zoe sighed and did her best to put a brave face on. "It's not been a great day. Crew and Eli were pretty banged up, too, but they mostly healed before you guys got back. Other than that, everyone is okay."

"What about Abel? Leif?"

At the mention of the other alphas' names, Zoe chewed her lip nervously. "Abel is in decent condition, though he's still unconscious and really sick or something. Super strange, since his shifter metabolism should make him pretty much impervious to disease. The healer isn't sure what the hell is going on with him, but she's fairly sure whatever experiments Simon put him through weren't too intense. I think we may have saved him in the nick of time, but we'll have to wait and see."

Abel was alive—that was the main thing I needed to remember. Anything else could be dealt with later. We'd been so sure that he had died in the jungle. Having him back with us, safe here in Haven, was nothing short of a miracle. I had to look at the bright side and pray Simon hadn't done too much damage to him.

"And Leif?"

"That's a little touchier," Zoe said. "He woke up, but was *super* feral. Like, for really *real* pissed off. Crew has him locked up in a holding cell. He had it built while creating Haven on the off-chance they ever needed to imprison anyone or anything." Zoe glanced toward the door. "Speaking of Crew, he wanted to meet with you whenever you finally woke up. He wants any info you have on Simon's lab. In case we decide to infiltrate it again later."

"Again? We all almost died last time. Without you, we wouldn't have made it out."

"I know, I know, it's not in the plans," Zoe said quickly. "Jeez, calm down. We just want to get a better sense of what's going on there *if* we end up going back there again."

I breathed a sigh of relief. "Okay. Sorry, I freaked out. That does sound smart. Let's get that over with, then. While it's all still fresh in my head."

Zoe led me to the meeting room, where Crew, Eli, Mika and Wyatt were already seated. Chelsey was also in the room, but she was on a wooden bench as far from Crew as she could get while still being in the room. As soon as he saw me enter, Wyatt rose and hurried over to me.

"Hey, sleepyhead," he said, putting an arm around me as we walked to the table. "I was wondering when you'd get up."

A large sheet of paper with a crude, hand-drawn map on it covered the table. Simon's lab. They were trying to recreate the layout of the place from memory. As I looked it over, I spotted several problems.

Pointing to a hallway, I said, "This intersection isn't here. It's farther up."

Crew raised an eyebrow and glanced at Wyatt. "You were right," he said with a grin.

Wyatt smiled broadly. "I told you. She's one of the best I've ever seen. Memory like a steel trap."

Ignoring the praise, I sat down. Plucking the pencil from Eli's hand, I made adjustments to the map, speaking as I worked. "Simon was really hung up on the fact that I somehow *helped* him develop all this stuff. He tested a drug on me as a kid. Forced my first shift, and somehow, from that one drug, all this other research was born. He treated me like an honored guest or something. Gave me a tour of the place. I didn't get to see everything, but I memorized what I *did* see." I erased an entire section. "This isn't a meeting space. I saw it when the door was open. It's a bunk room of some sort. I think it's where the staff sleeps."

"You're saying Simon walked you through the whole facility?" Crew asked, surprise written all over his face.

"Yeah. It was weird," I said.

"Hang on, go back," Eli said, holding up her hand. "You have history with Simon? From when you were a kid?"

Sighing, I put the pencil down and glanced at Wyatt and Zoe. Wyatt gave me a reassuring nod.

"Right," I said. "No reason to hold back now, I suppose."

I gave them an abbreviated run-down on what I *thought* had happened to me as a kid, then the true story Simon gave me and everything in between.

"So," I went on, "I actually *was* a latent wolf. Had Simon not interfered, I never would have had access to my inner wolf."

"Holy shit," Wyatt muttered. "This is crazy."

"That's what I thought, but it's all true," I said. "Whatever this potion or drug is that he used, it not only reversed my latency, but also caused the wolf that came out to be an alpha. He used the same drug on himself."

"Wait, wait, wait, hang on, hold the phone," Zoe said. "Why would a fae scientist use a shifter drug on himself?"

"That's where it gets even weirder. You saw him in the facility. You watched him shift, Wyatt. You got there late, Zoe. The wolf that attacked us was Simon. His mother was a fae, but his father was a wolf shifter. He'd been latent as well, but when he took that drug, it brought his wolf out. He's a shifter-fae hybrid now."

Zoe's eyes bulged. It was a combination that, quite literally, was almost unheard of. Female alphas like me were incredibly rare, but it was still ten times more likely to happen than a hybrid species. Hybrids were so rare, they'd faded into the realm of myth.

"Are you fucking serious?" Zoe gasped.

"Dead-ass. Once he faked his death, he apparently dived head-first into research and ended up on Bloodstone. The fact that he's here at all leads straight back to me. It's like he and I are entwined somehow.

Fate keeps throwing us together in awful ways. Most of this is my fault."

"Nope," Wyatt said. "Don't do that. This asshole used you as a guinea pig. This is not your fault."

"People died, Wyatt," I snapped. "Everyone at the mansion, the people from Haven. If I'd never been born, *none* of this would have happened."

"Enough," Crew said, though his tone was gentle rather than commanding. I turned to look at him. "You can't go walking all the way back to childhood attempting to shoulder the blame. Hell, if we all went back five, ten, or fifteen years ago, we'd find some shit we would take back." Crew's eye flicked, for the barest second, across the room toward Chelsey before locking on mine again.

His words actually did make it all a little better. Were things my fault? Sort of, but it had all been done against my will. I thought back on the small and terrified child I'd been, covered in blood and sobbing in that cave. Looking at her in my mind's eye showed me the truth. She was blameless in all this, regardless of what had happened after.

I heaved a sigh and nodded, leaning into Wyatt's soothing touch as he rubbed my back. "Okay. No, you're right. But"—I jabbed a finger at the map—"if you're planning to attack Simon's base again, I want in. I need to help take this son of a bitch down."

At my suggestion of attacking Simon again, Crew's face grew somber. He cast a hesitant glance toward Chelsey. "Um, I'm not sure that's in the cards. At least not right away."

"Why not?"

"Things are far more dangerous now. First, with the mansion's defenses down, the creatures on the island are still riled up and running wild. Second, Simon knows we've found his base. He's going to buckle down now, increase his security measures. Plus, he has to know time is running low with everything going on. He's going to be more desperate to get prisoners for his experiments. I have to keep this place"—he gestured widely, indicating all of Haven—"and everyone in it safe." He sighed and glanced at Eli and Zoe. "I didn't even mention the damages these two did to his lab. That hurts us as well."

"What?" I spluttered. "How could damaging his lab be bad for us?" It made no sense.

"Because," Crew explained, "we did heavy damage to that place, destroying not only computers and magical grimoires, but also doors, security systems, and a dozen other things that kept the place running. We have to assume that quite a few of Simon's experiments fled. All of it together makes things too dangerous right now. We need to wait for everything to calm down."

"Not to interrupt," Zoe said, "but going back to that whole *Bloodstone is even more dangerous* thing... should we worry that some of the things on the island might get off at some point? I mean, I don't think it will be good for anyone if harpies and revenants are running up and down the streets of Fangmore City, right? If the wards fell from the mansion, does that mean they fell everywhere?"

"It's not the wards keeping the creatures here— keeping us here," Eli said, cutting into the conversation. "We've had scouts checking the area around the mansion. The wards there are faint. They may as well not exist. The stronger wards that surrounded the island stretched out almost a mile offshore, but those have faded as well."

Zoe's eyes lit up. "Well, that seals it. Let's get the hell off this rock."

Eli shook her head slowly and glanced around at all of us. "We had the same concern about monsters escaping. A couple of our most powerful magic wielders scried the area beyond the fallen wards. There's some kind of dark force still in place. It's something none of them have ever seen before, and whatever it is, isn't allowing anything to leave the island. While it's still there, we're stuck here like every feral, vampire, and all those other creatures in this place."

Something dark and powerful? It made no sense. What could be strange and potent enough that wiccans and fae couldn't even figure out what it was? As awful as it was to be stuck here, it only pushed me to fight back harder.

"Crew," I said, rounding on the leader, "we can't keep hiding. There are enough dangers on this fucking island that we can't *also* be looking over our shoulder for this mad scientist boogeyman. I didn't spend that much time with him, but what time I did spend with him told me that he's crazy, vindictive, and quick to anger. He may very well be hunting even harder for Haven, to destroy it as payback."

"Hold on," Mika said, holding a hand up. "I thought this place was fully hidden, right? How could he find it?"

"It's hidden, yes," Crew said, "But we don't have nearly as many spell casters as *The Reject Project* employed. We can't create an impenetrable barrier like they did. The best we can do is a really good glamor spell to hide the entrance, and a *lot* of magic and practical booby traps. We've also installed deterrent spells that keep non-sentient creatures away. But Simon? Or one of his assistants? If they find us, they could breach the entrance. It's part of why I always keep someone near the entry tunnel as a lookout. Day and night, twenty-four seven." He grimaced in irritation and looked at me again. "You may be right. Simon *may* be looking for us even harder now."

It was time to tell them everything I'd learned. They wouldn't like it, but it might get them on my side. We couldn't let Simon keep working. Not even for a day more.

"Simon is far worse than you realize," I began. "He's a mad scientist, yes, but he's more than that. He's an arms dealer. All this shit he's creating? He told me he's selling it to people on the mainland. Some of it is already there. The fucking heat serum that got me fired and rejected is his creation. He's going to be arming the packs, the fae, the humans—anyone—with these monsters and weapons. It's not about us anymore. Not the show, or Haven, or any of it. This is about the whole world. We can't allow him to do this. He *has* to be stopped. If not, those monstrosities will be stalking up and down the streets of every city and neighborhood on the planet soon. That can't happen."

Crew, Eli, and all the others gaped at me. The information was heavy, but they needed to know. Even Chelsey, who'd spent the whole meeting staring daggers at Crew, looked distraught and shaken.

"He's making these things to sell?" Crew asked.

"Like I said, he's already sold some of it," I said. "A lion shifter slipped me some of the heat serum. If that shit starts to get used on a bigger population, it'll be fucking chaos. Like, orgies-in-the-street chaos. And that's the least dangerous thing he's created."

"Hang on," Eli said, looking up with a smile spreading across her lips. She shared a look with Wyatt, who was grinning back at her. They'd both come to some conclusion.

"If he's sending this stuff to the mainland," Eli went on, "then these shipments are getting out somehow."

I could almost hear the lightbulb clicking on in my head. "We use those shipments to get ourselves off the island?"

"Exactly," Eli said, and looked to Crew for confirmation.

"It could work," Crew admitted warily.

Jumping in to keep the momentum going, I said, "Look, I have no clue what finally started the war, but if we have a chance to keep it from being even worse, we need to take it."

"Kira's right," Wyatt added. "I'm the last person who wants to see her in danger, but this is too big to ignore. She and I both swore an oath to protect people from dangers like this. We have to move against Simon. Stop him from causing any more harm than he already has."

"I don't know." Crew looked pained. "It's awful what he's done, but the people here in Haven have been through a lot. I can't put them in any more danger."

Crew was a good leader. Someone who didn't want to hurt his people or see them hurt. He probably harbored a massive amount of guilt from the people he'd already lost. I couldn't fault him for not wanting to jump back into battle right after the last one.

Thankfully, I didn't need to convince him. Chelsey spoke up for me. "We have to do what Kira is saying," she said.

Crew's gaze shot across the room to look at her, his look of consternation fading a bit.

"My family is on the mainland like everyone else," she continued. "My little brother and parents? Everyone I know and love? These things Simon is creating will tear them apart." She looked directly at Crew. "We can't hide here while the rest of the world burns. Not when we know we can stop it. If we do, then we're nothing but cowards."

Her words hung heavy in the air, none of us able to say anything that would push the argument any further. Crew chewed at his lower lip, knocking his knuckles absently on the table as he thought. When he finally looked up, I was sure we had him on our side, and I did my best not to smile in victory.

"Here's the deal," he said. "You're right. I can't, in good conscience, let Simon continue. We've got to stop him from sending more of that shit back home."

I let out an audible breath, but Crew held a finger up before I could speak.

"When I say plan, I mean a real plan," he continued. "We've got to come at him with everything we've got. We went in too fast for the rescue mission and took some hits. Two really good men died during that mission."

I winced as though physically slapped, remembering the men who'd died to save me. I kept my mouth shut, remembering that this was Crew's place. He was in charge and deserved the floor.

"I will not order anyone to join us," he said. "I'll do my best to convince the citizens of Haven that this is an important and worthwhile objective. I'll take volunteers who want to join the fight, but I will *not*, under any circumstances, force them to help. They can fight, or they can hide. Haven is not a dictatorship or monarchy. Everyone here has their own volition and agency, and I won't take that from them. Anyone who goes will be risking their lives, and that's a decision they need to make for themselves."

"That makes total sense," I said, relief and happiness battling to be the strongest emotion. "It says a lot about you, and I respect the hell out of that."

I had a suspicion that almost no one in Haven would turn down the chance to fight. They all looked up to Crew as an almost deific figure. Most would probably jump at the chance to both help Crew *and* get off the island.

"Eli?" Crew said. "Do you want to come with me? We'll need to talk to everyone. Small groups, nothing big. I don't want anyone to feel pressured by a group setting, so let's do intimate meetings to lay this out. Give them the whole story so they can decide on their own."

She nodded. "Yeah. Better sooner than later."

She and Crew turned to leave, and I thought I saw Chelsey and Crew exchanging another loaded look. This one had less anger from Chelsey. Possibly a good sign? Who knew at this point?

All I could really think about was striking back at Simon, destroying his lab and his disgusting creations once and for all. Hundreds of thousands of people back home depended on us, and I was desperate to keep anyone else from getting hurt. My parents and Kolton were already struggling with fighting other packs. I'd be damned if I let Simon send more weapons back to the mainland to put my family in even more danger.

Chapter 6 - Wyatt

I kept quiet during the meeting. The shock of what Kira said bounced through my head like a pinball, making it hard to add much to the conversation. Simon had developed the potion that put Kira into heat? None of the labs had been able to figure out the chemical component used in it. The fact that the same psycho who'd created that was on Bloodstone Island made my head spin.

Even worse was the fact that this guy had been the one to force her first shift all those years ago, and here he was again. Not content with ruining her life in childhood, he'd had his little fucking inventions following Kira through time and space, hellbent on destroying her. Unbidden, a flash of memory flooded my mind. Kira, sobbing and covered in blood. She'd spent her whole life thinking she was a killer. A murderer. A *monster*. From what I could see, she was putting on a good front, but she couldn't hide what she felt from me. There could be storms raging inside her, and she'd act like nothing was wrong. I wouldn't pry into that. She'd give me answers in her own time.

Until then, I wanted to make sure she was *physically* all right.

Once Crew and Eli had departed, I pulled Kira aside out of earshot of the others. "How are you doing? Any residual issues from yesterday? Weakness? Exhaustion? Anything?"

She gave me a faint smile. "I'm okay. Sleeping for eighteen-ish hours did the trick. Simon pumped me full of some sort of potion or drug or something that weakened me and made me tired and worn down, but other than that, nothing out of the ordinary. Whatever it was might have been a precursor to the *actual* chemical he was going to give me to finish the experiment or whatever. I think you guys got to me in the nick of time. I'm fine, really."

"I know you," I said. "You could be dying, and you'd pretend you were fine. All you need to do is tell me if you feel anything weird, okay? No judgment."

Kira rolled her eyes and patted my chest. "You sound like you're getting back to your old bossy and nagging self."

"Forgive me for wanting you to be safe," I said, my tone jovial and sarcastic, playing along with her. "The last thing I need is for you to get in trouble *yet again.*

I'm still trying to get over the damn heart attack you gave me when you went missing in the first place."

She quirked an eyebrow and grinned back at me. "Wow! Seriously? I didn't realize I *planned* to get kidnapped, drugged, and terrified by a mad scientist." She glanced down at her wrist like she was checking an invisible watch. "Oh, that's right, I'd actually planned on that happening the day after tomorrow. Damn, I got my crises mixed up. My fault. Yesterday, I was supposed to get swallowed by a kraken. I really need to get a personal assistant to coordinate all these things."

"Oh, it's always been in the plan, then? Good to know," I said, nodding along. "I was afraid that after all these years, you really were as clumsy as I thought. Whew, that's a load off my mind."

"I mean, planned or not, you can't help but jump in to try and rescue me. Do you get off on it, Wyatt? Is it some sort of sexual kink? Do you get a boner when things get tense and dangerous?"

We bickered back and forth like we used to before coming to the island, but the dynamic had changed. Instead of irritation in her voice and frustration in mine, there was a softness, a playfulness to the banter that had never been there before. It was the fact that we loved each other. That's what had changed. We no longer fought that or pushed back on the feelings we'd had for so long.

Kira was in the middle of making another dirty joke when I lunged forward, kissing her, cutting her off mid-sentence. After a moment, I pulled away and looked into her eyes, serious again. "I mean it. Tell me if and when you're not a hundred percent. We need to be in top shape to take on Simon."

A memory tickled the back of my mind. The scientist casting a spell at Kira in the hall, forcing her to shift. With everything that happened afterward, I'd pushed it away, but now it made me uneasy.

I mentioned it to Kira, but she waved it off. "It was a spell, Wyatt. If he'd cast it at you, the same thing probably would have happened." She shuddered. "It *did* freak me out, to be honest. You know how few times I've shifted. I'm still not used to the sensation, that's all. We'll need to watch out for that next time, though. If he can force me to shift into my wolf form, then that spell may work both ways."

Her explanation made sense, but I'd never heard of a spell that could do that. Maybe this Simon guy had developed new magical abilities during his studies, or maybe he had more power, being a shifter-fae hybrid. Either way, it did little to ease my worries.

Kira put her hands on my cheeks and kissed me again, the warmth of her lips washing away my anxiety. "I promise, Wyatt. If anything is off, you'll be the first to know. Now, can we go check on Leif? I can't stop thinking about him. He looked miserable in the lab."

"Yeah, okay," I said. "I'd like to see him, too. Crew told me where his holding cell is."

Kira remained silent on the trip through the tunnels and corridors. Shadows flickered in the light of the candles and fae lights along the walls. When we stepped into the chamber, both of us froze in our tracks. J.D. was sitting in front of Leif's cell, gazing at the other alpha. The sadness on his face damn near broke my heart.

Leif paced back and forth in the cage in his wolf form. He snapped at the air madly, like he was biting things only he could see. He snarled and growled, pawed the ground, and even spun in place to bite his tail and legs. He had the textbook look and movements of a fully feral shifter.

Kira cleared her throat, and J.D. turned his head to us. Leif lunged at the cage, chuffing at our presence. J.D. got to his feet and walked over to meet us, wrapping his arms around Kira. He sank into the embrace, almost like he had trouble standing once Kira took hold of him.

She rubbed his back. "How are you doing?"

J.D. pulled away, his cheeks tinged pink. "Don't worry about me. How are *you?* I've been feeling awful about you getting caught up in all this. The whole time you were gone, I had this terrible guilt."

Kira patted his shoulder and grinned. "I'm fine, J.D. Don't beat yourself up. I'm okay."

J.D. sighed and nodded. "Good. I was terrified you'd end up like..." He trailed off and glanced back at Leif pacing around the cage. "Well, you know. I didn't know what Simon would do to you once he had you."

As they continued talking, my eyes remained on Leif. I'd never seen anyone look more feral. We all knew there was no way coming back from that. My heart cracked, and my anger at Simon swelled into a raging fire. Even if Leif's current state had been forced on him, I had little hope that there was anything we could do to save him.

For his part, J.D. didn't have the same defeatist attitude I did. "We'll get Leif back," he said. "I know we will." He looked back and forth between Kira and me, a surprisingly determined look on his face. "If this Simon guy made him this way, then something in that lab will fix him," he added.

"Crew did say some of the healers thought there might be a chance to save recently turned ferals," Kira said. "If the transition wasn't natural, it could be easier to reverse. Have you talked to everyone? The healers?"

J.D. shrugged, his eyes downcast. "No. I've... well, I've mostly been here with Leif. I didn't want him to be alone."

"Why don't we go and talk to some people?" Kira suggested "The magic users may have a way of helping him. Zoe should be our first stop. She's got some tricks up her sleeve. Come on."

"Sure," J.D. mumbled, throwing a glance over his shoulder at Leif before following Kira. "I can't thank you guys enough for bringing him back."

"It's fine, J.D.," I said. "We would have done it for any of us."

"Still. You'll never know what it means to me," he said.

Down the hall ahead of us, I spotted Crew talking to a few Haven citizens. The people he spoke to looked at him with such intense excitement, I could practically feel the crackle in the air. From the look on these people's faces, they'd walk through fire for him. No matter what he asked them to do, they'd say yes.

Kira flagged down a guy walking down the corridor. "Have you seen Zoe? Do you know where we can find her?"

He pointed down another hallway. "I think I saw her that way. She's with some witches, trying to help that guy you all brought in. The one who's unconscious."

"Thanks. Come on," Kira said, taking J.D.'s hand.

"You guys go ahead," I said. "I need to have a word with Crew."

Kira nodded, and they hurried down the tunnel. As the three Haveners moved away, conversing softly among themselves, I made my way to Crew.

"Wyatt." He nodded at me.

"Crew." I tilted my head toward the group that was heading down the hall. "How's it going? Any takers yet?"

Crew sighed and gave me a rueful grin. "That's only the second group I've talked to. Just about everyone is chomping at the bit to throw down with Simon. A lot of them have lost friends to that psycho. Can't say it makes me feel good, knowing so many of my people are ready to jump into danger."

"Well, that's what I came over to talk about. I wanted to offer my services. If you have some people who might need some sort of training."

Crew raised an eyebrow. "Seriously?'

"Yeah. I think Kira would be on board to help as well. We're trained Tranquility operatives, skilled in hand-to-hand, blades, and firearm combat. Do you have anyone else in this place with that kind of experience? You've already told us that a lot of the people here are victims of circumstance. Most probably don't even know how to hold a gun, much less how to put someone into a chokehold. Right?"

Crew shrugged one shoulder noncommittally. "Some of our people are pretty dangerous and have skills. Like the folks who used to work for *The Reject*

Project." He heaved a sigh, and his face softened. "I also may or may not have a guy who used to be an accountant. So, yeah, they could use some help."

I turned my hands out in a gesture of supplication. "Then we're here for you. Say the word, and we're on it."

The look on Crew's face was a combination of relief and gratitude. "That would be amazing. Honestly, it would take my stress down about three or four notches, knowing my people will have a fighting chance. I have to tell you," he added, leaning close, "there are some people here who have no business fighting. The problem is, I'd be a hypocrite if I didn't let them. I promised I wouldn't order anyone *to* fight. I can't turn right around and order them *not* to fight."

"I get it," I said honestly. "Again, we'll do what we can."

"Thanks," he said. "The other problem I'm having is getting my head wrapped around the timeline. It could take days to get everyone ready for a full assault on the lab. Kira made it sound like Simon's shipments of specimens and weapons could go out at any time. I think our initial attack might have slowed down that timeline, but not by much. We might have bought a day. The war is only going to increase in intensity. Those fuckers pushing for it back home will be *desperate* to get their hands on something to give them an upper hand.

"We're going to do our best to plan fast and be ready to stop Simon, but I've gotta admit that I'm not hopeful. If it comes down to it, I'd rather focus on simply hijacking the shipment transportation and getting everyone off the island, even if that means we don't stop Simon."

What Crew was saying a lot of sense. Everything was moving so fast now. We'd thought we had a good plan before, but we'd been surprised by the sheer amount of lackeys Simon had. It had caught us off-guard, and we'd almost failed to make it out with Kira and the others. We'd lost two people in the process, and we didn't have the element of surprise now that Simon knew we'd discovered his lab.

"How about this?" I said. "We play this as plan A and plan B. Plan A is that we launch an assault on Simon, destroy his research and experiments for good, and then hijack the shipment to escape. Plan B is that we aren't able to plan the assault in enough time, and we drop back to only worrying about the hijacking. I want your people to be safe, too. Either plan works for me as long as Kira gets out of here alive."

Crew nodded, relief emanating off him. "The same goes for me with Chelsey. The last thing I want is to see her hurt again. I'll keep talking to people, see where everyone's thoughts are."

"All right. I'll see you later."

I patted Crew's hand and left to find Kira. Following the tunnel she and J.D. had gone down, I didn't make it more than a hundred feet before a hand fell on my shoulder. I stopped mid-step and turned to find Gavin behind me. My mood had been improving, but the sight of his face sent it crashing back to the ground.

"Oh. Gavin. What can I do for you?" I said, trying to make it obvious that I had places to be.

"I need a minute with you," he said.

"Look, if this is more shit about Kira belonging to you, and you wanting me back off, I'm really in no mood for that. You'd do better to shut your mouth and walk away."

Gavin rolled his eyes and huffed out an annoyed sigh. "Well, since Kira went ahead and professed her love to you on live television, and the fact that the two of you can't keep your fucking hands off each other, I don't really have a leg to stand on. I'm not going to encroach. But"—he held up a finger—"if we do figure out and fix the broken fated mate connections, and Kira really is meant to be with me, you need to be ready to back off."

"Gavin, for real, can we not—"

"I know, I know, we can save that for a later date," he said. "What I really wanted to talk about is the plan for when we get back to the mainland."

This was getting us nowhere, and I really wanted to find Kira. "What part, Gavin? A lot of shit will be happening *if* we get back home."

"If the war is really getting as bad as they say, then I doubt your little unofficial *pack* will be faring too well. It'll be hard enough for the real packs to deal with the fighting and stuff." Gavin put a hand on his chest and then extended it to me. "I wanted to offer you a deal. I'll let you and your unofficial pack join me and what allies I have remaining in the Ninth Pack. In return, I'll want your help to overthrow Jayson and then merge the remnants of my pack with Kira's

Eleventh Pack. That will make things easier to protect the Eastern Wilds as one unified force."

I stared at him, blinking rapidly. This fucker was still concerned about power grabs and grudges? We were fighting for our lives and the future of the godsdamned world, and he was hung up on fucking over his big brother?

"Okay," I said. "You'll *let* us join? Who the hell said we wanted this blessing or whatever?"

Gavin smiled, though it was more of a sneer. "Wyatt, you and I both know your little band of misfit wolves need protection more than anyone."

"You see," I said, getting more irritated by the moment, "my *misfit* lone wolves are independent. We don't bow to anyone. In fact, we're fierce warriors who've been through more shit and can handle themselves far better than the spoiled wolves in the official packs. Trust me when I say we are doing fine without you. We stay in the Eleventh Pack lands because they offered us their hospitality. We didn't beg for a favor, and we aren't mutts begging for scraps from the table. Understand that." I jabbed a finger into Gavin's chest, making him stumble and take a step back.

"Hey—"

"I'm not trying to use this war as a way to play politics and overthrow a pack. All I care about is making sure my and Kira's loved ones are safe. You can go fuck around and slap-fight with your pansy brother by yourself. Whichever one starts crying first can kick rocks, for all I care. Now excuse me." I pushed past him to look for Kira.

"Wow. Thanks for that," Gavin called after me, the sarcasm in his voice grating on my nerves even further.

Rather than retorting, I picked up my pace, trying to get away from him as fast as possible. By the time I arrived at the room where Abel was being held, Kira had already left. The other alpha looked dead to the world. Eyes closed, breathing deep slow breaths. The healer stood above him, monitoring his condition.

"Hello," she said to me. "Did you want to spend a few moments with your friend?"

"Uh, no, it's fine," I said. "He's still sleeping. I was actually looking for Kira. Do you know who I mean?"

The witch nodded. "Yes, she came to speak with Zoe. They left not long ago. I believe your friend said she was still hungry. Perhaps try the dining hall?"

I nodded and smiled. "Thanks."

Before turning to leave, I gave Abel one last glance. What had happened to him was awful, but a dark and embarrassing part of me was glad it was him and not Kira on that bed. The thought alone filled me with shame. Hurrying away, I did my best to scrub the thought from my mind.

Kira was exactly where the witch said she'd be. She was seated at a table, eating what looked like soup or stew. When she saw me step into the room, she put the spoon down and smiled.

"Hey. How'd it go with Crew?"

Falling into the chair beside her, I shrugged. "I think we've got things figured out. I volunteered both of us to help train the people of Haven to fight. That way, they'll have some skill when the attack happens."

Kira nodded and picked up her spoon again. "Good idea. I hadn't even though of that. I'm still starving," she said, gesturing to her food. She took a few bites while I sat in silence, then wiped her mouth with a napkin and eyed me suspiciously. "Why do you look like someone pissed in your cereal?"

I chuckled, despite myself. No reason to keep anything hidden. "Gavin caught me in the corridor.

He's trying to recruit me and my unofficial pack. Wants us as, like, mercenaries or something when we get back to the mainland. Extra hands to help fuck his brother over, I guess."

Kira dropped her spoon into the bowl and shoved it away in disgust. "Ugh. I still can't figure out why he's got his mind set on this. It's stupid since it's all moot, anyway."

"What do you mean by that?"

"The whole system he's trying to bend to his will—it's all done for. In my opinion, once this war finally ends, the whole pack system is going to collapse. If you ask me, it's past time for it. I mean, hell, most other shifters aren't as regimented in their pack structure as we are. It's time for something new."

Her words struck me as completely out of the blue. Kira Durst, the person who was more loyal to her pack than anyone else I'd ever met, was talking about the whole system falling apart?

"Looks like this island has changed you," I said, raising an eyebrow. "Never thought I'd hear you say that. What flipped your opinion?"

She leaned forward and gave me a lascivious look. "This big sexy lone wolf showed me the truth. Real caring and protection doesn't come from packs or alphas or hierarchy." Her face softened, and she reached forward to take my hand. "It's all pointless if you don't have more. People should *choose* their pack. Like you did. Being here? Living with and watching out for other shifters who aren't in my pack? It's like what the fuck are we doing, separating ourselves?"

"When you put it that way, it makes a lot of sense," I said. "I never expressed it verbally, but that's kind of how I feel. Everyone else in the unofficial pack, too."

"Right. I'd be happy with a pack made up of people who *actually* care about each other. My parents and Kolton." She squeezed my hand. "A few other people, too."

"Oh, shit," I muttered.

Kira grinned. "What? Do you think I'm talking about someone else? I mean you, you big dumb idiot."

I laughed, but shook my head. "No, it's not that. When you mentioned Kolton, it reminded me of something. With everything that happened, I'd forgotten all about it. Before the mansion fell, I managed to get a hold of him through a communication device they had in the basement. He told me he was working on a plan to get us off this island."

"Wait, what?"

"I know. We've been trying to survive, and I pushed it to the back of my mind. I can't be sure he's even working on the plan anymore. I'm sure everyone back home knows what's happened at this point. For all I know, he thinks we're both dead. Plus, he'll be dealing with protecting the pack lands."

Kira's eyes had widened in surprise and shock. "Kolton would never believe we were dead. Not until he saw our bodies in a coffin. If he said he was planning something, then you'd better believe he won't stop. He can be a go-with-the-flow guy most of the time, but for important stuff? He's just as stubborn as I am. You know that."

"True," I said, chuckling.

"So, this means we may have a secondary plan if things don't work out with this shipment hijack?"

"Maybe. We had to cut the conversation short, so I didn't get a full breakdown of his plan. Like you said, he very well may still be working on it."

The idea of having my best friend come swooping in to save us at the last second was a nice fantasy.

Regardless, we still had to worry about Simon. Until I saw Kolton storming the beaches of Bloodstone with an army at his back, I had to keep my thoughts on what I could deal with. We had to stop Simon and, if possible, get off the island alive.

Chapter 7 - Kira

Thinking about Kolton or my parents made my heart hurt. I missed them all so much, and there was no guarantee that I'd ever see them again.

To keep from going too far down that path, I changed the subject. "You said we were going to train people?"

Wyatt's face softened. "Yeah. Crew was a little hesitant when I first offered, but he knows most of his people have no experience. It'll go a *little* smoother if they have some idea of how to protect themselves in a fight."

That was putting it mildly. From what I'd seen, most members of Haven didn't even go out to scavenge or scout. Those duties were left to Crew, Eli, and one or two other capable citizens. By and large, most of the inhabitants here were normal, everyday people who'd found themselves in this place by mistake, happenstance, or because of betrayal. If they were thrown into a fight, they wouldn't stand a chance.

"I'm down to help any way I can," I said. "You and I are better suited to it than anyone else. I've never trained fresh recruits, though. That might be a learning curve."

"It will," Wyatt agreed. "But the people here are fired up and ready to fight. I'm sure they'll be receptive and willing to learn."

Were they ready for everything that came along with fighting? I'd spent hundreds of hours planning missions and operations. All possible scenarios had to be taken into account when you went into a dangerous situation, and it was vital that you understood you might be going to your death. Could these people handle the reality of casualties? You couldn't really train people to be ready to see their friends die beside them. Hell, I still wasn't okay thinking about it, and I'd spent my whole career preparing for exactly that.

"How many people do we have, anyway?" I asked. "I've never seen them all gathered in one room."

Wyatt rubbed at the stubble on his cheeks and shrugged. "Not sure. I'd say they have maybe a few dozen people here at most. How many of those will fight? Who knows?"

I exhaled and went over what I'd seen in the lab again, piecing everything together in my mind. I'd been shocked at the sheer number of people working for Simon. They were also well-supplied and armed. As badly as I wanted to stroll into the tunnels under the volcano and kick Simon in the balls, I wasn't sure we had the ability. Even if we spent the next two or three days training the people of Haven, we would still be underpowered against Simon.

"I know what you're thinking," Wyatt said.

"And what's that?"

"We're fucked," he said with a wry smile.

"Not exactly fucked, but we don't have good odds. If we had a couple of weeks to prepare properly, I'd feel better about it. The problem is, we *need* to hit Simon in the next two or three days. It's not an ideal timeline. If we rush in too soon, I can't help but anticipate a huge number of casualties. Simon will be on his guard; he'll have his staff and security on high alert."

Wyatt grimaced and nodded. "Yeah. We won't have the element of surprise on our side this time. I've got a feeling the shock factor was the only reason we were successful in getting you, Abel, and Leif out."

"I guess that's one more thing for us to worry about," I said ruefully. "I'll think about it. Maybe some grand plan will pop into my head."

Wyatt chuckled. "Good luck with that."

We got up. I put my empty bowl in the large wooden tub near the door, then followed Wyatt out of the dining hall. At the end of the corridor, I spotted Crew trying to catch up to Chelsey, who was assisting some other Haveners with chores. Pausing, I watched the interaction.

Crew approached Chelsey and tried to engage in conversation, but she didn't even make eye contact with him. Rather than speaking to him, she addressed the people she'd been helping, then headed toward the healing area. Crew watched her go, a look of profound pain on his face. The other Haveners had noticed the awkward interaction and quickly dispersed.

Crew and Chelsey needed to sort out their shit—and soon. The last thing we needed was the leader of Haven less than focused.

Putting a hand on Wyatt's arm, I asked, "What are you getting ready to do?"

Wyatt gestured down the corridor. "I'm gonna see if I can round up some people who might want hand-to-hand combat training. You coming along?"

"You go ahead," I said. "I'll meet up with you later. There's something I need to work on."

"All right." Wyatt leaned forward and kissed me.

Blinking in surprise, I asked, "What was that for?"

He grinned and rolled his eyes. "See you later."

Crew stood in the hall, hands on hips, staring down the corridor Chelsey had taken. The rest of the Haven people had hurried away, leaving him alone.

"Seems things aren't going well," I remarked, stepping up next to Crew.

He flinched as though I'd startled him. "Oh, Kira, hey. Uh, what do you mean?"

"Chelsey. That's what I mean," I said, nudging my head in the direction she'd gone. "None of this makes any sense to me."

Crew tried his best to act like his normal, composed self. "What do you mean by that?"

"I mean, Chelsey told me all about her rejection. It was brutal and petty and heartbreaking. She's obviously not over you, but since she showed up here, *you've* been acting like you aren't over *her*." I gave him a hard look. "Tell me the truth, did you really reject her? Or was she spinning some woe-is-me story that isn't true?"

Crew's face had crumpled into misery. He ran his hands through his hair, obviously frustrated. "I *did* reject her. She isn't lying. It's complicated, though."

Crossing my arms, I asked, "What could be complicated?"

He leaned against the dirt wall and slid down until he was sitting. Shaking his head, he stared down between his feet for so long, I thought he wasn't going to answer. Finally, though, he started talking.

"Rejecting Chelsey was the worst thing I've ever done in my life. The biggest regret I have. I never *wanted* to reject her."

"Then why—"

"*Please* let me finish," Crew said. "When I was paired with Chelsey, I was thrilled. A lot of people find their fated mate, and they aren't what they expected. At least, that's how it's been in the last couple of generations, but that wasn't the case with Chelsey. As soon as I met her it was like… I don't know, my life became complete. I was drawn to her in a way I can't even describe. The problem was her pack's low standing. My family was upset." Crew laughed bitterly. "That's putting it mildly. They were irate." He glanced up at me. "You probably know my parents, Felix and Bianca Crew?"

I swore my eyes actually bulged out of my head. Felix Crew was an esteemed beta in the First Pack. The richest and one of the most powerful people in all wolf-shifter society, probably second to only Mika's father Garth. Bianca was known mostly for being a socialite.

Now I understood why they were both enraged that their son had been paired with a woman from the lowly Twelfth Pack. It was one of the myriad reasons I wanted to see the whole system upended.

Seeing the look on my face, Crew grunted. "Yeah. You see where this is going. It didn't go well."

"I get that your parents wanted you paired with someone of higher standing, but you could have told them to go to hell. Especially if you really *did* love Chelsey." Him bowing to his parents' wishes and severing ties with a woman he loved struck me as cowardly. In the short time I'd known him, Crew came off as anything but a coward.

Crew looked as if I'd punched him in the gut. "You don't get it. We fought about it, but my parents wouldn't hear any of it. I defended Chelsey, tried to get them to see my side of it—that Chelsey was amazing, and I wanted to spend my life with her, but they're too set in their ways.

"I told myself I didn't care what they said or what they wanted, that I'd be with Chelsey no matter what. We were happy for a few months. I sent word to my parents that they would be invited to the mating ceremony, but if they didn't come, they could enjoy life without me." His lip curled in disgust. "That's when I received a *visit* from my dear parents."

A chill went up my spine when he looked into my eyes again. I didn't dare speak. Whatever he was about to say was obviously painful, and I didn't want to interrupt.

Tears welled in his good eye as he continued his story. "They came to my house and gave me an ultimatum. I reject Chelsey and choose a more *appropriate* mate, or there would be...consequences. They handed me a folder full of pictures of Chelsey and her family that had been taken from a distance. Simple pictures of them going about their lives. Her parents, her little brother, one of her cousins she's really close with—the whole family." He let out a bitter laugh that broke my heart. "My mother pointed at her little brother and said, 'It would be a shame for this little boy to have his brains blown out in front of his sister.'"

"Holy fucking gods," I breathed, putting a hand to my mouth.

"Then my father said he'll have every one of them killed if I chose to mate with Chelsey. He looked me in the eyes, Kira—the man who taught me to ride a bike, who gave me hugs and kisses on my birthdays. It was like he was a whole different person. He said, 'I'd rather not have a son at all than have a son who would mate with and put his dick into trash.' He called Chelsey trash, and..." A sob tore out of him. "I couldn't even defend her. They were serious. They would do it. Nothing is more important to Chelsey than her family. I couldn't let that happen. So," he paused and took a steadying breath, "to save her and her family, I rejected her. My parents forced me to do it with the media present so I couldn't take it back."

Crouching, I put a hand on Crew's knee. "I am *so* sorry, Crew. I can't imagine how awful that was for you."

He nodded and wiped at his remaining eye. "It gets worse. Afterward, my parents acted all fucking happy and shit. They started parading in all these vapid rich women from other packs. Only those from the First, Second, and Third Packs, of course. They wouldn't allow me to mate with anyone lower than that. They got more and more frustrated when I turned them all away. One good thing did come from me rejecting Chelsey: it broke me out of that perfect son mold I'd been in. Nothing mattered anymore. No matter what I did, my parents would always find something new to try and control me with. I'd just figured it out too late to keep Chelsey."

"Is that how you ended up on the show?" I asked. "To rebel against them?"

"Ha, yeah, that would have been a better story," he said bitterly. "No. First thing I did was dig up dirt on my parents. I wanted to lash out, fuck them over. I snooped around and found all kinds of shit. After a few months, I'd basically thrown back the hood on all the underhanded and dirty deals my parents were part of. Not just them, but *all* the upper packs. Twisted shit. Affairs, assassinations, blackmail, murders, embezzlement, and some really shady connections with people they had no business dealing with. I thought I could use everything I'd discovered to expose them and the other packs." Crew looked miserable. "I was naive. I figured once the world knew what they were, I'd renounce my pack, then win Chelsey back. Explain what happened, why I rejected her. Get her to understand, and then go live together as lone wolves."

Sighing, I leaned against the wall beside Crew. "You had to know they wouldn't let that happen." The thought was too outlandish to consider.

"I should have," Crew said, kicking a frustrated foot against the opposite wall. "But they were my *parents*. No matter how much shit I dug up, I believed they were decent people deep down. All that got thrown out the window when the private investigator I'd hired flipped and told my parents what I was doing. They confronted me and said they were sending me to *The Reject Project*. My father told me if I survived and won a better mate, they'd accept me back into the pack, and all would be forgiven. If I didn't agree to go, then Chelsey's family would be free game. Not only that, but they'd go after Chelsey, too." He looked at me imploringly. "I *couldn't* let anything happen to Chelsey. I took the deal, came to the island. During the very first challenge, I escaped and used some of the tools the show gave me to found Haven." He shrugged. "I spent all this time assuming Chelsey had forgotten about me and moved on. At least until the other day when she walked into Haven."

"Well," I said, "you can forget about that. She told me the story of her rejection, and it pretty much broke her heart. She's been torn apart since the day it happened, Crew. The misery of losing the one person she loved is what pushed her to join the show."

Crew banged his fist against his forehead gently. "Dammit. All I wanted was to keep her safe. I never wanted her to come here."

"She didn't even know you'd gone on the show. Apparently, watching anything to do with fated mates depressed her," I explained.

"You aren't making me feel any better," Crew groaned.

"Sorry, but it's true."

"I haven't stopped thinking of her since the day it all happened. Every morning, I wake up missing her, and every night, I go to sleep wishing she was with me. I can tell she hates me. All this time wanting her, and now that she's here, she won't even talk to me. Barely looks at me. I can't blame her." Crew gave a feeble shrug. "If it was reversed, I'd probably feel the same way. I should probably leave her be, stay out of her hair."

It was the most tragic fucking thing I'd ever heard. Both Crew and Chelsey were dealing with terrible heartache. I understood why he'd done what he had, but the only way this would be resolved was for Chelsey to give him a chance to explain.

As I got to my feet, I gave Crew a friendly pat on the shoulder. "I'll see if I can make any headway with Chelsey. Maybe if she hears you out, you two can smooth things over."

Crew snorted. "Sure, yeah. I'm not holding my breath. I pissed on her heart and kicked her out the door. I don't know why she'd ever give me a chance to redeem myself."

Leaving Crew to wallow in his misery, I went to find Chelsey. The first thing I had to figure out was whether she actually hated Crew as much as she let on, or if it was only heartache and sorrow making her act that way.

My search didn't take long. Chelsey stood with her arms crossed, face cloudy with some emotion I couldn't pinpoint, leaning against the wall of a storage room. The place was filled with a couple dozen sacks labeled with words like *oatmeal, rice, quinoa*. Sundries stolen from *The Reject Project* supply drops.

"Chelsey?" I said carefully.

"What?" Chelsey asked without looking up, her voice flat and emotionless.

For five seconds, I debated whether I should try to be subtle or if it would be easier to come out and ask. Then I remembered we were under a time crunch. This needed to be taken care of fast. The issues Chelsey and Crew were dealing with were huge, but lives were at risk.

"Do you hate Crew? Like, *really* hate him?"

"Ben?" Chelsey asked, using his first name. "What do you mean?"

An exasperated sigh escaped my lips. "You know what I mean. Everyone in this place sees how you're treating him. Do you hate him? If so, you need to let him know there's zero chance he can make up for past mistakes and be done with it."

Chelsey stared at me for several seconds like I'd spoken a foreign language. Then, a moment before I was going to ask again, her eyes filled with tears, and she shook her head.

"I *want* to hate him. Kira, he hurt me so badly. It's been two years, and I still haven't recovered."

All I could do was nod. She devolved into sobs, and I let her cry until she was composed enough to talk again.

Chelsey swiped a sleeve under her nose. "I've tried to forget about it. I *really* have. No matter what I do, I keep picturing him as that loving and tender mate he was before the rejection. It hurts me to see what's happened to him on this island." She gestured toward the door. "He lost an eye, for the gods' sake. He's been through more than I could ever imagine." She put her hands in her hair. "I never even knew he was on the show. That's the kicker—I never watched it. I do remember a friend calling me one night, telling me to turn on the show. That there was something I needed to see." She chuckled and shrugged. "I freaked out and told her never to mention the show again. Looking back, she probably wanted me to see Ben was on the show. I've been walking around in this haze of heartbreak."

"It's all right, Chelsey," I said. "You're allowed to be hurt. Maybe there's still a chance for you guys. If you talk to him, you may find out that things aren't as they appear."

It wasn't my place to tell Crew's story. That would have to be something he revealed to her in private.

Chelsey snorted. "Yeah, sure. Even if I wanted to try, it's obvious he's got another person for company."

Furrowing my brow, I narrowed my eyes in confusion. "What? Who are you talking about."

Rolling her eyes, Chelsey groaned. "Oh my gosh, it's obvious, Kira. Crew and Elianna? The one they call Eli? I can totally tell they're together. It makes my inner wolf furious just thinking about it."

I slapped a hand to my mouth, not out of shock, but to keep from laughing. For a smart girl, Chelsey wasn't seeing things for what they were. Her mind was too consumed with pain to understand what was really going on.

"I can assure you," I said as I stifled a laugh, "that there is nothing going on between Crew and Eli. From what I've seen, those two are more like siblings than lovers. I've spent enough time with them to know there is literally *zero* romantic attraction between them."

Chelsey eyed me suspiciously while chewing her lower lip. "Really? Are you sure?"

"Look, you need to talk to Crew. Talk—nothing else. Get all this out and hear his side of it. The guy can't focus on anything if you're within five hundred feet of him. I promise you, if you go in with an open mind and hear him out, you'll see everything in a new light."

She wanted to speak to him, I could see it on her face. The problem was that she was too terrified of getting hurt again to allow him back in.

Chelsey stared at the floor. When she finally looked up to meet my eyes again, a wary hope glimmered on her face. "I'll talk to him," she said reluctantly. "But what if it's all for nothing?"

"What do you mean?"

"Our connection," Chelsey explained. "What if we talk and make up, but then find out our fated mate connection was a mistake, like you said the other night on the show? Maybe Heline's acolytes didn't process our bloodwork correctly, and Ben and I were never meant to be together in the first place?”

That idea had been at the back of my mind for days leading up to the fall of the mansion. It had worried me at first, but now? The further I strayed from following the old dogmatic beliefs our society had clung to for centuries, the easier it was to see that none of it mattered.

“When people feel as strongly about each other as you and Crew do, who gives a damn what some acolyte in a dirty robe says?” I laughed. “I mean, the only *true* way to know what connections are real would be to talk to Heline directly.”

As soon as the words were out of my mouth, a lightbulb went on in my mind. My joke was more than that—it was a glimpse at a path forward. If we found Heline, the moon goddess herself, we could get real answers. We could show her the proof that her acolytes were meddling with the connections. There might even be a chance that Heline would step in and stop the war.

My heart rate sped up, and chills coursed through my arms.

"I guess you're right," Chelsey said. "I'll do it. I'll talk to Crew. All I can do is pray he won't end up hurting me again."

She made to leave, and I put a hand on her arm. "Be honest with him, and listen to what he has to say. That's the only thing I can tell you."

She nodded and gave me a weak smile before vanishing down the corridor. As soon as she was gone, I hurried away, eager to tell Wyatt my idea. Searching out the moon goddess terrified me, but the more I thought about it, the more sense it made.

Wyatt was in the meeting room with Mika. I caught a snatch of their conversation as I made my way down the hall toward them.

"...the magic users more so," Mika said. "They're the ones who'll need to be trained how to fight the most."

Wyatt frowned. "Mika, I'll train everyone, but the magic users *have magic*. Don't you think people with less experience and no extra abilities should get the bulk of training?"

Mika shook his head fervently. "What happens if they get into a situation where they can't use their magic? They'll be screwed worse than a shifter. Right?"

"What is up with you?" Wyatt asked him as I walked into the room. "You've been going on and on about the magic users the whole time."

"I know what's going on," I cut in with a laugh.

They whirled around, surprised to find me in the room with them. Mika's eyes were wide and terrified.

Smirking at him knowingly, I said, "Don't get your panties in a wad. Zoe is all bubbly and goofy most of the time, but that doesn't mean she's helpless. She's one of the reasons we got out of Simon's lab the first time, remember?"

Mika's face turned red, and he scowled at me. "But what if Simon has something that can nullify magic? Zoe would be defenseless."

As soon as he'd finished speaking, a look of horrified surprise took over his features. He'd more or less admitted to being interested in Zoe.

"Wait," he stammered, closing his eyes. "I, uh, I didn't mean *just* Zoe. Um, I meant all the magic users. Uh, well, I..." He trailed off helplessly.

Wyatt and I burst out laughing. Seeing the ever stoic and broody Mika Sheen all tongue-tied and flustered, talking about a girl and trying to cover his tracks, was too much.

"Mika," I said quickly, not wanting him to think we were making fun of him, "don't get the wrong idea. We aren't laughing at the thought of you and Zoe together. In fact, I think you'd be a cute couple."

"Who said a *couple*?" Mika demanded, his voice going up an octave. "I didn't say that. No one said that."

"Calm down," I said, patting the air with my hand in an easing gesture. "It's all right. I know a lot of packs aren't keen on interspecies relationships, but fae are very open-minded about it, and Zoe is even more open-minded than most fae. Her family is the same, so I think you've got a good chance with her. If you want to pursue it."

Mika blinked rapidly. He'd obviously thought any chance with Zoe was too outlandish to truly consider. If I had to guess, he'd probably told himself that if anyone found out about his feelings, they'd tell him to forget about it. That I was encouraging him was a confusing surprise.

"Um, yeah," he mumbled. "Thanks. I need to, uh...I need to go." Mika stood and hustled out of the room without another word.

Wyatt watched him go with wide-eyed amazement before turning back to me. "Zoe and Mika? Seriously? When did you become a matchmaker? You're getting soft in your old age."

I swatted his shoulder. "I'm not even twenty-five yet, jackass."

Wyatt put both hands over his heart and batted his eyelashes at me. "A hopeless romantic, even at such a tender age."

Rolling my eyes, I took a seat next to him. "Enough. Time to be serious. Mika does have a reason to be worried. This attack on Simon is going to be dangerous. People are going to get hurt and killed."

Wyatt's grin faded. "It's like any other mission. Unless we get incredibly lucky, there will be casualties."

An idea had been tickling at the back of my mind for a little while, and I wondered if it was even worth considering. "I can't help but think that whatever happens will, in part, be my fault. This attack is mostly my idea. Maybe there's a way to even the odds somehow. A way to give us a leg up on Simon."

"And what would that be? A tactical nuclear bomb?"

"I'm working on it. It is a little strange, but I'm keeping it to myself until I'm comfortable talking about it."

Wyatt groaned and rubbed a hand over his face. "Well, that doesn't sound at all ominous. I know that look on your face. This little *idea* you have is going to put you in danger, isn't it?"

I shrugged helplessly. "I wouldn't call it *dangerous* per se, but it might be risky."

"I can't let the woman I love dive into something *risky* on her own. I guess I'm in this with you. Whatever it is."

My stomach gave a happy little flip, as it always did whenever Wyatt told me he loved me. The words came easily for him, like he'd been saying them his whole life.

Grinning back at him, I reached forward and poked him in the stomach. "You know you love my little plans."

Wyatt groaned again, then laughed. "Yeah. We'll see about that."

Chapter 8 - Wyatt

The next morning, I woke just as the artificial fae lights of Haven brightened in a sort of simulated sunrise and sunset the magic users of Haven had set up after Crew created the place. Kira lay curled against my side. As I looked down at her peaceful face, I found it surprising how natural and *right* it felt to have her there with me.

Sneaking around on *The Reject Project* had stressed me out. Hiding our feelings and desires had been one of the most exhausting things I'd ever done. Even before the show, I'd spent years concealing my feelings for her. I'd done such a good job of it, I'd believed my own lies. But the more time I spent with Kira, the more everything seemed to fall into place. Like I was where I'd always belonged.

Easing my arm out from under her, I slipped out of bed without waking her up. The light wasn't bothering her, and she snored lightly as I dressed and left the room. After closing the makeshift wooden door to our quarters, I headed down the hall to check on Abel.

The other alpha still hadn't regained consciousness. I wanted to be one of the first to speak to him and find out if he knew more about whatever serum they'd injected into him and Kira.

Unfortunately, Abel was still unconscious. A witch stood above him, running her hands an inch over his body as she murmured under her breath. She paused when she saw me.

"Good morning," she said. "I'm afraid your friend hasn't come around yet."

"Has there been *any* change?"

"He's more stable. No more strange night sweats, and his heart rate is back to normal." She put her hands on her hips and looked at Abel like he was a puzzle she couldn't figure out. "Not sure what else we can do for now. We're discussing it, though." She looked up quickly, like she'd just remembered something. "I *did* try a few spells on your other friend. The feral one? His name is Leif, I think?"

"Really?" I stepped forward, eager to hear any good news. "Did they help?"

She shrugged. "It calmed him down some. I wouldn't trust him in Haven, but he has been a little less feral. Zoe got up early this morning to work with him."

My eyebrows shot up. "She's there now?"

"Yup. Down the corridor, if you want to check in. A few of your other friends are there, too."

"Thank you," I said, giving a wave as I hurried down the hall.

In the enclosure room, I found Zoe, Mika, and J.D. Leif sat in his cell in human form, still looking wild and crazed. Instead of rocking in place and trying to tear his hair out, though, he sat on his knees and stared dazedly at Zoe. She was kneeling in front of the steel bars, her hands up as she cast her spells.

"Morning," Mika whispered as I stepped in.

J.D. kept staring at Leif and Zoe, chewing his thumbnail. He didn't spare me a single glance.

"How's it coming along?" I whispered to Mika.

"Not great." He sighed. "The spells they cast last night pulled him out of his funk, but it's not enough for him to be considered okay. He still reverts and has outbursts."

As if on cue, Leif jumped up. "This isn't working. I can't feel any-fucking-thing!" He kicked the wall of his cell, sending up a clod of dirt, then began muttering and mumbling to himself. Grabbing a handful of his hair, he tugged hard, trying to rip a clump out.

Zoe heaved a sigh as she rose to her feet. "I'm sorry. This isn't really my wheelhouse. I've got some fun tricks, but healing has never been my strong suit. Especially when I have no clue what caused the issue to begin with. Spell? Potion? Drug? Hypnosis? Gods only knows what that fucker did to cause this." She cracked a bittersweet smile. "If Leif wanted his fur a different color, I could do that in a snap."

"Hey," Mika said, stepping forward, "you're doing your best." He lifted an arm like he wanted to put it around her, but stopped himself.

Zoe lowered her eyes. "Doesn't feel like it."

"He's definitely less feral," J.D. said, his eyes still trained on Leif. "That's something to be happy about. You guys have done that much, at least."

"Exactly," Mika added, finally forcing himself to put a hand on Zoe's shoulder. "Zoe, without you, this would never have come as far as it has. You and the other wiccans and fae here are doing a *really good* job."

I stared, trying to stop myself from gaping at Mika. I'd never heard him sound so... *sweet.*

For her part, Zoe seemed to respond to the flattery. She flashed a brilliant smile at Mika. "Do you really think so?"

"Absolutely," he said enthusiastically.

"Do you guys want a minute in private?" I asked, grinning at Mika.

The other alpha snapped his head up at me, face flaming with embarrassment. *Stop*, he mouthed.

Zoe, oblivious to my joke, shook her head. "No, I can work with people around. It doesn't bother me."

"I'm starving," J.D. said with a heavy sigh. "I'm going to grab a bite and come back." He looked through the bars at Leif. "I'll be back as soon as I can, okay?" he said to him.

Leif, having calmed down again, nodded. "Okay. Yeah, you need to eat something. I'll, uh..." He glanced around at the ten-by-ten cell. "I'll be here, I guess."

"I'll go with you," Mika said to J.D. "Zoe, do you want me to bring you something back?"

"Yes, please. Either oatmeal. Or oatmeal, or if there's no other option, I'll take the oatmeal."

Mika chuckled. "Good one. I'll be back in a bit."

Leif walked to the lone bunk at the side of the cell and lay down, mumbling in that mad way of his.

"So," I said to Zoe, "how have things been going?"

Zoe rolled her eyes. "Oof. This place has been busy since Mika showed up. After him, you guys got here, and then?" She blew out her cheeks and used her fingers to simulate a bomb exploding. "Full crazy ever since."

"Why was it busy when Mika got here?"

"Oh, that," she said, then lit into one of her rapid-fire stories. "See, I never really talked a lot about the names of everyone on the show. So, when I told Crew we were going to rescue this Mika guy, I never told him Mika's last name because, like, who cares, right? So, Eli and Crew and I went out to where Kira said Mika would be, and when the guy came running out of the jungle to us, I was all like, 'Hey, we're here, let's get out of this place.' He was at first like, 'Oh, thank the gods, you're such a beautiful and caring soul to rescue me from this awful fate.' Except then, Crew and Mika caught a look at each other and then it was like, 'Record scratch, holy shit, I know you!'"

"Oh," I muttered, unable to get a word in edgewise.

"Exactly," Zoe said, clapping her hands together. "So, these two beefy beefcakes were in the same pack together and their dads are apparently both douches, but they were like rich kids. Now, they're living together in this big ball of dirt like a couple of earthworms or something. Ugh, what are the odds?"

I chuckled and decided to give a little nudge. "Yeah, and who knew a broody alpha from the First Pack would have a thing for chatty fae girls?"

Zoe rolled her eyes and punched me in the chest with surprising force. "Very funny, Wyatt. Go back to teasing Kira, because that stuff doesn't work on me. Besides, I can't play make-believe while trying to un-feral Leif."

"I'm very serious, Zoe." I wiped the grin off my face. "He's into you. Like, a lot. But he's a little skittish about admitting it."

Zoe stared at me stone-faced, either processing what I'd said or trying to figure out if I really was pulling her leg. "You're serious," she finally said in a monotone. Her face was devoid of any expression.

Uh-oh. Had Kira and I misread this whole thing? Did Zoe even like Mika that way? This could go very poorly, and I'd be the one to blame.

"Well, uh, yeah. He's got it bad for you, but if you don't—"

Zoe squealed, her face breaking into a massive smile. "Oh my gosh!" Zoe flitted about the room in quick zig-zags.

"Does, uh…" I frowned. "Does this mean you're happy?" I asked dumbly.

"Happy? Oh, gods, from the moment I laid eyes on him, I thought Mika was the sexiest, hottest alpha on the whole show."

"Well," I teased, "not to sound too full of myself, but I was on the show, too, Zoe."

She looked over her shoulder at me, her eyes tracking down my body. "I said what I said. No offense."

"Ouch. Okay."

She stopped abruptly, nibbling at her lip. I didn't know her as well as Kira did, but it was easy to see she was planning something in that fae head of hers. "Oh, I'm going to have to turn on the charm. Turn the flirt up to eleven. Make some new outfits." She looked at me again. "Do you think Crew would be mad if I walked around in a string bikini? Thong?"

"I don't…uh, I'm not sure I'm—"

"Morning," Kira said from behind us.

Oh, thank the gods. I could have kissed her.

"Can I talk to you real quick?" Kira asked me. "In private?"

"Sure." I went to follow her.

On the way out, I caught a bit of what Zoe said to Mika, who'd returned with her oatmeal. "Thanks for this. I'm starving. Mika, have you been working out? Look at these arms. Oh my gosh, so big!"

I didn't bother turning around. I could only imagine Mika's face.

"What's up?" I asked Kira once she and I were alone and out of earshot.

"Remember yesterday, when I said I had an idea?"

"Of course. You only have a few a year. They're memorable when they happen."

Grinning, Kira shoved me in the chest. "Very funny, asshole. No time for jokes. I'm serious."

"Yeah, yeah, you said it was strange. Are you ready to spill it?"

"The Shadowkeeper."

Any remnant of a smile I had faded, and my heart stuttered. "What?"

"She's bound to hate Simon as much as we do. He's fucking around on the island she calls home. Why don't we go looking for her? She could be an ally for us when we go against him."

My mind drifted back to the time I met her under the waterfall, and then again before getting to Haven. The woman, or being—whatever she was—didn't seem the type to readily help mortals in their affairs. We risked pissing her off just by trying to find her. It could be dangerous, and it would be difficult to find her to begin with.

When I mentioned all that, Kira acted like it didn't matter. "I think she wants to do something about it, too," she said. "Do you remember, right before she transported us to Zoe, she said something about *meddling*? I think that was her saying something was wrong on the island and she wanted to fix it."

"But like I said, how do we even go about finding her?"

Kira sighed and glanced around to make sure no one could hear. "We'll figure it out. Look, I know we're going to help teach these people to fight, but if we go against Simon like we are now, with no backup, it's going to be ugly. Lots of these people are going to die, and I don't know if I can shoulder that kind of blame. I *have* to try."

Gods, this was a fucking dangerous idea. The Shadowkeeper could kill us all with a snap of her fingers. But the look on Kira's face sealed it for me. She was right that we didn't have a large enough force to go against Simon. Plus, as fired up as Kira was about this, there would be no stopping her. I'd known her long enough to be sure of that much, at least.

"Okay," I finally said. "If you think it's worth a shot, I'll help."

Kira's shoulders sagged in obvious relief. "You will?"

"Of course. I can't think of anything more fun than running off to meet death. I mean, at least I'll get to be with you. How do you want to go about this?"

Kira glanced over my shoulder at the others in the room behind us. They were eating. J.D. had slid a plate through the bars to Leif. None of them were looking our way.

"Do we tell Crew?" Kira ventured. "Tell him our plan and that we're going to search the island for the Shadowkeeper?"

"Not a great idea," I said. "He's tense as hell about attacking Simon's lab again. Haven is locked up tight. He'll freak if we say we want to go wandering around the jungle right now and veto any plan to go out. He wants to keep everyone as safe as possible. I don't see him budging on that."

"Do we sneak out?" Kira asked, dropping her voice to a whisper.

"No other way to do it. Especially when we've got so little time to work with," I said. "And if we're going to do this, we need to go now. Before time runs out and I talk myself out of helping with this crazy shit."

Kira nudged me aside. "Hey, Zoe? I need you for a minute."

"What are you doing?" I hissed.

"We need her to get past all the traps and security measures."

"Hey, what's up?" Zoe asked, joining us in the hall.

Kira glanced at me first before whispering her entire plan to Zoe and that we needed her help to get us out of Haven.

Zoe simply stared at Kira. "Hang on. What?"

"You heard me," Kira said. "I'm not explaining it all again. Will you help us?"

Zoe heaved out a long, dramatic sigh. "Ugh, curse my powerful magic and my undying loyalty to my friends." She put the back of her hand to her forehead in dramatic emphasis. "The burdens I must bear."

"Is that a yes?" Kira deadpanned.

Zoe rolled her eyes and grabbed Kira's hand, leading her down the corridor. "Of course it's a yes, dumbass. Come on."

Zoe led Kira and me through the maze of tunnels that made up Haven. On the way to the exit, my stomach started doing nervous flips. The Shadowkeeper. I shuddered. There was something about her that inspired both awe and terror. Also, the way she'd so easily dealt with the creature Simon had created? Kira and I wouldn't stand a chance. I imagined the two of us reduced to nothing but bloody red spots on the jungle floor, but I shoved the thought away before it could really take hold. I had to believe the Shadowkeeper would see it was in the island's best interest to get rid of Simon. She lived here. Surely she'd want to keep her home as peaceful and calm as possible.

At the exit tunnel, a member of Haven stood, holding one of the few firearms I'd seen here.

"Good morning," Zoe said to him cheerily as we approached.

He looked up, startled. "Oh, hey, Zoe. Morning."

Zoe pointed over her shoulder with a thumb. "Go get some breakfast. I'll watch the entrance while you're gone."

"Seriously?" he said in surprise. "I just got on guard duty two hours ago. It's a little early for a break."

Zoe shrugged. "I have nothing else going on. Figured I'd be nice and give you a few minutes. Go on, before they run out of slop."

The guard, a panther shifter by his scent, glanced nervously at me and Kira, but hunger won out. "Okay. I'll be quick. You want my rifle?"

Zoe wiggled her fingers. "I have all I need with these babies."

He was already moving down the tunnel. "Be back soon. Thanks again."

Zoe waved. When he rounded the corner, she turned to us. "Let's get you out of here quick. I know that guy. He eats like a fucking horse, but he's also fast. Kinda disgusting to watch, honestly. We won't have long."

We followed Zoe out, waiting for her to disarm the magical wards and the standard spring-loaded traps.

"This one was my idea," Zoe said, releasing a trap with several pieces of bamboo sharpened to wicked points. It looked designed to spring forward and stab anyone who hit the tripwire. Zoe touched the tip of one skewer and showed us where the trap would hit an intruder. "Crotch level. Anyone who gets hit by this is gonna have a real bad day. They'll also have a few new holes to pee out of."

I winced. "Very exciting."

At the mouth of the cave, Zoe grabbed Kira and hugged her. "I'll keep my mouth shut, but I'm only giving you guys a few hours. After that, I'm spilling the beans to Crew. Got it?"

"Got it," Kira said, extricating herself from the embrace. "We'll be back soon. Promise."

Zoe went back down the tunnel, rearming the traps and wards as she went.

"Where to first?" Kira asked.

I pointed to the south, in the direction of the mansion. "I'm pretty sure I can find the waterfall where I first met her. I can't think of a better place to start than there. We can try to catch her scent while we work our way toward the river."

"Okay. Lead the way."

The jungle was already roiling with noises, even as early as it was. The attack on Simon's lab and the fall of the mansion had the creatures and beings of Bloodstone in a state of agitation. Kira and I spent the first twenty minutes of our trek hiding from passing beasts, one of which was another of Simon's abominations: a weird combination of snake, bear, and tiger. A bloody hunk of something humanoid hung from its serpentine mouth.

Once it had moved on, I nudged Kira. "Come on. This way," I whispered.

Moving quickly and stealthily, Kira and I made good time. The section of the island we found ourselves now traversing didn't have many creatures lurking about. Not at the moment, anyway. After thirty minutes, I caught the cool and crisp scent of moving water. The river. We were getting close.

"You smell that?" I asked, turning to Kira.

She was nodding, a smile forming on her lips. The smile faltered as she sniffed again, and fear crept into her eyes. Before I could take another whiff, a half-dozen hissing, spitting, and decrepit vampires exploded from the jungle to our right.

"Shit!" I shouted as they descended on us.

I shifted and lunged at the first attacker. To my surprise, Kira also shifted and began fighting off the creatures. As I tore the head off one vampire, a second jumped on my back, clawing and biting at me. Thankfully, my thick fur made it impossible for his teeth to find purchase. Flipping over, I crushed the creature against a tree, leaving it twitching and broken on the forest floor.

Turning, I found Kira had killed one of the vampires, but three more had leaped upon her, almost overwhelming her strength with their own. One of them had Kira's ear in his mouth. She yelped in pain and stumbled.

The sound of her in pain, the sight of that *thing* biting into her, sent me into a blind rage. My vision went red, and my inner wolf shoved aside any semblance of control. All I could remember were the growls and screams. When I shifted back to my human form, I found myself standing in the center of devastation. Vampire body parts lay everywhere, quickly desiccating. My hands were clenched into fists, and my breath heaved in and out of my lungs.

Kira shifted back and stepped toward me. "Wyatt? Are you all right?"

Seeing her safe and unhurt eased my rage. I opened my mouth to ask if she was okay, but an ear-piercing shriek erupted around us. Kira and I slammed our hands over our ears. A fucking banshee. Through the trees, I caught sight of the shadowy creature pushing through the foliage toward us.

Before it could let out another shriek, I grabbed Kira's hand and ran. Taking a full blast from that thing could not only burst our eardrums, but actually *kill* us.

Somehow, in our mad dash away from danger, I still managed to keep us on the right track. The last thing I wanted was to add to the time we were out in this godsforsaken jungle. The banshee fell behind us as we trampled through the jungle with all the speed we could muster.

Noticing a fallen palm tree to my right, I pulled Kira toward it. The fronds had formed a natural alcove, and we crawled under it. Hidden on all sides like we were in a tent, we sat silently, waiting to see if any other creatures were around.

"Come here," I whispered to her. "Are you okay? Are you hurt?"

I ran my hands over her body. She had a few scratches and bites, but they all seemed to be healing rapidly with no trouble.

"I'm fine, Wyatt. Really."

Her words did nothing to ease my fears. All my life, I'd prided myself on being able to control my emotions, but lately, that control snapped whenever Kira was hurt or in danger. My inner wolf freaked out in such a way that I had almost no control over him. And not only when it came to injury and danger, but other things as well. Like the night at the mansion when she'd been forced into heat by that potion Von had given her. The other alphas had noticed, and some—like Gavin—had gotten worked up. But *none* of them had reacted as strongly me. It had almost felt like I was feral.

Could that be what was happening? Maybe I'd been away from my unofficial pack long enough that some feral instincts were coming out? Or was something else going on?

Kira moved my hands aside. "For real, I'm fine. Stop fussing over me."

I inhaled, trying to steady myself. "You're such a pain in the ass. I never should have let you talk me into this."

Kira grinned at me. "I didn't hear you arguing."

"What was I supposed to do? Let you come out into this hellhole by yourself?"

"Aww, is big bad Wyatt Rivers worried about me?"

"Holy shit. Have you not been watching? I'm *always* worried about you. This place is so fucking..." I trailed off, the good-natured smile on my face quickly fading as a new scent caught my attention.

Seeing my face, Kira's grin vanished. "What's wrong?" she whispered.

I gripped her forearm tight, a signal to stay quiet. My eyes darted around, panic welling up within me as I became sure the scent was what I thought it was. Kira's eyes widened. She'd noticed it, too.

Pressing my mouth to her ear, I spoke, my voice barely louder than the terror-filled breaths I was taking. "We have to run. It's close."

Kira nodded. Holding up three fingers, I lowered them in a countdown. When my last finger lowered, we leaped up and rolled out from under our cover. An angry wet hiss came from behind us as a massive silver blade sliced through the palm fronds. The revenant stood, glaring at us from under its moth-eaten black hood, glowing red eyes pinning us in place.

Lifting the scythe again, it opened its mouth, black tongue flicking over rotting gray teeth. We must have stumbled into the territory it had claimed for itself. We couldn't fight it; Kira and I didn't have the skills to do that. We'd need *powerful* magical weapons to even have a chance, and then it would still be almost impossible. Running was the only option. It's what I'd done last time I'd come toe to toe with this thing.

"Go!" I screamed.

We bolted, leaving the revenant behind. The creature let out a hungry yowl of rage and chased after us. I spared a glance back, shocked once more by its speed.

"Faster. We have to go faster!"

Nodding, Kira shifted, and I followed suit. We were faster in our wolf forms, but the fucking nightmare behind us somehow sped up even more, its huge scythe slicing down trees and vines as it followed.

Unable to keep track of where we were going, I didn't notice until it was too late that we were on a downhill slope. The hills on either side of us had risen as we moved farther downhill. A sinking sense of terror flooded me. Ahead, the hills had become jagged rock walls, ending in a right angle. The lips of the walls extended twenty feet into the sky. A complete dead end.

Kira and I skidded to a stop, then shifted into our human forms. We tried to climb, but it was of no use. Water drizzled down the stone from a creek above. All the rocks were coated in mucus-like mold and lichen. Behind us, the revenant hissed again.

I turned. Dread poured through me, turning my blood to ice. The thing was stalking toward us. Kira gasped in terror at the sight of it. Pulling her back, I put myself between her and the revenant. We were going to die. There was no way out. We would fight—that wasn't a question—but the idea that Kira and I would be dead within the next few moments sent a wave of nausea through me.

The revenant raised the gigantic scythe high overhead and moved toward us. Thick, gelatinous saliva dripped from its black lips.

Kira dug her fingers into my back, grabbing a handful of my shirt. "I love you, Wyatt."

My heart broke at the fear and acceptance in her voice. Reaching back, I grabbed her free hand. "I love you, too."

When it was twenty feet away, the revenant rushed at us, hissing in rage. My own bellowing roar echoed back toward him. If he wanted to kill us, then he better come the fuck on and try it.

The scythe, glinting in a ray of sun shimmering down through the canopy, swung forward, ready to part my head from my body the way it had cut Tate in half.

We were saved so fast, I almost didn't realize what was happening. A flash of shadow, a burst of air, and a woman's lithe body stood before us, facing the revenant. She grabbed the blade of the scythe like it was nothing more than a plastic toy.

"I believe you have been warned about encroaching on my domain," the Shadowkeeper said to the revenant.

The creature thrashed and yowled, trying to pull the blade free, but even its otherworldly powers were no match for the Shadowkeeper's strength.

She lowered her voice to a dangerous whisper. "You've been warned once. That is more than many receive. I believe it's time you departed this plane."

With her free hand, the Shadowkeeper snapped her fingers. Kira and I flinched as the surrounding darkness of the forest coalesced and descended on the revenant, moving like liquid snakes. The shadows enveloped the creature, and it continued to spit and hiss its rage as the smoke-like tentacles suffocated it. In seconds, all I could see was a mass of writhing blackness where it had once stood. Then, in a single rush and with a sound like ripping fabric, the shadows pulled away.

The revenant split apart, torn asunder by the Shadowkeeper. Instead of blood or gore, only dust and black clumps of sludge exploded from the body.

The tendrils of darkness rushed back to their original hiding places while the remains of the revenant lay steaming on the forest floor. The Shadowkeeper tossed the scythe down, the blade already turning to dust. She turned her dark and uncaring eyes upon us, taking a breath as though smelling fresh air again.

"Ah, much better. That little nuisance has been here for almost fifty years. I never did like him."

Chapter 9 - Kira

I couldn't help but flinch away from her. The intimidating power she exuded was almost palpable.

The Shadowkeeper lifted an eyebrow. "You two again? Hmph, strange. You should really be in hiding, my dears. The mad one is out and about." She gave a disgusted sniff. "Stirring up trouble in his search for the hidden ones."

"The hidden ones?" Wyatt repeated.

"The little enclave." She slid a finger across my shoulder. "I'm sure you know. You have the smell of the place all over you."

"You're talking about Simon Shingleman? The 'mad one?'"

"Hmm, is that what the hybrid calls himself? Very well."

As I looked at her, my mind whirred with everything I knew about the being standing before me. She'd always been a huge question mark on the show—only appearing at random intervals, sometimes years apart, always bestowing gifts or power and favors. There had even been a course in TO training—

Unknown Beings and Their Histories—that had two full chapters devoted to her. From what I'd seen her do, she reminded me of some type of wraith. But wraiths had no scent, and no wraith could have taken down a revenant.

My gut told me what she was, but the thought was too crazy to seem real. They were all *known*. None were hidden. Were they? Could she possibly be what I thought she was? And if so, how did no one know?

"Are you a goddess?" I blurted.

Wyatt glanced at me like I'd said the craziest thing ever.

The Shadowkeeper, for her part, only gazed at me with an introspective look on her face. Then her stoic expression burst into a surprised smile. She thrust her shoulders back and raised her chin. A look of excitement that I'd guessed her deepest secret glittered in her eyes.

"My, you are a clever one. Correct. I am Lucina. Younger sister to Heline. Goddess of darkness, shadows, and night."

Wyatt's mouth fell open, and he croaked, "What?"

Ignoring him, Lucina continued talking to me. "In ancient times, I was much more well-known. A goddess worshiped by the ancients. Especially those creatures and beings who hide in the night and shun the daylight. Vampires and shifters were counted among my greatest followers. But"—her forehead wrinkled—"gods fall from favor and can be forgotten. My time came to an end. When worship wanes, so does a god's power."

"Why are you here, though?" I asked. It made no sense for something as powerful as a god to remain in a backwater place like Bloodstone Island.

"I chose this place as my isolation. As my followers dwindled, so did my powers. Rather than live in a world that had forgotten me, I came here." She lifted her arms and gestured to the surrounding jungle. "Many creatures here still revere me." She glanced down in disgust at the remains of the revenant. "Minus those created by my lesser siblings and cousins. I have chosen not to meddle in the lives of mortals for many centuries, choosing instead to remain here in a small kingdom of my own."

"But we need help. Simon—"

My words were cut off as my own shadow swirled up to press against my mouth. The feeling was strange, like both water and fabric over my lips.

"I was not done speaking, my dear," Lucina said, her voice lowering dangerously.

Wyatt stared in wide-eyed horror at the shadow that clung to my lips. Like me, he was probably thinking of how easily the shadows had torn the revenant apart.

"My sister Heline has chosen a separate path to mine, causing trouble and dabbling in things we gods should be above. An entire mortal war has begun. Not only that, she's decided to play with the little mating connections you people hold dear. It appears my time of isolation is at an end. If she will not stop meddling on her own, then I must step in."

My shadow slid away from my lips, returning to the forest floor. Heline was causing trouble? That made no sense. Why would the moon goddess cause trouble with the fated connections?

"Heline?" I asked, dumbfounded. "Not her acolytes and priests? *She's* the one who's been screwing with the fated mate connections?"

"Indeed," Lucina said with disgust and disappointment. "Such a simple thing to stay out of, yet my older sister seems to have grown bored with the status quo."

If Heline had truly fucked around with fated mates for the last few decades, it would make sense that things had been going bad for years. We absolutely *had* to find Heline and find out what the hell was going on.

"Since you've pleased me by guessing my truth," Lucina said, "I shall help you destroy the mad one."

"Why didn't you destroy him before?" Wyatt asked. "If you're a goddess, couldn't you have swatted him off this island at any time?"

Lucina shrugged. "Mortals don't understand the view of the gods. Many things have happened and *will* happen. Mortal life is short, and things tend to work themselves out without our interference. I had assumed this hybrid creature would eventually go away, but now I see that things have come to a head. To avoid a greater, long-lasting disaster, an example must be made. I shall step into the fray, but only under one condition." She held up one long, slender finger.

"Uh, and that is?" I asked.

"That Bloodstone be left in peace as a place for me and the darkness to remain in undisturbed isolation."

If the show remained off the air, I had no idea why anyone would ever want to come back to this place. That meant if we were successful, it was a promise we could keep. I opened my mouth to agree, when I suddenly remembered what Eli said about getting off the island. A *dark* force surrounded the island, preventing any of the creatures from getting out.

"Wait... are you the one keeping all the beings on Bloodstone from getting out?" I asked.

"Of course, dear. My minions are those that creep in the darkness. This place was created as a refuge for them when they become too dangerous to reside in the world of light. When the mansion fell, the creatures here would have attempted to escape. I increased my entrapment wards to maintain control. Once the mad one is dealt with, I will make it easy for you and your friends to leave Bloodstone. There is no dark in you, and as such, no reason for you to remain here."

"What's the plan, then?" Wyatt asked. "How will you help us?"

Lucina smirked at him. "I'll be there when you need me."

"What does—"

Before Wyatt could finish his question, Lucina's robe of shadow burst off her, and she devolved into a swarm of bats that rushed away into the jungle, leaving us alone.

Wyatt stared off after the last of the bats and shook his head. "It fucking worked? How the hell did we do that? We have a goddess on our side now?"

"I know," I said, grinning like an idiot.

As determined as I'd been to find her, I had assumed the Shadowkeeper would be much more difficult to entice into helping us. With her agreement, we were no longer hopelessly outmatched or stranded. We had a fighting chance now.

"Let's get the hell out of here," I said. "I'm sure Zoe will try to stay close to the entrance to let us back in, but if we don't hurry, someone will ask why she's hanging around so long."

Hands clasped, Wyatt and I began the hike back to Haven. Lucina's presence must have terrified any creatures in the vicinity, because he jungle was much quieter than it when we'd set out. We still had to skirt a group of feral tiger shifters, but otherwise, the return trip was comparatively mundane.

"There's something I didn't have a chance to ask her," Wyatt said after we'd been walking in silence for half an hour.

"What's that?"

"When I found her the first time behind that waterfall, she spoke to me. Said I was a *pawn* in her sister's game. I had no clue what that meant or who her sister was. But now that I know it's Heline, I wonder what the hell she meant. I don't want to be a pawn. Even the thought of it pisses me off."

I couldn't argue with that. Our lives were supposed to be our own, and we should be able to do what we wanted. We had free will. The idea that Heline had not only been screwing with big things, but taking time out of her day to mess with Wyatt and me directly was equal parts irritating and terrifying.

The trees ahead of us parted to reveal the fake rocky outcropping that concealed Haven. Zoe was waiting for us, and beside her stood a very angry Eli.

"Hey, bestie," Zoe said with a wave, but the smile on her face looked strained. "I really hope you did what you said you were gonna do." She cut her eyes to Eli and blushed.

Eli took a couple steps toward us, her arms crossed over her chest as she glared at us like we were the dumbest people she'd ever met. "What the hell were you two thinking?"

I shrugged and gestured back to the jungle. "We went out to—"

"Of all the dumbass things I could imagine doing, this has to be at the top," Eli went on. "Do you have any idea how dangerous this was? Simon could be out there looking for you." Eli stepped forward until she was right in my face. "We lost *two* men saving you. And how do you repay that? By strolling out into the jungle to get kidnapped *again*? That's a really heartless way to say thank you."

Shame, intense and visceral, spread through me. I hadn't thought of how this would look to those who'd lost friends. I hadn't even known the two men who'd died. Eli was right, and the knowledge filled me with remorse and contrition. Our mission had been important and successful, but this place belonged to these people. We were their guests, and Wyatt and I had spat on that kindness by being reckless. The fact that I liked and respected Eli and Crew made it all worse. We were assholes.

"Eli," I said, holding up my hands. "I'm sorry. I really am. We didn't mean to be disrespectful. I can't imagine what you guys have been through. You've lost people, and that is part of why we went out. We don't want anyone else to die if they don't have to, so we went to find help."

Eli snorted. "Yeah, Zoe told me. That was fucking dumb. You went *looking* for the Shadowkeeper? Gods almighty, do you have any clue how powerful she is? She could kill you with a snap of her damn fingers."

"We know," I said. "We...uh, saw. She saved us out there. And she agreed to help us when we go for Simon."

Eli blinked and shook her head, all traces of her anger gone. "Are you serious?"

"Yeah," Wyatt said. "She agreed. Didn't give us details, though. All she said was that she'd be there when we needed her."

"Um..." Eli's mouth opened and closed, like she couldn't quite process the information. She looked like we'd just told her water was no longer wet. "Well, all right, then. I guess that's, um, really good news." She regained a bit of her composure and pointed at us again. "Even so, that doesn't excuse what you did. This is your one and only warning. Got it?"

"Yes. We're sorry," I said.

Eli let out a heavy sigh and waved toward the entrance. "Get the hell in there, then. Go see your friend."

"Which one?" Wyatt asked, sounding confused.

Zoe, who'd been uncharacteristically silent, finally perked up. "Oh, yeah. Abel's awake."

At that news, Wyatt and I couldn't get into Haven fast enough. Having to take our sweet time while Eli and Zoe guided us through the security measures was misery. Probably a good punishment for our recklessness.

I tried to focus on my hope for success against Simon as we made our way deeper into Haven. With Lucina's promise to help, I couldn't help but imagine getting off this island soon. The thought had a weird, surreal feel to it. I'd only been on this island for a few weeks, but if someone told me it had been years, I would have believed them.

Once past the entry corridor, Zoe, Wyatt, and I and through the dirt tunnels to get to the medical area. As we entered the room, Abel looked up weakly. His face was deathly pale, and he looked like he could fall asleep at any moment. Still, he managed a smile when he saw us.

"Hey, guys," he said.

Wyatt and I went to his bedside. "How are you feeling?" I asked.

"Like I've been hit by a truck," he said. He pinned me with his eyes. "Kira, thank you. They told me what happened. I can't tell you how much it means to me that you saved me. That...*man.*" Abel shuddered. "He's a fucking monster. A psychopath. You have no clue how awful he is."

I actually had a pretty good idea, but I refrained from telling him that as I put my hand on his arm. "No problem. Hell, I owed you one for rescuing me from that basilisk."

"Abel, do you remember anything about what Simon did to you?" Wyatt asked.

Abel flinched at hearing Simon's name. "Not really. It's all a big blur. I don't even remember what happened in the jungle. One minute, we were all together and those weird creatures were attacking us; the next, I was in the lab. I was fucking terrified, man. Simon let his vampire assistants feed on me, then he hooked me up to this weird machine. After that, nothing. Just black. That's all I remember. Sorry."

"It's all right," Wyatt said, patting his shoulder.

Abel nodded, but tears sprang into his eyes, and he swallowed hard. "I'm not feeling great. I think I need to rest."

"Yeah, okay. You take a nap." I nudged Wyatt toward the door.

"Sorry about earlier," Zoe said when we were walking down the hall. "Eli asked why I was hanging around the entrance. She's...well, she's pretty intense. I tried lying, but she saw right through it. Anyway, she'd come looking for you two because there's a group of people ready to start training. She left them to work on their own until you were ready to help. Do you want to head that way?"

"Sure. It'll get my mind off everything else," I said, again feeling a weird mix of excitement and shame at what we'd done. Excitement for our success, but shame at betraying Eli and Crew's trust.

"Hey, guys," Zoe said as she led us into a big antechamber-type room. A half-dozen Haven citizens were gathered there. They looked at us expectantly.

"Okay," Wyatt said. "Let's get started, I guess."

The next two hours were spent teaching the group grappling techniques, disarming moves, ways to combine magic with hand-to-hand combat, and explaining the best ways to dispatch vampires, as it seemed Simon had quite a few of those in his employ. In no time at all, Zoe and everyone else was soaked with sweat. It was pretty basic, especially for me and Wyatt, but everyone else looked excited to learn new things.

As I helped a couple of younger witches learn some simple joint locks, my gaze kept straying to Wyatt. He moved around the room, pointing out flaws, coaching, and assisting. He took to leadership roles easier than anyone I knew, though I'd never really noticed it before. I'd spent too much time trying to ignore him or butt heads with him to really see what he was capable of.

"Watch how Kira and I do this." He waved me over. "She's going to attack me, and I'm going to use her own momentum to take her down."

"You sure about this?" I asked, cocking my eyebrow.

Wyatt nodded and grinned back. "Come on, hotshot. Let's see what you've got."

Smirking, I lunged at him. He parried my attack with fluid, effortless skill—grabbing my wrist and spinning, then knocking me to the ground. My breath left me in a huff as I landed.

Wyatt leaned over me. "Wanna go for round two?"

With a growl, I flipped onto my feet. "Let's give them a good show."

The trainees all gathered around, eager to see their two instructors fight. This time, Wyatt was the attacker. He moved damned fast, but I lashed out a foot, catching his shin. He tumbled forward, and I chopped my hand down on the back of his neck. I held back, not really wanting to hurt him, but I made sure he felt my power. The strike finished his fall and sent him face-planting into the dirt.

"You see, everyone," I addressed the crowd, "men have all those big muscles, but it can make them a *little* top-heavy."

Wyatt chuckled as he wiped dirt off his face and stood. "Fair enough. Let's see what else you've got."

We went back and forth, grappling with each other. Our bodies intertwined, sweat mingling, and our faces were so close together, our breaths became one. There was a sexual element to the fight that couldn't be ignored. From the way Wyatt was looking at me, he'd noticed it as well.

At one point, Wyatt had me wrapped me in a headlock, my back to his chest. His cock was hard against my ass.

"Oh, for fuck's sake," Zoe finally said, rolling her eyes. "Get a room."

The crowd tittered with embarrassed laughter. Wyatt released me and stepped away. "Okay, everyone. Uh, break time. Head out and get some lunch. We can do more training afterward."

The Haveners filed out. At the end of the line, Zoe looked over her shoulder at me and mimed giving a blow job. I bared my teeth at her, but she just laughed and hurried off to lunch.

Wyatt grabbed my hand and pulled me out through the opposite door. In the corridor, he pressed me against the wall and claimed my mouth. His hands roamed over my body, fingertips trailing up my hips, hands kneading my breasts through my shirt. His hunger and desire for me were exposed by his every movement. My own need sent pulsing waves of heat between my thighs. The tingly sensation on my nipples and clit, like an itch that needed to be scratched, made me dizzy.

I pulled away, gasping. "We've got a lot of training to do over the next couple of days. Are you gonna get this worked up every time?"

Wyatt growled and pressed his face into my neck, licking and sucking at the skin below my ear. My eyes rolled back, and I clenched my thighs together, needing the friction as he nibbled at my sensitive skin.

Putting his lips to my ear, he whispered, "Who cares? We don't have to hide anything from the people here. Everyone knows you're mine."

You're mine. Words I would have scoffed at from any man a few months ago brought a smile to my lips. I *was* his, and he *was* mine. Something about that made me feel content in a way I couldn't describe. I couldn't even make fun of him for saying it.

"If I want to call a break every ten minutes," Wyatt went on, teeth scraping against my earlobe, "to take you back to the room and have you, then I will. Screw anyone who wants to say something about it."

My breath came in lilting gasps. "Is that what you're gonna do? *Have* me?"

Wyatt pressed his hips forward, grinding himself against me, and I could feel the thick rod of flesh in his pants hardening. "Is that what you want?"

There was nothing I wanted more in that moment. "Let's go, before I fuck you right here against the wall."

Wyatt grinned and took my hand again. We sprinted back to our room. As soon as the door was closed, I shimmied out of my pants and panties. The garments were still around my ankles when Wyatt pushed me face-first onto the bed. A moment later, I felt his warm breath on my thighs, and then he slid his tongue into me. Arching my back, I gasped in pleasure as he probed deeper into me, then slid out to flick my clit.

"Oh, fuck," I moaned. "That feels so good."

Wyatt took hold of my ass and pressed his face even closer, almost suffocating himself against me to shove his tongue deeper. The world around me seemed to vanish until all I could feel was Wyatt fucking me with his mouth. My eyes half-lidded, my mouth agape, soft groans flowed out of me as he brought me to the brink of climax. One finger rubbed at my clit while another fucked my pussy as Wyatt swirled his tongue around my butthole.

Just as my orgasm threatened to burst free, Wyatt pulled away. I huffed in disappointment. Rolling over, I found him tearing off his clothes, and I kicked off the garments bunched around my ankles and pulled my shirt over my head. When his throbbing cock sprang free of his pants, I licked my lips. I took him in my mouth before he'd even gotten his shirt off, sliding my lips to the base and massaging his balls, fingertips trailing across the velvety skin of his scrotum.

Wyatt thrust his hips toward me, shoving his cock even deeper into my mouth. Taking hold of his shaft, I stroked him while suckling at the head. Wyatt ran his fingers lovingly through my hair as he fucked my mouth. Things between us were always so intense. Like we couldn't stop, couldn't breathe, until we'd made each other scream in ecstasy. Coaxed out every ounce of pleasure we could.

My body hummed, desperate to be filled. Filled with *him*. The thought of the cock in my mouth slipping deep into my pussy was too much to bear.

Pulling him free of my mouth, I lay back on the bed, spreading my legs in invitation. Wyatt smiled and climbed up. A moment later, thick warm flesh pierced my entrance, and he thrust into me, filling me completely. Once he was seated to the hilt, he stilled, letting me feel all of him. His balls pressed against my ass, his cock twitched inside me, his hands held my breasts to steady himself. His muscles bunched and flexed. It was an erotic sight.

With no warning, he pulled his hips back until only his tip was inside me, then slammed back into me.

"Holy fuck," I moaned.

His movements grew faster, more insistent. His cock crashed into me again and again, faster with each thrust. I lost myself in the moment, almost hypnotized. I wanted more. Needed more. I couldn't get enough of him.

"Harder, Wyatt. Fuck me harder," I hissed through gritted teeth, sweat beading on my neck and chest.

"Like this?" he whispered, increasing the pace of his thrusts. The only sound in the room was our heavy breathing and skin slapping against skin.

"Gods, yes," I moaned, throwing my head back. "Harder."

Wyatt rested his weight on his elbows, his face inches from mine, and looked into my eyes as he fucked me even harder. I locked my legs around his waist, taking him in even deeper. Each time he filled me, another wave of bliss jolted through my body, like a live wire was being shoved inside me. But instead of electricity, it was pleasure. Wyatt's breath came in rapid gasps as sweat dripped from his forehead onto my chest, gliding across my nipples.

"Fuck, fuck, fuck, I'm gonna come," I yelped, my voice growing strained as I clenched my jaws in preparation.

"Come for me, baby," Wyatt whispered, kissing my chin.

A loud sound erupted from my throat, half-grunt, half-scream as warmth exploded from my pussy throughout my entire body. Wyatt continued thrusting into me, and each time, another pulse of ecstasy rippled through me. I couldn't even form words; all I managed to do was paw at him, slamming my hips up to meet his every movement.

"Fuck, Kira, you're gonna make me come," Wyatt grunted, his muscles tensing.

"Mmm." It was all I could manage. My eyes were closed as I continued to ride the waves of an orgasm so strong, it stripped me of all my senses.

Finally, with a final thrust and a loud groan, Wyatt's cock twitched and pulsed, and his cum filled me. He collapsed onto me a few seconds later.

"Gods," I panted. "That was amazing."

"Uh-huh," Wyatt moaned, face buried in my breasts.

The sound of his voice muffled by my tits made me laugh, and once I started, I couldn't stop. Wyatt chuckled as well, and soon we were both on our sides, arms and legs intertwined, laughing together.

Everything else could be forgotten for a little while.

Chapter 10 - Wyatt

Zoe clenched her opponent's forearm in her hands, then jammed her foot into the ground, pulling on it while slamming her hip into his. The man cried out as he flipped over. Zoe didn't release the arm, but yanked up and pressed her foot down on the man's throat.

"Easy on him!" I shouted at her. "He's done. He's finished."

Zoe flinched, tearing herself from her bloodlust, and looked down at the male wiccan who lay beneath her. His face was scarlet from lack of oxygen as her foot pressed hard into his neck.

"Oh, shit, Dave. Sorry." She let him go, and he rolled away, gagging and coughing.

I patted her on the shoulder. "Really good job, but try to remember we're all friends here."

"Sorry. Got a little carried away there," she said, though she looked more proud of herself than sorry.

On the far side of the room, J.D. and Gavin sparred against each other while Kira helped Mika. It was the fourth training session we'd done in less than twenty-four hours, and the citizens of Haven were picking up on things pretty quickly. Kira and I kept the lessons simple, using techniques that were easy to learn and the most beneficial.

Turning around to check on the others, I spotted Crew leaning against the entrance to the training room. He was watching the proceedings with a critical but approving stare. The night before, Kira and I had discussed the alliance we'd created with the Shadowkeeper. Eli had decided it would be better if we told Crew. We'd kept the Shadowkeeper's *true* identity hidden, but rather than being excited about the prospect, Crew hadn't warmed to the idea.

"I don't know if we can count on her help," Crew had said after hearing our story.

"She seemed pretty fired up to get Simon off the island," Kira had countered.

Crew shrugged. "In my time on Bloodstone, I've found it easier to rely on myself and my people than outside help. She could easily turn her back on us. These immortal beings are fickle, you guys know that. Oh, I'm also not really happy about you both traipsing out into the jungle without authorization. I'd ream your asses, but Eli says she already did a good job of that."

"Okay, I get it," Kira said, "but maybe we can look at her like a secret weapon? We train and prepare as best we can, and hopefully, she jumps in if we get in trouble?"

Crew nodded and stood to leave. "I can get on board with that. Don't spread this around, though. I want my people focused and ready. If they start thinking some magical creature is going to swoop in and save them when it gets tough, they might not train as hard. That, and they may not be as focused going into battle."

He'd left then, leaving Kira and me to discuss training for the next day. In all honesty, I agreed with Crew. And now, seeing the way he eyed his people while they learned to fight, I saw exactly what he was worried about. These people relied on him, and he didn't want to let them down. We *did* need everyone as prepared as possible, because regardless of what Lucina had told us, there was a chance she could back out and leave us out to dry. Gods didn't have the same moral compass mortals did.

Zoe swatted my shoulder to get my attention. "I'm going to go check on Leif, is that cool?"

"Sure. How's he doing?"

"Not sure. I've been working with one of the fae healers on a spell that might work. They were gonna test it on him today, so I want to see how it was going."

"Okay. Let us know if you need anything."

Zoe left, and I walked around, correcting stances and helping out with some of the more difficult moves. She was only gone five minutes before she came sprinting back into the room, beaming at me.

"Leif's had a breakthrough. Come on, hurry!" Zoe turned and dashed back down the hall.

J.D. nearly tripped over his feet to follow her. Watching his excitement as he rushed after Zoe, I couldn't keep the smile off my face. Kira and Mika followed him.

I turned to Crew. "Can you watch over the others?"

He nodded. "Sure. Okay, everyone, let's go over what Wyatt and Kira showed you earlier," he said to the group, stepping farther into the room.

Knowing the trainees were in good hands, I ran to catch up to the others. They were all huddled around Leif's cell. The other alpha looked better than he had since we'd found him. His face was pale and strained, but he wasn't rocking on the floor anymore. And he looked relieved see us, especially J.D.

"How are you?" J.D. asked. "How do you feel?"

Leif put a hand to his forehead. "Weird, but better." He eyed us warily. "Uh, this, um, it's not a hallucination, right? You guys are really here?"

"We are," J.D. insisted, taking hold of the bars and leaning close.

"Yeah, this is real," I confirmed.

Leif nodded, then winced and clutched his head.

"Do you have a headache?" J.D. asked, a worried tone to his voice. He turned to look at Zoe. "Do we have anything for headaches?"

"I'm all right," Leif said. "It's not that it hurts so much as it feels like…" He trailed off, his face crinkling in concentration. "Well, I guess I don't know how to explain it. All my memories are out of joint. In the wrong order, if that makes sense. I also have this weird, overwhelming *pull* to go somewhere on the island. Almost like I'm being called to return somewhere I don't want to go."

Kira and I shared a look, and she asked the question on both our minds. "Does it have something to do with Simon? The guy who did this to you?"

Leif shivered at the mention of Simon's name. "I can't go back there. Not to him. I can't."

The fear in his voice sent chills down my arms. He started to rock back and forth, slowly lowering himself to the floor, slipping back into his strange hypnotic state.

J.D., seeing him reverting, turned to Zoe and the other healer. "Can you do more? Whatever you did to bring him around? Please?"

Zoe and the other fae gave each other a helpless look before Zoe turned back to J.D. "We're a little out of our depth here. I think all the magic users here are. This is a bit beyond what we're capable of doing. All we've been doing is tweaking other spells to get them to work on Leif."

J.D.'s shoulders slumped. "So there's no hope?"

"I didn't say that," Zoe said quickly. "If we really can stop Simon and get back to the mainland, I think Leif has a chance. Whatever is going on with him in his head can get better, too. I think he needs a combination of things: standard medicine, magical intervention, as well as psychic healing. Back home, we can find a good psychic doctor who can get in there and fix whatever Simon scrambled up." She squeezed

J.D's shoulder. "The fact that we can help him at all with what we have here means he's curable. I know it."

"Really?" J.D. asked, the light returning to his eyes. "You think so?"

"For sure, yeah."

J.D. let out a sound that was a mix between a laugh and sob and pulled Zoe to him, wrapping her in a hug. "Thank you."

The bars of the cage rattled and shook as Leif suddenly lunged forward, shifting and snarling in rage.

Zoe pulled herself free of J.D. and stared at Leif's bared teeth. "Lover boy is still in there somewhere. Uh, I'll call that a good sign."

"We should probably let Leif calm down and get some rest," Kira offered, taking J.D. by the arm to lead him out.

"Yeah, okay. See you later, Leif," J.D. said.

Leif growled, but it turned to a sad whine as J.D. left.

"So, Mika," Zoe said. "Maybe, uh, you want to show me some of those techniques Wyatt and Kira were showing us earlier? Go a few rounds?" she asked, raising her eyebrows suggestively.

I rolled my eyes, but Mika was apparently too dense to get her subtlety. "Me?" he asked. "I think Wyatt or Kira would be of more help."

Zoe nudged him with her shoulder. "Yeah, but I learn better in a *hands-on* setting. And I think I'd like to have *your* hands on *me*. You know what I mean?"

Mika finally got the hint and became flustered. "Uh, well, I, um..."

Life was too short, and we might all be dead in a few days. There was no reason to hold back. I took a step forward and pushed Mika toward Zoe. "Have at it, big guy."

Mika stumbled forward, catching himself by embracing Zoe. Zoe bobbed her eyebrows up and down. "Oh, Mr. Sheen, I don't know what to say. I've never done something like this before," she said in a faux-shocked voice.

Kira laughed as we left the two lovebirds to their own devices. Hunger clawed at my stomach, so I suggested we head to the dining hall to eat. J.D. agreed halfheartedly, and Kira continued guiding him down the corridor. The poor guy was damned lovesick. Just looking at him depressed me.

In the dining hall, the first person I noticed was Crew. I needed to talk to him about possible strategies for the attack on Simon, but it seemed like such plans were the last thing on his mind. He sat with a half-finished bowl of food, staring across the table at Chelsey as she spoke to him. He gazed at the woman like she'd invented happiness itself, and all because she was finally talking to him. Chelsey didn't look upset, so maybe that meant they were figuring things out.

When J.D. headed off to get food, I tapped Kira on the shoulder and pointed toward Crew and Chelsey. "So, is everyone in this place falling in love, or is it my imagination? Aren't we supposed to be planning the downfall of a mad scientist? Not sending out save-the-dates?" I joked.

"I think it's nice. I mean, you and I have been having some fun on our own. Who are we to judge?" Kira eyed Chelsey and Crew as the two laughed quietly. "I'm happy to see it. I'm glad people can find someone who makes them happy whether it's *fated* or not."

She chewed her lip, her eyes narrowing.

"What's going on in that pretty little head?" I asked.

It took her a moment before she spoke again. "What do we do if we find out the fated mate connections really *are* messed up?"

"Easy. We celebrate," I said. "It means you were never meant to be with that jackass Jayson. That Serenity and I weren't supposed to be together. It shows I wasn't wrong for rejecting her, and you don't have to be upset that Jayson rejected you. We're free to forge our own paths."

"Right," Kira said, meeting my eyes. "Your connection to Serenity wasn't real. So...if there's a way for you to find your *real* fated mate, do you think you'll go look for her?"

The question caught me off-guard. I hadn't given that a second's thought. After Kira's rant on live TV about the connections being wrong, I'd never considered what it meant for me. I'd put fated mates behind me when I ran from my own.

"I haven't thought about it much," I admitted. "Wasn't planning on doing anything, really."

Kira moved to an unoccupied corner of the room and took a seat, beckoning me to join her.

"In hindsight," she said, "I can't believe I ever thought Jayson Fell could truly be my fated mate. It's crazy to think about it now. It's ridiculous. Now that I know the truth, I can't stop thinking there's someone else out there I was supposed to be looking for."

It was like she'd twisted a knife into my heart. I didn't want to talk about this anymore. Seeing her with Jayson had been bad enough, and the thought of her being with someone else was devastating. Even more so now that we'd admitted our feelings for each other. Internally, my wolf curled into itself, pressing its paws over his ears to try and block out whatever else she might say.

"Whatever happens," I said, trying to sound reasonable. "I want you to be happy."

"Well, you're a better person than I am," Kira said with a growl. "If I found out there was some other chick out there who's supposed to be yours, I don't think I could stop myself from tearing her to shreds."

Her words, violent as they were, sent a burst of hope through me. Maybe we didn't need to worry about other people. Maybe...my thoughts trailed off as a new and exciting possibility flooded into my mind.

Reaching over, I took Kira's hand, tugging her closer until I could wrap my arms around her. "Kira, what if there is no one else out there? What if we're meant for each other?"

She pulled her head back, staring at me in surprise. "Do you think so? The odds of that are—"

"I don't give a shit about odds. All I know is how I feel about you. There's no *way* anyone could make me as happy as you do. When I'm with you, it feels like I'm finally home."

Kira smiled hopefully and kissed me. That feeling of *home* swept over me again as the warmth of her lips and tongue met mine. Maybe, just maybe, despite the odds, we would end up together and happy once all this was over.

Our moment of bliss was shattered when the ground beneath us shook in a violent tremor. Kira jerked back from me as shouts of surprise echoed throughout Haven.

"Wyatt?"

"I don't know," I said, answering her unspoken question.

A fae woman leapt to her feet. "This is nature magic. Fae magic."

"Simon," I muttered.

Kira's eyes went wide with shock and horror. "Has he found us?"

The walls and ceiling began shuddering violently, and dirt and dust rained down on us.

The same fae woman ran for the door. "We're under attack. They're trying to bring the place down. Everyone out. Now!"

"Run!" Crew screamed. "Run! Anyone with magic, hold the walls up until we evacuate."

The call for magic users went out, shouted down the corridors. A wiccan joined the fae woman at the wall. The fae put her hand to the wall and scrunched up her face in exertion as she pushed her energy into the structure. The wiccan raised her hands high overhead and muttered counter spells. The struggle on their faces told me they were fighting against something more powerful than them.

Crew grabbed Chelsey's hand, pulling on her to follow him. "Eli! Evacuate. Evacuate." His voice echoed back to us as he rushed down the corridor.

"Leif!" Kira gasped, tugging on my shirt. "We have to save him."

"What about everyone else?" I asked.

"No one else is locked in a cage!"

Chaos had enveloped Haven. Shouts and screams and cries of terror mingled with the dull, rumbling roar of the magic that threatened to bury us all under a mountain of dirt and rock. A steady rain of dirt fell everywhere. As we ran, multiple magic wielders stood in various areas, working together to keep Haven from crumbling apart. They strained and groaned under the pressure of the attack.

There were only minutes left. We had to hurry.

In the enclosure and medical areas, we found Eli shouting at the healers to either run for the exit or help hold the structure up.

"Eli, help us with Leif!" Kira called out.

"What?" Eli's angelic face was smeared with dirt.

"Leif! Can you knock him out again so he's safe to transport?"

Eli closed her eyes, fighting back frustration, then nodded. "Let's hurry."

We found Leif huddled in the corner of his cell in human form, rocking back and forth. With no one here to fight back against the attack, his cell had already begun to fill with dirt, the ceiling caving in and threatening to crush him.

Unlocking the door, Eli thrust her hand out in front of her. Leif, terrified by what was happening and still out of his mind, leapt up and rushed toward her. Eli put her hand to his forehead, and Leif's eyes rolled back as he passed out.

"There," Eli said. "Get him the hell out of here. I have to check everywhere else." She was already running out the door.

I hefted Leif up and flung him over my shoulder. "Move!" I shouted, pushing Kira toward the door.

The attack was growing stronger. Some magic users had given up and were rushing for the exits. The rumble around us grew to a roar. Even the screams and shouts were muffled by the deafening sound of a mountain being crushed down upon us. Some ran with their arms loaded with food and supplies, but all I could do was run and ensure Kira was ahead of me. If anyone got out alive, I wanted it to be her.

Ahead of us, Mika and Zoe ran toward the exit. Zoe had her arms up above her head as she ran, pulses of her magic bursting from her fingertips, trying to hold up the ceiling. Right behind us, J.D. shouted at someone to hurry.

At the exit, a wiccan and Crew worked like mad, disarming the traps to let everyone out. Chelsey was right at Crew's side. Kira and I huddled with the others, pushing forward with the group. I could sense the crowd wanting to bolt, to stampede away from danger, but we'd be dead in seconds if the traps weren't disarmed.

Finally, Crew stood and waved toward the cave mouth. "Run! Go, go, go!"

We rushed forward, streaming out into the late afternoon jungle. When the fresh air hit my face, I released a shuddering breath. I put Leif down and turned to help whoever needed it. The noise from inside rumbled louder than ever. J.D. and two shifters ran past me, and he knelt to check on Leif.

I ran back to the entrance, ignoring Kira's call for me to stay. Fifteen feet inside, I found two healers dragging an unconscious Abel along, both women struggling and gasping.

"I've got him," I told the women. "Run!" I took Abel's hands and hauled him backward.

Before I got Abel out, Eli came running, completely covered in dirt. I looked up. From the tunnel, I saw a male and female wiccan followed by a big black bear shifter in his animal form. All three ran as fast as they could, the whole mountain seeming to shiver and shake around them.

"Hurry!" But it was too late.

I'd barely pulled Abel free of the tunnel before the entire cave system collapsed. The wiccans and the bear shifter vanished under a million tons of dirt, sand, and rock. I fell on my ass, gaping at the now-sealed entrance to what had been Haven.

"It's them!" a voice called out behind me.

Turning to look, someone was pointing off in the distance. Three shadowy figures stood, hands pressed to the ground. I recognized the three warped and corrupted fae I'd met on one of the last challenges.

Instead of taunting us in weird rhymes, they stood, eyes vacant, then rushed away like ink spilling across a page.

My rage at what had happened, how close my friends and Kira had been to death, sent me into a fury. I shifted and bolted after them. Gavin, having somehow escaped the collapse, joined me in pursuit, as did Kira, Crew, and Eli.

Eli and Gavin descended on the slowest of the three, tackling her. I sped off after the fastest, leaving the third and final fae for Kira and Crew. Heedless of danger, only furious about the loss of life, the destruction of the lone safe place on Bloodstone, I chased the fae. A moment later, another loping wolf figure appeared at my side. Mika.

She ran in the direction of the volcano, probably to go back to Simon and tell him what had happened. They'd found us, likely using their mystic talents to detect the magical facade that had kept us hidden, and destroyed Haven. If he knew, he'd release every one of his monsters to hunt us down. That could not happen.

The fae was fast, but not fast enough. I snapped my jaws around her ankle and forced her to the ground. Mika caught her hand in his mouth before she could cast a spell at me. Her bones snapped under his teeth as he tore off her hand. To my surprise, she didn't scream or even wince. Instead, she tilted her head at me, studying me with those mad eyes.

"Glad they're dead, I am," she said in that strange, singsong voice. "Crushed like a bug, rolled in a rug. In bed, they are tucked. Forever to sleep, forever to be fucked."

Her remaining hand snapped up, ready to attack. I lunged forward, biting down and tearing out her throat. We left her to bleed out on the jungle floor and ran back to check on the others.

The other two corrupted fae had been destroyed, and Crew and Eli were working to gather the survivors. I shifted back and took Kira in my arms, finally allowing myself to relax, knowing we were safe for the moment.

"We've gotta get out of here," Eli said to Crew. She glanced back at the jungle. "The noise is going to draw a *lot* of monsters and creatures here. What do we do?"

"Do we go back to the mansion?" J.D. suggested. "Maybe they've left it alone now. We could barricade it or something?"

Crew shook his head. "No. It's only been a few days since the wards fell. All those things will still be fighting over the territory. I've got a better idea."

"We're all ears," I said.

Crew pointed in a direction opposite the volcano. "There's an area I've scouted several times. It's a spot that doesn't get a lot of action from any of the creatures because there's not lot of fresh water, vegetation, or animals, which means little food. They stay away. It's still dangerous, but less than most places."

"Safer than here?" Gavin asked, pointing at the collapsed entrance to Haven.

Crew shrugged. "Depends. The whole reason I chose this location for Haven was its central location. It's close to water and supply drops for the show. You lose a little safety, but gain other things. This other place is the best option."

"That's all I need to hear," Eli said, then turned to the survivors. "Eyes on me. Crew's going to lead us somewhere to regroup. Stay close. As in, able-to-sniff-each-other's-asses close. If for even a minute you think you'll lose sight of us, hustle it up. Stay quiet, but stay fast. Understood?"

The crowd gave terrified nods and clumped together. Eli moved to the right of the group with Kira at the left. Crew took the point position, and I had the rear, effectively pinning the survivors in with the best fighters on the outside. Gavin and Mika, along with a few people who'd scouted with Crew before, could handle themselves.

"Let's go," Crew said, and he took off at a slow jog.

The going was slower than I'd have liked, with the group weighed down carrying the unconscious forms of Leif and Abel, but at least no one straggled behind or complained. The jungle roared with a cacophony of sounds. Behind us, I could hear the snapping of twigs and crunching of leaves as beasts rushed toward the destroyed Haven. There was a bit of heartache, thinking of that place crushed under all that earth. It had been a bastion of safety in a world devoid of it.

If I was feeling like this, then I couldn't imagine what Crew was going through. The place had been his baby. A society he'd built up with blood, sweat, tears, and more blood. He had to be heartbroken.

Craning my neck to peer up at the front of the group, I saw Chelsey right behind him, holding his hand. Maybe mending fences with her would be a comfort for him.

A snarling yowl came from the underbrush to our left. A dog-sized creature jumped forward right behind Kira and bolted into the cluster of people. A chupacabra. It bit into the boot of one of the only humans who'd been in Haven and pulled him off his feet.

"Good gods!" the man screamed as the chupacabra dragged him into the jungle. "Help me!"

Kira strode forward and kicked the beast under its jaw as hard as she could. The teeth released as its eyes rolled up, neck snapping. The dead thing tumbled into the weeds.

Bending, Kria grabbed the man and pulled him to his feet. "It's a fucking chupacabra, man," she hissed. "No need to scream like a baby. Move. Everything in a hundred yards heard you wailing."

"She's right," Crew said. "Double time."

Our light jog turned into more of a slow run. By the time we reached the area Crew wanted us to hole up in, the sun had slid below the horizon. A secondary mountain outcropping rose up at the side of a cliff overlooking the sea. He was right about there not being much here. No running water, and very little foliage other than a thick outcropping of palm trees. However, up a hill sat the perfect spot for a camp. On two sides, the mountain surrounded it, and the cliff abutted the other side, leaving only one path in or out. That would make securing it a little easier.

Crew led us up, and upon closer inspection, I saw a small abandoned cave that went back about fifteen feet into the stone. It was a good spot to get everyone out of the weather and to sleep at night, though it would be *very* cramped. Still, it was better than being soaked. It also provided an additional layer of protection from the prying eyes of whatever monsters lurked in the darkness.

The folks who'd managed to haul supplies from Haven took them into the back of the cave to inventory what they had.

Crew walked up to me and nodded back at his group. "We need to set up a watch system. Two on guard at a time?"

"Good plan," I agreed. "It'll give everyone time to rest, and no one will be alone on watch. It might be better to have four, though."

Crew glanced at the pathway leading into the new sanctuary. "Two here, and then two more scouting farther out?"

I nodded. "If something comes, I'd like to have a two-stage warning to give us more time to mobilize. Plus, the two scouts can look for water and any edible plants. Maybe do a bit of hunting, too. The supplies we managed to get out of Haven will last for two or three days at most, and that will be with rationing."

Crew drifted off and pulled four people aside, spoke to them for a few minutes, then sent them out. They were two shifters and two magic wielders—one on each team. Once they were off, Crew returned to me.

"They'll be on four-hour shifts, nothing longer. Don't want anyone falling asleep on duty," he said.

Behind me, Eli and Kira were working with Zoe and another fae to use magic to lift some fallen palm trees and hide the cave entrance.

Lowering my voice, I leaned in close to Crew. "How safe is this place? *Really*?"

Crew sighed and nodded toward the entrance path. "As safe as it gets at this point. I've never seen any territorial creatures here, so that's a bonus—those things are hard to fend off when you're in their lands. We're on the opposite side of the island from the thunderbirds, and they never fly over this area. That means we'll only have to worry about roaming monsters, the ones with undefined territory. I already told the team on guard that *anything* coming near us needs to be killed, not just scared off. When stuff on Bloodstone gets scared off, they have a really fucking bad habit of returning. And with reinforcements."

"I guess we'll have to hope nothing terrible happens," I said with a sigh.

We spent the next few hours trying to get everyone as settled as possible. Leif was still asleep from whatever spell Eli had put him under, giving us one less thing to worry about. Night had fully fallen by the time a simple dinner of roasted potatoes and canned peaches was served. Zoe had used magic to cook the food—we didn't want to risk a fire.

"Who wants the second watch?" Crew asked, squatting down in front of the group. "It's about time to swap out, and those folks need to eat."

"I'll go," I said. The next few hours would be the most dangerous. The creatures on the island tended to be most active in the five or six hours after moonrise.

"Me too," Mika said, standing and dusting his pants off.

Another guy—a wiccan—volunteered as well. Crew thanked him and added, "That works. I'll go on this watch, too. Eli, you'll relieve us in a few hours. Go ahead and figure out who'll be with you, then get some rest."

The four of us walked out to find the others and sent them back for food and sleep. Crew and I headed out to do the scouting, leaving Mika and the wiccan to watch the entrance. As the minutes and hours ticked by, I had a hard time not glancing up at the volcano in the distance, rising high above the dark jungle. Our one small slice of safety had been torn away. I grieved for Crew and the others who'd called Haven home.

Just past midnight, I stood in a small clearing a few hundred yards from our camp and glared in the direction of the volcano again. My anger rose with each second. We'd take Simon down. I made a silent vow, then and there. We'd tear apart his lab and destroy all his work.

Then? By the gods, then we'd go home.

Chapter 11 - Kira

A younger tiger shifter sat huddled against the wall of the small cave, hugging his knees. He barely looked eighteen. His eyes darted around at every small sound. I'd never seen someone so freaked out and terrified. From what I'd gathered, he was one of those unlucky souls who'd been sent here as punishment for some misdeed or another. Eli and Crew had rescued him.

"How are you doing?" I whispered.

His head jerked around. "What? Huh?"

"How are you doing?"

"Oh. Uh, okay, I guess."

I patted his knee. "Get some rest. We'll watch out for you guys."

His shoulders relaxed, almost like he'd been waiting for someone, anyone, to tell him it was all okay. I couldn't imagine how stressful this was for these people. Most had been tucked safely away in Haven for a year or more. Wyatt and I and the other contestants had been in the mansion, sure, but we'd also had to go out to face the dangers of the island almost every day. We'd been inoculated to the dangers somewhat. These people were in for a full-system shock.

"Thanks," he said. He lay down, still hugging his knees as he closed his eyes.

I doubted he'd actually go to sleep. All the survivors were in various states of stress or worry, either huddled in small groups or tucked away on their own. It didn't help that we couldn't risk a fire. Something about the light offered a sense of comfort— the way the heat and flickering flames pushed back at the darkness and enveloped you in a warm glow. It would have done a lot for morale. Instead, we sat in the dark, the only light the shimmer of the moon at the entrance of the cave.

We'd managed to obscure the entryway with some dead palm trees and fronds, but it was a far cry from the relative luxury of Haven, much less Reject Mansion. We couldn't stay here long-term. Hell, there wasn't even a bathroom; we had to make use of the rock outcropping ten feet from the entrance. Even in Haven, the magic users had managed a toilet system that, while not completely perfect, kept the sewage from being a problem. We had little food, no fresh water nearby. We'd have to move against Simon sooner than we'd initially planned—before our people became too weak to fight effectively. Plus, Simon was likely still looking for us. He'd sent his twisted fae out to kill us, and though we'd managed to kill them before they could get back to him, he had to know some of us would have made it out alive. If we didn't act on him first, he'd act on us.

"Kira?" J.D. hissed from the back of the cave. "Kira, hurry."

At the rear of the cave, barely visible in the moonlight, I found J.D. kneeling over Leif. The feral alpha was stirring awake from Eli's knockout spell.

"Shit," I mumbled. "I need to get Eli."

Before I could run, Leif's eyes sprang open, and he put a hand to his forehead. "Ouch. Where am I? What's going on?"

I let out a relieved breath. He seemed, for the moment at least, to be in his right mind.

J.D. leaned forward and hugged Leif. "You're okay."

Leif blinked in surprise, then a slow smile formed on his lips as he wrapped his arms around J.D. "I'm, uh, not totally fine, but I'm all right for now," Leif said, his words muffled against J.D.'s shoulder.

That was good. I had no clue how we'd have secured him out here in the open jungle. As long as he stayed mostly sane, we could deal with him.

J.D. released him, and Leif sat up, giving me a strange look. Almost like he was ashamed or saddened by something.

"Kira, I'm really sorry. Anything I did... I, uh, didn't do it on purpose. I wasn't myself. If that makes sense." He glanced around, and a look of horror crossed his face. "Oh gods, did I hurt anyone? You have to tell me if I did. Why are we out here? What's happening?"

Reaching out, I put a steadying hand on his shoulder. "Calm down. You didn't hurt anyone. Haven was destroyed. Simon did it with some of his little fucked-up minions. None of this was your fault. You're good."

"Yeah, man, "J.D. added. "Nothing you did was your fault. It was that douchebag and his lab."

Leif nodded and let out a heavy sigh, then leaned back against the stone wall. He winced and put a hand to his forehead. "I can't remember much of what happened while I was half-feral. It's all jumbled and mixed up. The last thing that's really clear, other than what happened in Haven, is when I was out in the jungle on that last challenge looking for you. I was walking through a grove of trees, and then...black. Whatever hit me got me totally by surprise."

"A lot has happened since then," I said.

Leif chuckled humorlessly. "Yeah. I can see that."

"Zoe says she thinks you can be cured once we get you off the island," I said. "A good psychic healer and some top-notch spellcasters—people fully trained in healing—and you'll be right as rain. This will all be a bad memory."

J.D. put a hand on Leif's knee, massaging his leg gently. "Yeah, and I'll make sure to replace all the bad memories with good ones."

Leif glanced over at J.D. Even in the moonlight, I could see the blush creeping into his cheeks. Wyatt was right—little romances were springing up all over, and I was happy to see it. We needed hope, and what better symbol of hope than love?

Down the hill, the typical island sounds of growling, howling, and hissing grew a bit louder. Nothing terrible or dangerously close, but I couldn't quell my worry for Wyatt. He was out there with gods only knew what other creatures.

The snarling sounds suddenly grew in volume. My heart fluttered as I listened to what sounded like a battle in the distance. Then the noise ceased, followed by a familiar howl of victory. A shaky sigh shuddered out of my lungs.

Beside me, Leif groaned. Something about the jungle sounds had triggered him. He pressed the heels of his palms into his eyes and started rocking again.

"Kira," J.D. said. "Something's wrong."

Leaping up, I turned and ran to the mouth of the cave where Zoe sat. I grabbed her shirt and tugged. "Come on. I need help with Leif."

The tone of my voice must have given away my concern. "What's wrong?" she asked.

"Come on."

Doing our best not to worry the others, we tiptoed around all the extended legs of the survivors as they slept, or pretended to. Abel, looking a hundred times better than he had earlier, watched us walk by.

"Is everything okay?" he asked.

"All good," I said. "We're helping Leif. You rest."

He nodded with some reluctance and rolled back over.

At the back of the cave, Leif was still rocking, but faster now. Along with the increased movement, he moaned louder than before. A few people near him had moved farther away, casting dubious looks his way.

"Well, uh, get you back to good," Zoe said to him. "Hang on." She raised her hand and cast a spell over him. "This helped last time, but it made him really sleepy."

As she moved her hand around him, I saw her wince. Something was wrong with her arm.

"Zoe, what's wrong with you? Are you hurt?" I asked.

Before she'd finished casting, she let out a gasp of pain and lowered her arm. "Shit, I can't. I'm sorry."

"What's wrong?" Now I had two people to worry about—three, with Wyatt being out in the jungle. "Is it your arm?"

She nodded, wincing again. "I didn't want to be a bother. A rock fell on my shoulder while we were escaping. I cast a numbing spell on it because I didn't want to be a bother."

"For fuck's sake, Zoe. You wouldn't have bothered us. Hang on."

I sprinted back to the cave mouth and found Eli. "Hey, Leif's awake. He's not doing well. Can you help him? I need to have one of the healers look at Zoe."

Eyes narrowed, she stood. "What's wrong with Zoe?"

"Oh, you know, being a dummy as usual. Hurry."

Eli worked on Leif while I had one of the skilled healers look over Zoe's shoulder. "Oh, dear," the woman said. "This is bad. I think it may be fractured. How are you not screaming in pain right now?"

Zoe grimaced. "Numbing spell. It's...crap, I guess it's wearing off."

The healer clicked her tongue in disapproval. "You know the longer you let injuries go, the harder they are to heal. Come on," she said to me. "Help me get her out in the moonlight so I can see."

Assisting the woman, I helped Zoe up and guided her out to the small clearing beyond the cave's entrance. As the healer set to work, the breeze shifted, and I noticed Wyatt's scent. Turning, I saw Wyatt, Mika, and the others walking up the hill, finished with their watch. They all looked exhausted, Wyatt more so than the others. Crew headed inside to find the next group to send out for a watch.

Wyatt gave me a weak smile when he saw me. Rushing over, I checked him for injuries. "Are you okay? I heard the fight earlier."

"I'm fine," Wyatt said. "Took care of a couple of ferals. I saw worse while we were on the show."

"Zoe?" Mika gasped, looking at the healer, who was murmuring spells over my friend. "What happened? What's going on?"

He looked more alarmed and worried than I'd ever seen him. I grabbed his shirt. "Calm down, it's nothing serious. She hurt her arm in the escape from Haven. The healer's taking care of her."

The look in Mika's eyes told me he wasn't sure I was being truthful.

"Mika, Zoe's tougher than she looks," I said. "She only pretends to be a dainty little flower. I promise, she'll be all right."

Mika shrugged my hand off. "I need to check on her." He hurried off, joining Zoe, who smiled gratefully at his appearance.

"I cannot believe that's the same guy who came onto this island," Wyatt said. "He never smiled and barely spoke. Now the grumpy fucker is a plush little wolf when it comes to Zoe, and she's a smiley chatterbox. Like oil and water."

"No, not like that," I countered. "They're just different. Opposites attract. Mika had a rough life—no one on his side, lots of betrayal. Zoe is warm and kind and *severely* loyal. I think they suit each other."

Crew walked out of the cave, four volunteers following him. The four headed off to begin their watch, and Crew broke off and joined us.

"Zoe gonna be okay?" he asked. "Someone said she was hurt."

"I think she'll be fine," I said. "One of the healers is looking at her."

He nodded, glancing at Zoe and Mika, then back at the cave. Most folks were huddled inside, but a few were milling about outside, being sure to stay far from the cliff's edge.

Crew clenched his jaw as he looked at us again. "We need to hit Simon. Soon. I know we wanted a couple more days to prepare, but we're sitting ducks out here. I know we have people on watches, but if he finds out we're here and sends all his ferals or, gods forbid, those abominations of his? We won't stand a chance.

"I only see two options," he continued. "Either we run and try to find someplace safer than this, or we hit him with everything we have. If we manage to defeat Simon, we can take over the lab and use it as a new base of operations. Create a *new* Haven. Then we can be safe until these shipments come in. Whether they're by air or sea, we can hijack them and get back home."

Wyatt nodded and kicked at a clump of dirt on the ground. "I was thinking the same thing. We won't last long out here. It's..." He glanced up, checking the stars and the placement of the moon. "What, around two in the morning? Maybe later? When sunrise comes, it'll get hot. Without a ready source of water, it's gonna get bad real quick." He looked at Crew. "When were you planning? Tomorrow night?"

"Dawn, or sooner," Crew said without hesitation.

"Dawn? You mean, in a couple hours?" I asked, taken aback.

He nodded and pointed at the cave. "We have to move as soon as possible. Like Wyatt said, every minute we stay here, our people get weaker. Soon, they won't be able to fight. So far, we've been lucky that few monsters have come by, but that won't hold. This *is* Bloodstone Island after all. We move out, and hit him hard. If we're lucky, we can catch him off-guard again. Maybe he'll assume we're on the run and won't be able or willing to attack. It's the best plan I've got."

His voice was strained and thick with worry. Crew tried to put on the brave face of a confident leader, but deep down, he was worried about his people. He hadn't even had time to grieve the ones he'd lost, and now he was planning on leading the rest into battle, where even more of them were likely to die. It was a shit choice, but I didn't see any other way around it. He and Wyatt were right—we couldn't fortify this place and hole up for more than eight to ten hours.

"Don't forget our secret weapon," I said. "We have the Shadowkeeper on our side."

Crew snorted derisively. "You know, I'm not betting on her. I have no confidence she'll follow through. I met her a couple times and asked for help. I didn't say anything earlier because I didn't want to be a wet blanket."

"She said no?" I asked.

"It was a few months after I created Haven," Crew said. "There were only five or six people there at that point. I crossed paths with her while out scouting. I immediately asked her for assistance. All she did was turn her nose up at me and vanished. Didn't say a word. Five or six months later, I tried again, this time purposefully seeking her out. I wanted her to help the survivors. Food, protection, whatever she could offer. All she told me was that she was and always *would* be 'neutral.' She had no interest in helping us, and then vanished again, basically shaking her damn immortal tits at me as she did." He looked at me and Wyatt. "So, no, I don't put any faith in her assistance. From what I've seen, she prefers minding her own business and watching us struggle. She's as bad as Simon peering in on his experiments as they writhe and suffer." He took a step toward the cave. "Are we in agreement? Attack at dawn?"

"Sure," Wyatt said. "Sounds good."

"Same," I said. "We'll be ready."

"Okay. I'm gonna go talk to everyone about it. If we're doing this, we'll need to be ready to move in the next hour or so."

He turned and headed off to break the news to the survivors. His words about the Shadowkeeper haunted me. What if she was just playing silly games?

"I can tell what you're thinking," Wyatt said. "I can see it on your face."

"Keep it in your pants, big guy. No privacy for that kind of thing out here."

Wyatt snorted. "Not that. You know what I mean. Lucina."

I huffed. "What if she doesn't end up helping us? Do we even stand a chance?"

"Can't think like that," Wyatt said. "The die has been cast. There's no turning back now. We have to push forward. Either she helps us, or she doesn't, but either way, like Crew said, we're backed into a corner and need to fight our way out."

"You're right," I said. I needed to get my mind off this. I nodded back toward the cave. "I'm going to check on Leif. He woke up, but wasn't feeling great. Eli was working on him when I left."

"You do that. I'll see how Mika's doing. I think he's more upset than Zoe is right now."

Back inside, I found Leif sitting. He looked strained and upset, though not as bad as when I'd left him.

"How's it going?" I asked him.

"Not good," Leif said through gritted teeth. J.D. sat beside him, rubbing his back. "My head's fucked up. Elianna—er, Eli—is helping, but it's not enough."

"I'm trying not to put him to sleep," Eli explained as she waved her hands over him. "I'd like him to be aware and able to help if there's trouble." She shook her head bitterly. "Whatever that fucking scientist did to make him feral is something I've never encountered before."

"How the hell did you end up on Bloodstone, anyway?" I blurted to her. It had always been too busy for me to ask questions, and Crew's second-in-command seemed far too capable to be relegated to a place like this for certain death.

Eli sighed. "Bad luck, and too much honor."

"What does that mean?"

"Before I lost my wings, I was an archangel," she explained. "A soldier tasked with guarding another angel. An envoy, if you will. One of our kind who deals with diplomatic missions. During one of our missions, we escorted our envoys to the headquarters of the Tranquility Council in Fangmore City. During this week-long exchange, I discovered several of my brothers and sisters in the archangel regiment had become entangled in some shady dealings with a few of the high-ranking members of the council. It turns out several members of the council wanted my envoy to..." She gritted her teeth and shook her head in disgust. "To meet an inglorious end. Something that would tarnish their reputation, and in doing so, also leave them dead. I tried getting involved, to expose the truth, when I discovered my cohorts were planning to stab one of our own in the back. I didn't realize how deep the rot went. When I tried to voice the issue, I was framed as a double agent, trying to jeopardize the diplomatic mission. The main councilmember and several other archangels testified to it."

Eli's eyes were distant and troubled, as though remembering the situation was as bad as living through it again.

"I was stripped of my wings and my title, then they dumped me here to be dealt with quickly and quietly. Crew found me. That was a little over a year ago. Part of why I want off this island is to reveal the truth about the corrupt councilmembers and the archangels in their pockets." She shrugged. "That's the story. My story."

Hearing how deeply corrupted the Tranquility Council had become was like a punch in the gut. I'd spent years of my life dedicated to the organization, doing my best to keep every mission and every member of my team honorable and on the straight and narrow. Yet, hadn't I been terminated because one of Jayson's relatives had pulled strings? It had been obvious that I was innocent of any wrongdoing, but they'd still let me go. All because of the Ninth Pack's influence within the council.

Maybe it wasn't only the pack system that needed to be torn apart. Maybe our entire society, from Heline and the council to all the way down, was out of line.

An hour later, Crew had spread the word that we'd be attacking at dawn in the hope that we'd catch most of Simon's people unaware. Wyatt and Crew were gathering everyone together, preparing them for the hour-long hike to Simon's lair. Wyatt moved among the survivors, checking on each one. A hand on a shoulder there, a kind word here, a whisper of something to this one or that one.

Despite being born into one of the most corrupt packs, Wyatt was a true leader. The kind of person people looked to during a crisis even if they didn't know him well. Something about the way he carried himself and seemed to have time for everyone made it easy to see he had a strong moral compass.

Sensing my eyes on him, Wyatt sent a smile my way. Leaving the group he'd been talking to, he strode over to join me a few yards from the cliff's edge.

"Ma'am?" he said with a mischievous glint in his eye. "I couldn't help but notice the way you were undressing me with your eyes. Is there"—he looked me up and down before licking his lips—"something I can do to you—uh, I mean, do *for* you?"

I rolled my eyes. "Ugh, you're so full of yourself."

"What's that?" Chelsey's voice called out from the cave entrance. She stood, hand outstretched, a finger pointing out to sea.

Following her gaze, I immediately noticed what she was talking about. Hundreds of yards out in the ocean, blinking lights hovered above the water, flying toward the island with relative high speed. It took a moment until I realized the noise: the *thwap-thwap-thwap* of helicopter propellers.

The eagle shifter Zoe had told me about stepped forward and looked out to sea, squinting with his enhanced vision. "Choppers," he said. "Big ones. Look like transports." He turned to Crew. "Is this the shipment run you guys were talking about?"

"Shit," Crew muttered. "It came sooner than we thought."

We didn't have days or even hours. We had minutes. The choppers would land, and it would take time to get the bioweapons and creatures aboard them. But if we had any hope in hell of hijacking those helicopters before they took off again, we'd have to move. Now.

Forgoing quiet for efficiency, Crew cupped his hands around his mouth and yelled, "We go! I broke you guys into groups earlier, so fall into your platoons now. Wyatt and Kira will command group one, I'll take group two, and Eli and Mika will lead group three. This is it, people. It's time."

Nervous and terrified murmurs ran through the crowd. Leif, who'd been standing off to the side with

J.D. and Eli, flinched at the sound. I gasped as his face crumpled and his eyes became wild.

"J.D.!" I shouted. "Get away from him."

The group went silent and turned in time to see Leif shift. He fell to all fours, snarling. J.D. stepped backward, falling over on his ass. Eli, seeing that J.D. was helpless, stepped between him and the now fully feral Leif.

Leif lunged at her and snapped his teeth. Eli jerked back, just barely dodging Leif's teeth. The group of survivors shouted and called out for help. The noise sent Leif into more of a frenzy. Thankfully, instead of jumping into the group, he turned and sprinted off into the jungle. He was headed straight for the volcano.

"We have to go now," I said. "He's headed back to the lab. As soon as he gets there, Simon is going to force him to tell him where we are and what we're planning."

Crew nodded grimly. "We out of time, folks. Move. We go fast. There's no other way. Be as silent as you can not to draw attention, but speed is our ally here, not discretion. Let's go." With that, Crew turned, shifted, and bounded down the hill to the jungle.

I took Wyatt's hand, squeezed it, and led my team into the jungle after him. Above us, the helicopters swooped across the trees, sending waves of wind down onto us as they thundered toward the volcano.

Chapter 12 - Wyatt

The group's anxiety was a living, breathing presence around us. No one spoke as we rushed through the forest. Ahead of us, Crew's wolf led the way to Simon's lab. Kira and I stayed in our human forms to pass communication to the rest. The whirring of the helicopters had faded, then gone silent once they'd made it to the volcano. The urgency wasn't lost on anyone.

One of our only shots of getting off the island was already here. Every second that we weren't attacking Simon's lab was an extra moment the helicopters had to load up and fly back to the mainland.

Using hand signals, Kira and I kept our three attack groups organized. Our Tranquility Ops training was coming in handy. In fact, I couldn't remember a time when I was happier to have the knowledge and experience at my disposal.

The rest of our people had the wild-eyed look of people rushing toward what might be certain death. It was a look people got when they went on their first missions, or when soldiers went to war for the first time. Some of these people would surprise themselves and rise to the occasion, but that wouldn't be the case for everyone. They had little training, no experience, and were already exhausted from escaping Haven. They would panic, freeze up. They'd probably die.

It was a reality I couldn't allow myself to dwell on too much. We'd done all we could, and now we had to push forward. We'd mourn the ones we lost when this was over.

We made it to the volcano in record time, but the fact that we didn't run into any monsters nagged at me. Maybe the helicopters had scared them off? Or perhaps even the psychotic creatures on this godsforsaken island were afraid of what Simon was capable of. Either way, after only thirty minutes, Crew shifted back to his human form and called a halt to our run.

Kira, Eli, Mika, and I joined him to scope out the lone entrance we knew of. "They're ready," Crew whispered as he pointed through the foliage.

Sure enough, some two hundred yards ahead, three of Simon's lumbering monstrosities guarded the entrance like walking jigsaw puzzles of death.

"What's the plan?" Kira asked.

"I'll take my team in first," Crew whispered. "Get their attention, lure them away from the entrance. Once they're on us, Eli and Mika will bring in their team. Wyatt, you and Kira will hang back in case we need reinforcements. I'd prefer to keep at least one team hidden in case word spreads through the lab. Then they'll think there are less of us than there really are, but the team won't hesitate to jump in if it looks like we're in trouble."

"We'll be ready," I said.

"Once those things are dealt with, we move into the lab as fast as we can," Crew said. "Use surprise to our advantage."

Crew gathered his team, moving them closer to the entrance. They paused at the edge of the tree line, only feet beyond the reach of the spotlights Simon had installed. Behind Crew's group, Mika and Eli prepared their team. Kira and I took the rear with our own group. The tension reverberated like an electric current through the people under our care. They were makeshift soldiers about to go into battle.

When Crew sprinted forward, followed by the seven people on his team, a pressure release of sorts went through the group. A collective sigh of relief.

Crew bounded ahead. He and three of his team were shifters, and they all transitioned to their animal forms. The beasts guarding the door let out roars and squeals at the sight of the intruders. True to Crew's plan, the creatures rushed forward, leaving the entryway unguarded.

"Go!" Eli shouted as the two groups fell into a skirmish in the distance.

Mika and Eli led their team out, rushing the creatures from the back. Kira and I moved our own team up, waiting. From the bowels of the lab, a group of vampires erupted. They were not the decrepit half-starved things we'd been fighting in the jungle. No, these were lucid, well-fed, and well-prepared creatures of the night. They intercepted Mika and Eli before they could join Crew.

"Crap," I hissed. "Move. Everyone, let's go."

Not waiting for an answer, I sprinted out, rushing toward the fight that was rapidly devolving into chaos. The sound of my team following gave me a small sense of relief, which was dashed when five feral shifters loped out of the entrance to join the fray. Three wolves, a bear, and a panther.

The feral bear shifter slammed into Mika's group, one massive paw lashing out. It got one of the male wiccans in the throat. Blood spurted from the wiccan's neck as the bear shifter tossed him away, and I saw the light flicker out of his eyes.

Crew and his shifters had already managed to take down two of the three monsters. The third was being protected by Simon's magic users, with some strange spell condensing the water in the air, encasing the thing in a ball of water.

The panther I was battling struck out at me with his razor-sharp claws, slicing the air inches in front of me. Still in my human form, I prepared to shift, but before I could, Kira leapt onto the panther's back, wrapped her arms around its neck, and hauled its head back. A fae ran forward with a sharpened branch and slammed the stick into the beast's chest. It was dead before it hit the ground, managing only a yowl of pained surprise before its eyes rolled back and a final breath gurgled out of it.

"Behind you!" Kira shouted, pointed over my shoulder.

I ducked and rolled out of the path of an incoming vampire. Gavin shoved the thing in the back, and it tumbled right onto the dead panther. The same stick that had killed the panther pierced the vampire through the chest. Both enemies lay like some fucked-up kebab on the ground.

With the deaths of the patchwork creatures, Crew's team was free to assist us with the ferals and vampires. It was the most chaotic fight I'd ever been part of. Most of what we did in the TO was subtler. Undercover work, maybe some hand-to-hand combat and sometimes guns were involved, but never against more than four or five targets. This? This was war. Shouts, screams of pain, hisses, and howls cut through the air. In response, the beasts of the forest called back, sending the island into a fervor.

Eventually, we'd dealt with most of the enemies, but time was slipping away. We *had* to get inside.

Crew shifted back to his human form. "Wyatt, get in there! We'll finish these off and join. Move."

I whistled at my team. "Inside! Follow me!"

The remaining uninjured members of my team rushed after me. Kira broke off from fighting a vampire, leaving it for J.D. and Abel to finish off.

The doorway into the lab was still damaged from our last venture inside. Simon must have been too busy to repair it, assuming his creations and minions would be enough to secure it. He'd been wrong, but how many more surprises did he have waiting inside?

The bright glare of light inside the lab was a sharp contrast to the moonlight and darkness outside. We managed to get halfway down the entry hall before another group of corrupted fae appeared. Spells sizzled overhead, shooting toward us. A spell hit a member of my team, one of the few humans. He screamed as he was flung backward at breakneck speed. He tumbled out the door, bones snapping and breaking.

Zoe and Eli appeared a moment later, throwing up protective magic and spells, pushing the corrupted fae back until they managed to finish them off. Kira and I, followed by our team, moved deeper into the labs. Sirens wailed overhead as echoes of the battle outside died down. Crew's team had finished off the last of the outer defenses.

That was something, at least. But Simon had a lot of tricks up his sleeve. Even with Kira and I having each other's backs and the sheer aggression of our own desperate team of survivors, the hits kept coming. More experimental creatures, more ferals, more vampires filled the halls, slowing and eventually halting our progress. Had it not been for our magic-wielders, we'd have been annihilated by now. All three of our teams now fought together, but we were up against too big a force.

"Fall back!" Crew screamed. "Down this hall! Regroup!"

I took the rear along with Eli and Zoe, keeping our pursuers from picking off anyone at the back. The two magic wielders created a strong encasement spell around the door to keep Simon's security measures at bay. It wouldn't last long, but it would give us a minute or two to formulate a plan.

Crew knelt on one knee, sweet pouring down his face. Chelsey, who had blood dripping down her face from a rapidly healing cut above her eyebrow, put her hand on his shoulder.

"Holy shit," he said, looking up.

I looked at what he saw. We'd found ourselves in a broad corridor, one wall lined with windows looking out into what must have been the interior of the dormant volcano. The helicopters were parked on the broad expanse of black, volcanic stone. A small team was pushing cages of experiments, heavy cases of chemical and magic weapons, and enclosures filled with abominations into the transport choppers.

"We have to go out there and stop them," Crew said. "That's the main target."

"I'll go," I said, not hesitating. "We'll take a small team. Splitting up may divide Simon's forces and give us an advantage."

Crew nodded. "There must be a doorway out to the landing pad down this hallway. Hurry, that barricade spell won't last long."

I'd not realized how tired and beaten-down the group was. All around me, heads hung, lungs heaved, cuts bled. They were exhausted, and from the looks of it, we'd lost a few people since the start of the fighting.

"Any volunteers?" I asked.

"I'm going," Kira said, then jabbed a finger into my chest. "Don't even try to stop me."

"Me too," Abel said, wiping sweat off his forehead. "I owe this fucker some payback."

"I'll go with you," J.D. added.

Two more Haveners volunteered. The rest would follow Crew deeper into the lab to find Simon and take him down once and for all.

"On my six," I said, heading farther down the hallway.

My small team followed, Crew led the rest of our people to a T junction and departed in the opposite direction. Sure enough, as Crew had guessed, I spotted a door a dozen yards down the hall that led to the interior of the volcano. J.D. and I slammed into it, using all our enhanced-shifter strength to break the lock. On the third strike, the metal bolts gave way, the door swinging violently outward. J.D. and I tumbled forward, landing on the cool black stone. The men loading the helicopters turned at the noise, frozen at our appearance. Kira and the others rushed through the doors as J.D. and I scrambled to our feet.

We were met with a familiar face a few seconds later. Leif, fully feral in his wolf form, came running from behind one of the transport helicopters, teeth bared and a low growl emanating from his throat. He set himself up between us and the choppers, the men moving at a feverish pace to finish loading the shipments. Two more feral wolves sprinted toward us.

"Leif," Abel said, holding a hand up. "It's us. Your friends. I know you're still in there. Simon messed with my head, too. Calm down."

Leif lunged at Abel, teeth snapping and spit flying. Kira yanked Abel back by the scruff of his shirt a moment before Leif's jaws would have severed a few fingers.

One of the Haveners stepped forward. "We need to kill him. We're running out of time."

"No," Kira snapped. "We don't kill him. He's our friend."

We tried to subdue Leif and not seriously hurt him. Problem was, Leif had no qualms about hurting us. Plus, the two other ferals were doing their level best to rip our guts out. Each time one of us tried to leap on Leif's back or grab a leg, he lashed out with his teeth and claws, and the other wolves snapped their jaws at us. Leif nearly tore Abel's ear off at one point. A few seconds later, he was bare inches from tearing into my scrotum.

Behind him, one of the choppers was fully loaded its back hatch closed. The pilot ran for the cockpit to start the engine. We were out of time. Would we *have* to kill Leif? The thought made me sick to my stomach, but what other choice was he giving us? Anyone who tried to run past the three wolves was attacked.

The chopper's blades began to spin slowly as the engine started. Kira looked up, gritted her teeth, and bolted, trying to run past the Leif and the other two wolves. Leif jumped toward her, and J.D. threw himself between Kira and Leif's tearing jaws. Leif bit deep into J.D.'s chest instead of Kira's stomach, and blood bloomed on J.D.'s shirt. J.D. let out a bloodcurdling scream as the teeth sank deep into his flesh.

The noise of the man he loved screaming in pain appeared to snap Leif back into his own mind. He let go and blinked in horrified shock at J.D. sprawled on the ground, clutching his wound as he grimaced and gritted his teeth.

Sensing weakness, the two other ferals bolted toward J.D., ready to tear him to shreds. Leif spun on them, growling in rage, and jumped into attack. Awed, I watched Leif single-handedly tear out their throats in a matter of seconds.

I got my head on straight and sprinted to help Kira. By the time I'd joined her, she'd dragged the pilot out of the first aircraft. Together, we subdued or knocked out two other pilots as well as the team loading the chopper, managing to prevent them from unlocking any cages and releasing creatures in the process.

We weren't fast enough, though. The third chopper managed to take off. It was hovering twenty feet in the air by the time we got anywhere near it. The aircraft rose until it was above the lip of the volcano and headed in the direction of the mainland.

"You filthy sons of bitches!"

I spun, finding Simon striding out of a large, rolled-open metal door, flanked by nearly a dozen vampires and shifters.

"I am trying to bring the world things it has never seen." Simon sneered. "Wonders the likes of which you've never dreamed of, and you"—he leveled a shaking finger and me and Kira—"have done all you can to destroy my dreams." He shook his head sadly at Kira. "And you, my girl? Such wasted potential."

Simon raised his hand, casting a spell toward our team fighting behind us. A massive fireball appeared and slammed into the fae next to J.D. She never had time to deflect or counter-cast. The fireball enveloped her, killing her instantly. There wasn't even time for her to scream.

"Watch out!" I yelled. I shifted, dodging another spell Simon sent our way.

The vampires and ferals under his command encircled Simon, protecting him while he continued to lob spells at us. From behind Simon, Crew and the rest of the Haven survivors poured forth. Relief rushed through me when I saw our reinforcements, but we were still outnumbered.

"Crew?" Kira shouted. "Attack Simon."

Crew gave a thumbs-up, but his team of survivors were already deep in the fight. The circular chamber at the center of the volcano erupted in the sounds of battle. Screams, howls, the crackle of magic, the agonized yells of the injured and dying—I'd never encountered anything like this. Even the battles in the halls leading here hadn't been this chaotic. Simon had every member of his team here, trying their best to kill us.

Simon was aiming a spell directly at Abel, who was fending off a vampire trying to attack Chelsey. In the fray, I had a single moment to see the wicked grin on Simon's face as he cast his spell. It slammed into Abel, and the alpha's face went slack. He turned and grabbed Chelsey, trying to choke her.

What the fuck was going on?

Crew saw Chelsey was in trouble and broke away from the main battle. I tried to join, but I was bogged down with a feral bear. Abel growled and snarled. Chelsey screamed, desperately trying to fight him off. Zoe sent a spell into the bear I was fighting, and it collapsed, unconscious. Turning, I watched Crew, now in human form, leap through the air and kick Abel in the back of the head.

Abel fell forward, his head thudding against the hard ground, and went limp. I prayed he'd only been knocked out, not killed. My prayers were cut short when a vampire leaped onto my back, spitting and snapping its teeth at my neck.

Some of Simon's people attempted to get to the remaining air transports, presumably to pilot them off the island. Crew saw them as well, and the battle moved like a slug across the stone field toward the helicopters. The fight wasn't like a war anymore. Not how I imagined wars, anyway. It was more like a rugby scrum—chaos, blood, and screams. I was going to have terrible fucking nightmares for years to come if we somehow managed to survive this.

After seeing what Simon had managed to do to Abel, I kept close to Kira. He'd commanded Abel like a puppet, and I couldn't help but think it was due to whatever experiments he'd done on him. I'd never heard of a spell that controlled someone's mind like that. I feared Kira might be vulnerable to a similar attack.

Almost as though he'd read my mind, a similar spell went whizzing past Kira's head while she fought off a feral wolf. My inner wolf, seeing how close she'd come to danger, lost control. I shifted and dived into the mass of writhing, fighting bodies, drawing closer to Simon with every step.

"Come, you mutt," Simon hissed, watching me press into his circle of protective vampires. "See what I can do."

Simon shifted, becoming the mangy and bizarre-looking wolf I'd seen on our last attack. He didn't hesitate, lunging at me before he'd even finished shifting. We rolled, biting, clawing, and snarling at each other. Again, I was shocked by how strong he was. His strength equaled my own.

The battle began to turn. We were losing. Through the haze of my own battle with Simon, I could hear our people calling out for help, Simon's staff shouting out in victory. We were going to lose. I could feel it. Was Crew still alive? Eli? I couldn't see anything but Simon's snapping jaws.

A vampire reached out, clamping down on my muzzle. Unable to bite or fend Simon off, he reared back, jaws wide, white teeth glittering with saliva, and brought his mouth down toward my throat. A moment before he could rip my life away, Kira barreled into him, knocking him aside.

Shaking the vampire free, I took a moment to dispatch him before turning back to find Kira, in her wolf form, snarling at Simon. With Kira helping, we were able to push Simon back, but he was still a surprisingly difficult enemy. All around us, the sounds of our defeat grew even louder. Simon's forces were rallying, pushing the Haveners back, cutting Kira and me off from our support. I couldn't even hear our people's voices anymore above the dull roar of Simon's staff.

A sliver of fear gnawed at my gut. We were going to lose. They were too strong, too prepared, unwilling to give up. This was where we'd die. I growled and bit at Simon's paw in rage. If we did die here, I would do it beside Kira, and I would do it without surrender. If it happened, then I was determined to make sure this fucker was bleeding out beside me at the end.

Simon stood, snarling at Kira and me. A strange, victorious gleam shimmered in his eyes. He took a step toward us, then halted. His look of triumph faded, turning into one of confusion.

That's when I noticed it. Cold. A pervasive, bone-aching chill.

A great swarm of bats swept over the lip of the volcano, descending into the fight. They merged together and became a pale-skinned, terrifying woman. She stood between us and Simon.

Lucina cocked an eyebrow at the scientist. "You have caused me great irritation, fae," she said. All around us, the cacophony of battle ceased as even the ferals turned to see the new arrival.

Simon shifted back and glared at her. "Watch your tongue, old god. I am not just a fae; I am a fae-shifter. You would do well to remember that, pathetic, powerless creature that you are."

"Pathetic and powerless, am I?" Lucina cooed dangerously. "We shall see about that."

She snapped her fingers. Every shadow within the volcano sprang up like some strange, black, living liquid, and they rushed deep into the lab. Another slithering snake of darkness swept back across all of Simon's forces, crushing, breaking, and eviscerating them where they stood. From within the lab, explosions, crashing sounds, and the distinct melody of shattering metal echoed out toward us.

Simon flinched as Lucina destroyed everything he'd worked so hard for. Even his experiments on the choppers screamed and howled as her shadows swarmed over them, destroying them as though they were nothing.

Lucina moved her shadows like a conductor commanding an orchestra, her long, delicate fingers dancing through the air, sending shadow snakes to decapitate vampires and booming shadow waves to crush one of the two remaining helicopters. Then, she turned her eyes on Simon.

He must have realized he'd overstepped and was in trouble, because he cast a spell on himself a moment before Lucina's shadows caught him. The few vampires and ferals that remained alive toppled over as though every ounce of life had been sucked out of them. A faint, shimmery light flashed from their bodies back to Simon as they fell. A moment later, the fucker vanished, escaping death by less than a second.

Around us, his forces lay dead at our feet. Glancing back, I saw Crew, obviously exhausted by the fight, being helped to his feet by Chelsey and Eli.

Lucina pulled her shadows back to shroud her in darkness once again, then stepped forward, staring down at the spot where Simon had been a moment before.

"Pity. I was looking forward to taking that one. Stronger magic than I thought." She looked up as though scenting the air. "Unfortunate."

Chapter 13 - Kira

I didn't have a chance to be awed by what Lucina had accomplished with a snap of her fingers. Not when white-hot rage coursed through me. Simon had gotten away. All around us, his minions writhed or lay dead. Even through the thick walls of the volcano, the destruction in the lab had the familiar ring of a distant thunderstorm. Everything he'd been working on was gone, thoroughly ripped apart and destroyed by the Shadowkeeper's inky black tendrils.

"What was on the chopper that got away?" Crew asked. He was still leaning on Chelsey, even though his wounds were nearly healed.

"Nothing," Wyatt said. "It wasn't loaded yet. I think they were packing them in order. The guy piloting it bolted as soon as he could. We may have gotten lucky there."

Some of the tension in Crew's face eased. The knowledge gave me some relief as well. I didn't want any of Simon's monstrosities to wreak havoc on our friends and families.

Eli and a few Haveners moved to the remaining helicopter and unloaded the cases and cages. Lucina's shadows had destroyed everything inside them. Thankfully, the aircraft itself was undamaged.

Lucina approached me and Wyatt. She carried herself as though she hadn't just killed dozens of beings and wrecked millions of dollars of equipment.

"He's teleported himself somewhere else on the island, hasn't he?" I asked. "There can't be many places he could go. The mansion, maybe?"

Lucina sneered as she shook her head and gestured to the drained and desiccated corpses around us. "That last spell was interesting. He sucked the very life force from these poor things." She leveled her gaze at us. "It increased the power of his magic tenfold. He is no longer on Bloodstone Island. He is on the mainland."

"How is that possible?" Wyatt said. "I thought your boundary was impenetrable."

Lucina shrugged. "When the mansion fell and the fae and wiccan employees began to teleport back to the mainland in panic, I threw up a stronger wall of magic. I didn't want anything else to escape. I never expected a common fae to be able or willing to do something like this." She cast another look of disgust at the corpses. "Had I thought it possible, I would have increased the ward exponentially. I underestimated the hybrid again. I will not do so a third time."

Her shadows seemed to darken at her tone.

"That rat bastard," Wyatt hissed through gritted teeth. "What about the helicopters? How did they get through your wards? Did he cast a spell on them to allow that, too?" He waved a hand at the chopper Eli and her team were unloading. "How the fuck did the one that got away make it out?"

Lucina sniffed. "The spells encasing these vehicles are not Simon's doing. I know the scent of this magic. It appears my sister is even more involved than I was willing to admit."

Wyatt spat on the ground. "We need to go after him. Hunt his ass down like the dog he is. As soon as we're back home, we find him and kill that fucker."

The Shadowkeeper flicked her hand, and a shadow pressed against Wyatt's mouth. "This man has led a tortured existence. I could sense it in the few moments I was near him. He is driven by darkness, and his magic is powerful. He will make a good shadow. I would like to turn him into one of my children. A shade of the night, something wholly under my control." She smiled. "I ask that you find this Simon Shingleman and send him back to me. In return, I promise he will be at peace in the darkness and will never be seen or bothered by the living again. It will be a punishment both more merciful and more complete than mere death."

"How can you guarantee that?" I asked. "For all we know, when all this is over, *The Reject Project* will resume. They'll be back here doing the same shit as before."

A half-smile flashed across Lucina's lips so quick, I was sure I'd imagined it. "After *this* is all over, I plan to return Bloodstone Island to its former isolation. I see now I made a grave mistake in allowing that spectacle to film here. I will block this place off to the show, to my sister, and anyone else. As I said, Simon will never trouble the world again should you send him back to me."

Wyatt grunted, the muscles in his jaw ticking. He clearly didn't like the idea. I pictured myself choking the life out of Simon, my hands tightening around his throat. It was a pleasant fantasy. But if Lucina was telling the truth, it sounded like his imprisonment in her shadow prison would last longer than anything we could possibly do to him.

"Fine," Wyatt finally said. "If Kira agrees, then…ugh, fuck, I guess we'll *spare* him."

I nodded. It was for the best. "We will. Unless he gives us no other choice."

Lucina bowed her head. "Understood. I will not ask you to sacrifice your lives to bring him to me." A wall of flame sprang out of a doorway to our right, and everyone but Lucina flinched. "This place is not as safe as it once was. You'll be fine here for a while, but I suggest departing as soon as you are able."

Without another word, she burst into a cloud of bats and fluttered out through the top of the volcano.

J.D. was slumped on the ground, clutching his wound. His healing was slow-going, and the sheen of sweat on his face told me he was still in immense pain. All around, I noticed more and more people who'd been hurt in the fight. Several weren't shifters, so they would take longer to heal. These people wouldn't be ready to venture out into the jungle again anytime soon.

Crying and sad moans told me several of our people had died. We'd known not everyone would make it, but now that the battle was over, reality was setting in.

"How long do you think this place will hold up?" I whispered to Wyatt.

He glanced around at the destruction, the flames from the lab. "I wouldn't want to be in there right now," he said, gesturing to the inner compound. "I think we'll be fine as long as we stay in the interior until we regroup and heal."

Crew limped over to us, but he seemed otherwise unhurt. "We need to work fast," he said. "The Shadowkeeper was right about this place not being safe. The noise will have attracted a lot of creatures. The fires in the corridors and at the entrance will keep them at bay, but we all know they won't burn forever. Those things will make their way in eventually." He looked around at the devastation of his people. Zoe and several other magic users were doing their best to heal injuries. "We're safe here. For now. We're away from the fires, and the smoke is going out the mouth of the volcano, but we can't fight. Not again. Not after all that."

"How many can fit on this thing?" Wyatt asked, pointing to the helicopter.

"Eli says maybe fifteen people. *Maybe.* It's the smallest of the three that were here."

Wyatt and I sighed and looked around. Even after the casualties, the chopper would only fit just over half of our people. How would we decide who stayed and who went?

"Okay, let's take stock," Wyatt said. "Do our best to heal and rest. Once the sun comes up, we'll make the tough calls. Sound good?"

Crew nodded, though I could see he was already doing the math in his head. No matter how you fudged the numbers, there was no good outcome. He hobbled off to sit with Chelsey, and a healer started working on his leg.

Over the next hour, Wyatt and I moved among the survivors, doing our best to keep their spirits up as the healers worked. Abel's was face drained of all color, and he had a harrowed look about him. That spell Simon cast on him must have done a number. A smear of dried blood painted the side of his face. When Crew had knocked him away from Chelsey, he'd damn near split his skull open.

He grabbed my hand. "Kira, can you tell them I'm sorry," he said, nodding toward Crew and Chelsey. "I didn't do it on purpose. I promise you—"

"Abel, stop," I said, putting my other hand over his. "We know. We all saw it. Simon fucked with your head. No one blames you."

He nodded and gave a pained smile that told me he didn't entirely believe me.

J.D. and Leif were huddled together. Leif looked as bad, if not worse, than Abel. He kept touching the spot on J.D.'s chest where he'd bitten him, but at least he seemed to be mostly in control of himself. I had to believe that with Simon off the island, some of that magical influence might have dissipated. That, or hurting the person he cared most about had dampened Leif's feral side.

I returned to Wyatt's side, looking at the survivors sprawled on the ground, too exhausted to do anything other than sleep. "I need fresh air," I said.

"I wouldn't go that way," Wyatt said, gesturing to the doors that led into the lab. Flames still flickered inside it, smoke pouring out and rising up the walls of the volcano.

"I was thinking about that," I said. I pointed to a scaffold staircase that zigzagged up the wall of the volcano. Some hundred and fifty feet above, a steel catwalk ringed the lip of the mouth. "The sunrise might look nice."

"Why not?" Wyatt said, twining his fingers through mine.

The walk up wasn't as bad as I'd thought, and it only took about three minutes to reach the top. The view was as wonderful as I'd pictured. The jungle spread out below us in a vast green blanket. Far in the distance, I could just barely make out the slate shingles of Reject Mansion. Rather than look at that, I turned to gaze at the ocean, where the rising sun was barely coloring the horizon a pale yellow. Soon, the sky would be ablaze with orange streaks. Then we'd have to figure out who we'd leave behind. Who we'd leave to die.

"What do you think the plan will be?" I asked.

Wyatt continued to stare out at the ocean. "The whole reason I came here was to make sure you got home safe. No matter what, I'm going to make sure you end up on that helicopter and head home. I'll stay behind and help defend this place. Maybe you all can get help back in time to save us."

"Wyatt, now is not the time to play the tragic hero. Maybe we...Wyatt? Are you okay?"

His brow had furrowed, jaw clenched, and he leaned out over the railing, squinting at the ocean. I focused on the horizon and spotted a small, black speck.

"What is that?" I asked.

Wyatt squinted some more. After a moment, his face went slack. "Son of a bitch. It's another helicopter. A fucking big one." Horror and defeat marred his handsome face as he looked at me. "Simon. He must have sent another one when he got to wherever he teleported to."

"Oh my gods," I whispered. "We can't fight off more of them. Not unless Lucina comes back."

We took the stairs two and three at a time, rushing to get back down. By the time we reached the floor, the faint sound of rotors were audible.

"What's wrong?" Eli asked when she saw our worried faces.

Wyatt pointed up at the opening above us. "Helicopter inbound."

Her face fell. "Are you serious?"

"Unfortunately," I said.

The look of hopeless despair was only on her face for a moment before steely determination reappeared. She turned to address the survivors as the whir of propellers grew louder. "Get ready everyone. Prepare yourselves. Looks like we have another fight ahead of us."

"What's going on?" Crew asked, hurrying over to join us.

Before anyone could fill him in, the aircraft's engine thundered above us as the helicopter flew over the opening of the volcano. Shouts of surprise and worry rippled through the group. A lead weight dropped into the pit of my stomach. The helicopter was *massive*, at least twice the size of the one we had down here. It was large enough to hold dozens of people. Gods only knew what kinds of horrors Simon had sent to decimate us.

The aircraft hovered above us for several long seconds, then lowered. I frowned at its wobbly descent. It paused, then continued lowering, as if the pilot was unsure of his skill.

"Back up!" Crew shouted. "Against the walls. Back."

The survivors scurried back, clumping together in a single unit, ready to face whatever hell poured out of the huge helicopter.

Five feet from the ground, the chopper again bobbled, inching down slower than I'd anticipated. The landing gear touched, rose again, then touched heavily down, the ground shuddering beneath us. I gripped Wyatt's hand, and he squeezed back. Terror swirled in my stomach like a swarm of bats as the back hatch lowered after the engine shut down.

From the back hatch, a shadowy figure rushed right at us, and a gasp went through the crowd. I gasped as well, but not in horror. No, my gasp was something more like shock, relief, and disbelief.

"Kiki? Kira?" Kolton shouted.

Tears burst from my eyes at my brother's voice, an emotional dam breaking in an instant. I broke free from the group and bolted across the black volcanic stone floor, my boots thudding as I sprinted.

"Kolton?"

His face broke into a massive grin, and he opened his arms for me. I leaped into his embrace, so many emotions rushing through me as sobs racked my body. I'd been worried that he might have already died in the war, that I would die here. Part of me had been convinced I'd never see him again.

"I thought we were too late," he murmured in my ear. "When we saw the smoke coming from the volcano, we decided to check here first. Are you okay?"

I nodded against his shoulder, swallowing down my tears to speak. "I'm okay. Oh, shit, hang on." Turning away, I waved at the survivors. "It's okay. It's friends. We're safe."

They'd already guessed as much by my reaction, but my words sent a ragged and weak cheer through the group.

Wyatt, grinning like a little kid, strode forward. "You know how to make an entrance, don't you, asshole?" He grabbed Kolton and hugged him.

Laughing, Kolton hugged him back. "You know me. Although, I should be punching you in the face for worrying me like that." He looked at both of us and smiled, tears shimmering in his eyes. "We were worried. When the show ended so abruptly..." He trailed off, then cleared his throat. "They sent out a message saying that unfortunately, due to situations beyond their control, the mansion had been overrun, and all the *all* contestants had been killed. They spouted some horseshit about Von Thronton battling hordes of creatures as he tried to save you, but only he managed to get out alive."

"Of course they did. Gods, I hate that fucking vampire," Wyatt muttered.

Kolton shook his head. "We couldn't believe you were gone. Couldn't allow ourselves to accept it. We knew—like, absolutely *knew*—if anyone could survive Bloodstone, it was you two."

"You keep saying 'we.' Who are you talking about?" Wyatt asked.

"Sorry to break up this lovey-dovey shit, but we got stuff to do," a baritone voice said.

I glanced up at a broad-shouldered wolf shifter stepping out of the helicopter. He was vaguely familiar. I didn't know him, but I was sure I'd seen him once or twice before, if only fleetingly.

"What are you doing here?" Wyatt asked, his face breaking into an even bigger smile.

The man stopped walking and rolled his eyes, waving Wyatt over. "Fine. Let's do the whole hug thing. I know you like that pansy shit."

Wyatt laughed and hugged the other man, slapping his back. Now I remembered him. He'd come around our house once or twice when Wyatt had meetings with my dad. This was Wyatt's *other* best friend. The only person who came close to the bond he and Kolton shared.

When they'd finished their bro hug, they walked over to us. The big man nodded to me. "You're Kira." He said it like a statement rather than a question, and he put a thumb to his own chest. "August. August Evander. I figured I had to come save my alpha's ass."

I frowned at Wyatt, who rolled his eyes before punching August's shoulder. "Unofficial packs don't have alphas. Not a *leader* alpha, anyway. I keep telling you that."

August shrugged. "Whatever."

Crew joined us, and his relief was palpable. "Are you here for us? Can we hitch a ride home?'

August looked over Crew's head at the people huddled by the wall, then at the ruination Simon and Lucina had wrought. He nodded. "I suppose we are.

No offense, buddy, but you all look like a shit smear on the ass of a harpy."

"Thanks," Crew said wryly. "We feel even worse. You have no idea how happy we are to see you guys."

August pointed a thumb over his shoulder at the helicopter. "Get your folks on there. This place isn't safe. Honestly, we're shocked you're all alive. Outside is a disaster. Flames all over, smoke pouring out, and even from up there we could see a shit ton of nasty beasts milling around. Once those flames die down, this place is gonna be overrun."

"I had to beg him to fly over the top to have a look down," Kolton said. "Between the smoke and monsters, it looked like hell. When we saw all you huddled down here. Somehow, I *knew* it was you and forced him to land."

"Sorry about that landing, by the way," August said. "Only had a week of training on flying this thing. Even with the controls magically enhanced, it's not easy."

Crew and Eli were already calling people over to get in the helicopter. People hurried by, shouting their thanks to August and Kolton as they went. Kolton nodded and waved, but August looked uncomfortable with the attention. Our small group of four moved aside, giving them room to help the injured onto the transport chopper.

August frowned at the people streaming past. "Can someone explain to me how in the blue hell there are so many people here? This *is* Bloodstone Island, right? The most dangerous and inhospitable place on the planet?"

"I thought this place had nothing but the mansion and hundreds of dangerous creatures and beings," Kolton said. "What is all this?"

"It's a long story," I said. "I can fill you in on the way home."

Exhaustion was finally starting to creep into my bones. It had been a *long* few days. It felt like weeks since the mansion fell, years since I'd first set foot on this island.

Then another thought occurred to me that dampened my hope. "*Are* we going home, Kolton? With the war going on?"

Kolton's face fell, and he and August exchanged a grave look.

"How are things back home?" I pressed. "Mom? Dad? The pack?"

"It's bad," Kolton said. "All the packs are fighting. We'll have plenty of time on the flight back. You tell me what's been going on here, and we'll fill you in on the war. For now, though? I'm just glad you're both safe. And we want to keep it that way. Let's get out of here, okay?"

"Deal," Wyatt said, pushing me toward the helicopter.

Eli, Crew, Chelsey, and Zoe helped all the injured survivors into jump seats lining the walls. The aircraft really was huge. I looked at all the empty seats. This thing had enough room to have gotten everyone in Haven out. Crew had lost ten or fifteen people between the two assaults on Simon's lab and the cave-in. The senseless loss of life hurt more than anything.

"Where did this thing come from?" I asked Kolton.

"It's a Chinook transport helicopter. It's designed to carry up to forty men and equipment into war zones. It's used more by humans, but our mysterious benefactor pulled strings and got this one for us."

"I suppose you'll tell us who that is soon?" Wyatt asked, strapping himself into a seat.

"Don't worry. We'll give you all the details, boss man," August said as he walked toward the cockpit.

"I'm not the boss. Ugh." Wyatt huffed, patting the seat next to him for me to sit.

Once buckled in, I looked at Wyatt. "Is this really happening? Are we finally going home?"

He took my hand. "Looks like it."

The whine of the engine starting muffled the murmurs of conversation. The survivors shared looks of relief, hope, and sadness. Some of these people had lost friends and loved ones on the island, most of which had happened in the last two days. I couldn't imagine how strange this moment was for them. Wyatt and I had only been here for a few weeks. Some of them had been stuck here for a year or more.

As the helicopter took off, wavering as it rose higher and higher, I looked out the window, stifling my horrified gasp. The flames had died down in the hallways around the open area. Now, ferals, ghosts, and other horrors flooded into the place where we'd been only ten minutes ago.

I didn't bring this up to anyone—no reason for them to know how close we'd come to death. I thanked whatever gods there were that Kolton and August had arrived when they did.

I gazed down at the monsters covering the area like ants on candy, then we were gone, over the lip of the volcano, and heading toward the ocean. Out the window, the lush trees gave way to a strip of blond sand, then the emerald ocean beyond. A quivering sigh escaped my chest as we left the island behind.

Once we were about a hundred yards off the coast, a shadowy ripple appeared around the entire island, and was gone in the blink of an eye. One of Lucina's new wards. A fortress spell to keep anyone from ever trying to use the island for evil again.

From this distance, Bloodstone Island looked like paradise. The horrors that lurked there were invisible. Like most things, its true nature was hidden until you were right upon it.

Much like people. From far away, a person might appear to be smiling, but once you stood next to them, you saw the smile was actually a hungry grin. That the gleam in their eyes was really madness.

Chapter 14 - Wyatt

Once we'd leveled off and were far enough away from the island, Kolton joined us. "You guys can take off your seatbelts and move around if you want. We have about a few hundred miles to the coast, where we'll need to refuel, and then another couple hundred miles or so to our pack lands."

The survivors mostly stayed put, but several others unsnapped their seatbelts and stretched their legs, enjoying their new freedom. Kira stood and walked closer to one of the viewports out the side. Joining her at the window, I stood behind her, watching the ocean zip by beneath us.

Finally, I leaned forward, lips close to her ear. "It took longer than I wanted, but I'm happy I got you off that damned island."

"*You* got me off the island?" Kira said, turning and giving me a knowing smile. "Um, pretty sure it was actually my brother and your buddy who got us off the island. Or did I miss a step somewhere?"

"You know what I mean," I said, poking her in the stomach.

Kira scrunched up her face. "I could say the same thing, you know. Maybe *I* should be glad *you* got off that island. I seem to remember trying to get you sent home. Then you had to be all tough and stay. The macho martyr, right? Or were you trying to impress me or something?"

I flicked her nose. "Are you still holding that over my head? You've got to let that go."

"I don't know," Kira said, running a finger down my chest. "It's gonna take me a while to get over how dumb that was of you."

A retort was already forming on my lips, something to keep the banter going, but I noticed Kolton from the corner of my eyes. He was leaning against the wall of the helicopter, arms crossed. The cargo area had been enchanted in some way to keep the roar of the propellers from drowning out the conversation inside. He'd been listening to our whole flirtatious conversation.

Despite myself, heat rose to my cheeks.

Kira noticed him as well and quickly pulled her hands away from me, tucking them behind her back. We looked like a couple of teenagers who'd been caught humping in the back of a car. Would Kolton be pissed? I still remembered the goofy wrestling match we'd gotten into back in Fangmore for the mega-fans event.

Kolton's laugh spluttered out of him. "Relax," he said to me. "You don't have to hide that stuff anymore. The show is over, right? Hell, Kiki confessed her love for you on live television."

"So, uh, we're all good?" I asked hesitantly.

"Here's the deal," Kolton said. "I suspected long before that confession. I think the whole world could see what was happening in every episode." He cocked his eyebrow. "I still want to slug you in the nose for good measure, but only because that's what brothers are supposed to do. I'm happy for you guys. Like, seriously." He laughed and slapped me on the shoulder. "Now my best friend is gonna be my brother-in-law."

Brother-in-law? His assumption that Kira and I would mate and marry surprised the hell out of me. I wanted to be with Kira, but something *that* important needed to be discussed between us. We'd been too busy surviving that anything beyond getting to the next day alive seemed like something too far away to even contemplate.

Kira gaped at her brother. "Would you shut up? We are *not* talking about this right now. There's a war happening back home. Can we look at the big picture, please?" Her cheeks were an adorable shade of red.

It was all I could do not to laugh. Ninety percent of the time, she was the biggest badass in the room, but once you started talking about feelings and things, she got all freaked out. It was cute and funny, mostly because it was so out of character for her.

Deciding to throw her a lifeline, I changed the subject. "How are my people doing? The unofficial pack?"

Kolton's grin faded, and he nodded for us to follow him. "You should talk to August." He led us to the cockpit. "August, your buddy here wants to know how your pack is doing."

August glanced away from the windscreen and grinned at me. "The pack is kicking ass and taking names, bro. Most of these other *official* packs talk a big fucking game, but when the shit hits the fan, it's the loners like us who know what's up. Some of these official packs are on the verge of collapse, already splintering, and those wolves are shitting themselves. Us? We're cruising."

Kira squeezed my arm so tightly, I thought she would cut off the blood flow. "Wait," I said. "Did you say the packs are collapsing?"

Kolton nodded. "Several of the packs have already splintered into smaller packs. It's absolute chaos. The few that haven't splintered, like ours... let's just say there's a ton of tension." He looked at Kira. "Several elders are pissed that August and the rest of Wyatt's pack are still on our land, even though they're the *only* reason we haven't been overrun. It's the same old prejudices. It's fucking stupid. Dad's held us together through the tension, better than almost any of the other packs. It's pretty impressive, honestly."

Kira glanced over her shoulder at Gavin. He sat, head back against his seat with his eyes closed. The steady rise and fall of his chest indicated that he was asleep.

"What about the Ninth Pack?" Kira asked, turning back around.

Kolton and August grimaced. "Those guys are the biggest assholes we've had to deal with," August said. "They want the Eleventh Pack lands. *Bad.*"

Kolton nodded and patted August on the shoulder. "These guys have been a godsend. Like I said, without them, the Ninth Pack would have invaded and very likely eviscerated us." Kolton chewed the inside of his cheek as he turned back to Kira. "Jayson and his pack elders have accused our pack of orchestrating the assassination of Jayson's father. They're trying to push into our territories to kill off as many of our pack members they can get a hold of. We're already one of the smallest packs. We can't afford to lose more members."

Most of shifter society would have been taken aback to learn an unofficial pack was not only helping an official pack, but doing a damn good job holding off a bigger, more powerful pack. It didn't surprise me in the least. The Eleventh Pack had been the only pack to show us any hint of kindness. Not only that, but Kira's father had allowed us to *live* on their lands. That type of trust and friendship instilled loyalty. We would never bow down to Kira's dad as our alpha, but we would uphold our end of the bargain and fight off anyone who wanted to mess with us or them.

Kira chewed at her lip.

"I promise, as soon as we get home, we'll make sure Jayson knows he picked the wrong fight," I said to her. "The Eleventh Pack won't fall to the Ninth. Not unless it's over my dead body."

"I appreciate that," Kira said. "Let's just try to not have *any* dead bodies, maybe?"

I wanted to kiss her. Even when she was worried, she had that glint in her eye. The one that said she would be okay. All I wanted was to pull her in close, but I refrained. With Kolton standing right there, I had no idea how to act, and I didn't want to make things more awkward.

Being with Kira was the most natural thing I'd ever experienced. It was like we'd always been together. Kira felt the same—I could tell. Yet, it would take time to be open with our relationship. After hiding everything during our time on the show, it was difficult to figure out how to even have a normal relationship.

"You know, Wyatt," August said, looking back at me and Kira, "I'm gonna be a very rich man when we get back home."

"And why is that?" I asked.

"You see, almost every member of the pack has had this bet going. Being the intellectual I am, I was the only one who thought you'd ever bite the bullet and get with Kira. We all knew you had it bad for her, but none of them thought it would ever happen. What I'm saying is, you're welcome. I was the only one of your packmates to have faith in you, so thanks for making me a few hundred bucks. I appreciate you."

Kira laughed at my expense. "August, why did they think it was so unlikely? I have to know."

"Mostly because they didn't think you would *ever give* this dumbass a chance," August said, elbowing me in the gut.

Kolton laughed, winking at Kira. He moved his forefinger in a circle next to his temple and crossed his eyes. "Crazy."

"Get back to piloting, flyboy," Kira said to August. "And you shut up," she snapped at Kolton, her face going red again. "I'm going to go check on Zoe."

"Sounds good," I said.

Kira turned to head back to the rear of the cargo area. I made to follow, but Kolton's hand on my chest stopped me in my tracks. He waited until Kira was out of earshot.

"Look, bro, I am really happy for you guys. I can't tell you how relieved I am that you're both safe. I wanted to, uh..." Kolton looked away, blinking away the tears forming in his eyes. "I wanted to thank you for protecting my sister. I didn't have any doubt you would, but...thanks."

The emotion on Kolton's face showed me exactly how worried he'd been. How many times had he watched the show and seen how close to death we'd been? And then when the showrunners told the world we'd all died. I couldn't imagine the horror and grief he went through, even if he never *truly* believed that we were dead.

"I'd look after Kira no matter what. Haven't I always?" Trying to change the subject and get his mind off what might have happened, I patted the wall of the helicopter. "Speaking of saving people, how the hell did you get this thing? A military helicopter? While a war is going on? I mean, who in their right mind would hand that over to a couple of idiots like you when it might be needed for whichever pack or army owned it?"

August snorted. "You got the 'idiots' part right."

"It's complicated," Kolton said. "Couldn't have done it without August, though. It's not quite the same craft, but he's flown planes before and at least had some idea how to do it."

I chuckled and looked at August. "He makes it sound like you flew fighter jets." Turning my attention back to Kolton, I said, "He used to fly those dumb planes that have the advertising banners on the back. The ones you see at the beach."

Kolton didn't laugh and was having a hard time meeting my eyes. "What's really weird is how we got this thing. One day, we get this message—well, I got the message. A wire transfer came through to my account, along with a letter delivered by a wiccan courier. The letter told us what the money was for, and gave the name and contact info for a human arms dealer. He said if we told him who sent us, we'd be taken care of."

"He?" I asked, frowning. "Who are we talking about? This thing had to cost a few million. Who the fuck has that kind of money?"

August glanced at Kolton, and the two men shared a look. Kolton sighed. Oh, I wasn't going to like the answer. I swore, if they told me Jayson Fell or Von Thornton paid for this fucking helicopter, I would jump out the door and drown myself in the ocean.

"The wire transfer was from, uh, your dad. Lawrence Rivers," Kolton said.

The words slammed into me so hard, I took a step back. Confusion warred with disbelief. My father? The same man who'd barely blinked when I left our pack to become a lone wolf?

"Hey," Kolton said, hurrying on, "I know you left your pack for a good reason, and I've never pushed you to tell me what happened, but he really wanted to help save you. He told us he wanted you to contact him as soon as you got back…er, if you were alive, that is. Which you are…so that's good."

My mouth moved, but no words came out. I put a hand on the wall to hold myself up. My father? I hadn't spoken to him in years. Not since I'd walked out the door the day after I rejected Serenity. Hell, until I called my Uncle Rob to get put on the show, I hadn't spoken to *anyone* in my family, much less my father. I'd pretty much made up my mind that he didn't give two shits about me anymore, that he'd already written off the son who'd disappointed him. The kid who'd shamed his father, the second-in-command of the Second Pack.

"Crap," Kolton said, seeing the look on my face. "I fucked up, didn't I? I never should have accepted this gift. I'm sorry. We were freaking worried about you guys. This was like a miracle we couldn't turn down. All I could think of was saving you and Kira. We were—"

"Chill," I said, forcing a smile onto my face. "It's fine. You saved us. More importantly, you saved Kira, and I can't fault anyone for that."

Kolton sighed, and his shoulders relaxed. "Good. So, uh, are you gonna get in contact with your dad when you get back? I'm not saying you *have to*. That is, I was only wondering."

I thought about it for a moment, then shook my head. "Most likely not."

"Damn. Seriously?"

"Yeah. My father has never been big on family ties. There wasn't much in the way of love in my home growing up, at least not the fatherly kind. The only reason he'd want to save me, or talk to me, would be for his own personal gain. It's always been that way with him." I looked around at the interior of the helicopter. "I see this as some kind of repayment for all the years of his apathy, but nothing more. He'd need to do a lot more to get me to contact him. Not after everything that happened when I was younger."

Kira returned then, Eli in tow.

"How's Zoe?" I asked, eager to change the subject. "All good?"

"She's fine," Kira said. "She's hanging with J.D. Eli put Leif back under at his request."

"He was worried about being enclosed in here and going feral again," Eli said. "Can't say I blame him. The tight quarters make me claustrophobic, too. Your friend Abel wasn't doing well, either. Not sure if it was regret from what he did, or from the spell Simon cast on him. I put him under, too." Eli looked at Kolton and gave him a respectful nod. "I want to thank you for showing up when you did. Even fifteen minutes later, and we'd all have probably been dead. I'll tell you this—I'd be honored to have a brother as faithful and devoted as you are to Kira."

Kolton's eyes flicked across the face of the fallen angel, and I could see a spark of interest in his face. He grinned at her. "Um, well, it's no problem, really. Anyone would have done it."

"I highly doubt that." Eli placed a hand on Kolton's shoulder, and I thought I saw pink tinge his cheek as she did. "Well done, and thank you." She glanced around him at the empty co-pilot seat. "Do you mind if I have a seat there? Talk to the pilot about our route?

Kolton's face spread into a smile. "Oh, uh... no, yeah. I mean, yeah, you can. Sit there, I mean. In the seat."

Eli frowned, but a second later, she grinned. "That is where one usually sits."

Kolton's cheeks grew ever redder. "Right, yeah. Sorry. Uh, let me get out of your way."

The three of us moved toward the rear cargo area. I looked over my shoulder, where Eli and August were studying the route chart. Once we were out of earshot, I nudged Kolton. "Eli's pretty gorgeous, right? I didn't know you had a thing for fallen angels."

I hadn't thought it possible, but somehow Kolton's blush darkened to the point his ears glowed red. "What? No. What? I didn't...I wasn't..."

"She's single," I added. Kira snorted.

Kolton gritted his teeth. "That's not what was going on. I was, uh, just intrigued. I didn't know there were angels on Bloodstone. That's all."

"She's not as angelic as she looks," Kira said. "She can handle herself. Look, if I can fall in love with a lone wolf and throw out all our pack's old ideals and beliefs, I think you're free to get with an angel. That's if she'd give you the time of day. I mean, have you seen her?" She smiled, raising both eyebrows, then gestured to Kolton. "And have you seen *you*?"

"Very funny," Kolton said, but I didn't miss his lingering look at the cockpit. "Anyway, why are you guys teasing *me*? I should be doing that to you two. My best friend and my sister *doing* stuff to each other?" He made a gagging sound. "So gross."

"Yeah, yeah, we get it," Kira said. "Let's change the subject before you actually vomit. Can you give us more info on how the war is going? We need details."

Kolton looked relieved to get our attention off his obvious attraction to Eli. "Yeah, sure. The first skirmish, the one that started the whole war, was actually between our pack and the Ninth. It was right after they accused us of assassinating Jayson's dad. There were lots of smaller engagements on the borderlands. The real issue, though, was that our fight set off a bomb among the other packs. There's fighting happening around Fangmore City among the other packs. The city itself has locked down its borders to try and prevent rioting and fighting in the streets. That's where all the top alphas and betas, along with the highest-ranking members of the Tranquility Council, have taken refuge. Right now, it's the safest place." Kolton growled. "There have even been reports of wolf shifters fighting in wiccan and human cities. Fae towns as well. Everything is spilling over. And the pack leaders and the council are still pumping out all this propaganda that the hierarchy still stands, that the only way to get through this is to obey the alphas. Even while their own packs are splintering, the head alphas have locked themselves away in fucking penthouse suites in Fangmore, waiting for the worst of the fighting to blow over."

"Good gods," Kira said, shaking her head. "So it's really as bad as we thought."

"Worse," Kolton said grimly. "All of Heline's acolytes have been rounded up and imprisoned. Rumor is, they're going to be executed on live television in the coming days. They've been telling us that all the *mix-ups* with the fated mate connections is because the acolytes have grown lazy and gave faulty readings on the blood tests."

"Wait," I said. "The acolytes? Why are they bothering with that? Don't they have bigger problems to deal with?"

"Yeah," Kira added. "I'd think having enemies trying to break your door down would be a bigger threat."

Kolton looked back and forth between Kira and I like we'd lost our minds. "You of all people should know why, Kira."

"Huh?" She frowned at him dumbly.

"You're the catalyst for all this. The whole war."

She stared at him for several long seconds, confusion written all over her face. "What do you mean by that?"

Kolton chuckled. "Your speech on the show. The one where you called out the fated mate connections for being bullshit...that sparked all of it. The Ninth Pack claimed it was proof you never wanted to be with Jayson in the first place, and you were trying to justify what happened with you and Wyatt. They also said it was proof the Eleventh Pack assassinated Jayson's father. Other shifters heard your message and realized the truth in it. Groups immediately marched on Heline's temples." He paused, his face somber. "Then the in-fighting began. Heline's temples and the blood tests were no longer trusted, nor was the pack hierarchy that had always defended them both. Packs splintered, and more and more fights broke out. The first couple hours were the worst. It was chaos. The real bomb that set the fire was right before Fangmore locked its borders off, though. People were pissed at the upper packs, and a group of lower-pack shifters broke into some of the office buildings in Fangmore. Before anyone knew what was happening, they found and chased down the most powerful shifter in the world: Garth Sheen. He's dead. Killed in the street like a common criminal. The alpha of the First Pack, murdered by a bunch of lower-pack shifters. A reporter caught it on camera, live. When that happened, shit went downhill. *Fast.* An hour later, we were told that Reject Mansion had fallen."

The news was the most shocking thing I'd ever heard. So much had happened in only a few days. Garth Sheen was dead? Holy fuck. Looking over my shoulder, I spotted Mika sitting with Zoe and J.D. The three of them were talking quietly, smiling. What would Mika think when he heard?

It seemed we both had some daddy issues to deal with.

Chapter 15 - Kira

I'd started the war? That made no sense. I was...well, I was only me. A nobody. How could I have started a war just by telling the truth?

I'd only done it because people needed to know the reality of the problem. My plan had been to get a conversation started, to get people to question Heline's temples and the work they were doing. I'd never have believed—not in a million years—that a war would break out because I'd said a few words on camera.

In reality, what I'd *really* wanted was to end *The Reject Project*. To show the world how fucked-up it was to toss a bunch of people onto a nightmarish island to compete for the hope of getting a mate. I'd never meant for things to get this out of control. People were being murdered in the streets. Heline's acolytes were going to be executed. Packs were falling on each other like vultures.

All because of me.

As Kolton spoke and gave us more details about how the world was literally falling apart, thanks to me, a nervous ball of nausea coiled in my stomach. I wanted to throw up, and my skin beaded with cold sweat. If what Kolton was saying was true, how could I fix this? And I *had* to fix it before more innocent people died.

"Stop that," Wyatt warned.

"Stop what?" I asked.

"You know. I can see it on your face. This isn't your fault."

"I didn't say it was," I said, doing my best to act calm.

"You didn't have to. I can see your face."

"He's right, Kiki," Kolton said. "All you did was say what everyone's been thinking. We all had it in the back of our minds; you just voiced it and brought it to the forefront. If it hadn't been you, it would have eventually been someone else."

"But it *was* me," I insisted.

"You went on the show precisely to stop this," Wyatt said. "You went on that show, knowing damn well you were gonna game the system and take Heline's gift rather than a mate. You did that so you could stop a war and protect your pack. I know you carry some kind of guilt for that, but your reasoning was honorable. Stop trying to make yourself the villain when you aren't."

His words rang hollow. The devastation and destruction going on all over the world were my fault. No amount of sugar-coating would make it not be true. I should have kept my mouth shut, played the game, and done things the right way. If I had, I might be in Fangmore right now, asking Heline for her favor and stopping this whole war before it could've started.

But then, of course, I wouldn't be with Wyatt. Could I really give that up?

Gods, why was this so awful?

Wyatt, seeing I still didn't believe him, grabbed my shoulders and turned me to face him. "You have inspired change, Kira. Lasting change. You said the things that needed to be said. No one ever brought about change like this without there being some growing pains. Do you really think people should have continued mating with people they weren't meant to? Think about yourself. How miserable would you be if you were sitting at home with Jayson as your mate right now?"

Picturing that was like a slap in the face. It sank in better than anything else Wyatt had said.

"Kiki," Kolton said, "Wyatt's right. What you said that night? It was like a kick in the gut. The mating connections and the corruption of the packs? They were all things I'd noticed, but I pushed them to the back of my mind. I didn't press the issue because I wanted to be a good pack member. I didn't want to rock the boat. But you weren't afraid to do that. Are shitty things happening? Yes. But is it any worse than what was going on before? It's just different and more open." He leaned forward and wrapped me in a bear hug only a brother could give. "You did nothing wrong. Now, we need to get home and make it through this war."

"More than that," I said as he released me. "We need to protect our home and survive, but we also need to find Simon and Heline."

"Seriously?" Kolton asked.

"How the hell are we going to find the moon goddess?" Wyatt asked. "I doubt her address can be found on the internet."

"I'll figure it out," I said. "We find Simon and stop him from making more experiments and hurting people. Those weapons of his *can't* be allowed to be part of the war. And once we deal with him, we find

Heline. Part of this war is because of her fucking meddling with the mating connections. People are pissed, as they should be. The Shadowkeeper told us this was all part of her sister's game. That tells me Heline may be guiltier than we think. Shifters are too scared to call her out, and now they're gonna murder her acolytes when she's behind this."

Having a goal, a plan, helped focus my mind. It got me out of the self-loathing spiral I'd been about to drift into. If I could keep my eyes on the mission ahead, I could stop thinking I'd ruined everything.

Wyatt looked thoughtful for a moment. "Maybe we could figure out how to find Heline."

"You've got an idea?" I asked.

"She's shown up at the end of every season of *The Reject Project* to bless the new pairing between the two winners. If she's always there, that means the showrunners *must* have some way of communicating with or finding her. Right?"

I saw where he was going and smiled. "I'd *love* to kick a few of those assholes in the balls and get them to tell us where she is." They'd been so shitty to me and Wyatt when they came to chew us out at the mansion. I wanted some payback.

"I don't like the idea of testing our luck on *another* goddess, but I think we've got to give it a try." Wyatt rubbed his face, and it was the first time I really noticed how exhausted he looked. "That's enough for now. Let's get some rest."

Kolton checked his watch. "We should be at the coast in about five or ten minutes. We'll refuel there and then head home. You guys have a seat. We can figure all this out once we're safe back home."

We trudged back to our seats and fastened our seatbelts. What I wanted to do was discuss my plan more. Flesh out the details and the leads we should track down. But that all flittered out of my mind as soon as I rested my head on Wyatt's shoulder. Within seconds, a deep, dreamless sleep claimed me.

When I woke, I jolted forward with a start, panic and terror filling my mind. Where was I? Simon's lab? The jungle? I flinched when Wyatt put a hand on my arm.

"Hey, hey, calm down," Wyatt cooed softly. "You're awake. We're home. It's all right."

Blinking away the remnants of sleep, I realized we were still on the helicopter. The events of the last few hours rushed back to my mind, and I trembled from sheer relief

"Did you say we're home?" I asked.

Wytt grinned and nodded toward the back of the helicopter. The back hatch was slowly opening, letting in afternoon sunshine. I must have been asleep for a few hours.

That was when I realized the engines weren't on. We'd landed. Were we really back in my pack lands? My hands trembled at the thought. Home. I was really going home, after all this time.

In my haste to get off the aircraft, my fingers slipped on the seatbelt buckle. "This stupid fucking thing." I yanked at it in irritation.

"Here, let me," Wyatt said. He unclicked it so easily, I growled.

As soon as I was free, I jumped to my feet and sprinted down the ramp to the ground below. Outside, I hit my knees, running my fingers through the grass, inhaling the familiar scent of the field we'd landed in. *Home.* As much as I wanted to be here, at the back of my mind, I'd convinced myself I'd never see it again. In the depths of the worst horrors on Bloodstone, I'd pushed away any real belief that I'd return. Now here I was. It was like a dream.

"Kira? Baby?"

I gasped, choking on the lump that formed in my throat as tears stung my eyes. "Momma?"

I looked up to see my parents running toward me. My mother rushed forward ahead of my father, whose arm was in a sling. I stood and sprinted for them, grabbing my mom and collapsing into happy sobs as she hugged me. I was a child the last time I let her hold me like that.

Dad joined us and wrapped his good arm around me. We stood like that for several long moments before I managed to get myself back under control.

Releasing them, I eyed Dad's injury. A thick bandage bulged at his shoulder under his shirt. The wound there reeked of silver.

"Are you okay?" I asked, touching his arm gently.

He waved me off with his good hand. "It's fine. The Ninth Pack got their hands on some silver weapons. It's a shallow stab wound, but you know how it is. Silver heals slowly. But enough about me. How are you? Are you all right?"

Wiping my eyes, I nodded. "Yeah, I'm all right."

Dad leaned forward, looking into my eyes. "I want you to know how proud I am of you."

"Thank you, Daddy. I—"

"I can't believe they stopped the show," Dad said, cutting me off and shaking his head. "Those bastards ended it before you could win back honor for our pack. You were close to getting everything you went there for. I could see you were going to win."

My joy at being home vanished in a blink. Before I could stop myself, I poked an angry finger in my father's chest.

"Can you stop? All this crap about packs and hierarchy and honor and all that bullshit is over. Can't you see it? This outdated ideology of the packs has gotten so many people killed, it's ridiculous. You have no clue how awful that show was, Dad. They glammed it up for the viewers, but it was a hellhole. If they *hadn't* stopped the show, I'd probably be dead now. Is that what you want?"

My mother huffed a little breath, her nostrils flaring. "I, for one, am glad that the barbaric show is over. Good riddance. I hope it never comes back on. It's sick."

Dad looked at us both in confusion, like he didn't know where he stood. I couldn't hide my surprise at my mother's reaction. Mom had acted like she'd been on Dad's side when I left. She'd told me she was happy that I was going on the show, that it would be an avenue to restore our pack's reputation. Had that all been lip service to please my father? Or had she seen through the shiny veneer of the show, seen the rotten, awful thing beneath and now regretted letting me go?

"Mr. Durst?" Wyatt called from the helicopter. "A minute, please?"

Dad hurried off, ready to be away from two pissed-off women.

Crew and Eli had led all the survivors off the helicopter and were now getting them into a group. Crew continued acting as their de facto leader, and all of them accepted it, even though they were back home now. The way he moved among them, calming them and getting them settled, told me why. Wiccans, fae, demons, humans—all of them looked to Crew for guidance.

Mom and I strolled over arm-in-arm to see what was going on. Crew and Wyatt pulled Dad aside.

"Mr. Durst?" Crew said. "I want to thank you for your hospitality, letting me and my people come here. I know it's a dangerous time, and you didn't need to allow this. Thank you." He put his hand out.

Dad nodded and shook Crew's hand. "You're welcome. I couldn't turn people in need away. That's not how the Eleventh Pack does things."

"It's common courtesy to defer to the alpha of the land you're in," Crew said. "I am asking for your blessing for sanctuary for my people. To stay in your lands long enough to heal and figure out where to go from here."

My father mulled it over. He glanced at Wyatt, who gave him an encouraging nod. But rather than smile at Wyatt, Dad's frown deepened.

Finally, he said, "That'll be fine, I think. You'll need to abide by our rules, and pull your weight when it comes to defense, but that should work for us. Can't have too many allies these days."

Crew's face broke into a relieved grin. "Thank you. You have no idea how much I appreciate that."

From the edge of the field, a few of our neighbors appeared, carrying bags and boxes of supplies. As they drew near, I noticed it was all food, clothing, and medical supplies. August and Kolton must have radioed ahead while I was asleep. They'd had time to prepare for our arrival.

Mom took a box from a friend and moved forward to help the survivors.

"I'll carry that, Mrs. Durst," Wyatt offered.

Mom glanced at Wyatt and gave a dismissive sniff before turning away, ignoring him. I cringed at the sight. Wyatt, not realizing I was watching, slumped his shoulders and stared down at the ground. I hadn't seen him look that downtrodden in a long time. My mother had changed her mind about the show, but apparently, her old-school ideas about lone wolves hadn't changed. She obviously wasn't excited that I'd proclaimed my love for a lone wolf on live television. If I had to guess, Dad probably felt the same way.

Wyatt had always been a secondary concern to them. Just a valuable ally, with his unofficial pack helping to improve our defenses. And he was Kolton's best friend. They'd always *liked* Wyatt as a person, but that was very different from welcoming him as a mate for their daughter.

I remembered Chelsey and Crew's story. How silly it all was to think someone was below you and not worthy of mating, even if you loved them.

The dejected look on Wyatt's face didn't last long. He shook it off and walked over to me, looking as carefree as ever. "I'm gonna go check on my pack," he said. "August says they're camped with your pack's best fighters. They're guarding the perimeter."

"I'll stay here and help get everyone taken care of," I said.

"But first, there's something I need to do."

Before I could ask what that was, he wrapped an arm around my waist, pulled me flush against his chest, and kissed me. Hard.

The group of survivors hooted and cheered, and in my daze, I could make out Zoe, Chelsey, and J.D.'s especially loud voices. Wyatt's show of affection surprised me, especially in front of everyone. My parents, my brother, and a bunch of pack members? All of them seeing this for the first time, understanding that it wasn't a show for TV. That we really did love each other.

The kiss brought me fully back to reality, as though our connection here in safety had finally severed the part of our life that had been on Bloodstone Island. The real world.

It should have been a happy moment, but if we were in the real world again, that meant real problems now stared us in the face.

Regardless of what Wyatt said, I couldn't shake the thought that we both might have *true* fated mates out there somewhere. Would he still love me and want to be with me with that knowledge?

As good as we were together, could it be even better with a fated mate?

"I'm sorry about my parents," I whispered as he finally pulled his lips from mine.

He winked at me. "No big deal. I've got what I want. They'll come around."

"See you soon?"

"Sure thing. See you in a bit." After squeezing my hand one last time, Wyatt shifted and sprinted off to the west.

Standing there, I gazed out, watching Wyatt until he vanished into the forest. Even when I couldn't see him anymore, I kept staring off into space. There was so much running through my head, it was hard to figure out what to worry about first.

Zoe tore me from my thoughts by wrapping her arms around my neck. "You need to chill," she said with a grin.

"About what?"

"Chick, I can read you like a book. If I didn't know better, I'd think you were still on that island, looking for danger or monsters around every corner. Enjoy this. You're home. You're safe. You've got that big slab of man meat undressing you with his eyes every five seconds. Even better, you aren't a slave to the showrunners anymore. Live it up while you can."

"Easier said than done."

Zoe released me. "Look, if your pack wasn't in the middle of some big standoff right now, you'd better believe I'd be breaking out the margaritas and launching some fae fireworks to celebrate." Her smile faltered a bit.

"What's wrong?"

Zoe looked at me, but all her cheeriness had vanished. "Um, I need to go check on my family," she said. "This whole war is spilling over, and fae tend to end up getting wrapped up in wolf-shifter conflicts more than other beings. I need to see if everyone is okay."

"I get it. Go on. You need to make sure your family is safe."

Zoe rolled her eyes, her smile returning. "I'm not gonna leave you high and dry. I'll be back soon. I want a front row seat to you kicking Jayson Fell in the balls. Plus, I want to help you guys get that bastard Simon. I'm sure you and loverboy have a bunch of plans, and I'm all in."

"Well, you aren't going alone."

"Huh? What do you mean?"

It was my turn to roll my eyes. "There's a war going on. Cullman is a pretty long way from here, well outside my pack lands. I don't want you out there with no one to watch your back."

"Who the hell do you have in mind? Are you coming with? A girl's trip?"

Looking over her shoulder, I noticed the Haveners. Most of them were shell-shocked from being back in the real world after all that time on Bloodstone. Among them, a broad-shouldered alpha was handing out bottles of water. I grinned at Mika and waved him over.

He probably hadn't heard yet that his father had died in the riots. Once he did, he'd have some sort of grieving to do. His dad had been a piece of shit, and maybe Mika would mourn for the man his father could have been, or something. Either way, having Zoe around would help. As goofy and talkative as she was, I wouldn't want anyone else to help me deal with something heavy like that. Plus, her family was *super-*accepting of everyone and would welcome him with open arms.

That was something I thought Mika might need as well—acceptance. From what I'd learned, he'd never had that before.

"You really have become the little matchmaker, haven't you," Zoe whispered to me as Mika walked up.

"What's up? Is everything okay?" Mika asked. He spoke to me, but he only had eyes for Zoe.

"Well," Zoe said, trailing her fingers down his chest, "I have a *very* dangerous mission for Agent McBroodypants. Are you up for it?"

"Depends on what it is," Mika said with a grin.

"Your mission, should you choose to accept it, is to keep me safe on a trip to check on my family. To make sure they're safe."

Mika's grin widened. It was nice to see. He'd smiled so rarely on the island. He was handsome, and more than that, he was a kind and gentle man. All the things his pack wasn't, and everything Zoe deserved.

"I think I'm up for it," he said.

"Good! I'm sure my parents and grandparents will want to meet the hottest alpha from the final season of *The Reject Project*."

"Okay," he said. For the first time since I first met him, he actually looked excited.

Zoe turned to give me one last hug. "See you soon, bestie." She jabbed a threatening finger into my nose. "No getting into danger while I'm gone."

"No promises," I said, cracking a grin.

"Ugh, you shifters. A real pain in my ass." Zoe raised an eyebrow at Mika. "Though, sometimes a pain in the ass can feel really good, if you know what I mean."

Mika smiled, then frowned. "Wait, what?"

They vanished a moment later as Zoe teleported them away.

Behind me, angry shouts erupted. And it sounded like my dad. I spun to find him jabbing a finger toward Gavin.

"That fucker has ten minutes to get off my land," Dad growled. He turned to Crew. "I said your people could stay, but not that Fell piece of shit. You hear me? If he's not gone in ten minutes, he's a dead man."

Crew only blinked at my father. I couldn't blame him. I'd *never* seen my father so angry in my whole life.

"Hang on," Gavin said. "I helped keep Kira safe. I spent my whole time on the show, trying to protect her. There's also a pretty good chance she and I are fated mates."

"Excuse me?" Dad spat, his face a mask of derision. "What are you on about?"

"Look," Gavin said, holding his hands out pleadingly. The rest of the Haveners had moved away, terrified of being in the line of fire of my Dad's rage. "I want to join your pack. Ask Kira. We talked about it on the show. I want my old pack destroyed, and those who survive to join yours."

Dad sliced a hand through the air, silencing him. "I don't give a damn what kind of plan you had. We are at war, and your brother is threatening to tear our throats out. I cannot and will not allow someone who could be an enemy in disguise to stay on my land."

Gavin gritted his teeth, preparing himself to argue further. If I didn't step in, this might turn into a real fight. Someone needed to calm the tension.

"Dad, hang on," I said, stepping forward to put a hand on his shoulder.

My father paused to look at me, some of the anger draining from his face. "What the hell is he talking about? Fated mates?"

I shook the question off. "He's misinformed," I whispered. "Don't worry about that now. What I do know is that he's being honest about hating his pack. He despised his father and hates Jayson. He told me he wanted to overthrow his pack."

"But that's even worse," Dad argued. "He's a disloyal wolf, dammit. How can anyone trust a wolf who'd turn on his own pack?"

"The same pack who wants us dead?" I asked. Did he not see the irony?

Dad sighed heavily, looking like he was having some sort of internal argument with himself. Finally, he turned and pointed at Gavin again. "One night. You got it? You stay one night, and it will be under observation. You do one fucking thing that arouses our suspicions, and my pack will rip you apart."

Dad stomped off to join Mom with helping the survivors. Gavin caught my eye and nodded his thanks to me. He looked relieved, like he'd been spared death.

I hoped I wouldn't regret helping him.

Chapter 16 - Wyatt

Shifting back to my human form, I strode out of the forest to the one of the small forward patrol encampments that ringed the Eleventh Pack's lands. Tents and campfires dotted the area. In the distance, I could see some of the members of my unofficial pack patrolling in wolf and human form. Some even carried firearms. Eleventh Pack members intermingled with them.

"I'll be dipped in shit. You're back!" a voice called out to me.

Putting my hand up to shield my eyes from the sun, I saw a big, burly shifter walking toward me with a huge smile on his face.

"Darius? Are you telling me August didn't kick your ass out while I was gone? I gave him detailed instructions," I said with a laugh.

'Oh, fuck off," the big man said and wrapped me in a hug.

Darius was one of the few people I knew who was bigger than me. His shiny bald head and dark brown skin were a sight for sore eyes.

"Didn't think we'd ever see you again, boss," he said.

"Don't start with the 'boss' stuff. How's it looking out here?" I asked.

Word spread, and soon more of my pack members came to greet me.

Darius waved at the camp. "It's good. Lots of Ninth Pack fuckers keep trying to break through here and there. Every time they try, we give them a bloody nose. For all their talk, they're basically little pussies."

I took the time to shake hands and hug all my pack mates. Everyone was jovial and excited, but I could sense their lingering unease and worry. The release of all that tension was palpable now that they saw I was alive and well.

"Thank you all for holding the fort down while I was gone," I said. "It really means a lot. I can tell you the Eleventh Pack folks are appreciative. Not sure if they've told you that."

"Oh, they have," Darius said. "First time since I became a lone wolf at fourteen that I've been this beloved."

A few of my pack mates had some significant injuries from silver weapons. The fighting must have been really intense. Part of me had hoped things weren't as bad as everyone made it out to be, but the haunted looks in their eyes told me otherwise. These were people on the front line of a war. It was bound to change them.

The fact that the official packs were willing to kill other wolf shifters to claim their territory was insane. All they cared about was clout, power, money, and prestige. Kira was right. We needed to tear down the pack hierarchy and build a new and better world in its place.

"Level with me," I said to none of them in particular. "How bad is it out there?"

A younger woman named Camilla spoke first. "I went out scouting yesterday. Curiosity got the best of me, and I ventured off the Eleventh Pack's lands." She shook her head sadly. "It's mayhem out there. The lower packs are attacking the upper packs left and right. Have you heard about Garth Sheen?"

"I did. He's dead," I said.

"Yeah." She nodded. "The lower packs think the messed-up mating connections are due to the upper packs corrupting Heline's temples. They think they've got the acolytes in their back pockets or something.

Everyone is out for blood. I also headed out to some other areas. Lake City, the human capital? They've barricaded the streets so no one can go in. The vampire enclave on the other side of the valley, Dark Hollow? Same thing. All the other beings are getting ready for this thing to spill over into their territories. I've never seen anything like it. Even the stories of past wars are nothing like this, Wyatt. If this doesn't end soon, it's not gonna be just a wolf war. It'll be a world war."

"What's the council doing to help?" I asked.

In response, I received groans and muttered curses. Darius spat on the ground. "Not a damned thing, that's what," he said.

"What do you mean, *nothing*?" I asked, shocked.

"Exactly what I said. The operatives have all taken sides, most of them going along with their own packs. All the regional offices have been cleared out. There is basically no council or ops right now. The councilmembers themselves are in Fangmore, hiding in their fucking tower and waiting for this to blow over."

I couldn't have been more surprised if Darius had unzipped his face to reveal he was a kappa in disguise.

The council had run? The operatives had all scattered? I'd spent my career doing the bidding of those people. Our entire purpose was to protect. And now that people actually *needed* the council more than ever, they were hiding like cowards?

Kira had been screwed over by them, yes, but deep down, I'd hoped it was due to Jayson's family pulling strings with one or two corrupt people. But maybe things were worse than I wanted to believe. Tearing down the whole system was beginning to make more and more sense with each passing minute.

My fellow operatives were good people and did good, important work. It was their leaders who were too weak to maintain control. Instead of letting the operatives join in on the conflict, they should have used them to help keep things calm. I gritted my teeth, my hands curling and uncurling.

Shaking off my anger, I turned my attention back to my pack. "Do you guys need anything? Supplies or weapons or anything?"

Darius shook his head. "Nah. Mr. Durst has been taking care of us." He glanced over his shoulder, then leaned in so only our group could make out his words. "His people are a little freaked out. Trigger-happy, you know? Not used to the dangers of the outside world like we are."

"Right," I said. "Not surprising. Do your best with them. Where's everyone else?"

Camilla pointed to the north, then to the south. "We have groups like this scattered along this boundary. The eastern border is ringed with mountains and too treacherous for anyone to breach. The only other way in is the main road into and out of the Eastern Wilds, and we have a larger force there."

"Sounds like you don't even need me." I shrugged. "Guess I'll head back to Bloodstone. Get a massage from a succubus or something."

"Just make sure it doesn't give you a happy ending," Darius chuckled. "I think Kira might get mad about that."

He winked at me, and the group laughed at my expense. It was good to be home. I'd missed the banter, camaraderie, and the familial feeling of my unofficial pack. People who didn't think unofficial packs were worthy of consideration were out of their minds. In my experience, when people *chose* to form a pack together, the pack was far stronger and better adjusted than even the best of the official packs.

"I'm going to head back to the Dursts' place," I said as I turned to go. "If you need anything, let me know ASAP."

They waved me on and resumed their duties.

Shifting, I plunged into the forest again, running back the way I'd come. This forest was different from the jungles of Bloodstone. It was cooler, less humid, and not as densely packed with foliage. This was home. I supposed it *was* home. I'd lived in the Eleventh Pack's lands almost as long as I'd lived in the Second Pack's territory. It was weird to think about, but true.

Plus, Kira was here. She was my home, wherever she was. Knowing I'd see her soon, I picked up my pace, letting the cool forest air blow through my fur as I sprinted back to her.

When I got back to the Durst house, things were a bit less hectic. The helicopter still sat in the field across from their home, but Crew and all his people had gone. Probably sent off to whatever living quarters Kira's dad had figured out for them. I'd only been gone for a few hours, and already things were getting back to normal. As normal as it could be under the circumstances.

When I stepped in the front door, the delicious aroma of cooking food slammed into my nostrils. Saliva poured into my mouth. When had I last eaten? A few potatoes prior to attacking Simon's lab? That had been at least eighteen hours ago. I was starving.

In the kitchen, I found a familiar scene. Kolton and his dad sat on one side of the table, Kira and her mother on the other. I'd seen it a million times over the years, but for some reason, this felt more *real*. In the past, I'd found them like this when I stopped by to see Kolton. Back then, I'd have found some way to irritate or needle Kira. Push her buttons to get a rise out of her. *Anything* to get her to give me attention. Now, as I walked through the threshold, she turned and smiled at me. No need to bug her—she *wanted* me here.

Although, her parents didn't seem to share the sentiment.

"Wyatt." Kira beamed up at me and patted the seat beside her. "Sit. Kolton, get him a plate."

Kolton put his fork down. "Yes, ma'am. Is there anything else Mistress Kira would like? A foot massage, perhaps?"

"Shut up and get him some food, jerk."

I sat, putting my hand on Kira's thigh.

"I was just giving them a rundown on everything that happened on the island," Kira said.

"Nice," I said. "I love reliving nightmares. How far did you get?"

"She's, uh, to the part where she was slipped a drug during dinner," her dad said. He didn't look up as he said it, instead keeping his eyes on his food.

"Right," Kira said. She started into her story again.

Kolton returned a moment later and put a plate in front of me. While Kira relayed our adventures on the island, I ate, chiming in with my own descriptions and details every now and then. Kolton was transfixed, his food forgotten as he listened to our story.

Kira's parents, however, seemed less interested. Her mother hadn't said a single word to me, and her dad kept shooting irritated glances at my hand laying atop Kira's.

For my part, I did my best to ignore them. If Kira and Kolton noticed their parents' iciness toward me, they didn't show it.

I should have expected this reaction. The Dursts were the head alpha family of the Eleventh Pack, bogged down in traditions and proprieties. With me having been a lone wolf and now part of an unofficial pack, they probably didn't believe I was worthy of being with their daughter. It stung a bit, but as long as I was with Kira, I didn't care about their disapproval.

"You want more potatoes, babe?" I asked when Kira took a breath from explaining how Simon had kidnapped her.

"Sure," Kira said.

"'Babe?'" Mr. Durst repeated. "I think you mean *Kira*, don't you?" He glared at me with thinly veiled animosity.

Finally noticing the situation, Kolton did his best to defuse the tension. "Dad, did you know Wyatt saved a bunch of people on the island? He's basically a hero. Zoe told me all about it on the flight home."

Without taking his eyes from me, Kira's dad said, "Very good of him."

I shared a look with Kolton, who nodded and said, "Um, anyway, some of the families here donated a bunch of supplies for the Haven refugees. The folks who are too injured to help out are set up in a couple vacant houses nearby, and the rest went to the border camps to help with defense. Bentley Crew wanted to talk to both of you when you were free. He took his people out about an hour ago. Maybe the three of us can head that way after we eat?"

Kolton was doing his level best to steer the conversation away from my and Kira's relationship. Kira's mother gave me an icy glare, and her dad went back to his food, jabbing at his potatoes harder than was necessary.

Kira either hadn't noticed or was doing a good job of ignoring the tension. That worried me a bit. She'd always been so loyal to her parents and her pack. Would those old tendencies weave their way back into her mind now that she was back home? I didn't think so, but it still made me nervous that she'd push me away again. The stress and danger of the island was gone now. Without that, would she revert to her old self?

"You know what?" I said. "I'm full. Let's head that way now, shall we?"

"Sure," Kira said, putting her napkin down. "I can fill you guys in on the rest later."

Kolton pushed away from the table, relief flashing in his eyes.

"Thanks for the meal," I said to Kira's mother, who gave me a distant half-nod.

Kira hugged her parents and joined us.

"Which border camp did you visit earlier?" Kolton asked me.

"Not sure if the camps have specific names, but the one where my packmate Darius is stationed. Do you know it?"

"I do," Kolton said, nodding. "Crew and his team went farther north to one of the camps with the fewest reinforcements. It's where August is headquartered."

"Let's go, then," I said.

Kolton gave his sister an uncomfortable look. "Um, do we need to drive, or are we walking? It'll take a few hours if we're on foot in human form."

Kira grinned. "You forget things have changed, big brother." In a flash, she shifted, then turned her wolf eyes on us before racing off into forest.

Kolton let out a low whistle. "She looks even more impressive than she did on TV."

"Yup," I agreed, pride in my voice. "Let's hurry. Kira's fast, and I don't want her making fun of me for being slow."

Together, we shifted and bolted after Kira. Our speed allowed us to make it to the camp before sunset.

Crew was moving through the camp, assisting his people as well as some of my packmates and Kira's to prepare their defenses. He was a born leader. When he saw us approach, he raised a hand in greeting.

"Welcome to the front lines," he said.

"You seem pretty chipper for someone who's in a war," I said, shaking his outstretched hand.

"If I had to choose between fighting off angry ferals, wendigos, and thunderbirds versus pissy, spoiled assholes from the Ninth Pack, I'll take spoiled assholes any day."

I chuckled. "How's it going here?"

"Pretty good." Crew turned and gestured toward the rest of the camp. "August is over in that tent, said he was working on some leads. Not sure what that means. I've gotten the remainder of the camp organized into platoons. I made sure one of my magic users is in each one, which should help with defenses. If those Ninth Pack assholes try anything, they'll be in for a surprise when we start lobbing spells and magic at them."

"Any word on how he's doing?" Kira asked, nodding to the far end of the camp. A sullen-looking

Gavin sat there, a few Eleventh Pack guys standing around him. One of the men held a pistol.

"He's not happy about being considered a possible enemy, but he's glad he's not been turned out into the wilderness to fend for himself. I hope he does what he says. I don't think your dad was joking when he said he'd rip him limb from limb."

Eli and Chelsey came over to us, and Chelsey hugged Kira. Kolton blushed and did a poor job of trying not to check Eli out. Was *this* why he really wanted to join us out here? I stifled a smile.

"We still need to figure out safe transport for Chelsey," Eli said to Crew.

"Transport to where?" I asked.

Crew sighed, his eyes downcast. "Back home. She needs to check on her family. Problem is, Twelfth Pack territory is on the *opposite* side of the Ninth Pack's lands. We'd have to go through their whole territory to get her there. That's pretty much impossible right now. Even the highways are being patrolled, so using a car is out."

"I really need to see them," Chelsey said, and the look on her face was one of desperation. "They think I'm dead. I can't imagine what my brother and parents are going through. I tried to call them, but the signals into Twelfth Pack lands have been blocked or something. Apparently, lots of cell towers and magic relays have gone down in the fighting. Service is super spotty right now."

"I think we'll need to use that helicopter. It's the safest way," Eli said.

Before our discussion could go any further, August came sprinting out of his tent. "I've got news," he said.

"Good or bad?" I asked.

"Depends. A guy I've been talking to just sent me an email. He's a private detective, a bear shifter. He and I have been doing some digging. Wanna know what we found?"

"Are you drawing this out for dramatic effect?" I asked, impatient. "What the hell did he tell you?"

"Looks like the Tranquility Council is a lot farther down the drain than we realized," August said. "His investigation pulled up a wire transfer for several hundred thousand dollars from the beta of the Seventh Pack to three of the highest-ranking members of the council. He hacked the guy's email and found the exchange. They spoke in code, but it was easy to crack. An operative was sent in, under cover of night, to murder Jayson's dad."

"A Tranquility Operative assassinated him?" I asked, astonished. "Are you sure?"

August nodded. "Unfortunately. No idea who, though. There's only so much we could dig up, but do you know what this means?"

Kolton gave a tight nod. "We can destroy the Ninth Pack."

"What do you mean?" Kira asked.

"Jayson hasn't done shit to investigate his dad's death," Kolton explained. "As soon as he died, Jayson started pointing fingers at us. Rumor is, some of his pack elders and even the beta were a little pissed that he didn't look into it. If we leak this info, they'll flip their shit. It'll probably even split their pack. Jayson will be fucked."

"He's right," August agreed. "Once they split, there'll be infighting. It'll make it easier to hold them off and defend ourselves. We could even recruit some of their wolves to the Eleventh Pack, strengthening you guys in the process. A bunch of those people are innocent bystanders paying for the sins of the people running the pack. They'll want a fresh start."

"I'll do it," a voice said from behind us. "I'll leak the info."

We turned in surprise to find Gavin standing there, flanked by his assigned guards.

"You?" Kolton asked.

"This is dangerous, Gavin," Crew said. "I know he's your brother, but this is a fucking bomb you'll be dropping on the pack. He'll try to kill you."

"I'm fine with the danger. I can handle myself," Gavin said. "Once this gets out, it'll be easier for Kira's pack to swoop in and swallow the ones who break away from the Ninth."

"Stop. All of you," Kira said. "This isn't what I want. I don't want to steal another pack's territory or members. The main thing is to keep the Ninth Pack from attacking us. That's what the goal should be."

"That's what this will do," Gavin said eagerly.

"No, it won't," Kira said, shaking her head. "Not right away. It'll only cause more violence. More death and heartache. It's like August said—most of these people are innocent and simply following their alpha's lead. They're the ones who'll get hurt."

Gavin deflated. He didn't say anything, but I saw that she'd gotten through to him. He clearly hadn't thought about that. His single-minded determination to destroy his brother had blinded him.

Power blinded anyone at the top. It was the way of things. The ones in charge never thought about how their actions would affect those at the bottom.

"What's the plan, then?" I asked Kira. "You must have one. I know that look."

"A meeting," Kira said. "We bring this info. We meet with Jayson in private and show him that we had nothing to do with his father's murder. Once he sees the truth, he'll turn his attention to the Seventh Pack."

"Kira," Kolton said, looking exasperated, "how are we gonna get him to agree to that? He'll assume it's a trick."

She pointed at Gavin. "You use half of your plan. You'll deliver the message that we want to meet."

Gavin gazed at her dumbly for a few seconds, then, like a lightbulb clicking on, he smiled. "He thinks I'm dead."

"Exactly," Kira said. "Seeing you alive and well, and hearing that Wyatt and I are also alive, should surprise him enough to be intrigued. He'll want to meet with us. If nothing else, to figure out how the hell we survived and got off Bloodstone."

"I still think we should release the info, but I'll do as you ask," Gavin said.

"Good," Kira said. "Thank you, Gavin. The sooner you go, the better."

"Um...little problem there." Gavin nodding toward his guards.

"Let him go," Kira told the guards. "He's on a special mission for me."

The guard with the gun frowned. "Mr. Durst said not to let him out of our sight."

"I survived for three weeks on Bloodstone Island," she snapped back. "Do you really want to try me?"

The guards, seeing the fire in her eyes, relented and waved for Gavin to go. He said his thanks to Kira and even managed to give me a perfunctory half-nod before shifting and sprinting away.

Before Gavin was even out of sight, Crew addressed August. "You're pretty resourceful. Are you good at digging up dirt on everyone?"

"Maybe," August said, eyeing Crew. "What are you looking for, exactly?"

"My parents. Felix and Bianca Crew."

After a moment, August's eyes bulged in realization. "Holy shit. You're part of *that* Crew family? What do you think they're hiding?"

Crew adjusted his eye patch and shrugged. "Lots of stuff. Not sure how hard it will be to uncover it all. There's blackmail, corrupt associates, embezzlement...and murder, if I had to guess. I did some digging on my own a few years ago, but they caught me and destroyed everything I had. Gods only know how deep they've hidden it since then."

"Yeah, they're dangerous," August said. "That much is pretty well-known." He gave a big, toothy grin. "I like fucking with dangerous people. I'll get right on that. And don't worry too much. They can try to hide it, but me and my contacts are pretty damn good."

August headed back into his tent to get to work. Crew reached out to Chelsey, who took his hand.

"Once we've got transport figured out, I'll be heading to Chelsey's pack lands with her," Crew said.

"Really?" I asked, but didn't elaborate. The two looked to be on much better terms than they had been prior to Haven's destruction. In fact, Chelsey kept stealing adoring glances at Crew as we stood talking.

"Yeah. I want to make sure she's safe since we'll have to go past the Ninth Pack's lands and even part of the Fifth Pack's territory. I let her go once, and I'm not doing it again. Once she's settled in and safe, I'll come back and help you. You've done a lot for me and my people, and I need to repay the favor. I'll need to come back, anyway, to see what August digs up on my parents."

"I'm glad you want to take a stand against your parents," I said." I'm sure Mika feels exactly the same about the First Pack as you do. I'm from the Second originally, and I fucking hate it. Maybe we're the generation who will tear it all down. The official packs are already splintering. Another few nudges, and it might all come tumbling down."

"I guess we'll see," Crew said. "Anyway, I just wanted you to know. I didn't want you to be blindsided when I left. Eli will keep our people on point."

With that, Crew and Chelsey headed off. Eli drifted away to give orders to one of the scout groups preparing to head out on patrol.

As I stood there, looking around at it all, a feeling of awe fell over me. A couple of months ago, all this would have seemed like a fairytale. *The Reject Project* being canceled. The Tranquility Council and operatives found to be corrupt. Packs splintering. Riots, much less outright war? Was this real life? As surreal as it all looked on the outside, it was the way of the world, and somehow, we'd been the ones to start it all. Unwillingly, yes, but revolutions sometimes started with a mistake or a misunderstanding and snowballed.

"We need to get this sorted out," Kira said, pulling me from my thoughts. "We've got bigger fish to fry than Jayson."

She was still gazing off into the distance, but not in the direction Gavin had run. Instead, she was looking in the direction of Fangmore City.

"You're still thinking about Simon and Heline, aren't you?" I asked.

"Damn straight. They're the real threats here. Jayson is a speed bump."

If there was one thing I knew about Kira, it was that once she had a goal, she'd never stop until she'd reached it. She was determined in a way most people could never imagine. It was nearly impossible to change her mind once it was made up.

I loved that about her, but I worried that her mind still wasn't fully made up about me. A lot was happening, and I didn't want to lose what we had now that we were back in the *real world*.

Chapter 17 - Kira

I felt like I'd been kicked in the stomach. When Gavin sent us word that Jayson had agreed and told us the location to meet him, I'd almost called the whole thing off. Jayson wanted to meet on the mating grounds, where he'd rejected me weeks ago.

Had it only been weeks? It was difficult to keep time in a normal frame of reference. I'd gone through more in those weeks than some people did their entire lifetime. I was not the same person who'd been rejected in front of her entire pack. That wasn't hyperbole; I had completely changed since that day. Looking back on things, I'd built up all these walls and had kept almost everyone at arm's length because I thought I was a monster. If I was completely and totally honest with myself, I'd been a bitch. Harsh, unfeeling, and driven to the point of obsession. Now, what really mattered and what didn't were crystal-clear to me.

The idea that Jayson had chosen the meeting location as a *fuck you* to me was probably incorrect. This place was neutral ground, not on any pack territory at all and almost perfectly central to both our territories. It was as close to hallowed ground as a shifter could get, other than Heline's temples. It was actually the perfect place for a meeting like this, but that didn't change how I felt about it.

My father stood beside me. His arm was still in a sling, but his silver wound was almost healed. Standing next to him were Mom and Kolton. Wyatt, along with several of Dad's most trusted elders and his beta, waited behind us. Thus far, we hadn't seen any sign of the Ninth Pack's entourage. Dad and the others didn't have a great deal of faith in our ability to negotiate peace, though they'd been pleasantly shocked by the information August had dug up.

Dad had wanted to come with just his beta and a couple of others, but I'd held firm. Wyatt and I *needed* to be here—if only to prove to Jayson that we were indeed alive and home. Also, I knew it was probably best if I handled this directly rather than letting my dad do it. Jayson and I had history. Not great history, true, but more history than he had with my father.

"Are you okay?" Wyatt whispered from behind me.

"Sure. Fine."

"Whatever you say. Give the word if you aren't."

Truth was, I wasn't totally fine. As badly as I wanted to be here and deal with this, I was not looking forward to seeing Jayson again. After everything we'd learned, I was one hundred percent sure we were never meant to be together. I'd never had any real feelings for him, and I was now very much in love with Wyatt. The thought of seeing Jayson walk out into this clearing made my stomach somersault.

If this didn't go well, Jayson and his men might decide to fight. Maybe they'd look at the situation and decide it was better to take out the entire Durst family. That would crush our pack.

It was all so tiresome—the fighting and constant battle to survive. I prayed we could get this done without any violence, but I had to be ready for anything, which irritated me to no end.

"Where are they?" Dad grumbled. "We've been here for twenty minutes now."

I sighed and glanced around, searching for some sign. "He's late on purpose. This is a negotiation tactic. Make us wait, stress us out."

"That doesn't sound very honorable," Mom said.

"Kira won't be rattled," Wyatt said, leaning forward to wink at me. "She's got this."

"Thanks." I smiled at him and rubbed his shoulder before he leaned back, retaking his position behind me.

Mom and Dad watched the interaction between us. Over the last day, they'd slowly started to warm to the idea of Wyatt and me being together, but I could still see the disappointment in their eyes. As much as I loved them, they were stuck in that old-fashioned view of the world. They would never want me to be with someone outside an official pack, thinking it was beneath me and inappropriate. This lukewarm—and at times icy—reception they were giving Wyatt annoyed the fuck out of me. After everything Wyatt had done for us? After everything his pack had done for us? They should be treating him better.

"Finally," Kolton muttered.

Through the trees, a small procession of Ninth Pack members came into view, Jayson in the lead. Gavin walked behind his brother, and he looked pissed that he had to be here. If it had been up to him, he'd probably rather be on this side of the clearing with us.

"Son of a bitch," Jayson sneered as his group filed into the clearing. "Looks like baby brother wasn't spinning fake tales. You two are alive."

"I told you I wasn't lying," Gavin said through gritted teeth.

Jayson didn't even look at his brother. "Yeah, still surprising. You've always been full of shit."

Gavin kept his head down and clenched his fists, but didn't retort.

"Hello, Jayson," I said. "I hope you're doing well." Might as well start things off as cordially as possible.

Jayson ran his tongue across his teeth and eyed me warily. "You know, I was shocked when they put you on *The Reject Project*. I bet being *pretend*-famous really went to your head, didn't it? I didn't watch much of the show, but I wonder if you screwed with the other guys like you screwed with me."

Gods, he was insufferable. "Jayson, I never screwed with you," I said.

Jayson held up a hand, smiling. "You know, I say I didn't watch, but I did see the episode where you talked about how much you loved Wyatt. All that show did was prove that I was right. You were fucking him behind my back. Once a whore, always a whore."

"You watch your fucking mouth," Dad growled, taking a step forward.

Grabbing his shirt, I tugged him back. Wyatt was growling and muttering curses under his breath behind me.

"Let him get it out, Dad," I said, completely unperturbed. "Maybe being childish for a few minutes will clear his head." I glanced back at Jayson. "Can we get down to business? This stroll down memory lane has been lovely, but we have things to discuss."

Jayson's sneer turned into a grin. "Ah, yes. I should have known you'd come crawling back to me."

I wanted to be professional, to stay stoic, but those words broke me. I laughed so hard, I almost doubled over to catch my breath.

Jayson's smile morphed into a frown. Becoming pack alpha had somehow inflated his ego even more than it had already been.

"What is so fucking funny?" he demanded.

Wiping tears from my cheeks, I straightened, trying to regain my composure. "That was a good joke. You know, after everything I've been through, I can't believe I ever shed a tear over you rejecting me. It's kinda surreal to think I went on that show because of *you*. Ugh." I shook my head. "I spent five years forcing myself to believe you were my actual soul mate or something, when deep down, I *knew* our fated mate connection was wrong. I never felt anything for you, Jayson. Not an ounce of love or respect. Shit, I never even liked you that much. You're pretty obnoxious, and it appears power has made that even worse."

Jayson gaped at me, then seemed to find his voice. "You're as bitchy as ever. In fact, the only time I don't remember you being bitchy was when I caught you in that parking lot with Wyatt's cock down your throat."

"Unfortunately," I said with a sickly sweet smile, "we never actually got that far."

"You'll watch your mouth when you talk to my daughter," Mom spat at Jayson, heat rising in her cheeks.

"Yeah," Wyatt said. "Unless you're not planning on leaving this clearing alive?"

Jayson's eyes flashed in anger at the sound of Wyatt's voice. "Is that a threat, lone wolf? Is it?" Jayson rubbed his palms together greedily. "Because if so, I'd love to show you what a real alpha can do in a fight. Really show everyone how *pathetic* you unofficial wolves are."

"As everyone knows," Dad said, interrupting the threats, "Kira was injured and drugged. She never did anything that—"

"Enough," I said, raising my voice to be heard. "Jayson, we know who killed your father, and it wasn't anyone from our pack. We have proof."

Jayson stared at me for several seconds, then scoffed. "I don't care about whatever lies you want to tell. Why would I? All I care about is increasing my pack's standing and territory. We'll absorb yours first, then maybe the Twelfth or the Tenth, and prepare ourselves for when the upper packs eventually come for us."

"Are you being serious?" I asked, my annoyance building by the second. "You *should* care who ordered his death. What if they come for you next?"

The smile slipped from his face, his eyes boring into me icily. "Another threat?" He straightened and addressed his entourage. "This was a waste of time."

His men had grown restless, obviously agreeing with their alpha. Behind me, the members of my pack stirred nervously. This was going sideways fast. I'd really believed Jayson would be concerned with his self-preservation, but that didn't seem to be the case.

He was acting like he was above any danger. Above all of us.

Jayson pointed to Wyatt. "First thing we'll do is hunt down your little pack of unofficial mongrels. I'll save you for last, Wyatt. I'll make sure you watch all of them die. Then we'll take you out."

I took two steps toward Jayson, eyes blazing with rage. "You've never acknowledged it, but I'm an alpha, too. I *will* defend what's mine at all costs, Wyatt's pack included. If I could fight through the hell of Bloodstone Island and survive, I think I can handle your little pack of pussies like nothing."

Jayson opened his mouth, but I cut him off. "This is a make-or-break moment. You understand that, right? Either make peace with me and the Eleventh Pack now so we can move on and survive this war, or be an idiot. Keep fighting for nothing. Your pack will end up broken, your packmates dead or scattered, and you with a hollow throne to sit on. I am not messing around. Look into my eyes and tell me I'm lying."

Jayson considered my words, and for the first time since I'd known him, he actually looked impressed. "I have to say, you surprised me on the show," he said. "Finding out you weren't latent after all? Seeing that gorgeous wolf of yours reveal itself? Very impressive indeed." Musing to himself, he said, "It would be really nice to have a second alpha around to help manage things in my pack. What if..." He looked at me with suddenly hungry eyes. "What if we made up? The two of us form an alliance, and you *finally* take me as your mate. As you said, they're all fake, anyway. We can do whatever we want."

"The fuck you can," Wyatt growled, taking several steps forward and then shifting. He stood at my feet, snarling and glaring at Jayson.

The Ninth Pack contingent stepped back, nervously looking to their alpha for orders. But Jayson was still eyeing me, wholly unconcerned with Wyatt.

"What do you say, Kira?" he cooed.

After everything that had happened, all we'd told him, his only takeaway was power. He was too blind by all the stuff he thought was important to see the truth. With one word, I could start a fight that would end with bloodshed.

Instead, I snorted a laugh and stroked Wyatt's fur. "Jayson, if we'd been on the show together and by some weird twist of fate you and I became the last two contestants? I'd ask Heline to kill me rather than mate with you." I shook my head in disgust. "Peace talks are over. I gave you a chance to end this the right way, the only way that wouldn't end badly for you. We could have done this quietly. Too late." I turned to Gavin. "Tell them their alpha doesn't give a damn that the Seventh Pack and the Tranquility Council orchestrated their last alpha's assassination."

"What?" one of Jayson's men gasped. "Are you serious?"

Jayson flew into a rage. "Did I fucking say you could talk?"

The man glared at Jayson, as did some of the others. Maybe things in the Ninth Pack weren't as good as they seemed on the outside.

"It's true," Gavin said. "Jayson never investigated. All he did was point fingers like a child. Your alpha was murdered, and he didn't—"

"Enough!" Jayson snapped. "We're done here. Let's go."

Jayson strode away, and his men trudged along behind him. Several looked back at us, doubt in their eyes. If I had to guess, Jayson might have to watch his back in the coming days and weeks. The information we'd just dropped would spread quickly.

"Good luck, Jayson," I called sweetly.

He kept walking and didn't acknowledge my words.

It wasn't over between our packs. Regardless of how things went, we'd probably end up facing off again, unless a miracle happened. Jayson obviously had no intention of doing anything peacefully. The fact that he'd had the audacity to try to get me back when I was obviously with Wyatt made me want to laugh again.

"Well, sweetie," Mom said when they were out of earshot. "I'd never want to besmirch the goddess Heline's choices for mates, but I'm really glad you don't have to bed down with that walking pile of dogshit."

"Same, Mom," I said. "Same."

Chapter 18 - Wyatt

As Jayson walked off into the forest, my eyes burned into his back. Right before he shifted to run home, Jayson glanced over his shoulder at me. He was too far away for me to make out any emotion on his face, but I told myself there was a hint of fear there.

As there should be.

Once they'd shifted and sprinted off, I huffed out a breath through my nostrils. I wasn't scared of a fight, but Kira was set against more bloodshed. Jayson had been the exact version of himself I knew he'd be. He hadn't even tried to be charming or affable. Even greasy salesmen put the charm on to trick buyers.

But Jayson hadn't come here to negotiate peace. He'd come to see me and Kira, and try to get under our skin.

If there was anything about this meeting that put me into a good mood, though, it was the way Kira had refused Jayson's half-assed attempt to woo her back. When she'd rebuffed him, it had been all I could do not to smile. Not only had Kira told the world she loved me, but she'd rejected her *fated* mate in front of her family once and for all, turning the tables on Jayson and making sure everyone knew she wanted to be with me.

"Let's get out of here. I hate this place, and it's getting worse by the minutes," Kira said.

"Yes, uh, I can see what you mean," her dad said, still glaring off into the forest.

Our entourage shifted and padded toward the trees. Kira's father followed his people, limping slightly because of his injured foreleg. When Kira and her mother shifted and fell in behind him, I marveled at Kira in her wolf form. I followed, staying at the rear in case Jayson or one of his goons got any ideas about a sneak attack. While I ran, I watched Kira sprint through the forest, running free in her home land. Hopefully, she was enjoying it as much as it looked like she did. She deserved it.

She'd spent years suppressing an integral part of her and had been understandably miserable. Thinking about doing the same thing to myself made my heart hurt. I cursed Simon for subjecting her to experimentation, but I was happy that she now had access to this most basic and primal part of her soul.

Once we were far enough away from the mating grounds to be safe, I decided it was time to play. Running up beside Kira, I nipped at her flank. Never breaking her stride, Kira turned her bright golden eyes on me and broke off from the main pack to follow me. We sprinted through an open field ahead of the others before tumbling together and wrestling. If Kira still held any residual stress or anger from the showdown with Jayson, she wasn't showing it. If anything, she seemed more at ease and happy than ever.

Instead of leading her to her parents' house, we continued playing and moving in the direction of my unofficial pack lands that Kira's dad had granted us years ago. My house was there, along with several others—remnants of an abandoned neighborhood the Eleventh Pack didn't use anymore. Kira's father had given us the land not only because it was unused, but also because it was as far from the other home sites as possible.

My pack was tolerated, not *beloved*—at least, not by most. Even Kira's father's hospitality only ran so far. We didn't mind, though. A home was what you made it.

When we reached the wooded front yard of my house, I shifted back. Kira did the same and gazed around at the place. My nearest neighbor was August, but his house was nearly two hundred yards to the east and hidden in the trees.

"No wonder we stopped using this settlement," Kira said. "It's in the middle of nowhere."

"It's quiet, and I can commune with nature," I said with a smile.

"Commune with nature? Really?"

"All the trees and shade help with the electric bill, too. That's the main attraction," I said with a shrug.

"That sounds more like it. You know, I've rarely visited this area. I think I've only been to your house once or twice when I was looking for Kolton." She shook her head. "My own pack lands, and there are still areas I haven't explored."

"There's lots to see." I opened the front door and waved her inside. "Come on in."

The house had that musty scent that developed when it had been closed up for a while, as though the home itself had begun to forget you and taken on its own scent. I started opening windows to air the place out.

"I'd like you to sleep here with me," I blurted out before I could stop myself.

Kira chuckled. "Wow. You get right to the point, don't you?"

"All I mean is, I got used to you sleeping beside me in Haven. Last night was lonely." I shrugged helplessly.

Kira had spent last evening in her childhood room while I'd come home. I'd tossed and turned most of the night, wanting Kira's warmth beside me. I did *not* want to spend tonight in the same way.

Kira's smile faded. "Yeah. I barely slept last night without you next to me."

She moved around, studying the few items I'd decorated the place with—a painting of a rising moon, pictures of me and Kolton when we were teenagers, photos of me with my unofficial pack mates. Kira stopped in front of the display case and fingered the medals I'd received in the Tranquility Ops. Watching her move about my home, touching my things and looking so comfortable doing it, turned me on more than it should have.

Kira glanced at me as I walked over, gasping when I pulled her in for a kiss. She pressed herself against me, holding me tight as my tongue slipped past her lips.

After a few moments, I broke the kiss, but kept my lips a breath away from hers. "You telling Jayson to go fuck himself was one of the hottest things I've ever seen you do."

"Really?" Mischief glimmered in her eyes. "I'm pretty sure you've seen me do some naughty things."

"True. Still, I wish you'd told him off years ago. You always deserved someone better."

Kira gazed into my eyes for a few seconds, her expression turning thoughtful. "Did you mean what you said in Haven? About not bothering to find our *real* fated mates? Staying together? Choosing each other?"

"I meant every word of it." I laughed. "I've been choosing you for years. I just never admitted it to myself. I don't regret a moment of it, though. Not even when you drove me crazy."

Kira's face broke into a smile, and she slid her hands up my back. "I think it's the same for me. I've been choosing you, and now I see the truth was buried under all the shit in my head all this time. I kept pushing you away when all I really wanted was to admit to myself I wanted you close." She gazed deep into my eyes. "Wyatt, I want to be with you forever. No matter what we're up against."

She kissed me, but just as suddenly, she tensed and pulled away.

"You thought of something," I said.

"I can't help but think about what Kolton said. About you becoming his brother-in-law. It was…unexpected."

"Does that upset you?"

"No, I just…we don't have to make a permanent claim on each other to be with each other, right? We can belong to each other without the other stuff. I know it's a big commitment."

Putting a hand to her cheek, I looked into her eyes. "I want a permanent claim. We're together now, and I don't doubt my feelings. I never will." I kissed her again, tenderly this time. "I want it all. I want Kolton as my brother-in-law. I want your family to be mine. I want to claim you and have a mating ceremony—the whole nine yards. As long as you want that, too."

Her eyes grew misty, and she nodded her head fervently. "I want it, too. I want you."

Without taking my eyes off hers, I said, "Then come and take me."

With a hungry growl, Kira kissed me again. The heat of her body pressing into mine made my head spin. The passion with which she kissed me burned through my blood. It was like our souls were being fused together as the kiss deepened.

My cock throbbed, straining against my pants. I *needed* her with such desperation, I thought I'd go out of my mind if I didn't have her soon. Butterflies swarmed in my stomach. Was this really about to happen?

Stumbling backward, not taking my lips from hers, I led her to my bedroom. Kira's hands fumbled at my belt, finally unbuckling it, and her hands slipped into my underwear, cupping my cock. I gasped as her cool fingers wrapped around me.

"Already? That didn't take long," Kira remarked a little breathlessly.

She worked at my jeans as I pulled my shirt off and tossed it aside. Once she had my pants and underwear off, she pushed me back onto the bed. She trailed her fingers over my shaft, and my breath hitched. I reached out for her, but she gave me a teasing smile and stepped back.

Resting my weight on my elbows, I drank in the sight of her as she stripped for me. With each layer of clothing she removed, my cock grew even harder. Eventually, she stood, nude and beautiful, eyes locked on mine. She massaged her breasts, pinching her nipples gently, and the sight of it almost made me come.

Kneeling before me, she looked up with hooded eyes. "You look delicious," she whispered as she wrapped her hand around me.

My dick throbbed and nearly turned purple as she squeezed gently, then flicked her tongue across the head.

"Fuck," I hissed through gritted teeth.

She slid the tip of her tongue across the tip of my cock, flicking playfully around the hole. My heart raced as I forced myself to lay still and not thrust myself into her mouth.

"Do you want to feel my mouth?" she asked, dragging the nails of her free hand down my thigh.

"Yeah. I do."

She took me in her mouth, her tongue wet, slick, and hot as it glided over me. Gripping my sheets, I watched her move up and down on me. The wet, smacking sounds of my cock going in and out of her mouth were the most erotic thing I'd ever heard.

She worked me slow, so achingly slow. All the way down until I grazed the back of her throat, then back again. I rocked my hips in time with her mouth. Sensing my desire, she curled her hand around me and stroked in time to the movements of her mouth, her other hand cupping and massaging my balls.

"Kira," I rasped, "you're gonna make me come if you don't stop that."

She pulled her mouth away and looked up at me, still stroking with her hand. "Isn't that what you want?"

My mind was so consumed with lust, I couldn't think straight. "I do, but…"

Kira winked at me. "You're a big, strong man. I'm sure you have a couple rounds in you."

"Fuck," I moaned as the warmth of her mouth enveloped me again.

She moved even faster, tilting her eyes up to look at me as she glided her lips and tongue along my cock.

Her eyes held a command I couldn't deny her. She wanted me to finish. Wanted to see and feel me come.

I let go. Gasping, my hands curled into fists, bunching up the fabric of the sheets. Pulsing waves of pleasure burst through my balls.

Kira hummed happily, the vibrations of it sending me into a frenzy.

"Gods, Kira," I groaned, and the final vestiges of my climax spurted out of me into her mouth.

With one last languid stroke of her tongue, Kira released me with a slight *pop*. "Fun, wasn't it?" She patted my thigh. "My turn."

I was sweaty and still shaking from my orgasm as she slithered up my body and hovered over my face. With a hungry snarl, I grabbed her hips and yanked her down, forcing her to sit on my face.

"Fuck," Kira moaned as my tongue plunged into her. "Holy fuck. That feels amazing." She ground her hips against my face. Cool, insistent fingers ran through my hair, and she looked down at me while I ate her out. "Yes, baby. Fuck me with your tongue."

I slid my tongue across her folds, then closed my mouth over her clit and sucked hard. Kira let out a low cry of pleasure. Working a hand under her, I slid two fingers into her pussy, delighting in the squeal that came from her. My cock was already stiffening again.

Kira's hands twisted at my hair as she thrust her hips to my face, grinding her clit against my mouth. "I'm so close. Make me come, Wyatt."

She panted, her hips moving even faster. I flicked my tongue over that sensitive nub as I curled my fingers in a come-hither motion. I knew I'd hit the right spot when she groaned deeply. With my free hand, I reached up and clutched her breast, pinching her nipple.

When she came, her whole body shuddered against me, her breasts bouncing, her mouth open in ecstasy. Unwilling to stop, I fucked her with my fingers, her thighs twitching and shuddering on either side of my head.

Finally spent, Kira swung her leg over and settled on her knees next to me. She ran a finger across my chest.

"I told you you'd be ready," she said.

"How could I not be?" I grabbed her, flipping her to her back.

Lust flared in her half-lidded eyes. "I want to feel you inside me when I claim you."

"And I want to be inside you," I said as I thrust the full length of my cock into the hot, wet confines of her pussy.

Her back arched, eyes rolling back in ecstasy. We moved together, finding a rhythm as natural as it was ancient. With each thrust, a renewed sense of urgency flooded me. I was desperate to come again, to have her shatter into ecstasy below me.

"Come with me, Kira. I want you to come again."

She slid a hand between us, rubbing at her clit, the veins in her neck showing as her face went red with the exertion. "I'm gonna come, Wyatt. Claim me while I come. Please, baby."

At her words, my inner wolf, already ecstatic at the moment, became uncontrollable. A deep, satisfied growl rumbled in my chest as I lowered my face to the soft spot between her shoulder and neck. I didn't stop thrusting, my movements growing erratic as another orgasm raged closer with each movement.

As my lips touched her skin, hers touched my neck in that same spot on my shoulder. Peeling my lips back, I leaned forward and sank my teeth into her flesh. An instant later, the sweet, sharp pain of Kira's teeth pierced my flesh.

The pain sent us both over the edge. We cried out inarticulate screams of pleasure as something more than a simple orgasm rocked through our bodies. The claiming connection was almost more than either of us could handle.

As my hips spasmed and my cock twitched within her, Kira shuddered. Something else was happening between us, something unlike anything I'd ever experienced in my life. Already, our connection had surged in strength. I could almost *feel* her orgasm in my body as she came, and it rippled and mingled with mine. From the way she gasped and whimpered beneath me, Kira felt something similar.

"Fuck!" I roared. "I'm still coming."

I slammed into her again, every thrust sending a powerful wave of pleasure through me. Kira's hips rose to meet mine, and all that existed was her and me.

When we finally collapsed in absolute exhaustion, I tried to think how long our climax lasted. Ten minutes? An hour? I had no clue. All I knew was that my body felt like it had lightning running through it. Pulling Kira close, I wrapped her in a hug.

"Can you feel that?" I said, still shivering in postcoital bliss.

She nodded her head, her hair tickling my chest. "I've never...never felt anything like it."

As I held her, I did my best not to freak out. My senses were much more vibrant and heightened. I could hear more, smell more, sense more than ever before. At the same time, I caught glimpses and flashes of Kira's emotions. My inner wolf mewled happily, and for the first time in my life, he and I were complete. Until this moment, I'd never known he was so hollow inside, so desperate to find the one thing he longed for.

In a flash, I understood, and Kira did as well. I could feel her surprise fluttering through my head like an echo at the back of my mind.

A smile spread across my face. Leaning up on an elbow, I looked at her. "We *were* meant to be together," I said, then laughed. Had I ever been this happy in my life? I doubted it.

"I think you're right," Kira said, her voice barely above a whisper.

Swallowing hard, I went on. "This is why I always got freaked out if I thought you were in danger. Why I was desperate to save you, even though I know you can handle yourself." Another thought occurred to me. "And why my reaction was stronger than anyone else's when Von gave you that potion that forced you into heat." I trailed my fingers along her collarbone and across her breasts. "And why *this* is always so intense. Sex with you is like a life-changing event. Every single time. I've been trying to protect my true other half without ever knowing it."

Kira sat up, looking excited, happy, and confused all at once. "It explains a lot. Like when I lost control and shifted for the first time in a decade. When you were hurt and about to die. My inner wolf exploded forth. She wouldn't allow me to keep her suppressed when you were in danger."

She ran her hands through her hair and stared off into space, the look of confusion slowly erasing her joy. "How is this possible?" she asked. "How the fuck did we never know? All this time, and neither of us realized we were fated mates?"

"I don't know," I said, and I honestly didn't.

"Long ago, shifters found their fated mates naturally," Kira said. "Organically. It was up to chance instead of bloodwork. People would instantly *know* when they laid eyes on and caught the scent of the one they were meant to be with. We've known each other all this time, spent years annoying each other to death, yet we still missed this?"

"I don't care about all that," I said. "All I care about is that we belong together. I have no answers, but what I do know is that you're all mine and I'm all yours. I've never been happier in my life. Let's focus on that. Okay?"

Kira's radiant smile was the most beautiful thing I'd ever seen. She nodded. "Yeah. Okay." She bit her lower lip and glanced down between my legs again. "Ready for round three?"

"Bet your ass." I laughed and pulled her on top of me.

The rest of the night passed in an indescribable state of bliss. We made love again, this time feeling each other's emotions with every touch and stroke and kiss. It was mind-bending in the best possible way. We fell asleep, our limbs tangled together, only to wake a few hours later and make love again. It was like we couldn't get enough of it, that feeling of being coupled with the one person you were meant to be with. It was like a drug that made us giddy, and we couldn't stop.

The next morning, I woke to the echo of Kira's emotions. She was already awake and thinking. We shared the same blossoming wonder and pleasant shock of finding our fated mates, but something had her worried.

"What's wrong?" I asked, rolling over to find her sitting on the edge of the bed.

She chuckled. "I knew you were awake," she said, tapping her head with a finger. "I could *sense* it. This is weird."

"You didn't answer my question. What's wrong?"

"Don't worry about it. It's dumb."

"Nothing in that pretty little head can be dumb. I can tell you're worried about something, so spill it."

She grunted in frustration. "Ugh, it's my parents—and everyone else. What are they going to think about this? What are they going to say and think when they find out we've mated? It's fucking stupid. I talk this big game about tearing down the old ways, but I'm still worried my family won't approve of me being with a lone wolf. Like I said, it's dumb."

The fact that anything was keeping her from being completely blissful and happy irritated me. Sensations bounced around my mind, but before I could say anything to argue, Kira laughed.

"I felt that," she said, tapping a finger on my forehead. "You're irritated. I should have known you're the type to wake up grumpy."

I rolled my eyes and wrapped an arm around her, pulling her back down to the bed. I kissed her, then sat up to gaze down on her.

"Here's my thought," I said. "This new little empathetic connection we have needs more, shall we say, exploration? Let's see if we can create a feedback loop of pleasure." I slipped and hand under the covers and slipped my fingertips across her belly. "We can see if I can get you to orgasm over and over and over until you literally can't think of anything else. Nothing can worry you then, can it?"

At the back of my mind, I could sense Kira found the idea appealing. The thought of orgasming until she was limp with pleasure turned her on. She was on the verge of telling me to do it, but she pulled back at the last instant.

"No. Nope. Gotta be grown-ups," she said, though she looked disappointed by her own words. "We have important things to do. Jayson might attack us at any time. We need to get everyone ready."

"Ugh," I groaned. "Why do you have to be the adult? All I want is to fuck your brains out all day." I sat up. "You know, usually newly mated wolves get a week or two to be together until their hormones and pheromones calm down."

"I know. Too bad we're at war," Kira said, standing to get dressed.

"Fine," I pouted. "But no promises I won't pull your pants down and bend you over at an inopportune time." I held my hands up in surrender. "You've been warned, so you can't get mad at me."

She threw my pants at my face in response. I snatched them and watched her grab her stuff.

"Don't bother with all that," I said. "Check my closet. I have a surprise for you."

Kira frowned at me before opening the closet door. Inside, two outfits hung side by side. Tranquility Ops gear—one fitted for me, the other for her.

"What?" Kira turned to look at me. "How the hell did this get here?"

I shrugged. "When you got fired, they didn't even let you clean out your locker. I snuck in and got the rest of your stuff. I forgot about it until I came home and saw it. I figure that's a better outfit for a war than a T-shirt and blue jeans."

Kira smiled and ran a finger over the outfit, which was fortified with Kevlar, enchanted seams, fire-retardant spells, hardshell elbow-and-knee pads, and more. The perfect thing to wear into battle. Snippets of thought fluttered through her mind as she looked at the uniform. Feeling and hearing her thoughts was still so new to me—new, but amazing.

Her thoughts toward the gear was bittersweet. She'd missed wearing it, but was also angry about how and why it had been taken from her. I hoped she noticed my own thoughts slipping into her mind, telling her she'd never deserved to be fired, that she had been one of the best operatives the TO had ever recruited. She was amazing in so many ways, and I hated that anyone had ever made her feel like she didn't belong.

Her fingers lingered over the Tranquility Council patch on the chest. Anger swirled in her mind, hot and raging, and its intensity surprised me. Her smile faded a bit, then she tore the patch off, the *rip* of the Velcro the only sound in the room.

She tossed the patch on the floor and began to dress. Once she was in the uniform, her anger faded. What remained was determination and a reborn sense of purpose. I couldn't help but smile as I dressed in my own gear.

Kira glanced over her shoulder as she tied her boots and grinned at me. "I can feel you in my head. See anything you like?"

"Always," I said.

Once we were ready, the first stop of our morning was to check in with the border patrols. We arrived at Crew's camp an hour later, but he was nowhere to be seen.

"He and Chelsey headed out right before dawn," Eli said when we asked about him.

"Sounds good," I said. "Not surprising they'd want to leave soon, especially after the shitshow yesterday with the Ninth Pack. Things will get interesting fast, if I had to guess."

"Yeah," Eli said. "He was worried about getting Chelsey home safe." The fallen angel glanced over her shoulder, and for the first time since I'd known her, she looked a little uncomfortable. "Um, Kira, your brother came by early this morning to check on things. He, uh...well, we talked a bit. He thought you might already be here and was looking for you. He headed back home about thirty minutes ago."

Kira, noticing the same thing I did, smiled at Eli. "Is he okay?"

"Oh, he's great. Very driven and brave. Sensitive, too. I like that." Eli blinked, her perfect alabaster skin tinged pink. "I mean, in a fighter. In war, I mean. It's good to be sensitive to the needs of your soldiers. That's what I mean."

Kira nodded, stifling her laughter. "Uh-huh."

"Well, I need to go check on the patrols," Eli said. "I'll talk to you all later."

As she walked away, I leaned down to whisper to Kira, "Have you ever seen an angel that flustered? I didn't think they had it in them."

"Come on," Kira said, tugging at my shirt. "Let's find Kolton."

Another hour of running, and we were back at Kira's parents' house. Kolton stood outside, a cup of coffee in hand, talking to a few members of his pack and my unofficial pack who'd been tabbed as security for the Durst home.

"Morning," Kira said as we walked up.

Kolton glanced up, and when he saw us, he froze. His eyes darted to the bite marks on our necks, and the cup of coffee tumbled from his fingers, crashing on the ground.

"What the fuck?" he cried out, a broad smile splitting his face.

Before we could answer, he rushed forward, nearly tackling us as he threw his arms around both of us.

"You have some shit timing," Kolton said. "Doing this in the middle of a war is crazy, but I'm happy for you. I think I might cry."

I could sense Kira's embarrassment as she pushed her brother off. "If you're gonna cry," Kira said, "wait until Eli is around. Apparently, she likes sensitive types like you."

Kolton's smile vanished. "Huh? What do you mean?" He glanced around, then back at us. "Uh, did she really say that?"

The two siblings continued to poke fun at and tease each other. While they did, I glanced up at the house. In the big bay window overlooking the front year, Kira's parents stood, glaring down at us.

A knot of worry filled my stomach. They did not look pleased. There was no hiding the marks on our necks. Whatever reaction I'd been hoping for was obviously not going to happen. This would not end well. In their minds, I was the *last* person they'd have chosen to be their daughter's mate.

But I'd be damned if I let them rain on Kira's parade and ruin her happiness. While Kolton and Kira continued talking, I hurried inside to discuss things with her parents. Maybe I could smooth this over before they ruined what should be the happiest day of their daughter's life.

"Morning, Mr. and Mrs. Durst. I trust you slept well," I said as I stepped into the kitchen.

Her dad strode toward me, his finger shaking as he pointed at Kira and Kolton through the window. "I suppose you're gonna come in here with some crock of shit about *asking for my blessing*? I hope not since, apparently, it's already too late."

Kira was mine, and I was hers. Her father or not, I would protect what was mine. I leaned into the alpha side of my personality and took a step toward her dad.

Not threatening, but still aggressive enough to get my point across.

"I'm not *asking* for anything. What I'm doing is telling you that you had better watch yourselves when it comes to my mate. I'm not about to let you give her shit about our relationship."

"You watch your mouth, young man," her mom hissed.

I held up a finger. "No. I won't. You two have always put too much on her. Her whole life, she's kept her head down and done what was best for you. For the *pack*." I sneered at the word. "She's done everything she could to bring honor to the pack. She was moments away from mating with that piece of shit Jayson Fell. *Everyone* saw what an awful person he was. Yet, you two were too fucking happy to make an alliance with the Ninth Pack, even if it meant disregarding your daughter's feelings."

Kira's mother flinched. The truth struck deep, wounding her more than it did Mr. Durst.

"You two have always hated each other," her dad said, his voice growing testy. "Once you all got on that show, you screwed with her head with that act you put on—"

"Stop," I interjected. "You can't even *begin* to comprehend what Kira and I have been through together. You can't fathom what your daughter really feels. If you think your daughter is stupid enough to fall for some guy playing a game on a TV show, then..." I shook my head in disgust. "You don't know her at all."

"Well, regardless of how Kira feels now, you have to see what you've done," her mother said. "If you really loved her, you should have just gone away. Being mated to a lone wolf will destroy any social standing she has. You should have taken that into account."

"Exactly," Mr. Durst said. "You ruined her life, Wyatt. You've pissed on everything she worked so hard for on that show."

My fists clenched and unclenched at my sides. "You two should worry more about your daughter's happiness than fucking pack politics."

He snarled. "The packs are what makes our society what it is."

"They're the worst fucking thing on the planet," I hissed. "You're too blinded by tradition to see it. They're a damned cancer. All you need to understand is that your daughter will be loved, protected, and cherished for the rest of her life. If you can't be happy about that, then maybe you should look in the mirror and figure out what kind of parents you really are. Are the packs, the traditions, the social standing more important than your children's happiness?" Letting my inner alpha wolf have even more control, I sent out waves of furious pheromones and rose to my full height, glaring at them. "No one is going to make my mate feel like she's not good enough. Not Jayson, not her parents, not even fucking Heline herself. Not on my watch."

Kira's parents no longer looked angry. They were clutching at each other, eyes wide. As my rage faded a bit, I realized they were both startled at the power I possessed. I was even more dominant than Kira's father, who was the lead alpha of a pack. They'd never noticed it in all the years I'd been hanging around, had instead looked at me as some lowly, random lone wolf—their son's ragged friend and a thorn in Kira's side. The pack hierarchy said lone wolves would never and could never be as dominant as a pack wolf, much less a pack alpha. And here I was, showing them that, yet again, their traditions were built on shit.

I suppressed a grin, noticing they both appeared grudgingly impressed.

Chapter 19 - Kira

Kolton and I joked and laughed for several minutes until I began to sense something was wrong. A nagging tickle at the back of my mind told me Wyatt was nervous, then upset, and now he was pissed.

"Hang on," I said, putting a hand on my brother's shoulder. "I need to go inside. Something's wrong."

Kolton's face fell as he glanced at the window. "Crap. Not good."

I followed his gaze and saw Dad, finger pointed at Wyatt, face red with anger, saying something to him I couldn't hear.

"Son of a bitch," I muttered and headed up the steps.

Inside the foyer, Wyatt's voice rang out loud and clear. Defending me, telling my parents how much I'd sacrificed for them and the pack. I stayed out of sight, listening, feeling his emotions in my own mind. I couldn't remember anyone ever standing up for me like that.

It warmed my heart. I *loved* my parents, but Wyatt was right—they had to understand the world was changing. Things wouldn't continue the way they had before.

My whole life, I'd thought I wasn't good enough for my pack. Not worthy of my family's legacy. A broken shifter and a monster. Wyatt had seen beyond all that and showed me I was more. He'd always protected me, even when I didn't want him to. I'd been a brat and a bitch to him, but his loyalty had never wavered. I was lucky to have him as my mate.

Leaving Kolton by the door, I stepped into the kitchen and cleared my throat. My parents were almost cowering under Wyatt's fierce glare. When they noticed me, they almost flinched, and I saw shame on their faces.

Wyatt spun in surprise, shoulders relaxing at the sight of me. "Kira? Hey. Did you..." He trailed away, and his worry seeped into me.

"Yeah, I heard. Most of it, anyway."

The shame on my parents' faces deepened.

"Mom? Dad?" I said. "I will always look out for you and the pack. I'll always love you, but no matter how this war goes, and no matter what the future holds, I choose Wyatt because I love him. All of us really need to stop looking at lone wolves and unofficial packs as this stain on society. They're all people who have been wronged by the official packs in some way. They've been betrayed, pushed out, ostracized, or threatened with their lives."

Dad shook his head. "Sweetheart, I understand what you're saying, but when you're older, you'll see. It's about honor. If these things happened, then these wolves should go to the council and—"

"The same council that took money from Seventh Pack to kill Jayson's father? The council that fired me because some bigwig was related to the alpha of the Ninth Pack? *That* council?" I asked.

Dad lowered his eyes, staying silent.

"I've thought a lot about it," I said. "After some introspection, I plan on joining Wyatt's unofficial pack. The official packs are going to splinter and fall apart, anyway."

"What?" Mom gasped, putting a hand to her chest. "They will *not*."

Dad looked even more horrified at my pronouncement. "You think the packs will splinter? No, there's no way. The pack system has stood resolute for centuries. A single war wouldn't change that."

"This isn't a regular war, Dad," I snapped. "This is bigger. Yes, the pack system has been around a long time, and that's exactly why I think it's doomed. The world revolves around change and evolution—the packs are a relic, unchanged since the Middle Ages. It's time, and it's already happening. We've had reports of several packs already fracturing."

Wyatt looked at me with a mix of surprise and excitement. He took my hand and grinned. "Are you sure about this?"

"I am."

His face clouded, and the smile slipped a bit. "It's a big change. Things won't be like they are here."

He was afraid I'd regret my choice. I could see it in his face, sense it in his mind.

"I know what I'm doing," I said. "We're mates now. From now on, wherever you are, I'll be there, and vice versa. Forever. Or as long as we survive," I added. "Speaking of which, we need to go get ready to fend off the Ninth Pack instead of arguing about things that have already been decided."

"She's right," Kolton said from behind us.

When I turned to look at him, he had his eyes locked on our parents, a sad determination on his face.

"I'm happy for Kira and Wyatt. You two," he said pointing at our parents, "are going on and on about how *great* the hierarchy is, and all it sounds like to me is a bunch of propaganda from upper pack leaders."

Dad flinched as though he'd been slapped. The lower packs had always considered the upper packs too spoiled and pompous. Many of the lower-pack leaders had always thought of themselves as stronger and more honorable. In reality, they were all slaves to an antiquated system.

The fact that Kolton was speaking out like this showed how much he'd grown while I was away. Before, he'd been too afraid of disappointing our parents to say what he truly believed or thought. A soft-spoken beta wolf by nature, Kolton had gone along with the flow and never rocked the boat. Now, he was asserting himself. I'd never been prouder of him than now, when he was hearing sticking up for me.

"Come on, Kira," Kolton said. "I think they need to think about some things." There was a hint of disappointment in his voice, and our parents wilted beneath it.

Leaving them to stew and reassess their worldview, Wyatt and I followed Kolton outside. As we walked down the steps, Wyatt took my hand again. "Are you really sure about joining my pack?" he asked.

"Why are you asking dumb questions?" I asked with a smile.

Wyatt didn't return my smile. "I know how important your pack has always been to you, and I'd never want you to turn your back on that. Especially not for me."

"You know what I think?" I said. "These *official* packs aren't very natural. What's the difference between them and *unofficial* packs? Who the hell even came up with those terms? What makes them official, anyway? Do you know how many hundreds of thousands of wolf shifters there are? And only twelve packs?" I smiled. "If you look at actual wolves in the wild, they form packs based on family and the others they care about. I care about you most of all, Wyatt. We're family now, which means even if it's you and me and no one else, we'll be a pack from now on."

He grinned, and the love he felt for me rushed through me, as did the happiness he felt. It still boggled my mind that we truly were fated mates.

"I agree wholeheartedly," Kolton said, slugging Wyatt in the shoulder. "I'm really happy for you guys. Though, it'll take some getting used to you two being a couple. I mean, now I can't go and complain to you when one of you irritates me, so that sucks."

"I'm really glad you're looking at the important things. I'm very sorry for your loss." I laughed at him.

"You know what I mean," Kolton said, bumping against me. "Even if it takes Mom and Dad a little while to come around, I think you're a good match. Hell, I think you're fated to be together."

"I really wish you could have figured that out before you punched me at the mega-fans event," Wyatt grumbled.

Kolton shrugged and gave Wyatt a cheesy grin. "Hey, I was looking out for my baby sister." He went mock-serious and leveled a finger at Wyatt. "And don't think for a second I won't do it again if you mess with her. Got it, buddy?"

"Got it." Wyatt's eyes flicked behind us to the house, and the grin faded. Kolton and I turned to see

Mom and Dad standing on the porch, looking at us with chastened expressions.

"Kira? Wyatt?" Dad said. "Um, well, we..." He trailed off and cleared his throat. "We know that with the war, there's a good chance that bad things could happen. Your mother and I don't want what was said to be the last thing we ever say to each other."

Mom nodded vigorously, holding her fist against her mouth to keep her tears at bay.

"You're right that we may have some old-fashioned views," Dad said. "It's hard when your whole life has been turned upside down. It'll take time, but we love you, and we support you in anything you decide." He glanced at Wyatt. "Thank you for protecting my baby girl. I'm an ass for not saying that first. You did what I couldn't. Again, thank you, Wyatt. And, uh, I think you'll do right by her."

Wyatt nodded somberly. "Thank you, Mr. Durst. I will. I promise that."

Dad wiped his eyes and waved toward the forest. "You kids go on. You've got things to do. Just, uh, be careful."

I stood frozen as they waved and headed back inside. Part of me wanted to run up there and hug them, but some superstitious part of my mind told me that if I did, there would be a finality to it. That we might not actually survive the war.

Instead, I smiled and waved back.

"Well, I'll be damned," Kolton said when the door had clicked shut. "Didn't expect that."

"No, but it was nice," I said.

We strode off toward the forest, the air tense around us.

"As I was saying," Kolton said to Wyatt, "if you piss Kira off, I'll give you a black eye. Like, if you *really* bother her. Made her cry or something. Just so we're totally clear."

"You won't have to," I said. "He'll only make me cry with laughter. Or from disgust at his terrible jokes."

"You guys are funny. Really freaking funny," Wyatt said.

"This has been fun," Kolton said. "Family drama and all that, but I'm gonna head out to check on the border patrols."

"Say hi to Eli for us," Wyatt said with a smirk.

Kolton blushed, and he glared at us. "Don't be assholes."

He shifted and sprinted into the forest.

"We should get going," Wyatt said.

"I know, but I want to check in on Leif and Abel before we get too tied up with that. I've been thinking about them."

"They were taken to the Eleventh Pack clinic about a mile up the road from here. It's the closest we have to a hospital right now since most cities and towns are blocked off. Let's go."

We arrived at the clinic to find Leif, Abel, and, unsurprisingly, J.D. The two unhealthy alphas were in beds in the same room. J.D. sat on a stool by Leif's bed.

Leif was the first to notice us. "Hey, guys," he said, and I was happy to see how good he looked.

"Hi. How are you feeling?" I asked.

"They say I'm stable," Leif said. "I haven't had any issues since getting here, which I guess is a good sign I don't want to hurt anyone by accident."

"You won't. You're getting better," J.D. said.

Abel looked even better than Leif. The color had returned to his face, and he didn't look as lethargic anymore.

"How about you?" Wyatt asked Abel. "Feeling better?"

Abel nodded and fingered his hospital gown. "Can't tell much from my outfit, though. Looks like I'm about to get a liver transplant or something."

J.D. gasped in surprise. When I looked over, he was staring at me.

"What? What's wrong?" I asked.

He then pointed at my neck, then gasped again and pointed at Wyatt's neck. "Holy shit, you guys. Really? For really real?"

"Uh, yeah," Wyatt said. "For really real."

J.D. leaped from his chair and embraced us both. "I've been, like, the number-one Kwyatt fan since the beginning," he gushed. Can you guys sign my shirt or something?"

"That's great, guys," Abel said with a weak smile.

"I'm happy for you two," Leif added.

"Do you think there's any way to get back to our packs?" Abel asked.

"I'm not sure," I said. "Travel between territories is a little dangerous right now. What's up? Eleventh Pack not hospitable enough for you?" I joked.

"It's not that." He looked at our claiming marks again. "It's just that, now that we know the fated connections were all wrong, I've been thinking."

"About?" I asked, eyebrows raised.

"When I was rejected, it sort of broke my heart. Almost ruined me, but that was only because it was set up through the blood test. I assumed, as everyone did, that these tests were blessed by Heline and set in stone." Abel licked his lips and looked away.

A small smile tugged at my lips. "There's someone you want to see, isn't there?"

Abel nodded. "A girl. A really good friend, but, well, now that I know the mate I was originally paired with wasn't really my mate, I thought I could find her. We'd always had this really intense connection. It's why were such good friends. I'll be honest, I did the blood test hoping I'd get paired with her. Maybe, uh, maybe I can still have that happy ending. What if she's the one I'm meant to be with?"

I hated being the voice of reason and raining on his hope. "I don't know if you'll get to go back anytime soon, Abel. You're from the Fourth Pack, and the upper packs are seeing more fighting and skirmishes than the lower packs. It's probably too dangerous. But

I promise if things calm down, we'll be sure to get you home as soon as we can."

"I get it," Abel said. "No reason to rush home to get killed on the way. But I really am happy for you both. You guys deserve to be happy. So, since I'm feeling a lot better and will be here for a while, you tell me where you need help and I'll be there."

"I don't expect any of you to help," I said, holding my hands up. "You all went through enough on Bloodstone. This fight with the Ninth Pack doesn't have to be your fight."

"I know, but we want to," Abel said. "You could have left us to rot in that lab, but you risked your lives to get me and Leif out. That's a debt I have no idea how to repay, but helping with this fight might be a good start."

A lump formed in my throat as he spoke. By some miracle, I managed to keep my emotions under control. "You all worry about getting healed up and healthy. If we need assistance, you'll be the first we call. Deal?"

Abel gave me a weak smile. "Deal."

"We're in, too," J.D. said.

Leif cleared his throat. "I'm not sure I can be trusted on a battlefield, but you'll have me there in spirit, I guess."

After leaving the clinic, Wyatt and I headed straight for the border patrol camps. In the few hours we'd been gone, activity there had escalated exponentially. People were hauling gear, relaying messages, calling over radios to the other camps, and moving supplies.

"What's the word?" I asked Eli as she jogged over to meet us. "Something happening?"

Eli nodded grimly. "Our forward scouts sent word about fifteen minutes ago. Ninth Pack is amassing about a thousand yards from the border. The Haven survivors volunteered for the vanguard. They headed out about five minutes ago."

She must have seen the surprise in my eyes. "They volunteered to be the first to go in?" I asked incredulously.

She winked at me. "Our folks are brave. They also realize that you all took a hell of a risk letting us camp within your lands. They want to repay that kindness the only way they know how."

First Abel, now this. It filled me with wonder and hope. If all these people from multiple packs and species were willing to fight for what was right, then maybe we did stand a chance.

"I assume you want to be out on the front lines with them?" Eli said. "The vanguard is a third Haveners, a third Eleventh Pack, and a third Wyatt's pack. I'm sure they'd take heart seeing you out there."

"You couldn't keep us away," Wyatt said.

I nodded my agreement. "Let's go."

Eli led us the three miles to the border. Our teams were gathered, hidden behind trees, foliage, rocks, and any other natural camouflage they could find. We took our position behind a stone outcropping with a thick overhang of willow branches. The Ninth Pack had decided not to hide. Hundreds of them milled about, waiting. But on what?

"Why haven't they attacked yet? They've got us outnumbered," I said.

"No clue. Like I said, they approached and took up this spot, then stopped," Eli explained.

"Maybe there's trouble," Wyatt offered. "Could be Jayson is losing control of his pack. It might be splintering. You saw how that meeting ended yesterday." He sighed wearily. "*Maybe* Gavin wasn't worthless after all. He could be working behind the scenes to, I don't know, get the rest of the pack to see that Jayson's plan to attack us is as dumb as he is?"

"Possibly," I said. "But I'm not sure Gavin's info would sway them. The Ninth Pack has lusted after our lands for decades. I can't see them changing their mind if they've already amassed their forces here. Why back down now?"

"Shit! I guess not," Eli hissed, pointing.

In the distance, a group of Ninth Pack fighters charged toward the border.

Eli cupped her hands around her mouth. "Incoming! Prepare yourselves!"

"We're not too late, are we?" an out-of-breath voice asked from behind me.

I jerked around in surprise and saw my parents hurrying toward us.

"Dad? Why are you here? The fight is literally starting."

"This is my land, my pack, my family. If we don't fight for it, who will?"

Without another word, he and Mom shifted and joined the rest of our fighters in the charge toward the enemy. Kolton's gray wolf howled and bolted from a copse of trees to join them.

"It's time," Wyatt said, squeezing my hand.

I looked into his eyes and nodded. "Let's do it."

We shifted and joined the charge. The battle began in a small valley formed by an ancient, long-dead river. The Haveners and Wyatt's pack were the first to initiate contact, slamming into their opponents with the awful sounds of war—fists and claws on skin, jaws on flesh, screams of pain and rage, howls, snarls, growls, and cries of terror. It was so much worse than I'd thought it would be. This was somehow worse than the attack on Simon's lab. It was more personal, more visceral.

Even as I waded into battle, biting and clawing at the shifters charging toward me, I couldn't help but notice that only a third of the amassed warriors had charged. The rest stood high up on the hill, watching. Were they reinforcements that would join if the initial force faltered?

Jaws snapped at my throat, ripping me out of my thoughts. I tumbled into the wolf, biting its chest in response and tearing a great chunk of flesh from it.

Beside me, Eli blasted three shifters with her magic, sending them sprawling, unconscious.

Wyatt's wolf howled in rage as he tore into a group of five shifters. I could sense and hear his thoughts as he fought. They were faint, almost like suggestions in my mind.

Bastard, I'll show you.

Fuck, that was close.

Thought you could take me, did you, you little prick?

Then one directed right at me: *Yes, Kira, I can hear you.*

Had I been in my human form, I would have laughed in delight. The words were his. From his mind, somehow projected into mine. This connection we shared was amazing. I'd always known the mating bond was powerful, but I'd never expected this.

My inner wolf was full of bloodlust, but there was an undercurrent of fear at Wyatt being in harm's way. She was terrified that he'd be hurt or killed.

Two of Crew's people, a male demon and a human female, were in trouble. They'd been cornered by three wolves. I finished off the enemy I was fighting and tore through the forest to help them. Crap, I was too far away. I'd never make it to them.

The demon pushed the human behind him and growled at the shifters. Before any of the wolves could lunge forward, a new wolf sprang from the trees, slamming into the group and knocking them all aside. The wolf tore into one of the attacking wolves' throat.

Gavin. He helped the demon kill the three Ninth Pack wolves.

Before I could get there to help, they'd dispatched the wolves and moved on to fight together as a group.

Gavin's appearance wasn't the only surprise. Despite the Ninth Pack's superior numbers, we were winning, pushing them back. The rest of their forces still hadn't joined in the fight. What was happening? When I'd first seen how many fighters they had, I'd come to terms with the fact that, at best, it would be a coin flip on whether we won. Now, those of the Ninth Pack who *were* in the fight were tiring, backing up, giving ground.

Almost as though they'd heard my words, a new wolf came sprinting down, howling loudly. It rushed around the edges of battle, not engaging, but stopping every few feet to howl again. Jayson. He was attempting to rally his pack and call the remainder of his forces down to help. It wasn't working.

A few members of the attacking group had a resurgence of energy, but when they tried to re-engage in the fight, others from their pack snapped and bit at them, trying to drag them away, to retreat. Jayson howled in desperation and rage, glaring at the ones who hadn't joined the fight. He barked at them petulantly like a common dog.

He'd lost their respect, and we were watching it happen in real time.

The Ninth Pack fighters broke apart and retreated, and just like that, the fighting ceased.

I wasn't the only one shocked by what was happening. Wyatt's pack, mine, and Eli's forces all stood, mouths agape as the Ninth Pack devolved into chaos. Eventually, Jayson and the few remaining loyal members of his pack ran off, tucking their tails as they did.

Coward.

Chapter 20 - Wyatt

What the fuck was I seeing?

I stopped to leap onto a boulder, shifting into my human form as I did. Jayson was doing his best to rally his troops, but they were done. I could see it, they could see it, and now Jayson understood it as well. He hadn't even bothered to join the fight. Instead, he'd run around like an idiot, howling and begging the pack to help.

The small force that had actually been willing to fight turned on each other, and the entire team broke apart. A few dozen wolves followed Jayson away, but the rest stayed in the forest with us. The group on the hill drifted down to join the surrendering shifters.

One wolf shifted to his human form and raised his hands in surrender. "We give up!" he screamed, obviously terrified that we'd descend on them and finish the job. "We'll join you."

"Like hell!" Kira's father shouted. "The Eleventh Pack doesn't need any disloyal wolves."

I raised my voice to be heard over him. "If you all prove yourselves and can fend for yourselves and your families, my unofficial pack will take you in."

A ripple of unease went through them at my offer. Many appeared disgusted and distraught at the prospect of joining an unofficial pack, but a surprising number of them seemed open to the prospect.

"Who's the alpha of the unofficial pack?" one of them called out.

"He is!" Camilla shouted from across the battlefield, pointing at me.

"Yeah, that's our alpha!" Darius called out from where he stood beside a few Eleventh Pack warriors.

"Oh, for fuck's sake," I muttered to myself, rolling my eyes. I was *not* the alpha. We didn't even *have* an alpha leader.

Kira looked at me, a sardonic grin on her face.

With a sigh, I said, "If anyone wants to join the pack, I'll talk to them shortly. Until then? Sit your asses down. That way, we don't need to worry that the fighting will start again."

The group settled down while members of our forces surrounded them to make sure no one got any ideas about going back on their word.

Gavin ran up to me and Kira, a shit-eating grin on his face. "I can't believe we did it."

"Do we have you to thank for this?" I asked, my voice monotone.

He nodded eagerly. "Once word went through the pack that I'd survived *The Reject Project* and returned home, a lot of them looked at me with more respect than they ever had before. They all thought I was dead. Seeing me come back was, like, a miracle or something. They treated me like a hero." Gavin grinned wickedly. "That really irked Jayson."

I was not in the mood for Gavin's grandstanding and self-congratulations. "Get to the point, bro. How did all this happen?" I gestured toward the defeated army.

"Right. Once I explained that the Seventh Pack was behind my father's murder, a third of the pack voted to go and attack the Seventh Pack directly. Jayson flipped out because they refused his direct order to stay and prepare to fight you guys. They more or less said fuck off and went off to do what they wanted. Another offshoot group told Jayson they had no intentions of fighting you guys and wanted to stay put and defend the borders against attack and to let you be." Gavin tilted his head and made a face. "That...also pissed Jayson off. By the time it was said and done, all he had was a third of the pack who agreed to come out here, and even then, I was already working behind the scenes to get most of them not to attack. That's why only a few dozen actually fought." The smile on Gavin's face grew even wider. "The Ninth Pack is done. It's splintered into three different packs, and I don't see them ever getting back together."

His giddiness at the dissolution of his pack rubbed me the wrong way. It was for the best, yes, but there was no need to be so happy about it. I was with Kira that everything was falling apart, but that didn't mean it was something to be celebrated. Families and friends would split up, and the emotional carnage would be devastating. Older, more traditional shifters would be heartbroken and distraught. This would all be like a forest fire—devastating at first, but afterward, a healthy new growth would spring up. That didn't mean you needed to cheer on the fire while it was burning, though.

Kira looked pleased with the outcome, but there was a focus and intensity in her eyes that I'd seen many times before. "You know what this means?" she asked.

"I'm sure you're gonna tell me," I said.

"Now that the Ninth Pack isn't a threat, we're free to hunt down Simon and Heline."

"That's not the vacation I'd anticipated, but okay," I said.

The next hour was a blur. Medics were brought in to remove the wounded and dead—thank the gods, there weren't too many of the latter, and most of those were from the Ninth Pack. As awful as the work was, I couldn't stop glancing over at Kira. I wanted her again. After the mating bite, my inner wolf had become even needier and more possessive of her.

Back at the camp, we were hydrating and munching on some trail mix when me dirty thoughts were pushed aside by Mika and Zoe popping up out of thin air less than three feet from me. I jolted in surprise, dropping my water bottle.

"Holy shit, don't do that," I gasped.

Zoe grinned. "Easy, big guy. I know I'm hot, but you don't have to fall all over yourself. I've already got a date, anyway." She pinched Mika's ass.

"Ow, hey," Mika yelped.

Ignoring him, Zoe rushed over to Kira, squealing when she saw the claiming mark on Kira's neck.

"Holy shit! Yes, yes, yes! I knew you two crazy kids would figure it out. Come here," Zoe screamed.

The two women hugged each other and launched into a rapid chatter about what had happened to them in the time they'd been apart. Mika and I looked on.

"You'd think they hadn't seen each other in weeks," Mika said, amusement tinging his tone.

"I know. Anyway, how was meeting the fae family? Everyone safe and sound?"

Mika nodded, and the smile on his face caught me by surprise. He was happy. *Actually* happy.

"I've never met people who were so accepting and open," Mika explained. "It was like they'd known me my whole life."

"Most fae are like that."

"They didn't give a damn that I was a shifter. You know, my pack has always been a little more open to non-shifter relationships," Mika said. "Even then, I'd always been told that fae were flighty and eccentric oddballs, especially nomadic fae like Zoe's family. But they're not. They are *literally* the nicest people I've ever met."

Zoe, hearing him, slung an arm around him. "You're pretty nice, too, mister. You've got the seal of approval from my whole family. And why wouldn't you?" She ran a finger down Mika's jaw line. "Look at that sexy face."

Mika's face reddened. He opened his mouth to say something, but instead closed his lips and shrugged uncomfortably. The smile on his face and the happiness in his eyes were all the signs I needed to know that, as flustered as he was by it, he enjoyed being the target of Zoe's flirting.

"Are we too late to kick ass?" Zoe asked. "We went to your house first, but the people there said everyone was here getting ready for a fight." She glanced around at the wounded and bleeding and frowned. "I guess we missed the fun, huh?"

"The Ninth Pack is done," I said. "They've splintered into at least three new packs. Kira wants to go after Simon now."

"The Ninth Pack has splintered?" Mika asked, horrified wonder on his face.

"Yeah. It's happening faster and faster." I said. "I got word around fifteen minutes ago that there are rumors of a civil war within the Fifth Pack. I think Kira's theories are coming true."

"If we want this over as soon as possible, with the least bloodshed, we *have* to find Simon," Kira said. "Until he's off the board, there's still a chance he can use his past research to make more of those weapons and creatures. Just because we destroyed his lab on Bloodstone doesn't mean he's forgotten everything he did there."

"Okay," Mika said slowly. "Where do we start? I doubt Simon will have opened up a lab with big flashing lights pointing in his direction."

"We start in Fangmore City," Kira said. "It's the most heavily protected place on the planet right now. Plus, it has everything he'd need to get started again. Factories, labs, manufacturing, all of it. I'm sure whatever benefactor he has funding him is holed up there as well."

Mika groaned. "Are we sure that's the best place to start? The city is locked up like a fortress. I'm not looking forward to trying to break into the place where most of the upper pack leaders are hiding. It's gonna be a bitch."

"True," Kira said. "But the sooner, the better. All the chaos will help us. Everyone will have their eyes and ears on what's going on everywhere, so it might make sneaking in easier."

"Right," Mika said. "It's probably the best bet. You're right about him having a benefactor. I saw that lab he had on Bloodstone. There's no way he could afford that set-up without backing. The equipment and staff? Plus the high-level magic he'd need to get shipments in and out under the Shadowkeeper's nose? Yeah. Big money." He gave a shake of his head. "I wouldn't be surprised if my father was one of his investors."

Kira and I shared a look. Did he know about his father yet? Garth Sheen had been murdered in the street during the start of the rioting. Would we end up being the ones to have to tell him?

"Mika?" I said. "Um, have you heard about your father?'

Mika looked at me for a long moment before nodding. "I did. Yeah."

His expression was unreadable. He didn't look upset, but he also didn't look happy. Though, there was something going on behind his eyes. I doubted it was apathy he felt.

"Are you okay?" Kira asked as Zoe rubbed Mika's back absently.

He ignored the question. "If the First Pack doesn't have an alpha, I guarantee there's a ton of infighting happening back home. They'll all be trying to exert control, to prove who's the richest, strongest, and most powerful to try and take my father's place."

I wasn't sure what he meant by that. Did he want to go home and try to take the spot for himself? When I asked him that question, Mika snorted a derisive laugh.

"Go home? No. I was groomed from birth to take over as alpha. I couldn't give a flying fuck about that. They could put a harpy in the position, for all I care. Let them fight it out."

"You know, this whole devil-may-care attitude is super-hot," Zoe cooed.

"Oh my gods," Kira said, rolling her eyes. "Anyway, as I was saying, we need to start in Fangmore. Even if Simon didn't end up hiding out there, we have a secondary reason to go. The showrunners will most likely be in the city as well. They *have* to have a way of contacting Heline. She needs to be held accountable for this war. Her meddling with the fated mate connections started this fire burning. Now that Wyatt and I have learned that we were fated mates all along, I want to have a face to face with that bitch and find out why she's been up to no good."

"You know she's a goddess, right?" Mika asked. "Not necessarily the easiest person to have a heart to heart with. She could vaporize you with a snap of her fingers. I mean, you saw what Lucina could do, and she's not even that high ranking of a god. Her power is weak from being nearly forgotten."

"Hang on," Zoe said, gaping at Kira. "Did you say you two are *fated mates*? I thought you were sealing the deal by being regular mates, but you're *fated*?"

Mika blinked, then grinned. "Oh, wow, congrats, guys. This is crazy."

"Our heads are spinning, too," I said, unable to keep the smile off my face.

"Count me in for this crazy mission, I guess," Mika said, then looked at Zoe. "What do you think about it?"

"Oh, I'm going," Zoe said. "No way in hell am I getting left out of this."

"No," Kira said. "Zoe almost died on Bloodstone. I don't want her in danger again."

"Am I standing here?" Zoe asked sarcastically. "I feel like I'm standing here, yet you're talking about me like I'm not. Sorry, Kira, I'm going. End of story."

"It's not that you're incapable of defending yourself," Kira said. "But you ended up on Bloodstone Island because of me and almost died. If you went and something happened to you, I'd have even more guilt than I already do. Stay here, where I know you'll be safe."

"No can do, amigo."

I could see this had the potential to end up in a fight and decided to approach it a different way.

"The Ninth Pack still has some members who are loyal to Jayson. We watched them run off at the end of the battle. If we leave, we'll need someone here to help out if they decide to attack again." I turned to Zoe. "Why don't you help, Zoe? The Haveners know and trust you, and Kira's packmates know you as well. It would be a huge help to know we've got people we trust here."

Zoe's jaw clenched as I spoke. I could see she wanted to argue, but she must have heard the desperation in my voice. I did not want my mate to deal with the heartache of losing her friend if something went wrong.

At last, Zoe rolled her eyes and huffed a sigh. "*Fine*. I can take a hint, I guess. But, only if I get to keep my sexy bodyguard around." She tugged Mika close.

I looked at Mika, the two of us having an unspoken conversation as we stared into each other's eyes. Finally, he nodded, and smiled down at Zoe. "You got it. We'll hold the fort down while you guys are gone."

The four of us made our way back to Kira's house. Eli and two Haven wiccans joined us, returning to get more supplies for the patrol camps. As we stepped out of the forest, the familiar *thump-thump* of helicopter rotors cut through the air.

In the distance, the military chopper appeared, staying low to the ground. August had flown Crew and Chelsey out to the Twelfth Pack's lands early that morning. As the aircraft landed, I wondered if it was just August, or if the other two had returned as well.

The answer came five minutes later as all three of them strolled down the back hatch.

"'Sup, boss!" August called out as he walked across the field toward us. "Good to be home."

Chelsey and Crew followed behind, hands clasped together. As the three drew nearer, Chelsey's eyes grew wide when she spotted the mating bites on my and Kira's necks. Rushing forward, she smiled so wide, I thought her face would break. "I'm really happy for you guys. Seriously, I am. This is wonderful."

Crew shook my hand. "Congratulations," he said, but cut his one good eye over toward Chelsey.

I realized once again how terrible Crew had felt for rejecting Chelsey. He'd spent years pining for a woman who thought he hated her. Now that they'd made up, you'd have to blind not to see how much they loved each other. That meant not *every* fated matching had been messed up. These two belonged together, and I wondered why they were waiting to claim each other.

"How's everything with your pack?" Kira asked.

"They're okay," Chelsey said. "They haven't had any big attacks, just a few skirmishes here and there. It's the one good thing about having isolated pack lands. Easy to defend and tough to get to. The biggest problem is that they've lost electricity. A bunch of powerlines leading to the pack lands were destroyed in the fighting between the Sixth and Seventh Packs. Other than that, they're faring well."

Kira gave them all a run-down of the battle against the Ninth pack. She ended her story with our plan to head to Fangmore City.

I looked at August. "You up for another flight?"

"Shit," August scoffed. "I'm not only flying you; I'm going in there with you. Penetrate that city like I penetrate...uh..." August glanced at Chelsey and Kira before clearing his throat. "Well, you know what I mean."

"I can't ask you to do that," I said. "This isn't your fight, August."

"Bullshit. You got to see all the excitement on Bloodstone, so it's time for me to get in on the action. Besides, I'll be there, anyway, if I'm flying you. Might as well watch your back while I'm there. This is gonna be exciting."

"Your idea of excitement is the same as Von Thornton's," I said grudgingly.

"Speaking of," August said. "What happened to that guy? He sort of vanished as soon as the show was canceled. He was a funny guy. Over the top, and all fake fancy and shit."

"There's nothing funny about Von," Kira growled. "He tucked tail and ran as soon as things went bad. He left at least twenty staff members of the show to die to save his own undead skin."

"I'm going as well," Crew said, changing the subject. "I've got a bit of a grudge against Simon. I lost a lot of people to his experiments and the assaults."

Chelsey pulled Crew close, looping her arm in his. "Me too, especially if you're gonna go after the showrunners. Those bastards almost got my brother killed."

"A small team is best," I said. I wanted to talk Chelsey out of going, but the look on Crew's face told me he wouldn't be separated from her. I didn't think the same tactic we used on Zoe and Mika would work here. "Easier to sneak in if our team isn't too big."

"Well, I think six is a nice round number," Eli said.

Turning on my heel, I found her standing behind me. "Are you sure about this?" I asked. "There's no guarantee we'll make it back in one piece."

She nodded toward Crew. "We've been through a lot together. Might as well fight side by side at the end, too."

We needed to move. Before long, everyone and their brother would be volunteering to go. Time was of the essence, and as much as I'd have liked to say goodbye, or let Kira see her parents once more, all the goodbyes would drag out. Minutes would tick by, and each one was important. We'd learned that on Bloodstone.

I pushed August toward the chopper. "Start that thing up. No time like the present. Does it have enough fuel?"

August grinned at me with that cocky smile of his. "We're rocking and rolling. Come on in."

As the aircraft took off, I reached over and took Kira's hand. I did not relish the thought of what we had to do. Seeking out Simon would be difficult enough, but we also had to find the showrunners, wring any info out of them, and finally find the moon goddess Heline herself.

"No big deal, just another Wednesday," I muttered to myself.

"What was that?" Kira asked.

"Nothing."

Chapter 21 - Kira

The flight was quiet. Not only because the helicopter's interior was enchanted to keep our eardrums from exploding with the noise of the engines and rotors, but because none of us spoke. The atmosphere had turned anxious as what we were going to attempt sank in. We were thrusting ourselves into real danger. The reports said the fighting was strongest around the exterior of Fangmore City, and as we approached, I saw that was true.

Through the viewports behind each seat, I could see the way the landscape had changed in the days since the war started. Suburban neighborhoods had been transformed into battlegrounds, forest areas had been burned, and fields had pitted, churned-up soil where fighting had taken place.

"Tower One, this is the Eleventh Pack transport helicopter tail number N398CH, requesting landing status at Fangmore Airport, over," August said from the cockpit.

Seconds ticked by, and I waited to hear some sort of response to our radio calls. August winced in concentration as he listened for a return call through his radio.

"Any luck?" Wyatt called. It was the third time August had radioed for landing clearance, and we were only ten miles out from the city walls.

"Nothing yet," August said.

"What happens if we don't get clearance?" Chelsey asked, a tremor in her voice. "Will we get in trouble for landing without it?"

"That would be *if* we land," Wyatt said. "Without clearance, and with the war going one, that's not guaranteed. The city is on lockdown. Worst-case scenario, they'd blow us the hell out of the sky with missiles or magic projectiles if we try to land. The reports say they haven't raised a magical barrier as of yet, but that doesn't mean they don't have plenty of other countermeasures."

"Oh," Chelsey said, her eyes going wide, probably imagining our helicopter falling from the sky in a massive fireball.

"Tower One, is that you?" August asked, sounding excited.

We all stood and went to stand by the cockpit entrance.

"Yes," August said. "No, I understand, I just—well, we have—no, no, that makes total sense, but could we get a waiver or something to..."August slammed a fist into the armrest of the captain's seat. "Understood, Tower One."

August ripped his headset off and slammed it onto the padded seat beside him.

"Not good news, I take it?" Crew said.

"Fuckers," August hissed through gritted teeth. "They denied our landing request. Didn't even bother telling me why they ignored me for the last hour. Fuckers," he repeated with more venom.

"What option does that leave us?" Chelsey asked.

"A shitty one," Wyatt said. "We land outside the city and sneak in."

"Outside the city?" Chelsey repeated. "You've seen what it looks like down there. It's like hell on earth."

"I know, but I think this is the best chance we have." Wyatt leaned over August's seat to peer through the windscreen. "How close can we get before they target us with weaponry?"

August sighed and clicked his tongue against his teeth. "I'd say at any normal time, five hundred yards.

Now? With how fucking trigger-happy everyone is? The closest I'd want to get is about a mile."

"A mile through a war-torn battlefield?" Crew asked. "Sounds like a walk in the park."

"Find us a good spot. Preferably as far from fighting as you can get," Wyatt said.

Below us, bursts of light lit up the neighborhoods as spells arced through the sky. It looked like some packs had either hired wiccan or fae mercenaries, or some of those folks had decided to take the fight to the wolf shifters before they came knocking on their doors. Distant flashes of gunfire were also visible— silver rounds, most likely.

Nothing about this would be fun. The closer we got to Fangmore, the more encampments I spotted, similar to what we'd put together back home on our borderlands. This was not just a battle, but a siege. If we didn't hurry, the leaders of Fangmore might get itchy and put up a magical barrier, and then we'd have no chance of getting in.

"Are those vampires?" Chelsey asked, pointing out the side door.

I looked down. In the dim light of late afternoon and early evening, a group of two or three dozen forms rushed from the sun-safe forest and descended on a group of wolf shifters.

"My gods," Eli said. "This really is a full-scale war. It's not isolated to the wolves. It's everyone, isn't it?"

Wyatt gave a tight nod. "Wolf shifters are the most powerful shifter species in the world, and shifters outnumber all the other species or beings. I've always known that if such a war broke out, we wolves would use our power to pull in allies, or the others were going to band together to fight us off before we came to kill them. We've got to stop this. If we can," he added uncertainly.

"I've got eyes on that spot out there," August said, pointing through the windscreen. "Looks like the nearest encampment is at least half a mile away. I don't see any weapon flashes. It's the best I can see. It's also a little closer than I wanted, but it is what it is. Fingers crossed we don't get a prostate exam from a missile." He steered the craft toward the location he'd pinpointed.

The sights below grew clearer and easier to see as we descended. Now I could see the bodies. Dozens were dead or writhing on the ground. I did this. My stupid rant on that show had tipped everything over the brink. These deaths were on me. With a few quick words, I'd overturned the whole world. Men, women, and maybe even children had been killed.

A heavy, icy knot twisted in my chest. Deep down, I knew some type of catalyst had been necessary. Nothing big ever happened without it, yet the enormity of it ripped at my mind. So many dead, so many hurt, and it was my all fault. No matter how much I told myself that this upheaval had to happen, the idea of all this suffering made me sick with guilt.

As the thoughts bounced through my mind, Wyatt put an arm around my waist. "I don't like seeing this, either, but it was coming. Nothing you did or didn't do could have stopped it. If you didn't say something to start it, someone else would have. You can't put all this on yourself. All we can do is focus on getting into the city and doing everything we can to end this."

"I know, it's just..." I looked down at the fighting again and shook my head. "It's so awful."

"Landing in fifteen seconds. Everybody, take a seat," August announced.

The five of us plopped down in our seats and strapped in. A few moments later, we landed with a small bump. August powered down the engines, then unstrapped himself from the captain's chair to join us.

"Still clear?" Wyatt asked.

"Same as what it looked like before landing. No fighting within a couple hundred yards of us, but that's the problem."

"I'm not gonna like this, am I?"

"I managed to get a look at the city," August said, his face grim. "I know why this area is deserted. There's a massive battle happening near the city walls ahead of us. We'll have to go through it, unless we want to spend hours circling around the walls to an area with no fighting."

Wyatt's body tensed beside me, and he shook his head. "Can't wait that long. If there's fighting this close to the walls, they could throw up barriers at any moment. We've got to hurry."

August reached up, slapped a button, and the rear hatch lowered. "That's what I thought. Let's go be dumb."

Moving down the ramp, we hurried to a bombed-out building for shelter before taking stock of the situation. The cacophony of war echoed everywhere around us. Magic, firearms, explosions, and howls bounced off the ancient walls of the city. Fangmore had been shifter capital for centuries, and the massive stone walls surrounding the city attested to the fact that it had always known war, though it had been at least a hundred years since it had seen anything of this magnitude.

"This way," Wyatt said, moving between two smoking structures that looked to have been homes until a few days ago.

The sun had fully slipped below the horizon, and the orange glow of sunset had rapidly faded to the gray light of dusk. Creeping through the shadows and hiding from roving bands of shifters, vampires, and enraged wiccans gave me flashbacks of the jungles, marches, and swamps of Bloodstone Island.

A group of what looked like human special forces operators moved down a street lined on both sides by burned-out automobiles.

"Holy shit," August hissed. "Is every species on the planet here? Are they handing out free kegs of beer if you join the fight or something?"

"Shh," Wyatt said. "Let them pass. I don't feel like eating fifty rounds of silver bullets, do you?"

"I would prefer not," Eli said. "And silver doesn't even bother me. But a bullet is a bullet, regardless."

The six of us inched closer to the walls, closer to the heavy fighting. A fairly large battle was taking place directly in front of the gates to one of the seven entrances to Fangmore.

"Wyatt, look," I said, pointing beyond the fighting.

A heavy steel gate had been installed at the entrance. Tranquility operatives patrolled in front of and behind it. They didn't look concerned by the fighting going on less than a hundred yards from their post. A ball of fire streaked toward the gate and exploded ten feet from the guards, deflected by a magical barrier.

"Son of a bitch. We're too late," I muttered. "They've already put a barrier up."

"Those guys are TO," Wyatt said. "Maybe we can talk sense into them and get them to let us in."

"We've come too far to give up now," Crew added.

"Are you all ready to go through that?" I asked, nodding at the fighting. "It's the only way to get near the gate."

"Ready as we ever will be," Eli said with grim determination.

Moments later, we broke cover, all of us shifting, with Eli following behind. At first, the combatants didn't realize we were moving through the battlefield, but after a few dozen yards, shouts went up as we were spotted. My nerves frayed as the fighters turned their attention on us, but the sound of Wyatt's thoughts at the back of my mind helped me calm down.

Thankfully, the battle in this particular area appeared to only be between rival factions of wolf shifters. No sign of silver weaponry or magic users. Using our new mental connection, Wyatt and I fought off several wolves who rushed at us. Crew and Chelsey stayed near Eli and August, and managed to scare off a group of dumbass adolescent wolves. The stupid kids probably thought this was fun. They'd end up killed if they weren't careful.

Staying close to Wyatt allowed my wolf to focus and fight better. It was as if we were one being, leaping, biting, and clawing exactly when the other need help. As brutal and awful as it was to need to fight, there was a beauty to the dance we were in. Thankfully, the majority of the shifters who were fighting didn't see us as much of a threat, and we made it a decent distance toward the gate.

Crew and Wyatt had cleared out a small party of shifters, sending them fleeing, when a whispered voice slithered into the deepest recesses of my mind. Almost like the way some of Wyatt's thoughts echoed in my own mind, only that was a beautiful and natural sensation. This felt...oily. Dirty. Like an unwelcome visitor in my head. Whatever it was, it beckoned me toward the city, urging me to leave my companions and sprint to the city walls without them.

Wyatt could sense something was wrong with me, but he was locked in battle with a scrawny light-brown wolf.

I managed to shake the strange thoughts off in time to dodge an attack at my back. A burly black wolf, almost the same shade as Wyatt's, was attempting to jump on my back and bite into the scruff of my neck. Rolling aside, I lashed out, biting his foot. He yelped in pain, and Eli sent a blast of magic into his side. Ribs broke with an audible *crack*, and he yowled in agony as he tumbled away.

In the distance, gunfire started, a staccato *pop-pop-pop*. Someone with firearms was moving closer to this part of the battle. We had to hurry.

Come, my little success. My dearest girl. My first one. Come to me.

That voice again, this time louder and more pronounced.

Fucking Simon.

My body went rigid as the battle raged around me. He was luring me to him, doing something similar to the way he'd taken over Abel and Leif's minds back at the volcano. My paws moved of their own accord in slow, measured steps toward the gates. I fought for control of my own body, snarling at myself, but still my paws carried me forward. A tremor of existential terror coursed through me. My greatest fear was going feral, and this felt exactly like how I'd pictured it. No control, unable to stop. Complete and utter madness.

Wyatt rushed to my side. Simply having him within my radius, right there where our fur could touch, helped snap me out of whatever Simon was doing. I shook my shaggy head, trying to clear my mind and push Simon's voice out of my mind.

The battle raged on around us, but Wyatt nudged me behind a half-crumbled wall of what might have been a gas station in the past. He shifted back, and with a small bit of difficulty, I did as well.

"What the fuck was that? Someone's voice was in your head, but it wasn't you." Wyatt's eyes were wide with terror.

I rubbed at my temples. "It was Simon. He has to be in Fangmore. There's no other explanation for it. I didn't feel him calling to me until we got close to the gates." I grabbed Wyatt's shirt and looked into his face. "He is *here*."

"Are you up for this? You can go back and hide in the helicopter or something."

"Bullshit. I want to get the asshole. I'm fine. Now that I know what he's doing, I can resist him," I said, though that wasn't sure that was entirely true. I hoped Wyatt didn't sense my uncertainty.

Behind us, a terrible, ear-splitting roar erupted from the battlefield. The sound of it sent gooseflesh racing up my arms and down my back. The look of recognition and horror on Wyatt's face told me I hadn't imagined it.

We raced out from behind the wall to see a horror laying waste to the rival shifters. One of Simon's abominations, some creature that looked like it had come slithering out of a nightmare. It had the long, serpentine body of a basilisk, but four thick and muscular arms of a tiger. Massive paws slashed at the combatants, spraying blood into the night sky. Below the tiger arms were four misshapen humanoid arms, making it look almost like a centipede. Instead of the deadly eyes or head of the basilisk, it had the serrated mouth and head of a small sea serpent. Bile rose up my throat.

Wyatt and I rushed into battle. None of the others besides those of us who'd spent time on Bloodstone had ever fought these things before. August had shifted back to his human form out of shock and horror and stood staring at the monster.

"Stay in the fight!" Wyatt called to him as we ran past.

Eli stood beside Crew as the beast turned its baleful gaze upon them. She raised a hand to send a forceful spell out, but the creature was faster than many of the others we'd fought. A tiger arm slashed out, slamming into her, and sending her tumbling away. Sharp, caustic fear bolted through me as she rolled and slammed face-down in the dirt. If that thing had killed her, I would never forgive myself. If not for Simon's influence on me, we may have made the gate by now.

Flying into a rage, I leaped under a slashing clawed arm, joining Chelsey at the rear of the beast. We bit down hard on the thrashing serpent tail and dug our paws into the ground, preventing the thing from advancing on Crew and Wyatt. August, shaking off his terror, shifted and joined the other men.

To the right, I spotted a power pole that had been snapped off, leaving a jagged, sharp prong pointing into the sky. I sent a flash of a plan from my mind to Wyatt, praying he heard it and understood.

Chelsey and I grunted as the creature tried to rip free and go after the men. In the periphery of my vision, I watched as August and Crew dodged the claws again and jumped up, latching their jaws onto an arm each. The beast screamed in rage and didn't see Wyatt circling at a full sprint. He leaped onto its back, raced up its spine, and jumped, shifting to his human form in mid-air. As he came down, he reached out and grabbed the great jutting brow bones of the sea serpent head, using all the strength of his body weight, along with element of surprise, to pull it down.

Off balance with two wolves on its arms and a surprise visitor on its head, the thing buckled, falling forward. Wyatt let out a shout of victorious rage as he slammed the head down onto the snapped pole. The point pierced the bottom of its jaw and then burst out through the top of the thing's head, coated in blood and gore. The abomination twitched for a moment before going still.

Our victory was short-lived, as the battlefield had gone silent. The other shifter groups stared at us in awe. My wish would have been for them to accept our elevated fighting acumen and depart, leaving us to our mission. Instead, they all decided that we were a bigger threat than they'd first realized and converged on us.

Crew howled, calling us over, where we circled ourselves around Eli's body. The shifters inched forward, growling and snapping at us, forcing our circle smaller. There were too many. We'd never be able to fight our way out. The realization that we were about to die turned my guts to jelly.

"Damn, that hurt," Eli muttered, pushing herself to her feet.

My relief at seeing her alive was quickly dampened by the thought that she'd be *actually* dead in a few moments.

She glanced around at the encroaching shifter wolves and grimaced. Looking at Crew, she said, "Get ready. This is gonna be bad."

Crew, still in wolf form, jumped on Chelsey, blocking her from gods knew what. Eli clenched her hand into a fist and, grunting with exertion, slammed her knuckles into the ground. An invisible, concussive blast burst out, slamming into the wolves around us. Dust, dirt, and debris spun through the air like we were in the middle of a tornado. Moving outward like a wall of wind, the blast sent the shifters tumbling, rolling, and cartwheeling away. Howls, yelps, and screams of terror echoed around us. When the blast died down, we were alone, our path to the gates clear.

We all shifted back into our human forms. "Good gods, Eli," I said. "I didn't know you could do that."

The angel looked pale and weak, barely able to stand. August stepped forward to put her arm over his shoulder. "It takes a lot out of me, but..." She shrugged and shot me a weary grin. "Better than being dead."

At the gate, the lead operative called out to us before we could even reach the glow of their floodlights. "Halt right there! Turn around and go back where you came from," he shouted.

"We need to get into the city!" Wyatt called back.

Even at this distance, I saw they were still wearing their typical uniforms, but instead of the Tranquility Council patches, they wore patches with the symbols of the First and Second Packs. These were operatives who'd shirked duty to be the tools of the upper packs. I wanted to throw a rock at each of them and crack their greedy little skulls open.

Taking Wyatt's hand, I decided to throw caution to the wind and pulled him forward. We stepped into the light amid shouts for us to get back and the chambering of silver rounds.

"Hey, they've got TO gear on!" someone shouted. "They're Tranquility operatives. Hold fire!"

A sigh of relief shuddered out of my lungs.

"Well, that was ballsy as fuck," Wyatt muttered under his breath.

"We both know I'm the one with the balls in this relationship."

"I'm so glad you can still joke under this kind of pressure."

The lead guard waved us forward. "Come closer. You two, not the others. Keep your hands where I can see them unless you want a silver round through your foreheads."

Wyatt and I did as we were told, moving toward them slowly and with our hands held out. A dozen operatives gathered to join their commander to see what we were doing outside the gates. We were ten steps away when one of the soldiers gasped in shock.

"Yo, no shit. Danny, bro, do you know who they are? What the fuck? They're supposed to be dead."

"Hudson, shut the fuck up," the lead op said. "What the hell are you going on about?"

The one named Hudson pointed a finger at me and grinned like a kid. "That's fucking Kira Durst, dude. And that big son of a bitch is Wyatt Rivers."

The rest of the operatives murmured in shock as they realized he was telling the truth.

Hudson stepped forward, ignoring his boss. "Guys, big fan. Like, huge fan. Team Kwyatt all the way, am I right? Ha! How the hell did you get off the island alive?"

"Fuck them!" another voice called out, and wad of phlegm was spat into the dirt at our feet. "They rigged the whole show, fucked it all up. You heard what Von said."

"Yeah," another agreed. "All this shit is happening because she couldn't keep her damn mouth shut."

Any operative discipline had obviously vanished in the face of war. The lead operative tried to calm everyone down, but arguments were breaking out. It appeared that every one of these people had watched the show.

A plan formed in my mind. It might work, it might not. Wouldn't know until I tried it.

Slipping into my old TV persona, I put on a big fake smile and stepped forward. "Calm down, guys," I said, and they quieted, turning their eyes on me. "There has been a *huge* mistake. When the Reject Mansion fell, my dear, *dear* friend Von rushed away, thinking we were dead." I swallowed back the vomit at calling Von a friend. "We managed, by only the skin of our teeth, to get back to the mainland."

One of the soldiers frowned in confusion. "But how the hell could you—"

"We need to find Von," I said, cutting the soldier off. "Unbeknownst to the fans watching, Von, Wyatt, and I had been planning a big reveal to prove our love for each other. We were going to claim each other on the show, but we went ahead and mated after we escaped." A few wide eyes went to the marks on our necks that were only just starting to heal. It was one of the few wounds that didn't heal fast for shifters.

"You guys are mated? Oh, wow," the one named Hudson said with a reverent awe that almost made me roll my eyes.

The lead operative looked ready to explode. "What the fuck does this have to do with you all getting through this gate?"

"Von doesn't know we're alive," I said. "We need to get in there and let him know. He was sure that by putting us on the show and proving to everyone our love was genuine, it would calm some of the hostilities. You know what they say...everyone loves an underdog."

Holy fucking shit, I actually said it. Ew.

The lead operative glanced behind us at the other four. "What about them? Who are they?"

"They're the ones who helped us escape Bloodstone. We *need* them to go in, too. That way Von can hear the entire story and make a whole spectacle of it. Please," I begged, putting my hands together and giving him a pleading look.

Hudson leaned in toward his commander. "Bro, if Von Thornton finds out we turned them away at the gate, he'll be pissed."

The lead operative let out an explosive sigh and waved to August, Crew, Chelsey, and Eli. "Get your asses over here. We'll let you through, but we're checking all of you for weapons."

Doing my best to keep the smile off my face, I stepped forward. It had worked. They were going to let us in. Once through the gates, we could search out Simon and Heline—if she was here. I couldn't believe our luck.

The lead operative took me by the arm. "We'll take you straight to Mr. Thornton. He's in a hotel a few streets down."

My face fell. "What?"

Chapter 22 - Wyatt

Once we were through the gates, I got the shock of my life. After seeing the destruction of the outlaying neighborhoods and towns on our approach, I'd assumed it would be the same on the inside. But I was sorely mistaken. A few areas had been damaged in the initial riots, but it was already being cleaned up. Most of the city was pristine and peaceful. Hell, there were even people waiting outside a restaurant.

"Are we dreaming?" August whispered to me. "Like, these people know a war is raging right outside their gates, right?"

"Apparently not," I said.

The people walking the streets were the rich and powerful. Anyone who didn't want to get their pretty little hands dirty had come running to Fangmore for safety and to continue living their lives of privilege. The scorched bricks, broken windows, and damaged signs had already been cleaned up and repaired. It made everything outside feel like a dream in comparison.

"So, can we stop and get a coffee or something?" August asked one of the operatives.

The man obviously didn't hear the sarcasm in August's voice. "Nope. It's evening, why would you want coffee?"

"Never mind, bro," August said with a little roll of his eyes.

I could sense Kira's anxiety. She—none of us—had anticipated an armed escort straight to Von Thornton. Her play had been genius. Once she realized all the soldiers were fans of the show, she'd thought fast, and it had worked in our favor. Except, now we were being led to the one person we didn't give a shit about.

In the big scheme of things, Von was small potatoes. Especially when we were dealing with a psychotic scientist who could destroy the world with his toys. And the *literal* moon goddess.

Von would probably have tons of security, and once he saw us, he might send us straight to a holding cell. *Boom*, mission failed. The thought that we could make a run for it appealed to me, but the soldiers outnumbered us two to one. They also had machine guns with silver rounds. We had nothing. They'd taken our only weapons—August's boot knife and a bottle of silver nitrate pepper spray that had been in Kira's TO gear. We'd left behind any other weapons in favor of moving fast, silently, and unimpeded.

"Which hotel is he staying at?" Kira finally asked.

The lead operative glanced back at her and grinned. "You know the one. It's where they always have you guys for the premiere. It's up ahead another block."

That was when I noticed the noise. A steady, humming roar of hundreds, maybe thousands of voices.

"Do you hear that?" I whispered to Crew and Eli.

They nodded, and Eli frowned in confusion. "Is it a riot or something? It sounds like lots of people."

"Not a riot," one of the operatives said with a malicious grin. "It's justice."

He said no more, leaving us to figure out what that meant. When we rounded the corner, some of what he said became clear. It definitely wasn't a riot. Thousands of people stood in the main city square of Fangmore City around a massive stage, similar to the one we'd all been on the night of the premiere. The difference was this one wasn't quite as tall, and it had obviously been slapped together at the last minute.

Instead of immaculate wood, stainless steel, lights, and crystal fixtures, this looked more like a giant hangman's tower from a hundred years ago. Plain two-by-fours and plywood had been hammered together to make a half-assed stage.

"What the hell is this?" August asked. "What are they watching?"

The crowd was nothing like what I'd seen at the premiere, either. These people weren't the lowly plain folk who were simple fans of a TV show. No, they were all families from the upper-level packs. It was ridiculous that they were all huddled away here, rubbing elbows while their packs were out fighting each other. Another fucking sham that proved the highest levels of pack society were so corrupt, they could do something like this. The First Pack had been ordering attacks on the Second Pack's factions while both pack leaders were hanging out here, sipping fucking wine together. They didn't give a damn that innocent people were dying. Why would they care when their mansions and yachts would all be fine and dandy once it all blew over?

I heard the familiar drone of those hovering cameras that had plagued us on Bloodstone Island. If I'd had a rock, I'd have thrown it at one of them.

"You call this justice?" Kira said. "What does that mean? What is all this for?"

An operative pointed at the stage. "This is where the acolytes who fucked everything up are going to be cross-examined before they're executed."

Kira looked at him like he'd lost his mind. "Cross-examined? By whom?"

"Callista Oborin," the soldier said with a grin. "She's using her psychic powers to determine who among them is guilty and who's innocent of intentionally messing up the bloodwork. It's like you said on the show, we all knew it was messed up. We just didn't have the guts to drag these sorry shits out and expose them. Man, I wouldn't want to be those guys."

"So, she's the judge and jury?" Kira bit out. Neither of us had any love lost for Callista after the way she'd pushed Kira at the mega-fans event.

"Yup. If they're the slightest bit guilty, then everyone gets the pleasure of watching the scumbags getting killed off on live television. Those pieces of shit will get what's coming to them for ruining people's lives and their chances at true love."

"This is such bullshit," Kira muttered, anger dripping from every word.

It was disgusting. We'd learned enough to be pretty sure the acolytes had nothing to do with the faked fated mated pairings. Or if they did, it was because Heline herself had ordered it. These people were being psychically tortured and would be murdered for a lie.

Something tickled the back of my mind a ball of fiery emotion. So strong that I stopped walking for a moment to collect myself. Rage. Bitter and violent anger. Uncontrollable. A small gasp escaped my throat as I realized what it was.

"Kira, no!" I called out a moment too late.

Her hot-headed nature had won out at the worst possible time. She shoved the guard next to her aside, and the man tripped and fell into the next closest operative. Kira bolted toward the crowd of shifters.

The men shouted and called after her, but she was too fast, too driven. She plunged into the crowd and pushed forward, elbowing her way toward the stairs leading to the stage.

"What the hell is she doing?" Eli demanded.

"Something stupid," I said through gritted teeth, and shouldered my own guard away.

The operatives, already confused by Kira's flight, struggled to get their bearings I rushed into the crowd after her. There was no way I would let her do another dangerous thing without me by her side.

The upper-pack shifters murmured their annoyance as Kira and I pushed forward. Curses and pissed-off mutterings slowly shifted to chittering exclamations as person after person began to recognize us. Once the word spread, the crowd parted, allowing us free access to the stairs. Behind us, I could still hear our escorts arguing with each other.

"You really know how to make an already dangerous plan more dangerous. You know that, right?" I said to her, taking her hand in mine.

"Danger is relative, Wyatt. Besides, I can't stand for this."

With that, we took to the stairs, ascending to find four acolytes tied to crosses, their hands and feet bound with leather straps. The four men were covered in sweat, thrashing and moaning as Callista Oborin stood before them, glaring. This was not the subtle, gentle probing she'd tried with me during our interview. This was torture. She was shoving into these men's minds, uncovering every secret they had in the most brutal way possible. It made me sick to see it.

Magical cameras, summoned by some producer offstage, swooped low to get a good look at Kira and me. The murmurs of the crowd had replaced the awful cheering and jeers that had been egging Callista on. Tearing her attention from the four men, she whirled around at the interruption. Her supermodel face was twisted in a sneer of sadistic glee, showing the true person beneath the famous glamor. A monster. When she saw us, her countenance of rage and brutality vanished, replaced with abject confusion and shock.

"Wyatt? Kira? You...uh...you're alive?"

Kira took a few steps closer. "You're probably getting off on this whole thing, aren't you, Callista?" she spat.

The crowd below grew silent, desperate to hear what we were saying. Glancing back, I saw that even the operatives had stopped arguing and were staring up at us.

Kira gestured to the four men. "You're thriving off all the drama and trying to make yourself look good. The sole judge and jury of these poor men."

Callista, visibly regaining her composure, swept a hand at the acolytes. "These men have created these problems. You yourself said—on live TV—that this war is caused by their wanton disregard for society."

Raising her voice to make sure everyone could hear, Kira said, "We cannot allow these men to have their minds ripped apart by a psychic. We can't even see what she's seeing. For all we know, she could be lying. These men deserve a fair trial." Kira pointed a finger toward the sky. "Before that, Heline herself needs to admit whether or not these acolytes actually messed up. That needs to happen before anything else."

The crowd stirred at her words, and at the fact that we were alive when everyone still believed we were dead.

Callista lifted a hand to her ear. "Do you hear that, Kira? They're all asking the same question I am. Why would you halt these lawful interrogations when you were the one who demanded their blood? You said they needed to be punished."

"Wrong!" Kira shouted. "I said the ones who were guilty needed to be punished. Big difference."

Callista shook her head derisively, swatting a hand toward us as if shooing a fly away. "Security! Get these two out of here. We have things to do."

Confusion rippled through the crowd as armed security guards pushed through and thundered up the stairs. Tranquility operatives, and not the same ones who'd been escorting us. These had patches on their uniforms showing they were loyal to the Third Pack.

The first to the top of the stairs was met with my boot in his face, shattering his nose and sending him tumbling backward, taking two of the others with him. The dry cracks of breaking legs and arms were punctuated by screams of pain as the three men fell in a tangle off the side of the stairs.

Shouts of shock shuddered through the crowd, and when the next guard crested the stairs, he was warier. I didn't recognize these men, which was good. I didn't want to beat the shit out of someone who'd been my comrade in arms.

A fist struck out toward my face, and I pivoted, grabbing the offending wrist. Yanking the wrist down, I simultaneously exploded upward and slammed my shoulder into the elbow joint. The joint snapped, bending the wrong way. My eardrums rattled with the injured man's bellowing screams. I shoved him back, and he fell down the stairs, his head bumping on each step. The whole way, he clutched his ruined arm and shrieked in pain.

By the time I turned to check on the last two operatives, Kira had already taken care of them. One lay on his back, bloody face slack and unconscious. She had the final operative in a headlock, and I watched the light go out of his eyes as she put him to sleep. He thudded to the wooden stage, and the sound of his skull bouncing on the wood had a strange finality to it.

More murmurs from the crowd. This time, a combination of shock and awe at how easily we'd dispatched the operatives. Kira and I were the best the council had ever trained. There were maybe a dozen other operatives in the entire organization who equaled our skills. These men were nothing. Not even enough for us to break a sweat. The crowd saw that these proceedings were not going to go the way they thought it would, and they were scared and excited all at once.

Callista laughed and clapped her hands. "Wonderfully done." She turned to address the crowd. "What a wonderful surprise. The two most controversial contestants in the history of *The Reject Project*, here to show off their skills. I'm very happy you two could join us."

She did her best to play this off as part of the show, but the look in her eyes told the real story. She was horrified, and furious, that our corpses weren't rotting on Bloodstone Island.

"Now, I know that the two of you, especially Kira, love attention, but I have work to do. These men need to pay for ruining thousands of lives. If you would be so kind, go back down the stairs and leave me to this."

"Not happening," I hissed. "We aren't leaving these people to be tortured when we have no idea if they've done anything wrong." My anger boiled over as I leveled a finger at Callista. "There are laws against aggressive psychic torture that you are obviously breaking. Plus, everyone knows that the information gleaned via psychic manipulation is tenuous at best. All we have to go off is your word, and I can't say that I find that trustworthy."

Callista blinked rapidly and put a hand to her chest. "You dare besmirch my honor?"

I decided to ignore what I thought was a ridiculously self-evident answer. "Kira is right. We shouldn't be looking to the acolytes for answers. We need to start at the top. Heline should be answering for these crimes against shifterkind. If Heline gave even a rat's ass about these acolytes who have dedicated their lives to her, then she would not be letting these people take the fall for what is possibly her fault. Can anyone here truly believe that these connections could be wrong without Heline knowing? The goddess in charge of them? Ask yourselves that."

An unsettled rumble of unease. The people in the crowd were clearly considering my words and understanding the logic. They weren't stupid. Rich, privileged assholes, yes. But not stupid. Kira looked at me and gave me a smile and reassuring nod.

Callista's eyes flicked toward the sea of people surrounding us, and a hint of fear marked her face. No longer content with murmuring, shouts rose up from the surrounding shifters. Angry and demanding. The rich were used to getting what they wanted when they wanted it. They now called out for Heline to show herself and take the stand on this stage to defend the accusations.

Fear turned to panic on the psychic's face, and she pulled a small device from her pocket. Callista spoke several rapid words into the device, too low for my shifter hearing to pick up. The crowd grew ever more restless and began to pelt stuff onto the stage—wads of paper, half-empty cups, water bottles, and more. This was taking a turn for the worse quickly, far faster than I'd thought. Similar to how Kira's speech at the mansion had started the war, my accusations against Heline had sparked something else in these people. A desire for the truth.

Moments after Callista used the device, dozens of Tranquility operatives, Fangmore City police, and what looked like *The Reject Project* corporate security flooded the city street, dispersing the crowd with threats, shoves, and tasers and non-lethal magic weapons. The moment these new arrivals showed up, the hovering cameras shut down and flew off to wherever they were housed.

With the cameras off and the crowd being herded away, Callista let the television facade slip away. Turning a baleful glare at us, she said, "You two annoying little shits had to show up now?" The vitriol in her voice was shocking to hear, even to me.

"Yes," Kira said, not backing down from the other woman. "To save innocent people? Of course."

"Are you really this stupid?" Callista asked, pointing toward the four tied-up men. "If I'd been allowed to execute these acolytes, it might have appeased the warring packs and stopped this meaningless war. Once all the old acolytes were killed, we could install new ones in Heline's temples, and then everything would have gone back to normal. Now, you've screwed it all up." Callista took several angry steps toward us, baring her teeth like she was a shifter instead of a psychic. She jabbed a thumb into her chest. "If you hadn't interfered, I would have been a hero. The woman who ended the shifter war. All you two did was make me look like an idiot."

"You didn't need us for that," I said, the words falling from my lips before I could stop them. "Only an idiot or a psychopath would condemn innocent people to death without a fair trial."

The fury on her face only got worse, warping the once-beautiful visage into something that was probably closer to the twisted and insolent person she really was underneath.

"You two have so many *opinions,* don't you? How fucking noble," she spat the word at us. "You just had to be such pains in the ass. Why couldn't you just die a nice and simple death on Bloodstone Island? Perhaps you'd like to discuss all this with the people in charge of *The Reject Project*? A live special? I'm sure the public would love to see the great Wyatt and Kira talk about their ideals." Callista gave a bitter laugh. "It would be nice to watch the world chuckle as you two tried to tell them about all these naive worldviews you have. You realize that morality is thrown out the door when there's a war going on, right?"

Kira's face was red with anger, her jaw clenched, ready to spout off at Callista. Before she could make a sound, a voice behind us spoke out, causing the two of us to flinch.

"Mr. Rivers? Ms. Durst? I'm here to collect you and your associates."

The man was dressed as a chauffeur—black suit, white gloves, and polished patent leather shoes. At the bottom of the stairs, a large stretch limo sat, its doors open. The remaining Tranquility operatives allied to the Second Pack were leading our friends toward the car.

"Hey!" I shouted, recognizing the man immediately. "Let our friends out of there. We don't need a ride. Go back to where you came from."

The chauffeur bowed his head slightly. "I'm sorry, but going with me is the best option. A warm bed, a fresh meal, and safety is preferable to the prison cell you'll end up in if I leave you here."

"Excuse me," Callista snapped. "I'm dealing with these two."

The chauffeur barely gave Callista a cursory glance. "Hmm, yes. I'm sure you are." Turning back to me, he said, "Come now, Wyatt. You've been away for too long. Let's head down the stairs, shall we?'

I growled, but Kira took a step toward him, realization dawning in her eyes. "Did your father send this car?" she asked me.

"Yes," I hissed. Calming myself enough to face her, I decided to leave it up to her. "Your choice. We go with them if you want, but I'm fine sleeping in a prison cell. Or in the gutter, for that matter."

"That's not fair, Wyatt. You can't leave it up to me. Either you want to see your father or not. This isn't about me right now."

"That's easy," I said. "I don't want to see him. Like I said, I'd rather sleep in the street with newspapers for blankets than see him."

"Hey!" August called from the rolled down window of the limo. "It's actually kinda nice here. I'd rather go with this guy than them." He pointed down the street.

A large group of Tranquility operatives were hurrying toward us. The patches on their uniforms were not for the Second Pack. They may even have been sent by the show, or Callista could have called them. We had about thirty seconds before they would be close enough to take us into custody.

"Shit," I grunted and took Kira's hand. "Fine. We go."

"You aren't going anywhere," Callista said. She reached forward and grabbed Kira's arm, tugging at her.

Kira spun without hesitation and slammed her fist into the psychic's nose. The cartilage snapped, blood squirting from both nostrils down her lips and chin. She tumbled backward with a miserable groan of agony, thumping onto her ass and cradling her ruined face.

Kira laughed. "For a psychic, you sure didn't see that one coming."

The chauffeur led us down the steps and opened the back door for us to climb in. Down the street, the operatives were screaming for us to stop. The driver slammed our door, then hopped into his seat and sped away from our pursuers.

It should have been a victorious moment, but all I felt was dread as we cruised through the deserted streets of Fangmore City. I was going to see my father for the first time in over a decade, and I had no clue what I would say to him.

Chapter 23 - Kira

"Wow," August said. "They've got a freaking minifridge with sodas in here." He lifted an armrest to reveal the lighted refrigerator built into the limo. "Anybody want one? There's bottled water, too."

"I'll take a water," Chelsey said. Like the rest of us, she was soaked with sweat and covered in grime.

He tossed one to her and looked at Wyatt. "You want anything, bro?"

Wyatt shook his head, doing his best to appear aloof and unworried. Our new connection let me peek into his emotions, and he was *far* from okay. Stress, anxiety, and even a small bit of panic were eating at him. My own nerves were making me jittery, so I could only imagine what he was going through. He was doing a good job of hiding it, though. Looking at his face, you'd think he was wholly unconcerned by the fact that he was about to see his father after years of estrangement.

Through the heavily tinted windows, our group watched the city roll by. It was striking how untouched it was from the fighting beyond the walls.

There must have been some type of curfew or something because the streets were suspiciously quiet. Nightclubs, bars, and other venues appeared to be closed as well. Basically anything that would be open late into the evening had been shuttered.

"I don't like this," Eli said, gazing out the window. "This whole city feels weird. Not like it usually does."

"Yeah," Wyatt said, keeping his eyes out the window. "Because the rich and powerful have decided to keep things as safe as possible for themselves. Honestly, I wouldn't be surprised if a lot of people were"—he smiled bitterly—"removed from the city. Middle and lower-class citizens or something. Can't let the commoners use up all the stored resources the rich need. Shit, they probably kept enough to man the restaurants, spas, and theaters. Maybe a few for sanitation and other services. Either that, or the rich fuckers were told to keep their asses inside unless told otherwise."

We turned down a side street that led to a less urban part of the city. The new neighborhood, lined with trees and shrubs, had more green spaces and parks. Along with that, there were also houses. *Very* large houses. I'd thought my parents' home was quite large, but these were full-on mansions with large, manicured lawns. Some even had fountains or small ponds out front.

The chauffeur lifted his hand and clicked a button built into the roof as he turned into a driveway. A large, wrought-iron gate swung open automatically and we drove inside. Two armed shifter guards stood sentinel, nodding to the driver as we passed. The car wound along a curving driveway lined with maple trees before revealing a gorgeous brick and stone mansion.

"This looks like the place I grew up in," Crew said, angling his head to take in the house with his one good eye.

Crew didn't sound wistful or nostalgic, but disenchanted and sad. Watching his face, I realized he hated everything about this city. Somehow, this shifter, who'd been born into this much privilege, appeared more at home in the wilds of Bloodstone Island than in Fangmore City.

Chelsey noticed it as well, and reached forward to take Crew's hand. A small smile creased my lips at the sight of it. After going through hell, they'd pulled through. The path they'd taken to find each other again was even more intense than what Wyatt and I had gone through. Crew and Chelsey figuring out a way to make their way back together gave me faith that things might work out after all. If they could find love again on Bloodstone Island, anything was possible.

The limo pulled up to a circular parking area in front of the house. Up close, the home was even more impressive. Hand-carved gargoyles stood on the eaves, the roof was an aged-green copper, marble accents on the stairs led to the front door, and a massive stone wolf stood in the center of a large fountain, a stream of water arching from its mouth into the pool around it.

"Holy shit, bro," August said, staring at Wyatt. "I knew you came from money, but damn, this place is nice." He pointed at the windows on the second floor. "Which one of these was your room?"

Wyatt ignored the question and pushed open the door. A butler or valet of some sort stood outside the car and assisted us, giving a hand to the ladies as we climbed out onto the cobblestone driveway. Chelsey, August, Eli, and I looked around, absolutely awed by the luxury around us. I'd thought Reject Mansion was nice, but this was a whole other level.

By contrast, both Crew and Wyatt appeared aloof and jaded by the whole thing. It wasn't that they were bored of it all. More like disgusted at and irritated by the spectacle of it all.

"Refreshments?" another butler asked. He'd appeared seemingly out of nowhere, with a silver tray laden with glasses of wine.

"Fuck, yeah," August said, snatching a glass of red wine from the tray. "It's been a rough day."

He proceeded to take two other glasses and poured them into the first, mixing red and white wine together. The look of utter disdain on the butler's face had me stifling a laugh.

The front doors swung open, and all conversation stopped. A handsome, middle-aged shifter stepped out and walked down the steps toward us. Wyatt's shock, recognition, and then anger at the sight of the man echoed from his mind into mine, and I knew in an instant that this was his father. Lawrence Rivers.

Wyatt must have taken after his mother, because he bore no resemblance to the man who strode toward us. Where Wyatt was broad-shouldered, this man was thin, almost wispy. Wyatt looked more like a football player, while his dad looked like a marathon runner, with blond hair so pale it could have been white and sharp blue eyes. Wyatt's dark eyes and hair was a sharp contrast to his father's features. If I hadn't known, I never would have believed they were related.

"Thank you for bringing them, Anthony," Lawrence said to the chauffeur.

"My pleasure, sir."

Lawrence turned to greet us all, but his eyes lingered on Wyatt and me more than the others. "Welcome. I'm happy to have you here as my guests. I would like…" He trailed off as his eyes flicked to the claiming marks on our necks. "My apologies. I'd like to bring you inside. I have rooms for all of you—food, showers, whatever you would like. You are guests here in my home."

"Thank you, Mr. Rivers," Crew said formally.

Lawrence nodded and turned his full attention on Wyatt. "Son. You've, uh, well you've grown into a far stronger alpha than I ever could have dreamed."

Wyatt smiled humorlessly. "Really, Dad? Is that where we're going with this?"

Lawerence's smile faltered a bit. "I don't—"

"Not surprising you see me different now," Wyatt said. "Last time you saw me, I was nothing but a neglected child. Left to figure out life with a bunch of tutors and instructors, and then that bitch of a fated mate. You never had time for me, didn't give a damn that Serenity didn't care about me. Did you even know she was fucking other guys? Did you care?" He snorted. "I doubt it. All you cared about was me pairing with her—screw my feelings. So yeah, Dad, I am different. Once I managed to get away from all this *shit*"—he waved toward the mansion—"I found out who I really was. A true purpose and identity. Not something you could ever understand. Thanks for noticing."

The tension between the two men was so high, it pricked at my skin. The rest of our group looked as uncomfortable as I felt. August chugged his glass of wine and kept shooting worried glances at Wyatt.

Lawrence, instead of looking angry or disrespected, appeared taken aback by Wyatt's outburst. He smiled weakly at his son. "You've become more vocal, that's for sure. You were always quiet as a boy."

I'd never known Wyatt Rivers to be quiet. A sad ache filled my chest, realizing he must have been quiet because he'd suppressed his anger as a child.

Wyatt didn't respond to his father's words, just crossed his arms over his chest and glared at the other man. Most people wilted under that stare, but Wyatt's father composed himself and addressed the rest of us.

"As I said, you are my guests. You can stay here as long as you are in Fangmore City. If you need it, I have several cars that will be at your disposal if you need transportation around the city. You all look like you've been through the wringer. My staff is preparing dinner as we speak. Go ahead and get cleaned up, then we'll have dinner." He gestured toward Eli and her wounds. "Miss? I have a healer on staff. I can send her to you if you'd like."

Eli glanced at Wyatt, then at Crew, who nodded to her. "That would be nice. Thank you, Mr. Rivers," Eli said.

"Please, call me Lawrence."

"Okay, *Lawrence,*" Wyatt said, sneering at the word.

A few staff members appeared to lead the others inside, but Wyatt didn't move, standing stock-still in front of his dad. I stayed at his side. His mind and emotions were a whirl that I could barely make out. Rage, sadness, disgust, heartache, nostalgia, betrayal. But deep, *deep* down, there was still a small glimmer of love for the other man, though it was buried in the trenches of his heart.

"I don't like being bought off," Wyatt said to his father once everyone else was inside. "A helicopter? A limo? A mansion? You think you can buy back what you threw away when I was younger?"

Lawrence shook his head and put a hand to his chest. "Wyatt, that's not what this is. Do you know that I've looked for you for years? Tried to find you over and over again, then *boom*, there's your face on *The Reject Project*."

"Really?" Wyatt asked, incredulous. "How hard did you try? Seriously? I've been in the Tranquility operatives for years."

Lawrence winced, and I had the impression that he was ashamed of himself. "True, and I have many contacts there if I'd only reached out to ask. I just never thought that was a line of work you'd go into."

Wyatt laughed bitterly. "No faith in your son. Not surprising."

"No," Lawrence blurted desperately. "I thought you'd choose a less dangerous trade. Finance, law. Medicine, perhaps?" He shook his head sadly. "When I saw you on the show, saw what you were capable of? I sat there saying, 'That's my boy.' The whole time I watched you, I started to realize that I never knew you. You're right. I was an absent father. Emotionally absent. I took you for granted, and when you rejected Serenity and became a lone wolf, I can admit that, for a time, I hated you."

Wyatt chuckled. "Really great, Dad. Good to know."

"Let me finish, please." He held up a hand and closed his eyes in a pained expression. "I hated you because I didn't understand what you'd gone through. All I could think about was the dishonor that the Second Pack went through when you left. But when I watched you on that show, fighting to bring honor back to our pack, I took it as a sign. A signal that you were ready to come home, to step back into your real life." He gave a little smile. "I'm happy I managed to help you enough to get you back to Fangmore City. Things can go back to the way they were supposed to be. You can stay here as one of the rightful leaders of shifter society."

Wyatt scoffed. "This is the problem with all you upper-pack wolves, Dad. You realize there's a war going on out there, right? *Rightful leaders*? Seriously? You all can sit here in your ivory towers, trying to make believe everything will blow over, but you can't deny the packs are splintering. You may need to find a new home soon."

Before his father could say anything in response, Wyatt walked away, heading for the stairs. I joined him, leaving Lawrence Rivers behind. When I glanced over my shoulder, the man looked both devastated and confused.

A maid met us inside and led us to one of the guest rooms. It was as nice as the suite I'd had back in the Reject Mansion. Once the door closed behind us, Wyatt allowed himself to vent.

"Can you believe that shit?" he growled.

I shook my head as I inspected the ornate carvings on the mahogany wainscoting. "No. Why on earth would your father bring us here and act like everything was totally normal? Was all this a ploy to get you back into his pack?"

Wyatt flopped into a leather chaise lounge by the window. "My father's mind has always been a mystery to me. When he's not mentally checked out and ignoring his responsibilities, he's spending time convincing himself the world is exactly like he thinks it should be." He sighed, and for the first time since getting into the limo, he looked sad rather than angry or bitter. "When I was a kid, I used to hate him. He was never around, never had time for me, always pushed me to do things I hated. That hate's gone now. I really thought that when I finally saw him again, I would lash out and be so pissed, but I'm angry at the situation, not at him. All I feel is apathy. I barely have any feelings for him anymore. After my mom died, things went downhill. After all these years, nothing has gotten better."

I could sense the emotions flooding his mind. His anger was focused on the words his father had said, not the man himself. The only emotion I could sense in Wyatt's head was disdain toward his father.

"What do you want to do?" I asked.

"I'm sure he's trying to manipulate us in some way. That, or he truly has deluded himself into thinking I'd want to come back to this pack after avoiding it for over a decade. Either way, it doesn't matter. We'll sleep here tonight, get our bearings, and then tomorrow we can get the hell out of here and find the remaining showrunners. Wring some information out of them."

Even as I nodded, my bones turned to slush. It had been an incredibly long day, and I was exhausted. We'd been through multiple battles and fights. Would my life ever be normal again?

The huge, fluffy bed looked like heaven, and I jumped onto it, grunting as I sank into the comforter and feather topper.

"That looks nice," Wyatt remarked.

"Join me."

"Don't mind if I do."

He leaped onto the bed and pulled me close, nuzzling my throat. The feel of his lips and nose against my skin sent an arrow of heat between my legs.

"Hmm? I heard that," Wyatt whispered.

"What?"

"You. Are. Horny."

"Ugh, this is weird. Good, but weird. It's gonna take some getting used to this whole connected-minds thing."

"You didn't deny that you're horny," Wyatt teased.

Chuckling, I palmed his cock, already throbbing and rigid. "Seems like I'm not the only one."

Wyatt leaned forward to kiss me, but before our lips met, there was a knock at the door.

"You in there? It's time for dinner!" August's voice called behind the door. "We're gonna eat, like, fish eggs and shit. Whatever rich people have."

Wyatt flopped back on the bed, releasing a frustrated sigh. "I swear to the fucking gods, I'm gonna kick him out of the pack. He can be so annoying."

I giggled and dragged him from the bed. "Come on. Let's go. Dinner awaits, and my stomach is about to eat itself."

"I'm starving, too," Wyatt said, eyeing me like I was a juicy steak. "But not for food."

"If you're a good boy, maybe you can have dessert later."

"We'll meet you down there," Wyatt called out to August through gritted teeth.

"Cool. See you in a minute," August said.

Once we were in the hall, Wyatt led me down the stairs toward the dining room. My stomach flipped at the delectable scents wafting toward us, and my mouth watered. The faint mumble of conversation echoed from the dining room, and when we stepped through the threshold, I saw that all the others were already there. Our friends, Wyatt's dad, and another figure I didn't recognize—a pretty woman in her early thirties.

Wyatt jerked to a stop, and I immediately sensed the blinding rage and disgust flashing through his mind at the sight of the woman.

"What the fuck are you doing here, Serenity?"

August, who had just popped a roll into his mouth, froze, his eyes going as wide as bowling balls. He slid his gaze to the woman sitting beside Lawrence.

Serenity smiled seductively and patted the seat beside her. "Come sit, Wyatt. We have some catching up to do, don't we?" The woman lifted a flirtatious eyebrow. "I won't bite unless you want me to." She glanced at me and gave a pitying smile. "You can leave the tramp from the low pack at the other end of the table where she belongs."

The audacity of this bitch. I released Wyatt's hand and stalked around the table toward her. The look on my face made her flinch in surprise. Crew and Eli both tensed, ready for trouble, and Wyatt's father had the decency to look confused. These two must have assumed their *upper-pack* intimidation would cow a lowly female like me. If that had been their game, then they were sorely mistaken.

Serenity stared up at me as I stood directly beside her chair.

"You may not bite, but I do." I leaned down, putting my face near hers. "Normally, I would ignore this sad, and"—I glanced down at the low-cut dress and her tits that were almost flopping out— "desperately *slutty* attempt to get even a passing glance from a wolf whom you treated like shit all those years ago. I can't ignore it, though. Maybe Wyatt can forgive you one day for messing with his head when he was a kid, but I don't have to." Pressing my face even closer, forcing her to lean away from me, I added, "If you ever cross my pack or Wyatt's again, I'll show you how well a lower-pack *alpha* female can ruin you. Bloodstone Island will look like a playground compared to what I'll do to you."

Lawrence adjusted himself in his chair. "Ladies, this isn't necessary."

"And *you*," I said, shifting my ire from Serenity to him. "Wyatt and I are fated mates. We've claimed each other, and that isn't changing. Maybe one day, you can yank your rich head out of your ass and realize you may actually want to get to know the amazing man who is your son. Look at him as a real person with his own wants and desires and successes, rather than trying to fit him into this stupid fucking world you think is perfect. Until then? Fuck off."

The servers appeared in the doorway from the kitchen, freezing at the sight of our standoff.

"Oh, good," I said, walking toward them. "There's a to-go option."

Yanking two plates from the hands of one of the servers, I turned to the hallway leading back to our room, nodding at Wyatt to follow me.

"Good night, everyone," I said to Crew, Chelsey, Eli, and August. The four looked surprised, amused, and uncomfortable with what they'd witnessed. "Enjoy your dinner." I cast a baleful look at Serenity and Lawrence. "If you can stomach the company."

Wyatt didn't say anything as we headed back to the room. I sensed his anger at his father and his disgust at seeing Serenity, but I also felt a surge of pride and happiness at what I'd done and said. Those emotions were far stronger in Wyatt's mind than any other. A pleased smile came over my face as we headed back into our room.

Once there, I set the food down and locked the door. "I cannot believe your father invited that bitch here." I wanted to punch something. No, I wanted to punch that bimbo downstairs. I'd have loved to slug her like I did Callista. "She's got some fucking nerve to try and—"

My words were cut off by Wyatt scooping me up and pressing his lips to mine. His emotions flooded into me as the kiss deepened.

"That temper of yours," he said when he broke away. "I've always liked it—when it wasn't aimed at me. It means more to me when you do stuff like that, claiming me so publicly. I think my inner wolf likes it even more."

I sighed and ran my fingers across his shoulders. "I lose my cool when I see you being mistreated. I'm not going to apologize for that."

"I don't want you to," he said. "So, about that dessert? Can we have that before dinner?"

Grinning, I leaned forward and kissed him again. Wyatt's lips crushed against mine as we allowed the lust and desire to take over. Hungry and demanding, our hands roved over each other's bodies, and a deep, overwhelming need to have him ignited in my chest.

Our new bond as fated mates plunged me over a cliff of sensation and emotion. His longing and need flooded from his mind into mine, sending my own emotions into a raging fire, like gasoline being thrown onto a torch.

Wyatt wrapped his arms around my waist and carried me to the bed. I tugged at his shirt, trying to get him naked. Once on the mattress, I nearly ripped his clothes off him.

"Are you in a hurry?" Wyatt asked with a smile as I yanked his pants down.

"I want to feel your skin on mine. I *need* it."

Before he could respond, I slipped my hand into his underwear and pulled his cock free, stroking it. Wyatt moaned, the ecstasy of the sensation filling his mind and spilling over into mine. I gasped, clenching my thighs. My pussy throbbed, dripping wet. It was like nothing I'd ever experienced.

I needed him inside me. Now. I would go mad if he didn't fill me.

Wyatt, sensing my need, sat forward and tore at my clothes. When his fingers brushed my breasts, I thought I would pass out. My pleasure bounced through his head, giving him even more. Our mingled desire surged through me, amplifying it. We were in a feedback loop like the last time we had sex. It excited and terrified me to see what this would be like now that our bond was fully complete.

Rolling me over, Wyatt finished undressing me and fell upon my body. His lips and fingers traveled all across my skin. I cried out in happy surprise as he took a nipple into his mouth, sucking and biting at it. Reaching out, I ran my fingers through his hair, urging him on with my hands and my mind.

When his finger slipped inside me, I almost lost it. It was too much, yet not enough, all at the same time. Writhing beneath him, he slid his finger in and out of me, all while continuing to lick, suck, and kiss my breasts and nipples.

"I need you, Wyatt," I said, my words strained as I spoke through clenched teeth.

Obeying my words and the thoughts and emotions he sensed coming from me, he released me and settled between my legs, his thick cock resting against my clit, sending waves of hot agonizing pleasure through me. He hadn't even started yet, and I was already quivering with anticipation.

Locking his eyes on mine, he slid into me. Breath rushed from my lungs, and I raised my head, looking down to watch as inch after inch slipped into the soaking wet confines of my body. I traced lines across his rippling abs with my fingers as he sank fully into me.

Before he moved again, he gazed down at me. "You're beautiful. Kira, I love you."

"I love you, too," I said, my voice slipping out in tiny gasps, preparing myself for what was to come.

I wrapped my legs around his waist, urging him on, digging my heels into him. Understanding, Wyatt rocked his hips against me, sliding almost all the way out, then back in. The more he moved, the more love and desire poured out of his mind. He had to have felt the same from me. Soon, we were writhing and thrusting with abandon. No longer chasing a climax, but rushing forward, trying to match each other's need. Giving, taking, sharing, and basking in more pleasure than I'd ever experienced in my life.

"Look at me," Wyatt gasped, sweat staining his hair.

I did. Time seemed to stand still. My gods, how long had we been going? I couldn't tell, but my body was coated with sweat. When I locked my eyes on his, the first tremble of release began to quiver between my legs and up into my gut and chest.

"I'm gonna come," I moaned.

"I'm close," Wyatt panted.

I gasped. "Harder, Wyatt.."

His slow thrusts turned into desperate, powerful movements. The aggression of his movements sent me over the edge. It was like I'd been floating on waves and now the water had vanished, sending me plummeting into an abyss of ecstasy. I came, digging my nails into his back, my mouth open in a silent scream.

I lost control of my legs. They twitched and kicked out as Wyatt called out my name and spilled his seed into me. As good as I felt, sensing his own orgasm sent bursting stars across my vision, and another crashing wave of the most wonderful pleasure swept over me.

I couldn't imagine anything else feeling as intimate. We were one, feeling everything the other did.

After what could have been a hundred years, the spell was finally broken, and we collapsed on the bed, Wyatt resting his head on my chest. We lay like that, catching our breath, all thoughts of his family and the war forgotten. For those few moments, the only thing that mattered was us.

Chapter 24 - Wyatt

The night before had been exhausting but also amazing. Kira and I had made love multiple times. I'd never understood how intense the fated mate bond could be, but now I understood why most couples honeymooned for at least a week. The constant desire was insatiable.

Now, we stood in the shower after a night of sex and intermittent sleep.

"You're getting frisky again," Kira murmured as I ran the bar of soap over her breasts.

"That's not true," I lied. "These are just so filthy and need to be cleaned. It's not my fault you're such a dirty girl."

She rolled her eyes, but didn't stop my roving hands.

"Want me to keep going?" I asked hopefully, growing hard just thinking about it.

Before Kira could answer, a loud pounding came at the bedroom door.

My face fell. "You've got to be kidding me. This place is as bad as that damn mansion."

"Maybe it's Von Thornton with a camera crew, ready to catch us in the act like last time."

I snorted a laugh. "At this point? I'd let them. The whole world can eat their hearts out while I have you for everyone to see."

The knock came again, more insistently this time.

"As great as it sounds to be a porn star," Kira said, "I think we need to see who that is. They're obviously not going to stop."

I grumbled and cursed under my breath as we dried off and put on robes. A third flurry of knocks came as I tied the belt at my waist. By the time we opened the door, I was ready to punch whoever was on the other side. That feeling vanished as soon as I saw it was Eli.

"What the hell is so important?" I asked.

Eli crossed her arms. "Where have you guys been? You missed breakfast."

"What time is it?" Kira asked. "We, uh, didn't check the clock."

"It's almost noon." The fallen angel scanned our faces, then grinned ruefully. "Been busy, I take it?"

Heat crept up my neck. I wanted to change the subject. "What's up? Do you have news or something?"

"Lots. Can I come in?"

Kira and I moved aside so she could enter, then closed the door.

"I can tell things between you and your dad are a little tense, to say the least," Eli said to me. "But having one of the richest and most powerful shifters on earth helping you has paid off. Do you want the good news first or the bad news?"

"There's both?" Kira asked. "I don't like that."

"Good news first," I said.

"We figured out where Simon Shingleman is."

Kira and I gaped at her. "What?" I asked.

"Your dad isn't on the board, but he's got stock in the company that runs the show," Eli said to me. "He received an email this morning, informing all shareholders that a replacement has been found for Garth Sheen's spot. That's the bad news. Guess who it is?"

"Simon?" I asked dumbly. "That psycho?"

"I don't understand why they're even worrying about replacing a board member," Kira said. "Do they not realize a war is happening? No one gives a shit about this show anymore." I could sense her incredulous rage.

"I agree," Eli said. "Your father was confused, too, Wyatt. Apparently, all the other shareholders he knew had discussed it with him. They all thought the show and the board would be dissolved. Maybe they could try a revival or reboot a couple of years after this war was over. They can't figure out why they added a board member now."

"Too dumb to realize their cash cow has been hacked up into hamburger," Kira muttered.

"There's more," Eli said.

"It gets worse?" I asked gingerly.

"A courier dropped off a message for you two about five minutes ago," Eli began. "It's a formal invite from Von Thronton for you guys to be on a live broadcast. They want you there within two hours if we want the whole world to know you're alive."

"Holy hell," I mumbled. "We can never get away from this guy."

"How did he know we were here?" Kira asked.

Eli gave Kira an incredulous look. "Dozens of people, including Callista Oborin, saw those Second

Pack shifters hustling us into that limo. They know who Wyatt Rivers and his father are. Not difficult to connect the dots."

"Eli, can you give me and Kira a few minutes? We need to talk about this."

The fallen angel nodded and departed.

"What do you want to do?" I asked my mate. I could sense the dread in her mind.

"I think we do it," she said.

"Seriously? That easy?"

"Yeah. The whole reason we came here was to find Simon and the showrunners. Now Simon apparently *is* a showrunner. There's a chance they'll be wherever Von is. It'll be like killing two birds with one stone."

"That's part of why I don't like it. This all seems too easy. It smells like a set-up. A trap to get us where they want us."

Even in the depths of her worry, Kira grinned at me. "We're pretty good at getting out of trouble. If we stick together, it should be no problem."

"You've got a lot more faith in us than I have," I said.

"It's our best bet," Kira said, the smile fading from her eyes. "If we don't go, then we'll end up wandering around this city with no real clue where to find anyone we're looking for. This is our best chance to get close to Simon, and possibly even Heline."

"All right," I said grudgingly. "I'll go along with it, but I'm warning you, if something happens that puts you in danger again, I'll never let you hear the end of it. This connection we have now? It's increased how much I worry about you, and I can't control that. Unless you want me chewing you out for getting into trouble for the billionth time, we need to keep our heads on a swivel."

"Deal," Kira said. "Let's hurry, time's wasting."

Once we were dressed and presentable, we headed downstairs and found our friends in the foyer. August was tapping away frantically on his phone, while Eli, Crew, and Chelsey stood off to the side. My father was nowhere in sight. Not surprising. He'd probably already forgotten I was here. That, or he was off somewhere trying to figure out some new angle to get me to return to this pack.

"There's supposed to be a car coming to pick us up," Eli said. "It should be here soon."

"Great," I muttered.

August let out a little whistle and turned to Crew. "Hey, bud? Remember when I said I'd look into your family?"

Crew's eye swiveled to meet August's face. "Did you find something?"

"I did some digging with a few of my contacts." He held up his phone and grinned victoriously. "Checked my email, and between what my people and I have dug up? It's a lot of dirt."

Crew looked ready to burst. "Is it enough to take them down? What are we talking?"

"I'll tell you, man," August looked at the screen again. "Some of this stuff is intense. If we release this, there's no way they would be able to keep their position in their pack. Doesn't matter how much money and power they have—best-case scenario, they go to jail for a decade." He grinned. "What's your call? This is your deal. You say the word, and my guys will start leaking this stuff."

Crew didn't hesitate. He was nodding before August had finished speaking. "As soon as possible. With the packs beginning to splinter, this information could help everyone remember we have one common enemy: corrupt leaders and a system that isn't working. All this fighting is pointless. Maybe if everyone sees this, they'll snap out of it. Stop fighting each other, and slow the war."

"He's right," Chelsey added. "That's the main thing. All the corruption and the messed-up mating connections. If those two things can be exposed and fixed, it'll help the world. It's obvious that the upper-pack leadership *had* to have known something was wrong with the blood tests. The more of these people we expose, then the more people will understand what the problem really is."

"This is good," I said. "Between this and whatever we can say during this interview, we might get some real change going. If we're *really* lucky, we can get Heline to show herself, too." For the first time since getting in that limo, I felt a flicker of hope.

Out the glass windows by the front door, I spotted a luxury SUV pull up in the driveway. Before I could mention it, the passenger door opened, and I almost shit myself. Von Thornton stepped out with a parasol shading his face from the sun.

"What's he doing here?" I muttered, and the others turned to see what I was looking at.

Kira groaned. "He came to collect us himself?"

"Come on," I said, opening the door.

"My lovelies!" Von called out as we stepped out onto the front steps. "It has been far too long."

Kira turned her head to me and hissed, "If he hugs me, I'm killing him. Just letting you know."

Von, having heard the words, laughed and pointed at her. "Ah, Kira, a spitfire as always. Such a charmer and..." Von faltered, caught off-guard by the sight of Crew standing beside Chelsey.

Very rarely had I seen the vampire caught wrong-footed, and this was one of those times.

"Uh, Bentley Crew? But I thought—"

"That I was dead?" Crew said. "Surprise."

"Well then," Von said, recovering. "It appears this truly is a day to celebrate. Not only are Wyatt, Kira, and Chelsey alive when we thought all hope was lost, but Bentley Crew as well? What a day!" He laughed heartily and added, "This must be how it felt for those poor people centuries ago when they went up against vampires. Thinking they'd killed a man, only to see them pop back up alive a few moments later." Von dabbed at his eyes. "You have no idea how I mourned for thee. I never thought I would see you again."

His joy at our miraculous return seemed genuine. That alone made me wonder what was really going on in that undead head of his. From what I'd learned, he actually *had* liked the contestants, but he also reveled in our misery and suffering. Such a strange and confusing man.

"Hey, bro," August said. "Can we get going? No offense, but you're kinda creepy."

Von glanced at my friend and raised an eyebrow. "Hmm, nice to meet you, sir. I have the feeling your blood would taste like bologna and cheese sandwiches." He wrinkled his nose in disgust. "You have nothing to fear from me. Come, everyone. See my new toy."

He led us down to the car. As large as it was, I saw no way for all seven of us to fit inside. I was about to tell him to forget it, that I'd have my father's chauffeur bring the limo around, when he opened the rear door. My mouth dropped open. The rear of the SUV looked to be at least double the size it should have been.

"Special enchantment," Von cooed. "It makes the inside larger than the outside." He leaned toward me and whispered, "*Very* expensive upgrade."

Climbing in, I felt a strange sense of vertigo.

Inside, another surprise awaited us. Von wasn't alone. A small, mousy-haired woman sat on one of the bench seats, scribbling onto a legal pad. She ignored us as we piled into the back.

Once we were on the road, the strange woman turned to look out the window.

Von noticed my gaze. "Personal assistant. You can't have too much help these days. The service sent her this morning. My usual one is out sick, apparently. I don't really need one on Bloodstone, but here on the mainland? Indispensable."

August was moving around the rear of the SUV, tugging on the arm rests.

"Is there something I can help you with, sir?" Von drawled.

August stopped and took a seat before grinning at the vampire. "My name isn't *sir*, it's August. I was checking to see if your little magic car was as cool as the limo Wyatt's dad sent. You need to step up your game. No built-in fridges? Kinda lame."

Von's left eye twitched. "Well, I will be sure to pass along those requests to the manufacturer, Mr. Autumn."

August scowled. "No, I said my name is Aug—"

"Anyway," Von cut in, "Kira, Wyatt, I must tell you how heartbroken I was that the show was shut down before we reached the climax."

"Yeah," I said. "You...what was it they said?" I frowned deeply as though trying to remember. "Didn't you fight valiantly to try and save our lives? The way the news portrayed it, you were slaying beasts left and right to get us out. Weird. I don't remember any of that."

Von chuckled and slapped a hand on his knee. "Hyperbole, my boy." He leaned forward conspiratorially. "You know how the press can be. They have this need to lift me up even higher than I already am. My personal security team wouldn't hear any arguments I had about staying. I assure you, there were many vociferous arguments, but alas, I was shuffled off to the helicopter and flown away in the night. My greatest regret is that we didn't get to have any more fun together."

"Fun?" Kira asked through gritted teeth.

"I know," Von said wistfully, ignoring Kira's tone. "I miss it, too. Honestly, it's been quite boring here. Stuck behind all these walls and security while that silly fighting goes on outside. Anyway, when you two popped up on Callista's broadcast last night? My heart simply fluttered with delight. I swear, I could feel the excitement in my ancient veins. I'm looking forward to seeing how we can shake things up even more."

I'd had enough of his pompous attitude. It was time to get down to business.

"Do you know Heline, Von?" I asked. My question was blunt, cutting him off while he yammered on about something pointless.

The vampire blinked slowly at me. "The moon goddess? That Heline?"

"Yes."

Von, regaining his footing, smiled and rolled his eyes. "My dear boy, one does not simply *know* a goddess. How silly. She is above these trivial matters for the most part." He laughed it off.

Something about the wooden way he'd answered, how quickly he'd tried to brush off my question, gave me the sense that he was lying. This man *did* know more about Heline than most. Whether that meant he was a friend, a slave, a confidant, or perhaps had some insight into her plans, I didn't know, but he was hiding something—I could see it in his eyes. Kira felt it, too. Her own thoughts went in the same direction.

Von snapped his fingers, making me flinch, and pointed at Crew. "Bentley, I have to say, seeing you again is an even bigger shock. I would love to get you to do an in-depth interview. You can tell the world how you managed to survive the dangers of Bloodstone Island for, what, two years? The uh..." Von tapped a spot below his own eye. "The injury there, would make for great drama."

Crew scowled. "An interview?"

"Of course. We would obviously use any information you gave us to help with hunting down any would-be survivors the next time." Von winced. "Having you survive all this time *really* dilutes the image of Bloodstone Island. It's supposed to be this place where one wrong step means death." He sighed heavily. "If anyone can live there, it's nothing more than a tropical resort, really. If it becomes too easy, then contestants will eventually run off all the time. And while I enjoy an exciting death as much as our viewers, it's only truly juicy if it happens on camera."

"Can you shut up?" Chelsey snapped.

"Yes, please," Crew agreed. "I forgot how annoying you were, Von."

If their words hurt the vampire in any way, he didn't show it. "I can see how some would think me less than truthful, but I assure you, everything I say is accurate. It's part of what helps my mystique, if you will." Von smiled slyly. "I am beloved by fans around the world. I shudder to think how much I would be missed if I was gone. Every immortal being dreams of hearing they would be missed if they vanished from this life. That is a gift I don't take lightly."

Thankfully, the car pulled up outside a skyscraper downtown before Von could continue waxing poetic about how much he thought everyone loved him. Two hulking demons opened the door. Things were fine until Eli stepped out of the car.

The larger of the two guards growled low in his throat. "Filth," he grunted.

Eli glared back at them. "Sulfurous prick."

"Big words from an angel who lost her wings," the other guard said.

Von clapped his hands. "Enough of that, boys. These are honored guests. Please don't embarrass me.

Thank you." He drew the last words out like the end
of some chipper song.

The demons, though visibly still upset at Eli's
presence, had some professionalism and kept their
mouths shit. They stood behind us as we followed
Von, probably to make sure none of us ran.

Von's assistant, who still hadn't said a word to us,
hurried along ahead of us, forcing our group to walk
fast to keep up. Von led us to a private elevator at the
far end of the lobby, using some type of magical gem
embedded in a keycard to unlock the door.

Once we'd gotten inside and the doors closed, he
grinned around at all of us. "This is fun," he
murmured. "Such a coup, having the two of you here.
I cannot wait to see the ratings for this little special."
His smile slipped a bit. "Hmm, they won't be as big as
they should be, of course, what with all that silly
fighting going on. But it is what it is."

We passed floor after floor. Twenty, thirty, forty,
fifty, it went on and on. The hum of the elevator was
almost enough to lull me to sleep. How tall was this
building?

Eventually, the elevator car slowed to a stop. I
glanced up and saw we were on floor 107.

"Everyone off!" Von exclaimed.

The doors slid open, and we stepped into a large room that looked like some sort of set or media room. There were cameras everywhere, standard recording devices as well as the enchanted hovering cameras. Techs and assistants were testing audio equipment, adjusting lights and furniture. When I saw what else awaited us, I nearly laughed.

A large table had been set up at the center of the room, and the same board members we'd met on Bloodstone sat around it. Everyone was in attendance, even the mysterious woman in white. The only one missing was the deceased Garth Sheen. In his place sat Simon Shingleman.

Kira stiffened beside me, and a swirl of emotions flooded her mind. It made me momentarily dizzy. Along with the inevitable rage, the most prevalent emotion between the two of us was disgust. Part of me had hoped the news Eli had relayed to us would be wrong. Surely a person as unstable as Simon couldn't have been given such a place of power and responsibility. Yet, here he was, looking like King Shit of Turd Mountain. A self-important smile played on his lips. The others wore crisp, expensive suits, while Simon was wearing his ratty, stained lab coat.

There were a few other notable faces in the room as well: the mayor of Fangmore City, a few actors and musicians, a well-known billionaire tech mogul, and the starting point guard for the Fangmore Howlers professional basketball team. It was as though they were setting up for some sort of talk show and had no care about the war going on beyond the city gates. Very few people had the privilege of continuing their lives like nothing was happening.

To the left of the large table, Callista Oborin stared daggers at me and Kira. Her shattered nose had been magically healed, but that didn't help with her opinion of us.

Von strode across the room, and the others at the table turned in our direction. Not a single one of them looked happy to see us. Other than Simon, that was. The scientist beamed at us, but there was no way to know exactly what that smile meant. It certainly didn't hide the madness behind his eyes.

Simon's gaze locked on Kira, and my skin crawled at the way he leered at her. I tugged Kira aside, putting myself between her and the mad fae scientist.

My instincts were screaming that we were in danger. Had we walked into a hornet's nest? A trap? Would we ever see the Eleventh Pack's lands again? There was no way of knowing what to expect. All I could do was keep my mate safe if things went sideways.

Von and his assistant took a seat at the table. "Come now, everyone," the vampire said. "Have a seat. The show must go on."

Then the asshole winked at me.

Chapter 25 - Kira

The hesitancy I felt as we walked toward the table nearly made me freeze in place, but I pushed forward. I would *not* let these assholes see me weak.

Before each seat was a legal pad and pencil, as if they expected us to take notes or something. Wyatt took his seat, and I sat beside him, the mousy little assistant on my other side. The woman still hadn't said a word, which didn't surprise me. If I had to be around Von Thornton all day, I'd keep my mouth shut, too. The guy never seemed to stop talking. The poor woman had probably given up on speaking while at work.

Simon's eyes were still on me. Even without looking in his direction, I could feel them boring into me. In the deepest recesses of my mind, I could still catch small hints and whispers of his voice, calling to me. It was less like the connection Wyatt and I shared and more like a faint memory. Any hope I'd had that I'd imagined it vanished. That subconscious pull and tug toward him was still there; Simon still had some sort of control over me.

What had he done to me in that lab?

Von sat on Wyatt's other side. Wyatt was obviously not happy to be so close to the vampire, but he kept a neutral face.

"I'm sorry, dears," Von said, looking at Crew, Eli, and August. "This meeting is only for *current* cast members of *The Reject Project*. For one thing, you are mostly unknown to the public and would confuse viewers. You, Mr. Crew, are more difficult to explain. The viewers would, of course, recognize you, and as I said earlier, Bloodstone Island's reputation for danger has already been diluted by having these three lovely folks return unscathed. Another survivor would tarnish it beyond redemption." Von pointed to the rear of the room. "There's a bench over there. Help yourselves to the craft service table if you'd like."

August and the others walked away, grumbling and hissing under their breath. Crew glanced back and gave Chelsey a reassuring nod before moving to the back of the room.

Beneath the table, I took Wyatt's hand, trying to take solace in his thoughts and emotions floating through my mind. Anything to take the edge off. I was afraid Simon might cast a spell on me any second. I still remembered the vacant look in Abel's eyes during that final battle in the volcano. The last thing I wanted was to be that helpless and robotic—a tool for the fae scientist and nothing more.

Callista took a seat at the table, completing our group, and a moment later, the cameras hummed to life. My stomach flipped. I'd spent the last few weeks on television, but for some strange reason, this moment was more nerve-racking than almost anything else I'd done.

"Good afternoon, everyone. Welcome back to a very special episode of *The Reject Project*," Von said, facing the nearest camera. "I bet you thought we were done for, but you know what we always say: everyone loves an underdog. And we've most definitely been an underdog the last few days, but here we are." He clapped and chuckled.

He glanced around the table, waiting for the rest of us to join in his laughter, but he was met with stony faces. While Von kept spouting nonsense to the camera, I sensed another foreign presence in my mind, sharp and insistent like a fingernail digging under a scab. My eye twitched, and I turned to see Callista gaze at me hungrily. Bitch. She was doing her best to dig into my head again like last time. Every defensive wall I had went up, slamming like a door in her face.

She wrinkled her nose in dissatisfaction and leaned back, crossing her arms.

Von went around the table, introducing several people, though he skipped over most of the board members and his assistant. Finally, he came to Wyatt and me.

"Now, for the biggest surprise in our show's history," Von said as the camera panned toward me. "We have Wyatt Rivers and Kira Durst. Our star-crossed lovers, the game-rigging anti-heroes. Two dangerous and sexy shifters who we thought had succumbed to the terrible accident on Bloodstone Island. They are, in fact, alive and here with us. How exciting is that? Say hello to your rabid fans. They are, no doubt, shocked to see you all."

Wyatt and I waved half-heartedly at the camera.

"Also," Von said, a look of bloodthirsty glee on his face, "you may not notice, as the marks have almost faded, but it does appear that these two voracious lovers have claimed one another. Such a huge win for all those team Kwyatt fans. Since mating, they have been very busy. Some of you may have even seen them last night. Roll the footage."

Off camera, a monitor broadcasted what was being shown to the viewers. A reel of us trying to protect the acolytes from Callista's mental torture.

"Yes, Von," Callista added from across the table, her showbiz persona in full, million-dollar-smile effect. "But it appears after our little discussion last night, our couple may have their story mixed up. If you'll remember, Kira stated on Bloodstone Island that the fated mate connections had been mixed up or the results damaged in some way. Yet, there she was last night, defending these acolytes who identified and certified those connections." Callista turned her steely eyes on me. "Kira, your words that night instigated the riots that have turned into the war we face now. Are you going back on those words? Because if so, then a *lot* of blood is on your hands."

I cleared my throat, realizing she was pausing to let me or Wyatt speak. "I'm not sure that you truly understand the situation, Callista," I said. As I opened my mouth to keep speaking, I froze, blinking, feeling my eyelids growing heavy.

"I..." My head swam with confusion. "Uh..." Something was wrong with me. It had to be Simon. This was exactly what had happened to me on the battlefield.

Every time I tried to open my mouth, nothing came out. I must have looked guilty beyond belief. Wyatt turned toward me and saw the look of horror in my eyes. The fingers of his mind drifted into mine, and an instant later, he spun in his chair, angry eyes leveling on Simon.

"He's doing something to her," Wyatt snapped.

Simon adjusted his glasses and laughed. "Me? I'm doing nothing. Perhaps Ms. Durst is simply speechless with guilt for her crimes. Have you thought about that, Mr. Rivers?"

Veins bulged at my neck as I tried to force words from my mouth, but it was like a brick wall had been built between my voice box and my mouth. I stared down at the table, at the pad of paper and sharpened pencil I had before me, trying to make sense of what was happening. Around the room, the other guests and board members glared at me with dark, accusing eyes.

A hand touched my leg. Firm yet gentle, gripping my thigh. The fingers cool even through my pants. Von's assistant. Surprised, I glanced down at her hand.

In an instant, the mental blockage was gone, so was Simon's strange murmuring in my mind. My head was clear.

Callista was speaking again. "Kira Durst has apparently seen the truth of it and is trying to work up the courage to take it all back. I suggest—"

"I'm not taking anything back," I snapped. Callista flinched, and Simon narrowed his eyes. "The fated mate connections are real. As for the stupid blood tests we use to find our mates? Those are what's wrong, and I can tell you that for a fact. My blood test paired me with a wolf who made me miserable. Now I'm mated to my true fated mate. Wyatt Rivers."

A shocked murmur ran around the table.

"Hang on," Von said, looking uncomfortable. "You're saying that you two aren't just regular mates, but *fated* mates? That can't be possible. As you said, the blood tests—"

"Are wrong," I said again. "Pay attention, Von. See if you can follow along."

The vampire's eyes flashed at my impropriety.

"Very convenient," Callista scoffed. "It's quite easy to *say* you are fated mates. There is no way to prove that. For all we know, you two were rutting like pigs in heat and decided to claim each other."

"We don't need to prove anything to anyone," I said. "I'm not flaunting our connection. That's not what this is about. It's about what people are being led to believe. There is no question that fated mates are real. The part that's a lie is that most people are not with the person they are meant to be with."

I could see my point wasn't getting across, at least not with the people at the table. I changed tactics. "Tell me, exactly, what the acolytes have to gain from mixing up these connections?"

A few attendees appeared thoughtful. Even Von's forehead creased.

"See," I said, "they aren't getting rich; they aren't getting anything. I know who *does* gain something."

"Who in the world, other than the acolytes, would want to mess with these connections, Kira?" Callista asked, her voice dripping with suspicion.

I shrugged. "Ask Heline."

That caused more of an uproar than anything I'd said so far. Almost all of the people at the table were wolf shifters. People who'd spent their lives worshipping, respecting, and fearing the moon goddess.

"Now, wait one minute," a bearded board member said. "You can't go dragging the moon goddess's name into this. There is no proof she had anything to do with this."

The mystery woman in white beside the man shook her head, her nose wrinkled, but otherwise kept her mouth shut. Multiple voices around the room echoed the board member's assertion.

Ignoring them, I turned to the vampire. "Von, I'll admit, you may be insufferable, condescending, and self-important, but there is something you taught me when I was on the show."

A hint of a smile returned to Von's lips. "Oh? Do tell, darling."

"Immortals get bored. They lose their sense of empathy and end up entertaining themselves in some pretty terrible ways. After giving it a lot of thought, I think Heline is either delusional and making mistakes due to her advanced age, or she's like you. She's seen it all, lived it all, heard it all, and wants something new. An exciting change of pace. My theory is she's messing with the connections as some twisted form of entertainment."

"That is blasphemy!" a heavy-set bald man shouted, rising from his chair and slamming his fist on the table.

Callista leaned back in her chair, shaking her head derisively. The rest chimed in, aghast that I would dare besmirch the moon goddess.

"I would not want to be you," the bearded showrunner said. "The punishments you have coming your way?" He whistled. "You're a dead girl walking, that's what you are."

Wyatt slapped his palm on the table in a loud *pop*. The table went silent, turning to look at him.

"I suggest," Wyatt said, "that we talk to Heline herself. Get her opinion on this matter."

I sensed Wyatt's intent a split second before he moved. He snatched the sharpened pencil form beside his pad of paper, leaped from his seat, wrapped an arm around Von's chest, and placed the pencil above Von's heart. He pressed deep, puncturing the suit and dress shirt and the first few layers of skin, then paused.

Von let out a little squeal of terror as everyone around the table flinched, both at the sheer speed with which Wyatt had moved and at what he'd done. Von's eyes darted around the room in a panic. I'd never seen the man sweat before, but already beads of moisture were visible on his upper lips and forehead. His pale fingers gripped the armrests.

"I can't die like this," he gasped. "My *fans*. They're watching. If I die on air, it will be appalling."

Ignoring Von's pleas, Wyatt said, "Call for Heline, Von."

Von's murmured begging ceased. "Excuse me?"

"Of every person on this show, you've been around the longest. If anyone knows the moon goddess, it's you. You see her at the end of every damned season. Call her. Tell her to get her ass down here. Now."

"But...but...but," Von stammered. "My boy, I can't simply call to a goddess—aah!" Von's words cut off in a shriek as Wyatt dug the pencil in deeper.

"Von," Wyat said with a sad shake of his head, "I am *not* a fan of yours. Please don't piss me off. I've staked enough vamps in my day to know exactly how scared you are of this pencil."

I couldn't take my eyes off Von's face. The sheer terror I saw there was both sad and cathartic. He'd put us through so much shit, had giggled, laughed, and applauded over it. Now he was getting a taste of the danger he loved—and it seemed he wasn't a fan.

Wyatt dug the pencil in deeper and put his lips to Von's ear. "Tick-tock, Von."

"If you want to talk to her, then do it!" Von screamed. "She's right there!"

His shaking, pale finger pointed at the woman in white. My mouth fell open as I turned to look at her.

The woman glared at Von. "I suppose," she said with thinly veiled anger, "it is time to shed this disguise."

The woman stood, her white dress vanishing with a flash, replaced by a shimmering gray outfit the color of a bright full moon. Her face and hair transformed as well. The hair now tumbled down her back was a shimmery white, her face, already beautiful, became gorgeous beyond words.

There was a definite resemblance to Lucina. The moon goddess had been sitting there among us all along. She was terrifying to behold.

"Turn the cameras off. Now," she commanded.

All around the room, the hovering cameras drooped and fluttered to the ground. Heline glared at Von and didn't see the movement at the rear of the room. Eli rushed one of the lone cameramen and placed a hand on the back of his head. The man's eyes rolled up, and she and August caught his body, dragging it away. Chelsey turned the camera towards us, awkwardly trying to adjust the huge machine. Crew caught my eye and gave me a thumbs-up. It all happened in less than ten seconds, and no one was any the wiser. Everyone was too awestruck by the appearance of a goddess in their midst to notice what had happened. Whatever went down next would be broadcast to the world.

"You," Heline said, turning her gray eyes upon me. She looked both irritated and amused. "Such a clever girl you are. I underestimated you when I began this little game."

The assistant squeezed my thigh even tighter as Heline took a step toward me. The woman must have been as scared as I was.

"What you said was correct," Heline said. "You nailed the gist. After tens of thousands of years, I have become bored. These simple run-of-the-mill connections had no fire, no excitement." Heline stood directly above me now, eyes boring into mine with a fiery intensity. "Countless wolf shifters, countless simple mating connections. You can't help but get tired of it all."

"What was the point?" I muttered, surprised I could even speak.

"The point?" Heline repeated with a sad little smile. "To see how far I could push things, of course. I wanted to make life more interesting. I wished to test the limits."

"Of us?"

She nodded. "I am your chosen god. It is my prerogative to do as I will with my subjects. I twisted the pairings, hid the true matches, and put people with mates who made them miserable." She chuckled to herself. "It's the main reason *The Reject Project* came to be. In times past, rejected mates were quite rare. My fiddling created a problem, and this show was born. Of course, I had to have a seat at the table. I wanted to watch it all happen. Perhaps through my machinations, a pair I'd kept apart might find themselves surviving great dangers to be with one another." The goddess leaned down, her eyes level with mine. "After all these years, I saw you and Wyatt as a great test to my skills. You were fated and found each other at a young age. It had all worked out perfectly for you. I decided you would be my masterpiece. I did everything in my power to keep you apart, but..." She frowned and reached forward, an icy-cold finger running along the fading claiming mark on my neck. "It seems you have figured out you are fated mates. All the fun is gone now." She glanced across the table. "Simon? Do as you will. I'm done playing with this toy."

Chaos erupted. Simon leaped from his chair, laughing maniacally. The others around the table scattered, shouting in fear as he lifted his hand. Magic crackled in the air as Heline took a step back, clearing the way for Simon. Wyatt dropped the pencil, allowing Von to scamper out of the room like a mouse escaping a trap.

"Perhaps," Simon said to me, "we'll have you tear your handsome mate apart. Then I'll wake you to see the aftermath."

Wyatt was rushing around the table, trying to get to Simon, but magic was faster than any person. A dark spell burst from Simon's hands, black and writhing like oil dropped in water. When it struck me, a veil seemed to go over my eyes, and the part of me that was actually *me* plunged deep into the rear of my mind.

I could see what was happening, but only dimly, as though watching from far away on a dark night. I had no control over myself. My greatest fear had happened. I watched as the magic Simon had filled me with used my body as its own and stood. Shifting, I lunged across the room, pouncing on Wyatt a moment before he struck Simon.

Stop! Please no, don't hurt him. Gods, please stop, I screamed out at myself from deep in my mental prison, but through my internal screams, I watched as the jaws that had once belonged to me snapped and bit at Wyatt. He managed to hold me back, his hands under my jaw, but I was strong and he'd been caught unaware. I couldn't even hear his thoughts or emotions now. All I could see was the terror in his eyes as my teeth drew nearer his neck.

"Enough!" a shout erupted from behind me.

Even in the manic feral state of my body, whatever controlled me turned to see the mousy woman standing. She lifted her arms and a flash of magic shot forward, surrounding me in a net of darkness, the strands of it digging painfully into me. With a jerk of her hand, I was hauled away from Wyatt, leaving him blessedly safe.

Inside the strange magical net, Simon's influence melted away, the weird connection between us shattering. Suddenly, I was free. Freer than I'd felt since that night all those years ago. Whatever Simon had done to me all those years ago, what he had continued building in his lab, was gone. I shuddered with relief.

Dark, writhing snakes of shadow coiled around the woman's feet, and she vanished. Before us stood the stark beauty that was Lucina. Shadows rushed from every corner of the room and enveloped her nakedness. At first glance, she was the polar opposite of Heline. Dark hair and eyes, black dress, but the same milky skin and a shockingly similar face. They could have been twins.

"Holy shit!" a man exclaimed from the rear of the room.

Others expressed similar sentiments. The shock at seeing another mystical being along with Heline was almost too much.

Lucina flicked her wrist, and the shadow net containing me vanished. Shifting back to my human form, I crumpled to the ground. Wyatt was with me in an instant, cradling me in his arms.

Simon looked at me in indignation. "You've ruined her!" he bellowed, gesturing to me, then he looked at Lucina. "You ruined my greatest achievement, you bitch!" Spittle flew from his mouth as he shouted. I hadn't thought he could look more psychotic, but he did.

"You," Lucina said calmly, "are not meant for this world."

"Fuck you!" he shouted and cast a spell toward her.

Lucina batted it away like a fly and raised her own hands. Rippling shadows burst forth from her chest and enveloped Simon. The mad fae shrieked in horror as the shadows wound around his legs, up his waist and stomach.

"No!" he screamed, trying to push the shadows away, but his hands were sucked in. "Please no. Don't." His shouts were manic now, blind terror making his voice jump in octaves until he sounded like a terrified child.

Tendrils of shadow enveloped his face, shutting off his words. Once he'd been fully surrounded, a dark pulse shivered through the tentacles, and when they swept away a moment later, Simon stood, now nothing more than a living shadow. A faded outline that had once been a man.

Lucina grinned. "Time to come home, my child," she said, and snapped her fingers.

Simon vanished into the rest of the shadows, then flew to rejoin her. He was gone. That quick. That easy. The man who'd tortured my existence for my entire life was gone.

My horror at the way he'd been taken was nothing compared to the relief I felt being free of him and his influence. Did I truly never have to worry about him hurting me or anyone I cared about again?

Wyatt pulled me close, and his presence was like a blanket of warmth. He calmed and steadied me and my inner wolf. That was good, because things looked like they were gonna get worse before they got better.

Lucina and Heline glared at each other. Across the room, August had taken the camera from Chelsey and positioned it to get a better view. The bright red light on the viewfinder said it was still broadcasting.

"You know the rules, sister," Lucina said, a hint of disappointment in her voice. "You've pushed your little game too far. The mortals are at war because you became bored. I didn't realize you were so childish as to break one of the laws of our kind for simple pleasures."

Heline grinned maliciously. "You know, dear Lucina, I thought I sensed you nearby. Clever trick. *Fantastic* disguise. I couldn't even tell you were there under that pathetic face. You've not left your little island for centuries. I didn't really think you had it in you."

"Yes, I'm sure you didn't," Lucina said. "Is that why you chose to flaunt the rules? You know we are not to change the course of mortal history. *Nothing* changes things more than love and war, and you've meddled with both."

Heline's grin vanished, and she pouted like a petulant child. "Rules and laws are beneath me. But..." She stood straight, her face stoic, all other emotions bleeding away. "I'll put things right. It's no longer fun, anyway. You'll need to ensure they never know it was me who did this, of course. If the mortals knew, I'd lose their respect and worship. I would weaken, and I cannot have that. We'll place the blame, as I originally intended, on my acolytes. The rabble will love me even more for *fixing* the issue. After that, you can tuck your tail and run back to your island of misfit creatures."

Shrugging out of Wyatt's grip, I stood, clearing my throat. Both goddesses turned their eyes on me. The intimidation rushing through me made my knees shake and almost buckle.

"I wouldn't do that if I were you," I said to Heline.

Hot indignation flared through Heline's eyes. "*You* wouldn't do *that*? Why is that, you silly little wolf?"

"It's just that, uh...." I pointed toward August and the live camera trained on her. "That's not really gonna fly anymore."

Heline turned and registered the camera. A mix of emotions flashed across her face--confusion, understanding, shock, anger, fear, rage. Her face was even paler than before as she took in the truth. Millions had seen and listened to her admit to all she'd done.

Behind me, Wyatt chuckled. "After all this, I can't believe I'm happy to see a camera."

Heline's eyes widened, and I thought she was going to unleash a tirade on us. But instead, she grinned and laughed along with Wyatt.

"Yes, yes, yes, so funny," she chuckled. "Of *course* I knew that camera was there. Do you really think the great Heline would let anything happen to her acolytes? I care deeply for them. I would never allow harm to come to them for something I allegedly did."

"Really?" I asked dryly.

"I fully intended to make the fated mate pairings right again. I always did, my dear girl," Heline added.

The way she called me *dear girl* made my guts go watery and cold. The smile on her lips was no longer jovial. It looked like the kind of smile a predator gave a small creature before devouring them.

"I will make those connections right," Heline said. "In fact, I'll do it at this very minute...as long as you and Wyatt make the right choice."

"Excuse me?" I asked. Wyatt's hand found mine.

"Yes, of course. I'll make you a deal," Heline said. "Since you two were always meant to be fated mates, you can either keep the connection you've established, or I can remove that connection and end the war." She cocked an eyebrow. "Your choice. Love, or the deaths of thousands. I'll give you a hint...I know what the right option is."

Lucin sighed behind her. "Sister, you truly are growing tiresome."

Heline spun and leveled a finger at the other goddess. "Due to your interference, I am going to lose everything," she hissed. "My influence is already waning. I can feel it already. If I'm to be relegated, then I *will* have one last bit of fun."

I had no clue what to do. How could I give up Wyatt, give up this wonderful connection we'd established? Yet, there were hundreds, thousands, maybe even millions fighting and dying. I could end it all.

Turning toward him, I looked into Wyatt's eyes. He gave me a sad smile.

I understood the truth. Even without a fated mate connection, I would love him. I had always loved him, even without some magical connection binding me to him. Ending the war was the most important thing we could do.

"I know your answer, Kira," Heline said. "I can see it written all over your face. What of your beloved? This concerns him as well. What does he say?"

Chapter 26 - Wyatt

All eyes in the room turned toward me. Heline was right. I could see Kira's answer in her eyes. She was a protector. She would sacrifice anything and everything to save the innocent. That was one of the main things that made her good at her job, and drove me crazy. Always jumping into danger, always stepping over the line to help someone, save someone, rescue someone.

But what about her? Didn't she deserve happiness?

I didn't want to lose this special thing we had. It meant everything to me, had already become an integral part of my soul, even after only a few days of being mates. Could I be selfish? Would I be able to live with myself if I chose Kira over the entire world? I'd loved her for years, and now that love had grown to a wildfire in my heart.

Kira nodded, squeezed my hand, and said her mental goodbye. If we chose to end the war, we would never again see our thoughts and emotions in one another's minds. As painful as that thought was, I would at least have Kira by my side forever.

"End the war, Heline," I whispered.

"Ugh," the goddess groaned. "You two are no fun at all. *Fine.* I'll go about and defuse the war. There is quite a lot a goddess can do." She glared at the two of us. "Kira? Wyatt? You're both very disappointing. I don't deal with things that bore me. Stay out of my affairs, and I'll stay out of yours. Keep your little connection. I have no need of you any longer. Why should I care who you're with? Besides, your connection was fated. No one can change that. Not even a god. Why do you think I changed the blood tests?"

"Seriously? You were just fucking with us?" I snapped. How could a god be so flippant and childish?

Heline scoffed and turned back to Lucina. "I will not meddle in the affairs of mortals anymore. They bore me, and they are such tiresome creatures. As of today, all my acolytes will be relieved of their duties. These filthy animals can find their mates the old-fashioned way." She turned to glare at us. "They can hump legs, for all I care."

"So gracious of you," Lucina said with a sneer.

"Now, if you'll excuse me, it appears I must spend the next several days ending battles throughout the world. Feel free to help if you want, sister, since you've become concerned about these mortals. Perhaps you can call some of our other siblings or cousins. A god's work is never done."

Heline graced me and Kira with one last withering glare, then vanished in a flash of light.

Lucina nodded to us, and if I wasn't mistaken, a faint smile tugged at the corners of her mouth. Instead of bursting into a thousand bats like she usually did, she raised her arms and the shadows enveloped her, then vanished.

"What the fuck?" one of the board members muttered. He sat in a corner, hugging his knees. He looked more like a scared child than a powerful businessman.

Movement caught my eye, and I glanced at our friends. August was talking hurriedly to Crew, who nodded and took over control of the camera. August then rushed over to take a seat at the table while Crew zoomed the camera in close to August's face.

"Good afternoon, world. I hope you enjoyed the latest episode of the new show, *What the Fuck?* I'm your host, August Evander.

"Now that I have a captive audience, I have some cats—er, dogs—to let out of the bag. I'm sure you'll all enjoy this. We all love dirt. Let's spill the tea, shall we?"

August rambled off the information he'd dug up, starting with Crew's parents. He proceeded to discuss the Tranquility Council's corruption, the assassinations carried out by Tranquility operatives, pay-offs, embezzling, blackmailing, paid-off judges, murders, and more. Nearly every alpha and beta from the upper packs were named in some dirty dealing or another.

At first, we stood transfixed by August's rapid-fire delivery, but eventually, the board members snapped out of the shock from seeing two goddesses fight in front of them. Especially when August began to name several of them in his reports.

"Stop him!" the bearded board member shrieked.

Several of the showrunners scrambled over like children to yank the power on the camera, finally ending the broadcast.

August sighed in disappointment. "Aw, man, I was just getting into the sex scandals. One of the pack alphas likes getting pegged by his beta's wife. We even got video evidence. That was going to be my cherry on top. Damn."

"We're ruined," a dark-skinned board member groaned. "The world knows the show was Heline's personal sadistic fucking playground. It's all over."

"More than the show is over," Crew said. "With everything August just dumped on the world? I think the ball is really going to start rolling on dissolving the packs, and shaking up the council leadership. We did it." He looked at me and took Chelsey's hand. In all my time knowing him, Crew rarely smiled, but he did now. "We've started something here."

I grinned and glanced at the group of distraught showrunners. "Maybe you can keep your show on, but you'll have to change a *lot*. Maybe play a different angle. You could try to work on finding *real* fated mate connections, and do away with all the violence."

"No violence? On Bloodstone Island?" a showrunner asked, gaping at me.

"You'll never go back to Bloodstone Island," I said. "As of now, that place is completely off-limits. I'll see to it that it remains unbothered. If you want to try to go back there, you can deal with me, or Lucina the Shadowkeeper. Your choice."

"Plug that camera back in," Kira ordered.

One of the showrunners shook their head. "No way. We can't."

"I said do it," Kira growled. "You all are probably going to jail, anyway, but I can make sure you go with plenty of broken bones. Now, plug in the fucking camera."

Deciding that discretion was the better part of valor, the man grabbed the plug and jammed it back into the wall. Crew gave Kira a questioning look, and she nodded. Crew shrugged and tilted the lens toward her face.

Once the camera was focused on her, Kira spoke. "To anyone still watching, there are going to be some major changes coming. It may take some time as most of the packs, especially the larger ones, are splintering. Once the cleanup and recovery have taken place, I think many of you will be open and ready for new ideas and traditions.

"The old ways led us to this. Old prejudices pushed us to hate one another. But now we know the truth. It wasn't the upper packs versus the lower packs. It was a spoiled god wanting to have fun.

"That's the whole problem. *Upper*? *Lower*? Who gives a damn? We weren't meant to be shoved into these massive packs with no connection to our alphas. We should do things as we did in the distant past. Small packs, normal hierarchies—family, friends, fated mates. It was never supposed to be so cold and calculated as sending in a vial of blood." Kira's face creased with distaste. "We were supposed to find our mates naturally. Everyone deserves to be in a pack full of people who care about them." She glanced at me. "They deserve to be with someone they truly love. I hope we can do that. All of us."

Kira nodded to Eli, who unplugged the camera again.

Crew stood over the cowering showrunners, hands on hips. "Sit down."

"We are sitting," said one.

Crew sighed. "At the table. Don't be dense."

The group scrambled up. August escorted the celebrities, who had likely been brought here at Von's behest for added star power, to the elevator.

Once the board members and our small group were seated, I once again witnessed Crew's ability to lead and command a room.

"Okay, everyone," he said. "Time to figure things out."

Chelsey glanced at him. "The alphas?"

Crew grinned at her. "Exactly. You people," he said, addressing the showrunners, "are going to call all the upper-pack alphas. You may not be successful, since after everything we just saw and heard means they're probably running for the hills. Fucking cowards. If they won't answer, call their betas, or the pack elders. We need *someone* in charge of these packs here to answer for these crimes."

As Crew and Chelsey worked together like only fated mates could, my mind drifted. We still had a dangling thread. Von. He'd run off the moment I let him go, and that irked me to no end.

Sensing my annoyance, Kira leaned over, putting her lips to my ear. "I think these two have it handled. Wanna go hunt a vampire?"

Grinning, I took her hand, and the two of us hurried out of the room, leaving Chelsey, Crew, and Eli to do the work the council should have done years ago. We hurried down the hall to the elevator.

"He must have gone downstairs, right?" Kira asked.

"Yeah. He'd never stay in this building. He may have hidden at first, but he would have gone for the lower levels as soon as the coast was clear."

The elevator trip was spent in silence, each of us basking in the other's happiness and relief. Kira's emotions bounced through my mind, and I was ecstatic that we hadn't lost this deep, binding connection.

At the ground floor, the doors slid open and we were met with two voices, one mewling and begging, the other pissed.

"Told your ass not to run, didn't I? And my name is fucking *August,* not Autumn!"

What the hell was going on?

"Please, you must let me go, you must. I have fans. Oh, gods, it hurts. What do you want? Money? I can get you girls. Boys, if that's your speed? Whatever you want!"

Von?

I turned to look at Kira, and her eyes were as shocked as mine. We sprinted from the elevator and around the corner. Von was pinned to the wall with the broken leg of a chair. The makeshift stake pierced him in the shoulder rather than the heart. August stood before him, using a hand to hold the vampire's head up. Seeing us coming down the hall, he let Von go, letting the host dangle six inches off the ground.

"Found this piece of shit hiding down here when I escorted the celebs out," August said. "The little bitch made a run for it when he saw me. Told him to stop, but I guess his ears are as full of shit as his mouth."

"You didn't kill him?" I asked. August wasn't exactly known for his self-control.

August shrugged. "I figured we could use him. He knows a ton of dirt. He may even know more about Simon's lab and how it was funded. That deserves to be investigated, too. Plus..." He trailed off, looking embarrassed.

"Yes?"

"Well, maybe I *missed*. It all happened so fast," August said with an embarrassed shrug.

I laughed and patted him on the shoulder. "Probably for the best that you did. You're right. We can use him."

"Let me go, for fuck's sake!" Von howled, thrashing against the stake, then wincing in pain.

I had to admit, it was wonderful seeing Von flustered and annoyed for once. His entire showman facade had slipped away. He was nothing more than a rat in a trap.

"Calm down, Von," I said, standing directly in front of him. "You missed out on the show. Heline and Lucina hashed things out. Once all this fighting is over, there are going to be some big changes."

It would take a few days for that to happen, of course. For word to spread, for Heline to make her rounds, using her magic and remaining influence to stop battles. Once everyone realized that the goddess they'd worshipped had caused ninety percent of their problems, things would settle down.

"Changes?" Von asked, a hopeful gleam in his eyes. "I would be...uh, happy to assist with these changes." Now the showmanship was coming back. "Perhaps you and dear Kira need a public face for these changes? I would be happy to extol the virtues of these exciting developments."

"Shut up, Von," I barked. "Let's be honest with one another, shall we?"

The vampire's mouth closed, and he nodded hesitantly.

"I really don't like you. Personally. Like, I fucking hate you."

Von winced.

"I would actually love to pull that stake out of your shoulder and slam it into your heart. After all the shit you put Kira through, you deserve it. I would laugh while your body shriveled, and I would probably dance a fucking jig on the ashes that were left. But," I said with a smile, "I am a man of conscience. And I was given a choice a few minutes ago. That means I'll do the same for you.

"You can choose to go peacefully to the nearest Tranquility operative bureau, where I will personally find an upright, non-corrupt member of my organization to question you, or we have a helicopter outside the gates. My friend August, who I think you've become acquainted with, will drop you in the ocean, and you can attempt to swim back to Bloodstone Island since you love it so much."

Von's mouth worked like he was sucking on a piece of sour candy, and he didn't even try to hide the anger behind his eyes. "I will speak with the TOs if—and only if—I retain my career. A game show, a talent show, some other dating type show—it doesn't matter. My fans will follow in droves. I'll be happy with any of those options."

Kira snorted a laugh. "If we gave you another show, it would turn into another *Reject Project* in two seasons or less. I guarantee it."

"I would never!" Von whined. "Most of the dangerous bits were, uh...they were Heline's idea," he added quickly. "Yes, it was her."

Kira and I shared a glance and rolled our eyes. We knew exactly how much he'd enjoyed sending us out into hell. Heline may have gotten the ball rolling over thirty years ago, but Von had nudged things into ever more dangerous territory with every challenge and every season.

"Either way, Von," Kira said, "I think you overestimate the number of fans you have."

You'd have thought she'd just kicked him in the balls. His face crumpled, and he shook his head in disbelief, but thankfully kept his mouth shut for once.

I held up a finger in front of his nose. "You talk to the TOs, and only the ones I tell you to, and then you can deal with them. Maybe if you're lucky, they'll give you a plea bargain. If you play ball, who knows? You may end up with a great career, stocking grocery shelves. If you don't like that, then there's the option of throwing away that dumbass floating umbrella and your sunscreen and walking straight into the sun."

Von's head dropped, his chin resting on his chest. I couldn't be sure, but I thought he might have been crying.

"August," I said, "keep an eye on this one until I can figure out how to get him into custody. I think he's got enough in his head to bury his corporate leaders and most of the pack alphas. I don't want anything happening to him."

"You got it, boss," August said with a smile.

I needed to speak to Kira alone. Now that everything was wrapping up, I had to see how she was doing. Taking her hand, I led her back down the hallway to a private alcove. I kissed her, my lips lingering on hers for longer than necessary. All the stress of the last few days—hell, the last few weeks— finally felt like it was easing. Now we would have time to think and recover.

"How are you?" I asked. "After what Simon did to you in there?"

Watching her turn into a mindless animal had frightened me even more than when she'd attacked me. Seeing those soulless eyes glaring down at me while she snapped and growled had damn near broken my heart.

Kira took a steadying breath and nodded. "For a minute or two there, I really thought I might kill you. I had no control. The idea of killing my own fated mate was horrifying. I don't think I've ever been that terrified in my life. But it's over." That beautiful smile returned to her face. "Whatever Lucina did broke that spell. I don't think I'll ever have to worry about Simon's experiment again. I doubt Abel will, either, now that Lucina took care of that asshole."

"That's a relief. I was afraid for you."

"The worst part is over, but now we've got even more to do. At least we can do it together."

"Right." I grinned. "You know, you really shouldn't have worried that much. I totally would have saved you, even if Lucina hadn't been there."

"Oh? Is that right?"

"For sure," I said. "I was literally seconds away from shifting and putting you in your place. I totally would have whipped your ass. Then, when we shifted back, I'd have bent you over my knee and spanked you."

"Wow. Are you being serious right now?" She laughed and shoved me. "Maybe I would have liked that. Did you ever think about that?"

"You don't seem like the submissive type."

"You're a jerk."

"Yes. And you're a butthead, but what can you do?"

"Are we ever going to get along like a normal couple? Or are we gonna do stuff like this forever?"

I smiled and stroked her cheek. "I hope not. Because I don't want normal. I want forever. With you."

Chapter 27 - Kira

Moonlight streamed down from the waning crescent moon, casting a milky-white glow across the clearing. Home. The Eastern Wilds. For a time, I truly never believed I'd see it again. Now, here I stood, free and alive.

Breathing in, I noticed the things I'd always taken for granted. The green scent of the forest, the tang of the soil, and the sweet smell of wildflowers. We'd chosen this night as a symbol. Typically, mating ceremonies happened around the time of the full moon, but neither Wyatt nor I wanted to honor Heline in such a way. The fading light of the waning moon was our symbol instead. A way to show Heline's fading influence.

Smiling, I ran my hands down my dress. It was even more beautiful than the first one Zoe had made me. She'd truly outdone herself, and it was the most gorgeous thing I'd ever worn in my life. She'd even hand-painted all the swirling symbols—mating ceremony glyphs. I'd cried when she revealed it to me and thanked her a dozen times.

Through the trees, I could hear quiet, murmured conversation the voices low and respectful. Members of my pack. My new pack. After everything that happened, the packs broke apart just as I'd anticipated. Even the Eleventh Pack. My new pack was composed of former members of the Eleventh Pack, a few Haven survivors, a few new wolves who'd joined from other packs, and many of Wyatt's unofficial packmates.

The Eleventh Pack had been my family since I was born, and I'd truly believed they *were* family, but there were dozens of members I still barely knew, and even more that I'd never met. That wasn't a pack. These people, the ones I shared my life with now, were true *family*. People we would fight and die for, people who would comfort us when our hearts were broken, wipe our tears, and be a shoulder to cry on. They would laugh with us, hold each other's children like their own, and build their lives around one another.

Pack. This is what I'd always envisioned it being.

Three months, and all of shifter society had changed. In some ways, it seemed like it had been much longer, and in others, it seemed to have gone by in a blink. The war had wound down, and Heline had vanished into near obscurity. Lucina had not been seen since she'd saved me. She was probably residing peacefully back on Bloodstone with her creatures of the night.

Bentley Crew had stepped in as a liaison of sorts to help negotiate peace accords between packs and assist with the dissolution of the packs that had splintered. He'd also sat in on the *many* court cases that brought down the mightiest of our race, including his own parents. Crew had never planned on being an alpha, but he'd done such an amazing job and was such a charismatic leader, he'd soon found himself being the alpha he never thought he'd be. His own birth pack had dissolved, and he now commanded his own true pack, along with Chelsey. The two had officially mated days after the final takedown of Simon and Heline. They truly were fated mates, and I'd never seen two people happier to be together.

The members of Haven that hadn't joined my pack had chosen to join Crew and Chelsey in their new pack. Some weren't even shifters, and that strange combination of pack members would never have been allowed before the upheaval. Now Crew said it was "an experiment that might be worth it."

Who knew what the future held? Maybe things would look even more different in a few years. After all, look how much had changed in a few short months.

I walked down to get a better view of everyone. So many familiar faces. Chelsey and Crew, of course. Mika, with Zoe snuggled right up against him. J.D. and Leif, holding hands. Leif's body, face, and attitude were stronger and healthier than during our final days on Bloodstone Island. It had taken weeks of intensive work with spell casters, healers, and psychologists, but he'd fully recovered. No longer feral, he'd begun working with J.D. to form a nonprofit company to help shifters who were in danger of going feral or who had recently slipped over. He wanted to give everyone the same help he'd been given.

Abel had come with his new girlfriend, the woman he'd always thought should have been his fated mate. My brother Kolton stood beside Eli, their hands clasped together. Eli was even more beautiful than before. After we'd revealed all the dirty dealings of the upper echelons of the Tranquility Council and proven her innocence, along with the dirty truth behind her *disappearance,* her order had restored her wings and her title.

Gavin Fell had come, too. I'd invited him, but hadn't truly believed he would attend. He stood off the side, mostly keeping to himself. After the way the Ninth Pack had dissolved, he'd fallen in with some old members and created their own new pack. He'd finally come to grips with the fact that he and I were never meant to be together. The faint smile on his lips showed that he was at least sort of happy for Wyatt and me. Hopefully, he would find someone out there who was meant for him. As annoying as he could be, he'd done right by all of us. He deserved to be happy.

Not everything was happy, though. Wyatt's father hadn't been invited. If not for him, we might have died on Bloodstone Island, and he had sheltered us that night in Fangmore. There was good in him, but he was too deeply enmeshed in the old ways. Too blinded by ancient pack loyalty and the hierarchy. Once Crew released the acolytes and worked with people to ignite big changes, Lawrence Rivers had fled the city. Thankfully, most of the dirt August and his hacker and detective friends had dug up on Lawrence hadn't been too awful. Mostly money and investment issues. I hoped that one day, he and Wyatt might reconcile, but that day might be far in the future.

My own parents had learned to look beyond the old ways better than many. They stood beside Kolton and Eli, holding hands and smiling. They now saw the love Wyatt and I held for each other, the way we fit together like puzzle pieces, finishing a picture that had yet to be completed. They were able to look at me—their daughter, a female alpha, created by experimentation—and loved me for who I was. They looked at Wyatt—the renegade alpha, a lone wolf, member of an unofficial pack—and saw the way he treated me and took care of me, and they loved him for who he was now.

I sniffed and blinked, desperate not to ruin my makeup. Crying wasn't my thing, but sometimes emotions did what they wanted without your say-so. So much had happened, and it was only really hitting me now. Wyatt and I had gone through hell. Danger beyond description, and we'd come out the other side. Not only had we found each other, but we'd changed the world. We'd set shifters free of the ancient, toxic chains of hierarchy. It was early, but I thought the changes we'd brought about would alter the world for the better. Maybe years from now, people would look back on what we did and smile. The sheer scale of all we'd accomplished weighed heavily on me.

Wyatt finally appeared. A smile spread across my lips at the sight of him. He was clothed in the traditional mating clothes, with similar swirling glyphs and runes on his garments. I'd never seen a more handsome man in my life. This was exactly what I'd dreamed of as a young girl, before all the awful things Simon did to me. Before Jayson Fell, Bloodstone Island, and *The Reject Project*. I'd once dreamed, like most girls, of a day like this. A gorgeous dress, a man who loved me, family and friends, all together to celebrate a love that would last forever.

Wyatt and I had already claimed each other, but this ceremony was a symbol. A day we could look back on in twenty, thirty, even fifty years and smile at the memory of. No cameras, just the people who loved and cared for us.

Beginning my slow walk across the clearing, I wondered how long it would be before Wyatt and I could live normal lives again. Unfortunately, our celebrity status hadn't died down yet. In fact, we were two of the most famous people on the planet. It was part of why we'd kept our new pack here in the Eastern Wilds, far from prying eyes, reporters, and above all, no cameras. Out here, we didn't have to worry about our lives being broadcast to the whole world.

Wyatt and I, tasked with rebuilding the Tranquility Council, had been appointed directors of the Tranquility operatives. Our first order of business was inclusion and representation of other beings besides wolf shifters in both the operatives and council. There was no reason for two of the most powerful groups on the planet to be solely made up of one species. Those duties, unfortunately, took us to places like Fangmore and other large cities. When word of our arrival spread, we were treated like celebrities, even by other *actual* celebrities.

One of those being Von Thornton.

The vampire had done his duty: he'd rolled over and spilled his guts. His testimony alone had sent seven pack alphas, five pack betas, the entirety of *The Reject Project* board, nearly the whole Tranquility Council, and thirty percent of the Tranquility operatives to prison. Along with that, dozens of others had been taken down as well. Von had been given amnesty for his cooperation and had somehow managed to land on his feet. He was the new host of *Shifter Wives*, a dating show for all species of shifters looking for their fated mates.

Wyatt and I would have a short honeymoon soon, but once we were back at work, our main focus would be tracking down and destroying any of Simon's experiments that may have survived or lay hidden away somewhere. August, whom Wyatt had talked into joining the new Tranquility operatives as a forensic hacker, had dug up a lot of Simon's money transfers and shell corporations. With his help, I was sure we'd find every last drug, potion, and abomination the mad fae had hidden away.

Wyatt grinned quizzically at me as I finally took my place by his side.

"What?" I whispered. "What's wrong?"

"There is a lot going on in that head of yours," Wyatt whispered back. "If you're about to reject me, can I at least get a heads-up?"

Before I could retort, he kissed me. When he pulled back, I rolled my eyes at him. "Not a chance, big guy. We're too far gone to turn back. You're stuck with me, whether you like it or not."

"Kira Durst, that may be the most romantic thing you've ever said to me. It's a good thing I'm happy to be stuck with you."

The ceremony began. Vows were said, hands held, and the sound of my mother sniffling in the crowd made me smile. We exchanged kisses on our necks, our lips lingering on the claiming bite scars, marks that bound Wyatt and me together forever.

After that, we kissed each other again. All around us, cheers and whistles and shouts of joy erupted. It was hard to believe that the man I'd tried to make my worst enemy had ended up being the best thing to ever happen to me.

We still teased and poked one another, though those moments usually ended with us tumbling into bed together. Our relationship was playful and perfect. Most important of all, we had each other's backs. Forever and always.

While our friends and family cheered us on, I pulled my lips from Wyatt's and whispered into his ear, "You know you're my favorite former nemesis, right?"

"Good," Wyatt whispered back. "I was worried I was in second or third place. You'll always be my favorite annoying little brat."

I grinned at him. "I love you, too."

We kissed again, and the sounds of love and friendship echoed through the forest, up to the sky where the stars glittered and shone down upon us. Family, friends, and love. What more was there?

Printed in Great Britain
by Amazon

41977025R00324